The Atlas of Forgotten Places

The Atlas of Forgotten Places

JENNY D. WILLIAMS

THOMAS DUNNE BOOKS ⚏ ST. MARTIN'S PRESS NEW YORK

THOMAS DUNNE BOOKS.
An imprint of St. Martin's Press.

THE ATLAS OF FORGOTTEN PLACES. Copyright © 2017 by Jennifer Williams. All rights reserved. Printed in the United States of America. For information, address St. Martin's Press, 175 Fifth Avenue, New York, N.Y. 10010.

www.thomasdunnebooks.com
www.stmartins.com

Designed by Steven Seighman

The Library of Congress Cataloging-in-Publication Data is available upon request.

ISBN 978-1-250-12293-3 (hardcover)
ISBN 978-1-250-12294-0 (ebook)

Our books may be purchased in bulk for promotional, educational, or business use. Please contact your local bookseller or the Macmillan Corporate and Premium Sales Department at 1-800-221-7945, extension 5442, or by email at Macmillan SpecialMarkets@macmillan.com.

First Edition: July 2017

10 9 8 7 6 5 4 3 2 1

The
Atlas of
Forgotten
Places

***

LILY

December 2, 2008
Kitgum, Uganda

She leaves in the darkness before dawn, when she knows the guard, Kenneth, will be asleep, and before the rooster tends to crow. She doesn't need the alarm to wake her; she's hardly closed her eyes all night. She untucks the mosquito net and climbs out of bed, and in the ambient greenish glow of her lit cell phone display, she dresses in the jeans and T-shirt she laid out last night, cinching her money belt around her waist, her limbs tense and tingling.

Everything in the hut is put away. A dozen books lean against one another on the shelf in the main room, and she left a box with extra clothes, rice, tea, and sugar on the kitchen table with a note for Esther: *Take whatever you like! I'll miss you! Love, Lily.*

Next to the front door sits her backpack, a hulking beast of a thing, which she's organized and loaded and unloaded countless times in the previous days. She unzips it once more and runs her hands among the items inside, touching each in turn as if they were talismans: two changes of clothes; a sleeping bag and lightweight tarp; an aluminum water bottle; a Swiss Army knife; a ziplock with essential toiletries; and a first-aid collection that includes bandages, iodine tablets, a malaria self-testing kit, ibuprofen, and two courses of Cipro, because as much as she feels protected by the power of her convictions, a little medicinal chemistry never hurt.

Finally, snug against the spine of the pack, she finds the journal. She fingers the familiar, hard cover—a piercing azure, the way she remembers the sky over the Rockies—and thinks of the precious information contained within. She's been careful, she knows, but has she been careful enough? Her mind swirls with the stories she's heard, stories of the missing, the resurrected, the dead. She zips the backpack and hefts it on. She closes the door behind her without looking back.

Outside, the night is cool, the darkness cut by the light of a partial moon and two planets, Jupiter and Venus, joined in a rare triple conjunction. When Christoph told her about it yesterday at dinner, it felt like a sign: a blessing from the universe. Now she pauses to take in the clear, brilliant sky, the smiling moon, the planets paired like twins. So much has aligned to bring her to this point.

The most dangerous part lies ahead.

Hidden insects buzz from the low grass, and she treads cautiously, mindful of cobras; she'd ignored Kenneth's warnings for months and then nearly stepped on one last week as she left for work. She'd been thinking of something else when the snake snapped up and opened its hood, and she didn't even scream, just backed away slowly and called in a steady voice to Esther, who ran to get Kenneth so he could kill it with a *panga*. She was proud of how calmly she acted, how composed in the face of lethality. That, too, felt like a sign: that she is capable of anything, that she is stronger and braver than anyone would guess.

A shadow comes up beside her—it's Blue, the compound mutt, wagging his skinny tail in quick, low circles. He whines and licks her fingers, and she rubs his ears in response. "It's all right, boy," she whispers. "It's just me."

She's sad to leave him behind. When she first arrived she thought he was the most beautiful dog she'd ever seen: tawny with streaks of copper and black, elongated legs and huge pointed ears, coyote-like. He didn't have a name, so she gave him one that made her think of home. Now he trails her across the yard, past the garden with its rows of beans and groundnuts, past the shed where she can make out Kenneth's sleeping figure sprawled on the long bench inside, all the way to the gate. The latch is heavy but quiet, and she cracks open the metal doors just wide enough to slip her backpack through and then her slender self. Blue tries to follow but she blocks the way.

"You have to stay here." She closes the gate and reaches through the slats to lower the latch back into place. Blue whines again, scratching at the door. "I'll be back," she soothes, though her voice catches at the lie.

The Catholic Mission looms darkly alongside her as she skirts the building and heads for the front steps of the church. The dirt road that leads from here toward Kitgum town is deserted. She checks her phone: 4:12 A.M. An insect chitters shrilly, insistently. She tightens her backpack straps and shifts the weight higher.

Faintly, she hears the drone of an engine in the distance. Her muscles go slack and wobbly. Doubts swoop in like bats. She can still turn back, she can still change her mind.

But when she thinks of returning home like this, without even trying—she'd regret it the rest of her life. This is bigger than her fear, bigger than her grief, bigger than all of it. She steadies herself as the engine gets closer, and then it's here, and there is no turning back, and the planets and the moon spin in place, engaged in their elaborate illusion of closeness, pinned against a backdrop of finite, boundless black.

PART I

THE MISSING

CHAPTER 1

SABINE

December 24, 2008
Marburg, Germany

All around her, the world was white and bright and hushed; a pale sky pressed upon red-roofed buildings and was pierced by thin, reaching branches of trees made bare by cold. Sabine nuzzled her chin deeper into her turtleneck and clenched and unclenched her hands inside her gray wool gloves to keep the circulation moving, though her fingers were already stiff and painful. She knew they wouldn't get warm again until she was back in the animal shelter and could run them under the hot-water faucets. She still had twenty minutes till then, and she couldn't make the time go any faster.

That was okay; she had become accustomed to numbness. Winter this year had come hard and early to Marburg, and Sabine both hated the cold and relished it. Hated it because she had lived so many years without it, had adjusted to the thick, heavy heat of a different continent and forgotten how bone-biting a northern wind could be. But she loved the stark nakedness through which that wind swept. She hated the layers of clothing she had to don and discard every time she entered or left a building, but she loved the city when it was buried beneath a layer of snow, clean and quiet.

Aside from a few cars driving idly past, the streets were deserted as she walked the last few blocks down to the River Lahn, pausing every few steps to let Bruno sniff a clump of dirty snow. The bells of

Elisabethkirche had just rung the noon hour, and Sabine felt the stirrings of hunger. She'd take her lunch break as soon as she got back. Bruno hadn't really needed to go out—he'd had a long play session with another dog at the shelter, the two black Labs tumbling over each other in a slobbery wrestling match—but Sabine enjoyed the exercise, despite her frozen fingers. Together she and Bruno descended the stairs to the riverbank and wended their way along the river's curves. She saw that new parts of the river had frozen over since yesterday. How quickly the water turned to ice. She knew, too, given a sudden rise in temperature or even a light rain, how quickly it would turn back.

She thought of her niece, Lily, who was returning to the U.S. today after half a year volunteering in Uganda. It was Lily's first time in Africa. All those years Sabine had lived on the continent—in Ethiopia, Tanzania, Mozambique—Lily had asked to visit, but Sabine kept putting her off. When Lily graduated from college earlier this year and announced that she'd arranged to spend six months as a volunteer in Kitgum—a small town in northern Uganda, the site of Sabine's last assignment—Sabine had felt a flicker of foreboding, but all she said was, "Stay smart, stay humble, and if you're going to ride *bodas,* for God's sake wear a helmet."

For the past five months, Lily had e-mailed religiously once a week from the offices of the nonprofit organization where she worked, using an ancient computer she dubbed Old Reliable. She wrote about the children she counseled, the expats she met, the groundnut sauce, the smell of the earth after a heavy rain. Her messages reflected the standard surges of optimism and defeat, eagerness and frustration that plagued all first-timers with the unfortunate possession of innate idealism. Sabine was tempted to write long e-mails in return, peeling back the layers of naïveté that fostered such sentiments, but in the end did not interfere. Lily would learn the harsh truths of aid—and of herself—and come out stronger for it.

Then came Lily's last e-mail, three weeks back; Sabine recalled the precise words, the phrases so very American, so earnest:

Wrapping up things in Kitgum . . . a few weeks left in Uganda,
I figure I'll do some sightseeing . . . nice to get off the grid for
a bit . . . don't freak out if you guys don't hear from me before my flight!!!

There was no mistaking the emphasis of those three exclamation
marks. Since then, Sabine had dutifully managed to not *freak out*;
that is, she'd worried about her niece backpacking alone in East Africa,
but vaguely, distantly, in the way she worried about climate change
and the dubious fiscal responsibility of certain members of the European Union. She was concerned, she understood the risks, but it didn't
change what she ate for dinner.

After all, Sabine had once been young in Africa, too, and she remembered clearly the exhilaration that sprang from tossing caution to the wind, the thrill of making up your itinerary as you went.
Lily had turned twenty-two earlier this year, the same age as Sabine
on her first assignment abroad. That year Sabine had spent her R & R
hitchhiking around Ethiopia with nothing more than some camp-
ing equipment and a stack of U.S. dollars. That was before cell phones
and e-mail made transcontinental communication instantaneous
and cheap, before Couchsurfing and Lonely Planet built the temple
of budget travel in which every restless college grad worshipped.
Sabine remembered pitching a tent outside Lalibela and waking in
the morning to a band of local men in her campsite brandishing
scythes. After some animated discussion—mostly in the form of
charged gestures—she realized that they were afraid she had come to
steal relics out of the churches. They'd been drinking *tej* all night to
work up to a confrontation. When she assured them that she was only
interested in *seeing* the stone-hewed churches, perhaps with the assistance of a hired guide or two, their anger dissolved and everyone
was chummy.

But it could have been otherwise, and in those days pre–cell phones
and Internet, when things went wrong, they went truly wrong. Modern backpacking, with all its guidebooks and safety nets, seemed to

Sabine to be relatively benign—certainly more benign than the moral thicket of humanitarianism—and Lily had already managed half a year in Uganda on her own. After Lily sent her final missive from Kitgum, Sabine went about her life in Germany as usual, attending to the animals at the shelter, scattering salt on her balcony to melt the snow. Every so often she'd think of her niece somewhere near the equator, wearing flip-flops and getting tipsy on perspiring bottles of Nile Special, sleeping in hostels under mosquito nets with the sheets kicked off. These visions rarely lingered.

Now Lily's three-week holiday was over, and with it, her time in Uganda. If Sabine had the time difference right, Lily had landed in Denver hours ago. Steve—Lily's stepfather—was supposed to pick her up. Just last night Sabine lay in bed imagining Lily's plane somewhere above, perhaps passing over this very part of Germany on her way from Entebbe to Amsterdam and onward toward home.

As they turned the next corner, Bruno tensed and stopped, his eyes trained ahead. Sabine followed his gaze, looking through a screen of slender, tangled branches, and was startled by a movement at the edge of the river on the opposite side. A tall man clothed in all black stood on the icy shore. Sabine gripped Bruno's leash tighter.

Apparently unaware of Sabine's presence, the man kneeled down onto the packed snow and came on all fours, then—to Sabine's profound surprise—began to crawl slowly onto the frozen river.

Bruno growled low in his throat, and Sabine soothed him with a hand on his head. Meanwhile the man moved steadily forward, his gloved fingers brushing the ice ahead to feel the way. Sabine was baffled. The man seemed to be crazy. There was no way of knowing how thick the ice was—it could be newly frozen, fatal if it cracked and he went through.

No one else was around. The man was silent as he paused, knocked lightly on the ice, then crawled another few centimeters. Sabine held her breath. The moment felt uncanny, this strangely solitary man breaking into her own strange solitude.

Then she saw the swan. Obscured by the branches in the way, the swan's colors had matched the blue-white of the river and snow. Now she could make out the shape of its back, the writhing limb of its neck. It began to hiss, pumping its orange and black beak forward as if hoping to pull the rest of its body free.

Which, Sabine could see clearly now, would fail: the bird was trapped, frozen into the ice. Even its wings were pressed tight against its body. She knew this happened sometimes with ducks and other water birds that chose poorly where they slept the night. Usually they died. But swans seemed so big, so powerful; surely this one would have been able to thrash its way out?

Sabine looked again at the man's clothes and realized he was wearing full-body waders, like fishermen. When he turned slightly away from her to evaluate his distance from shore, she saw a hand ax tucked into his back belt loop. She dared not move, both for fear of agitating the swan further and because she didn't want the man to know he was being watched. Bruno sat and started sniffing the air. Sabine didn't remove her hand from his head.

The closer the man got to the swan, the harder the swan strained its neck. The man seemed to know the danger of getting too close; he stopped a few feet away, just out of reach, and pulled out his ax.

As gently as if stroking a cat, he began tapping the ax against the ice.

Bit by bit he chipped the frozen river away, taking care not to shift his body weight nor come within range of the swan's angry beak. Sabine watched, enthralled. Time was lost to her. The man's fierce concentration was contagious; Sabine hardly breathed. The world narrowed to the scene before her: the *scratch scratch scratch, tap tap, scratch scratch* of the man's ax, the swan's constant hiss.

A *crack* broke the trance; bits of ice bobbed in the water, suddenly loose, and the bird surged forward. The man got to his feet quickly and stumbled back, out of range of those massive, miraculous wings, as the sheet of ice shifted and groaned. He made it to shore just as the swan beat its way out of the river and into the air, and the ice broke away. The swan was gone in seconds.

Stillness returned to the sky, the river.

Then Bruno barked and Sabine remembered herself; she looked over at the man as he noticed them for the first time. He waved, unembarrassed, then gathered his things and trudged on in the other direction. Sabine watched him until his figure disappeared around a bend, even after she felt her phone begin to vibrate deep beneath her winter layers. Slowly, she removed her gloves and undid the necessary zippers to pull it out.

She was surprised to see Steve's name on the caller ID. In an instant the swan was swept aside, vanished as if from a dream.

"Steve?" she answered. "It must be four in the morning over there. Was Lily's flight so late?"

"She's not here," Steve said, his voice panicked. "Lily's not here."

"Not there?" Sabine said. Holding the phone to her ear, her exposed fingers were already white and trembling. "You mean it's delayed?"

"No, no, the plane arrived, but Lily—she wasn't on it." In the background of the call, Sabine could hear a low echoey airport announcement being made. "I just talked to the customer service rep at KLM," Steve continued. "They said she never showed up in Entebbe. Did she say anything to you about changing her ticket? Has she contacted you at all since she left Kitgum?"

"She was backpacking . . ." Sabine trailed off. "She said not to worry, that she would be out of touch for a little while. Remember? She said that."

"So you haven't heard from her?"

"No. Nothing."

Bruno had stopped whining and was now, bless him, sitting patiently, watching a pair of bullfinches chatter in the branches of a nearby tree.

"What does it mean?" Steve said.

"I'm sure she's fine. She probably just missed her flight." Even as she said it, a trickle of nausea snaked through her stomach.

"And didn't tell us?" Steve said. "Not a word?"

"She might be in the air right now." *Please let her be in the air right now.*

"*No,*" Steve said. "It's not like her. She would have found a way to contact me. Something *happened* to her." His desperation was escalating. "What was she thinking, going to Africa in the first place? Hannah would have talked her out of it."

At the invocation of her sister, a prickling of guilt wreathed Sabine's neck. "You don't know that."

"She was my *wife.*" A beat passed. She heard him exhale heavily. "I'm sorry. I'm a mess. What do we do?"

He was on the verge of splitting open; she heard it in his voice. How long had he been at the airport, waiting, sleepless? Scrutinizing face after face, his hopes repeatedly expanding and deflating as passenger after passenger exited customs and did not materialize into the singular shape of his late wife's only daughter? He needed her to pull him back from the edge, to take control.

"I'm sure there's an explanation," she said with a confidence she didn't at all feel. "You go home, get some rest. I'll call the U.S. embassy in Kampala."

"What about the police? Do we file a missing person's report?"

"Let me talk to the embassy first," she said. "They'll know what to do."

After they hung up, Sabine stood in the snow a moment longer, the phone still in her hand. The bullfinches were gone, and Bruno had lain down and was licking his front paw. Bits of lingering ice still bobbed in the river. The twin Gothic spires of Elisabethkirche impaled the sky. Impossible, Sabine thought, that the world hadn't stopped completely, that the church bells had managed to ring that morning at all. The assertiveness with which she'd spoken to Steve came easily; it was a familiar instinct, managing crisis with pragmatism. But stirring in the depths was something darker, more menacing.

The day she left Uganda for the last time, two years ago, she'd looked out the oval airplane window as they lifted off the tarmac and rose into the air over Entebbe: the undulating green hills below, the vast blue of Lake Victoria glinting all the way to the horizon. She'd known even then—hadn't she known?—that after everything, she couldn't just flee; it wasn't as simple as packing your bags and unpacking them on another, colder continent. She thought of Lily—earnest, eager Lily—and her knees nearly buckled with the weight of it.

She tugged lightly on Bruno's leash and he stood, and together they turned back toward the animal shelter. The doubts, the guilt, that gaping absence in the shape of a twenty-two-year-old girl—these and other things could be kept in abeyance so long as she focused on first one task and then another, as simple as putting her feet forward, left, right, left. The path ran straight from the river to the shelter, and she no longer felt the cold.

She called the Kampala embassy from her office at the shelter. As the phone rang, she picked up the photograph of Hannah and Lily that sat on her desk. It had been taken a decade ago, and the mother-daughter pair could have been mistaken for sisters: same constellation of freckles across the nose, same soft eyebrows, same closed-mouth smile. The primary difference was hair color: Hannah's was mousy-brown while Lily was dark haired, like Sabine. Hannah looked so young in the photo—she *was* so young. She had eloped at nineteen with an American student she'd met in Hamburg and returned with him to the States at the end of the semester without completing her degree. It was the single boldest act Sabine had ever known her sister to make. What other adventures might Hannah have had if she hadn't gotten pregnant so soon after arriving in Colorado? She'd never said anything to hint at regret, at fantasies unfulfilled, but Sabine wondered. While other American girls celebrated their twenty-first birthdays by taking their first legal drink—and second, and third—Hannah spent her twenty-first birthday eight months pregnant with the baby girl she'd already decided to name Lily, after the white-and-yellow flowers that bloomed in early spring in the grassy foothills of the Rocky Mountains.

At last, a recorded message: *Thank you for contacting the embassy of the United States of America in Kampala. We will be closed from Wednesday, December twenty-fourth, through Friday, December twenty-sixth, for the Christmas holiday. Normal business hours will resume Monday, December twenty-ninth. Please visit our Web site for more information. If this is an emergency, please contact our duty officer at . . .* Sabine wrote down the numbers that followed, then replaced the phone on its cradle.

She hadn't factored in the holiday. She knew it was Christmas Eve, of course; it was a hard thing to forget. She drove past the Christmas market outside Elisabethkirche every evening on her way home from work, the kitschy circus-like wooden stalls juxtaposed with the church's regal gray stone, the smell of fried dough and Glühwein and bratwurst seeping in through the car's heating vents as she passed beneath a lit-up banner that read, O DU FRÖHLICHE WEIHNACHTSZEIT IN MARBURG!—a joyous Christmastime indeed, Sabine thought, when you spent your days cleaning kennels and administering medications to surly felines and reluctant mutts. The animals at the shelter never took a day off, and Sabine always agreed to take the holiday shifts, along with a brusque young Polish girl who was currently tending to the rabbits. Their colleagues were grateful to spend the time with family, and it was all the same to Sabine; she hadn't celebrated Christmas in any meaningful way since Hannah died.

As girls, the sisters had made the annual trek from Stuttgart, where they lived with their parents, to Marburg, where their maternal grandparents had a house in the narrow cobblestoned streets of the *Oberstadt,* below the castle. *Oma* cooked the goose for Christmas

Eve, and *Opa* read them stories of talking ravens and glass mountains and siblings lost and found. The Grimm brothers had lived in Marburg in the early 1800s, and the town's hilly forests and half-timbered houses still retained an atmosphere of magic and wonder.

After Hannah expatriated to the U.S., and Sabine to Ethiopia for her first job, these Christmas pilgrimages were often the only occasions when the sisters would meet in person, Hannah with Lily in tow. Sabine watched chubby little Lily take her first unsteady steps in the same garden where Sabine had once broken her wrist during a clumsy cartwheel; she consoled Hannah during her divorce from Lily's father, while four-year-old Lily blew bubbles at the neighbor's cat, shrieking with delight when a gossamer bubble hit its mark and popped in a silent smatter of droplets that sent the cat bolting for cover. Sabine felt a painful nostalgia when she secretly observed Hannah tucking Lily in at night, reading stories of talking ravens and glass mountains and siblings lost and found.

The sisters had continued to come to Marburg after their grandparents died, and then after the death of their own parents, but after Hannah was gone, Sabine let the tradition slip away. It was easier to just keep working, and Lily seemed content to spend Christmases in Colorado. Then, when Sabine returned to Germany two years ago— she told people she needed a break, she was burned out after eighteen years of disaster zones, which was a portion of truth large enough to satiate their interest—Christmas felt too loaded, too weighty, to invite Lily to join her, and Lily never asked. The last time she'd seen her niece in person was a year and a half ago, when Lily stopped in Marburg overnight on a whirlwind summer backpacking trip with a college friend through Europe. Sabine remembered offering to pick them up at the train station and being surprised by Lily's cool confidence that they could find the animal shelter on their own. When they'd shown up right on schedule—Lily's laughter disappearing beneath the chorus of barking dogs—Sabine had a fleeting vision of Hannah as she must have looked upon arrival in the U.S.: sure-footed and beautiful and unafraid.

Another memory came: one Christmas, when Lily was seven and they were gathered at *Oma*'s house in the *Oberstadt*, Sabine and Hannah were standing together in the garden, facing the house, when they realized Lily had been quiet—too quiet. They turned and found her gone. After they'd spent twenty minutes scouring the neighborhood, calling Lily's name over and over again, they returned home to call the police, and there was Lily, emerging from the deep hedges at the periphery of the garden holding a sliver of wood, long rotted: part of an old rabbit hutch. Holding it as if nothing were amiss. Now, listening to the line ring for the American duty officer in Uganda, Sabine recalled this moment with a mixture of hope and unease. Could it be that easy, again?

A harried male voice answered. "Yes? Hello?"

"Hello?" she said. "I'm trying to reach someone at the U.S. embassy. Is this the right number?"

"Well, I'm the guy on call." His accent was unmistakably American. "What can I do for you?" In the background she could hear cars honking. She grasped the noise as evidence of Kampala—she smelled the fumes, felt the fine grit of dust and the bump of an anonymous shoulder jostling her in the crowd.

"My niece—she's been in Uganda since June. She was supposed to fly home yesterday out of Entebbe, but she never checked in for her flight."

"American citizen?"

"Yes."

"In Uganda?"

Why didn't he sound concerned? She rapped a pencil rapidly against the desk. "Yes—I think so. She left northern Uganda a few weeks ago, probably December second. Her last e-mail was December first."

"But she's in Uganda?"

Sabine's grip tightened around the pencil. "She could have crossed a border. She's been out of touch since she left Kitgum."

"Where?"

"*Kitgum.*"

"Hold on a sec." The line became crackly, and the seconds ticked by. She heard a muffled thump, and then he came back, and the background noise was gone. "Sorry about that, Mrs. . . ."

"Hardt. Sabine." She didn't bother to correct the *Mrs.*

"The thing is, I'm not in the office. Christmas Eve and all. I've been running around downtown. Just got back to the car. Okay . . . pen . . . paper . . ." She could hear something rustling. "Got it. Your niece, you said? What's her name?"

"Lily Bennett. *B-e-n-n-e-t-t.* She's twenty-two years old. She was volunteering with Children In Need. It's an NGO in Kitgum. The last time we heard from her was December first. She said she was leaving the next day to go backpacking." Sabine was aware that she was repeating herself, but the facts she had were so spare. She had nothing else to offer.

"*Bennett,*" he echoed. "And where was she staying? Which hotel?"

"I don't know."

"She didn't say?"

"She didn't make any reservations. She was probably staying in hostels."

"Was she traveling with friends, family?"

"She didn't mention any friends. No family," she said, then added, uselessly, "her mother died six years ago. My sister."

A respectful pause; then: "Did she keep a blog, Facebook, anything like that?"

A few days ago, Steve had mentioned that he'd been checking Lily's Facebook profile over the last few weeks, but there weren't any updates. "Not that I know of."

He sighed. "Look, I'll be frank with you. I'm just a clerk in the visa office who got the short straw as duty officer over Christmas. If you give me a number where I can reach you, I can make some calls here and let you know what I find out. But we haven't had any reports of an American citizen being hospitalized or detained recently."

"Detained? No, she's—that's impossible." But she knew it wasn't; it happened all the time. "She's just—out of touch." She couldn't bring herself to say *missing.*

"I'm sorry. I understand. It's just, from what you've given me, there's not much we can do. The local police have to conduct the investigation."

The word *investigation* sent a ripple of unease down her spine.

"So I should talk to them?" she said. "The Ugandan police? They'll be able to help?" Thinking of her previous dealings with the Ugandan police did not fill her with confidence.

"That's the official line," he said.

"Is there an unofficial line?"

"Local law enforcement can be hampered by bureaucracy." He seemed unaware, Sabine thought, of the irony in this statement coming from an employee of the U.S. government. "And three weeks without contact is a long time," he continued. "There's gonna be a lot of legwork involved, a lot of phone calls, *a lot* of dead ends."

Dead ends mingled with *investigation,* hanging bleakly in the air.

"What are you saying?" The dogs began to bark in their kennels. The light slanting in through her office window seemed diffuse. At once the image of the man and the swan returned to her from that morning: his gentle touch, the explosion of ice and energy and bird when the swan broke free, and then the wide, still, gray sky. She remembered a different brightness, an all-encompassing brightness—dust rising from a red-dirt road, a woman waving frantically . . . Then a shadowy place—a hatbox with something written there, an unfamiliar name, her grandfather's spindly handwriting, a terrible secret—

The American's voice cut back in. ". . . it's what a lot of families in your situation choose to do."

"Sorry, what?"

"It's what a lot of people decide," he said again. "If they can afford it, you know."

"Afford what?"

"A plane ticket."

And then she understood.

For a moment her voice didn't seem to work. At last she said, "Thank you for your advice."

"Good luck," he said. "I hope you find what you're looking for."

CHAPTER 2

ROSE

December 24, 2008
Kitgum, Uganda

The afternoon sun pressed like hands upon Rose Akulu's shoulders and neck as she made her way on foot through Kitgum town toward her brother's home. The air smelled of roasted groundnuts and burning garbage. A car drove past, stirring a haze of dust in its wake; two bony dogs trotted purposefully down a narrow alley between buildings. Otherwise the streets were mostly empty: here a slow-moving bicyclist, there a woman with a purple umbrella for shade.

Rose had spent the morning working in the dim, peaceful coolness of her rented room, transcribing interviews she and Christoph had conducted earlier in the week. He'd made her promise not to work over the holiday, but she enjoyed the rhythm of play, type, pause, type, rewind, fast-forward, pause, play. Christoph had provided her with equipment from his university in Switzerland—laptop, earphones— and the soft clicking of the letters on the keyboard beneath the fingers of her left hand felt as soothing as the patter of rain on a thatch roof. She was slow, as she could only use one hand to type; she'd lost her right arm years ago, and the scarred stump that remained—three inches past the shoulder—was of little use except in attracting unwanted gazes in public. But in her slowness she could be careful, methodical. This was her strength, Christoph said—the reason he preferred her to anyone else. And for Rose, as long as the sentences were divided into words and phrases, disconnected from one another, she didn't have to consider the meaning they carried as a whole. She could forget her body, be deaf to the grief that singed the edges of the voices in her ears, thinking only of capturing the English and Acholi words and pinning them down, accurately and in the correct order.

The patchy green soccer field next to the Bomah Hotel was empty of schoolchildren, and the shops along the main road had their doors closed and shutters pulled down. The wooden stalls of the market were bare; a breeze worried a piece of blue fabric caught on a broken stick. A man passed carrying two live roosters upside down in each hand, their legs tied with twine, wings loose.

Transcriptions hadn't always been the best part of her work. In her first such job years ago, when a Dutch academic had plucked her from the girls at the rehabilitation center to help him with his research, she'd preferred the interviews themselves: going into the community, speaking with people as if she were any other Acholi girl. Rose could ignore their distrustful looks so long as they answered the questions she asked on the *mono*'s behalf. The technology, though, made her nervous, so certain was she that she'd break any electronic thing she touched. But her employer had been patient, and with time she began to look forward to those hours of drifting, alone, when she was accountable to no one and nothing but that little black cursor, winking. It filled her days. When she made a mistake, the delete key never judged. People, she'd learned, were less forgiving.

Well—there was Ocen. Always Ocen. As Rose turned the corner and spotted a group of parked motorcycles, her heart made a small leap and she searched for the familiar red and blue tassels hanging off the back of his passenger seat. Ocen had sometimes worked this corner with a handful of other *boda* drivers, ferrying passengers around town for a small fee. It had been some weeks since she'd seen him. They'd had a fight, and she was angry, and then he left town and had not returned. She suspected he'd taken refuge at his uncle Franklin's house in Arua, where he could just as easily ply his trade, though she'd called Franklin and he said he'd not seen his nephew since spring. But of course if Ocen was fleeing her, he would hardly encourage his uncle to reveal his whereabouts. Perhaps it was only a test, time for them both to cool off; perhaps Ocen had already returned without telling her.

By the time she'd come close enough to see that his bike wasn't among them, she'd also seen the three drivers relaxing in the shade of a mango tree to the side of the road, and her disappointment was confirmed. One noticed her attention and sat up, calling out, *"Boda?"*

Rose shook her head and walked on. She circled the roundabout and crossed the bridge leading out of town. Below, the creek was stagnant and muddy. Two hulking Marabou storks stalked the reeds and trash along its banks. Thunderheads gathered in the distance over Agor, and she picked up her pace. Though the sun shone now, the weather was quick to shift, and she didn't want to get caught out in the rain. A few hundred meters later, she turned off the broad road for cars and onto a narrower dirt path for pedestrians that cut through the brush. Stalks of grass tickled her calves where her skirt did not quite reach. In a moment she entered the well-swept clearing of her brother's home, sending three clucking hens into a flutter.

Behind the round hut, her sister-in-law, Agnes, leaned over a large black pot, stirring millet. A baby was wrapped tightly on her back, his bottom supported by fabric that came around Agnes's front and was tied in a knot beneath her breasts; only Wilborn's scrunched face above the nose was visible. A green plastic cross hung around Agnes's neck, swaying slightly away from her chest as she bent forward. She glanced up as Rose approached.

"Apwoyo," Rose said.

"Apwoyo." Agnes stood straight and arched her back. Wilborn blinked his wet-black eyes, yawned, and closed his eyes. *"Itye maber?"*

"Atye maber," Rose said. "Is my brother here?"

A goat emerged from the surrounding brush and plopped down in the shade next to the gray mud walls of the hut.

"He is away."

Rose felt a momentary, selfish relief. She pitied her brother his passion and his pride—traits that in a different era would have been sharpened with the same attention and intention as an Acholi spearhead. But these times were past. James had been lucky to avoid both abduction by the rebels and recruitment by the government army. Now, in this so-called post-conflict northern Uganda—with the rebels scattered across the borders in Sudan and the Democratic Republic of the Congo—James was distinctly unsuited for the kind of menial labor opportunities a man of his little education could hope to get. Unemployment in Kitgum was high, and James had taken to the unfortunate endeavor that occupied so many frustrated men. He often started before noon, joining friends on hard wooden benches outside a neighbor's hut; a thousand shillings bought five small sachets of *waragi,* and the clear empty plastic packets would grow in piles at their feet as their conversation raged and quieted and raged again, until he ran out of drink and stumbled back home.

Agnes carried the bruises of his discontent. Rose had berated James many times and encouraged Agnes privately to pursue divorce, but her sister-in-law refused. And in the end, James was Rose's brother, her blood. The only family she had left.

"I've brought you something," Rose said as she took a small stack of bills from her purse and handed it to Agnes. Fifty thousand shillings was enough to buy food and pay rent on their hut for a month. In addition, Rose paid the children's school fees and gave money for books and supplies, and if anyone became sick, she would cover the cost of the medicine.

Agnes slipped the package in between the pages of a folded newspaper that sat on a stool nearby. "You are generous."

"You are family." Rose glanced around. "Where are the children?"

"Isaac is sleeping. Grace has gone for water."

As if on cue, a girl of nine emerged from the path in the brush, swaying beneath a yellow jerry can that was balanced atop her head; she had both hands up to steady it, but Rose could see dribbles of dampness on the front of the girl's red dress where the water had spilled. Grace set down the jerry can in the shade of the hut. The goat bleated but didn't move.

With her eyes low, Grace whispered, "*Apwoyo*, auntie."

"*Apwoyo*, Grace," Rose said. "Did you come from the river?"

Grace looked away.

"It is not clean there," Rose said.

"She went to the borehole," Agnes said. "Didn't you, Grace?"

The girl made the slightest indication of a nod.

"You were at the borehole?" Rose asked. "At St. Joseph's?"

"Eh," the girl affirmed, almost inaudibly.

Rose knew that the river was only a short walk down the footpath, while the borehole at St. Joseph's Hospital was a kilometer along the roadside, plagued by careless drivers. Neither was a good choice. "Make sure you boil it thoroughly," Rose said.

"We are not animals," Agnes said sharply.

"Of course," Rose said.

Soon she was kneeling, ankles demurely to one side like a proper Acholi woman, as she prepared the dough for samosas. Grace peeled potatoes while Agnes set aside the cooked millet and started another pot for stew. Rose watched them with aching envy: how easily they passed an object from one hand to the other, how natural it was for Grace to turn a potato in her left hand and grasp the peeling knife with her right. For the most part, Rose found that she could do almost everything with one arm that others could do with two; it just took longer and required greater care. But cooking was complicated—she couldn't hold an onion in place and slice it at the same time. She knew a woman, one-handed like her, who'd had a special cutting board made with nails pounded all the way through the wood so she could spike vegetables and keep them from slipping away. Rose was lucky: she never cooked alone.

The bells from the Catholic Mission next to St. Joseph's rang in the distance, carried and then whipped away by the wind that had turned sour and chilled, a sure sign of rain to come. Rose had already carried the dried laundry inside the hut, moving carefully so as not to disturb the sleeping boy, Isaac, who lay warm and sprawling on a mattress under a mosquito net.

On the ground outside she poured one package of Pembe baking flour into a large plastic bowl, then filled a steel mug with water, which she added to the flour a little at a time, alternately dribbling and setting down the mug to knead with her left hand, until the dough cohered.

"How is your work?" Agnes asked after a while.

"It goes well."

"This *mono* has not tried to bed you yet?"

Rose felt a flash of defensiveness toward Christoph. Though he was fine-looking enough for a white man, she had no feelings for him, and he had been nothing but professional in the eight months they'd worked together.

"It's not like that," she said.

"Shame," Agnes said. "With him you could really go somewhere."

Her sister-in-law spoke the truth; Rose had known it to happen with others. The idea of starting over somewhere else had its appeal. But even if Christoph had opened the door to that spacious, mon-eyed room of *life abroad,* how could she leave Ocen behind?

Unless he left her first. She took out her anger on the dough, pinching off smaller pieces with particular zeal.

"Is it the *boda*?" Agnes asked.

How like Agnes to cut to the quick. Rose was silent.

"You didn't arrive with him today," Agnes prodded.

"He is not around."

"Another woman? One whose dowry he can meet?"

Rose held her tongue. Of course Agnes would know the price James had set for her marriage and the unfair burden it placed on Ocen. It didn't please Rose to be speaking of these things, even to a woman she should see as a sister. Agnes had been begrudgingly welcoming when Rose returned to Kitgum after many years away, and she was grateful for the financial support Rose brought, but the two were not close. Agnes had suffered greatly during the war, and though she'd never blamed Rose directly, Rose knew the accusation was there, a splinter beneath the skin. How else should Agnes face such loss? Three brothers and a sister, all dead. Aunts and uncles, gone. Agnes's parents lived in Adjumani, a hundred and fifty kilometers away; she saw them rarely. None of the children she cared for were her own. Grace Aber and Isaac Onen were her brothers' children; the baby, Wilborn Okello, had belonged to her sister, who died in childbirth. That sorrow was still fresh. Agnes's only living sibling, another sister, was also in Kitgum but cared for four children, two of whom were orphans. Such was "peace" in northern Uganda: the few who remained, struggling to care for the loved ones of the many who were gone. The memories of violence remained palpable—in the absence of family members at a gathering, in the missing ears, missing noses. Missing arms. In the redness of men's eyes by midafternoon. In the abandoned schools, crumbling, burnt, reclaimed by wilderness.

"Did you see this operation in Congo?" Agnes nodded toward the newspaper. "Museveni is hunting the rebels in Garamba. They should find Kony and take him here, so that he can be killed in front of us."

Rose had long learned not to flinch at the sound of the rebel commander's name. "Should he not go to trial?"

"His death is the only justice."

Rose and Christoph had spoken often about this issue. Like many foreigners interested in the northern Ugandan conflict, Christoph was well versed in questions of justice and reconciliation between the government of Uganda, headed by Ugandan President Yoweri Museveni, and the Lord's Resistance Army rebels, led by Joseph Kony. The last chance at peace had been negotiations that took place in Juba, southern Sudan, in 2006 but were problematic from the beginning. The International Criminal Court had issued arrest warrants for Kony and his top commanders the previous year, and some people argued that these warrants were the reason—at least partially— why Kony was wary of appearing in person to sign a peace agreement. Why should he risk arrest? A movement had begun to promote the idea of traditional reconciliation, involving Acholi ceremonies of cleansing and forgiveness; the ceremony of *mato oput,* "drinking the bitter root," was touted as the best chance to move forward. But in order to perform such a ceremony with the rebel leader, he must first be found.

When the negotiations in Sudan failed, President Museveni turned to a military option. Ten days ago, on the fourteenth of December, his army—the Uganda People's Defence Force—began an aerial bombardment of the LRA's main camps in Garamba National Park, in northeastern Democratic Republic of the Congo. So far Museveni had made a lot of noise about success but had entirely failed to produce Kony. Rose was unsurprised. The rebel leader had ways of knowing things, of slipping beyond the government's grasp. And Museveni could not be trusted any more than the LRA. Probably there were other motives for putting soldiers on the ground in that place. *It's all so far away,* she told Christoph. *What good does it do to think of such things here?* And, she thought but did not say, what good to confront things she would rather forget?

She began to roll out the small balls of dough one by one on a rock. Grace had moved nearby, anticipating her needs, and each time Rose lay another thin circle on the growing stack, Grace dipped the tips of her fingers into a cup of oil and drizzled it on the dough in neat spirals to keep the layers separated. The girl was silent, her dark eyelashes so lovely.

Rose felt a pang of longing for this borrowed intimacy. She'd had a son once; he would be almost Grace's age now, if he were alive. His hands had been as tiny and fragile as blossoms. Rose pushed the memories away. From the tall stack of circles, she took a smaller stack the width of her thumb, then pressed the edges down to turn the many smaller sheets into one long, layered circle. This would become the flaky crust of the samosa. As Rose finished each crust, Grace set them on a growing stack on a hot, flat pan over a second cooking fire, whose smoke drifted Rose's way, stinging her eyes.

Evening was falling, along with the drone of insects and snatches of birdsong. The clouds had dissipated into scattered wisps. It seemed that the rain had passed them by after all.

"Ah, my sister," said a gravelly voice. "My sister has come."

James entered the clearing with a swagger.

"*Apwoyo*, brother," Rose said. Even without meeting his eyes, she knew they would be red. She kept him in her field of vision as he approached, though she did not look up from her work.

"What have you brought for us today?" he said. "Tomorrow is Christmas. You must have a big gift, you are working for a big man."

Rose wiped her hand on her skirt, leaving a light dusting of flour, and rose from her seat. She pulled out a white envelope from her purse and handed it to him. James fanned through the bills inside.

"This is all?"

"I must eat, too."

He eyed her sullenly but said nothing. At the open door of the hut Isaac emerged. He stood in the dim shadows rubbing his eyes. His T-shirt had a hole near the hem, showing a dark slit of belly, and he was naked from the waist down. He looked briefly at the people assembled there and then his face pinched. Grace picked him up—he held his arms out to her, his lips quavering—and she carried him to the edge of the clearing, where she set him on his chubby legs and he proceeded to pee into the bushes. When he was done, he picked up a rock and threw it with surprising force toward the seated goat, which bleated and scampered off. Isaac picked up another stone and began to examine it, turning it over in his hands. He was taking it to his mouth when Grace took it away, admonishing, "So sharp! You will hurt yourself, little one."

James sulked into the hut with the envelope, and Rose took the chance to speak to Agnes, hushed so Grace wouldn't hear. "When was the last time he hit you?"

Agnes turned back to the stew.

"Ocen says men who beat their women are cowards."

"He will not beat me," Agnes said firmly.

"How do you know?"

"I know."

James returned, his stash tucked away. "Where is the food? It's time to eat."

"It is not ready," Agnes said. "You must wait."

"I am hungry."

"You can wait," Agnes said again. On her back, Wilborn began to whimper. Agnes took the wooden spoon over her shoulder and tapped lightly on the fabric next to the child's body, saying, "Shh, shh." Rose remembered her own mother doing the same when she was a baby tied to her mother's strong, broad back, with the half shell of a hollow calabash over her head to shade her from the sun. If she began to cry her mother would tap on the shell with a stick—*tak tak, tak tak tak*—and it soothed her. Even now, when she typed on Christoph's laptop, sometimes the clicking would sound the same, *tak tak, tak tak tak*, and she would be lulled.

"I will wait," James announced. He swayed toward the stool and reached out for the newspaper. A jolt of adrenaline raced through Rose's body—she saw his movement as if in slow motion. "Stop!" Rose said.

But she wasn't fast enough. James picked up the newspaper, and the bundle of shillings fell out to the dusty earth in a flutter. He looked at the money dumbly for a moment, then turned to his wife in a rage.

"What did you do? Did you go to Acholi Pride? Did you spread your legs for whoever would pay?"

He lunged toward her, but Rose stood quickly and stepped between them, putting her good hand against his chest. "Stop!" she repeated. He was strong but sluggish, and she hoped the force of her tone would be enough.

"It was a Christmas gift from the *mono*," Rose lied. "For the children. I could only give it to them."

He breathed *waragi* into her face. "Get out of my way."

"Listen to me. I am your sister. Would I be false with you?"

"You are not my sister," he seethed. "You are a rebel whore."

He shoved her aside, then turned and kicked the pan where the dough had been slowly cooking; the stack went sprawling into the dirt, and the pan fell with a bright clang. Rose saw Grace move subtly in front of Isaac.

"You!" Agnes's shout cut through the scene, aimed at James, her voice a razor's edge. She shook her spoon at the spilled dough. "Eh! We have spent all afternoon. What shall we do now? What shall we eat tomorrow?"

Rose kneeled to pick up the upended pan. The pain of her brother's words throbbed dully; she had heard other people say such things, but to hear them from his mouth was something else entirely. She wished she could disappear—right this instant, right from this spot. Maybe she would reappear someplace else, somewhere new and clean. Someplace where no one knew her name, her face, her past.

"I will not share a pot with LRA," James said.

"You stupid man," Agnes said. "Come here. The stew is ready."

And so they gathered on woven mats set on the ground—three children, three adults; like a foreign fairy tale, Rose thought suddenly, like the stories Christoph told from his own land, blessed by triumphant trios and perfect symmetry. The pot of stew and the pot of millet sat in the center of their small circle; they had no plates or forks or spoons.

"A prayer, my child," Agnes said to Grace.

Rose tried to imagine this scene, transcribed: on paper, in black and white, the little letters lined up side by side. How could anyone make sense of such a thing? *It defies understanding,* Christoph sometimes said of the war. She knew the same could be said of everything that comes after.

Grace began to speak. "Dear Lord, we thank you for this bounty.

Please forgive us our sins. We thank you for the gift of your son, who died so we might be saved."

Rose felt her heart contract. *The son who died so she might be saved.*

In Jesus' name, Amen.

CHAPTER 3

SABINE

December 25

Outside the plane window, all was dark; inside, too. When they departed Amsterdam, the flight attendants had lowered the cabin lights so people could sleep, a courtesy Sabine's seatmate was now taking full advantage of. He was a heavyset Kenyan businessman—the finely tailored suit gave it away, along with the passport in his front shirt pocket—and his periodic snores punctuated the background noise of the aircraft.

The seat-back display stated that they were somewhere over Egypt. Sabine looked out to see if she could spot a city or even a cluster of lights, but there was only blackness stretching in every direction. It reminded her of flying across parts of the United States, where the land was cloaked in vast wildernesses that no longer existed among the manicured forests of Germany. Somewhere out there was Lily, alive or—

Alive, Sabine told herself firmly. She wrapped the thin airline blanket tighter around her shoulders.

She was amazed at how easy it had been to arrange everything once the decision was made. The flight had left Frankfurt yesterday evening, with a short layover in Amsterdam; she would arrive at Entebbe, Uganda's international airport, in another few hours. She'd called an old friend to meet her there. She'd fired off a mass e-mail to three dozen people from over the years, NGO colleagues and expats whose contact information she'd kept; they'd be scattered across the continent, probably across the globe—she imagined lights switching on in cities around the world like pins on a map—but if someone knew someone else who could help, she'd take everything she could get. In Marburg, a colleague had agreed to take over her shifts at the animal shelter until she returned. Her vaccinations were up to date. She'd put a travel notification on her bank card and pulled out a thousand euros from her savings account.

These practical considerations had kept her moving and occupied. Now, detached from solid ground and helplessly unable to do anything more, Sabine felt the magnitude of the situation anew. She tried to think objectively about what could have happened. The problem might be one of access—Lily was stuck somewhere, without Internet or phone to communicate her change in plans—but considering the pervasiveness of mobile technology in even the most remote villages, this was unlikely. She could have gotten sick somewhere along the way and was being treated in a local clinic. Sabine had once spent three days in a hotel room in a malaria-induced fever dream; one of the hotel staff finally checked on her and took her straightaway to the hospital, where she'd been half-conscious another few days. Lily might have come down with something a day or two before her flight and still be recovering.

Anything worse . . . Sabine couldn't—wouldn't—think that far.

Back in Denver, Steve said he'd monitor Facebook and find someone to hack into Lily's e-mail account in case she'd communicated with anyone else in the last three weeks. On the advice of a friend of his who worked for the police department, Steve filed a missing person's report in Colorado and would spend the next few days drumming up media involvement. He'd been reading about other cases of people who went missing abroad (*Had he slept at all?* she wondered), and he told Sabine that the U.S. State Department or FBI got involved only if subjected to enough public pressure—though they would still need permission from local authorities. "That's your job,"

Steve had said. "Convince them we're all on the same side. The only thing that matters is finding her."

As logical as this approach seemed, Sabine found it wanting. She knew how bureaucratic behemoths operated: lethargically, and with much griping. As the clerk from the U.S. embassy had said, there was so little to go on. Even if they brought in a search helicopter, where would it circle? Sabine, acting independently, could be nimble and swift. She could cover more ground in less time. She knew East Africa, she knew Uganda—she knew Kitgum. That was where she would start, she'd already decided: in the place Lily had lived, her last known location.

Throughout the flight, memories of Hannah and Lily surfaced at random—images that seemed utterly trivial, things she didn't even know her mind had filed away.

Hannah at eight, standing on a wooden stool at the kitchen sink elbow-deep in suds, helping their mother wash dishes while Sabine stood behind them to dry. Hannah wore a pink checkered apron with a white lace hem, and her wispy blond braid lay tamely down the perfect center of her back.

Hannah at thirteen, sharing an ice cream cone with Sabine: *here, I know vanilla's your favorite.* The look of surprise and hurt in her eyes when Sabine licked too hard and pushed the entire scoop to the ground. The overpowering shame Sabine felt when Hannah whispered, *How could you?*

Lily, in a home video, nine years old. She's wearing Hannah's rain boots and a floppy gardening hat, crouched in front of a line of Barbie dolls, placing a chunk of Play-Doh in front of each one in turn. Hannah's voice: *Can you tell Aunt Sabine what you're doing?* Lily looks up defiantly, squinting. *I'm giving food to hungry people,* she says. *And then I'm going to fly in an airplane and never come back.*

The lights in the cabin flickered on, accompanied by a polite ding and an announcement for everyone to please put away their tray tables and bring their seat backs to an upright position. Sabine's neighbor woke from his nap, shifted in his seat, and gazed past her out the window. Dawn had broken while they were over Sudan, and the crimson-streaked horizon gave way to a fierce blue. Sabine struggled to return to the present.

"I'll be happy when we're on the ground," the man said. "Are you traveling for business or pleasure?"

How could she begin to answer?

"Family," she said at last. Something in her tone must have indicated that she would say no more on the subject, and he did not press.

After they landed, as they shuffled down the cramped aisle, just before they exited the plane the man turned back to her.

"Merry Christmas," he said.

It took her a moment to realize. "So it is."

Outside baggage claim, Sabine's friend Rita Meier was waiting, her sleek brown bob impossibly perfect despite the early hour and humidity. Rita worked at the German embassy in Kampala; they'd met when Sabine had first arrived in Uganda in 2003 and Rita helped her sort through visa paperwork. Whenever Sabine had come to Kampala after that, for staff meetings or outward travel, she'd sought out Rita's company. It wasn't that they were so like-minded—their differences were more numerous than their commonalities—but there had always been something comfortable about their friendship. Never mind that Rita listened to awful, saccharine German pop songs, or that her bookshelves were filled with everything except books. They were both single women close to forty living abroad, and that was enough.

"Thanks for coming," Sabine said as they embraced.

"My God—poor Lily," Rita said. "Poor you." She held Sabine at arm's length and smiled tightly. "We'll find her. She'll be all right."

They shouldered through the glut of drivers who called out, "Kampala? Hotel?" as the women passed.

"It's been, what—three years?" Rita said as they walked to the parking lot. "Four?"

"Just two."

"It's good to see you again. I'm sorry it has to be under these circumstances."

"I'm sorry for bothering you on Christmas," Sabine said.

"*Quatsch*. We're happy to have you. And to help in any way we can."

"We?"

Rita smiled shyly. "I'm married now."

"Rita! That's wonderful." Secretly, though, she felt a pang of hurt, as if it were a betrayal of their friendship. They'd spent so many evenings discussing the pitfalls of marriage, complaining about unfair expectations that all women abroad have to have a man to keep them safe and sane. Safer and saner without, they liked to say.

"His name is Jochem," Rita said. "He's from Berlin."

"So you're not Rita Meier anymore?"

"It's Stücher now."

Inside the car, as soon as Rita turned on the engine, the space was filled with the whirr of cold air and the melodic crooning of Reinhard Mey. Some things, at least, hadn't changed.

Sabine sat up as they drove out of the lot and exited the airport, driving on the left-hand side of the road, a relic of British colonialism. The land was lush, the sight intoxicating, and Sabine could feel her limbs pulling outward, longing to press against the landscape itself. The roads were busy despite the holiday: minibuses shared the road with motorbikes, packed trucks, SUVs, and sedans, all drifting between lanes as if on a whim.

"*Arschloch*," Rita cursed under her breath as a minibus swerved in front of her and screeched to a stop at the curb so another passenger could squeeze in.

They'd only just left Entebbe behind when the sprawl of Kampala crept out to meet them. Kampala had never been Sabine's favorite city. Capitals in general were too busy for her, too self-important. She preferred the villages and the countryside. But after so long away from this place, every tiny thing felt significant: the pristine yellow

MTN billboards over the grimy streets, the ubiquitous minibuses with their blue checkered stripes, the woman selling pineapples out of a wooden cart, the way slender men wore shirts that always looked two sizes too big. Sabine lost herself in the crush of imagery.

"That wasn't there before, was it?" she said, pointing to a massive three-story shopping mall.

"They built it last year."

The city was louder, more crowded, more everything than she remembered. Kampala had always felt chaotic but safe; now it seemed vast and overwhelming—labyrinthine alleys wending in and out of one another, disappearing behind unfinished concrete walls and splitting into a hundred narrow gutter-lanes. How easy it would be for one girl, alone, to take a wrong turn and never resurface.

Lily's first e-mail after landing had been gushing with enthusiasm, everything in exclamation marks; had she felt fear, too? She never said. But even if she had, Sabine would have brushed her off as a stereotypical American, timid and gullible. Unease pinched her chest; she should have known the dangers. She should have prepared Lily better, inundated her with warnings, as Hannah surely would have done.

After a quick stop at the Garden City mall ATM—where Sabine withdrew some two million Ugandan shillings, roughly eight hundred euros—they proceeded to Rita's house in the high-class neighborhood of Kololo, on a hill overlooking downtown. The streets here were calm and green, shadowed by leafy trees; the fences were tall and the tops embedded with broken glass or barbed wire. Rita honked at the driveway entrance, and a Ugandan man peeked through an eye-level opening before swinging the metal gates wide. Inside, a large house stood handsomely in the compound, surrounded by foliage and a wide green yard sloping downhill toward the city.

Though Sabine was long accustomed to the strange decadence of expat life in Africa, the juxtaposition of splendor and poverty never failed to make her uncomfortable. She knew that these luxuries—a big house, a well-maintained yard, a guard and gardener, maids and nannies—attracted genuinely skilled candidates from abroad, who sacrificed other things to live here: closeness to family, access to top-notch health services. But no one forced them to come. And the ugly side of expat life—the feeling of being special, being granted automatic entrance to the upper echelons of society by the mere accident of one's birth, which was conveniently masked by the fact that they were there to "do good"—hung in the air wherever expats gathered.

At the same time, the thought of navigating downtown Kampala in the heat exhausted her, and in Rita's spacious, breezy living room she accepted the offer of a real cup of coffee—"not that instant Nescafé crap," Rita assured her—with sincere gratitude.

After coffee, Rita gave her a spare cell phone and a calling card with ten thousand shillings' worth of airtime. Jochem joined them from the kitchen, his hand outstretched to Sabine. She took it.

"It's good to meet you," she said.

"I'm so sorry about your niece." He had a dish towel slung over his shoulder, and his shirt was splattered with flour and something gravy-like.

"I really appreciate your help," she said.

"I wish I could do more at the German embassy," Rita said. "We've sent out an alert to our newsletter subscribers and posted to the Web site. If anyone's seen her, they'll contact us."

Jochem crossed his arms. "Someone must have seen her get on a bus, at least. The hostels she stayed in would have her name in their books. If she was backpacking, she'd leave a trail."

Rita squeezed her shoulder. "*Mzungu* girls don't just vanish—what's the phrase in English?—*into thin air.*"

But Sabine knew that *mzungu* girls didn't just disappear and emerge weeks later unharmed.

"Come on," Rita said. "Let's pay the police a visit."

A Marabou stork picked its way through a pile of garbage along the curb outside the Kampala Central Police Station, and another was perched on a billboard overhead. The one stalking near the station stood about four feet tall and was bald on the head and neck; a bulbous pink throat sac hung at its breast like a deflated sausage. Atop the billboard, the second one spread its massive black wings, flapped twice, and resumed its surveillance. No other capital city that Sabine knew was as infested with these ugly, carrion-eating birds as Kampala. She'd heard that the Marabous had arrived in droves during the seventies to feast on the dead victims of Idi Amin's dictatorship, but that was only rumor. Most likely they'd simply trickled in two by two, relishing in the uncollected trash and poorly regulated slaughterhouses dotting the densely populated city. Locals viewed them as a nuisance—the birds' droppings were acidic enough to dissolve the paint on a parked car—and Sabine had heard of people cutting down the branches of trees where the storks nested so that the chicks would fall to the ground and die of exposure. But most Kampalans understood that the Marabous, as unsightly as they were, played an essential role in the urban ecosystem, and until the government was prepared to deal with the garbage of a growing city, the storks would do their dirty work for them.

Inside the station, an officer pointed them toward the missing persons' room down the hall, where another officer in a khaki uniform and black beret sat behind a gray desk pecking at a yellowish computer keyboard. A dozen other Ugandans—civilians, by the look of their clothing, Sabine assumed—sat in plastic chairs along the wall or stood nearby, waiting. The officer glanced up as they entered and briskly waved them over.

"Yes, yes," he said. "What is it?"

Sabine felt ashamed at how easy it was to skip the line—*mzungu* privilege, present and accounted for—but did not demur. She explained the situation as succinctly as possible. The officer listened expressionlessly but attentively, taking careful notes on a loose sheet of paper. At the top he wrote LILLY BENNET—USA in block letters. When she was done speaking, he tented his fingers.

"Is there a reward?"

Steve had brought up the possibility; his police officer friend advised against it because of the torrent of false leads it would generate, and they'd have to be careful with wording and legal management. But at this point they didn't want to close any doors, and Steve said he'd look into fund-raising in the next few days. Their private accounts would be quickly depleted; Steve already had two mortgages, and Sabine had taken a significant pay cut when she traded aid work for the animal shelter. And none of this answered the far more difficult question of how to set a price on Lily's life; any amount seemed too little, too crass.

"Soon, maybe," Sabine said.

"Radio ads are also good," the Ugandan officer went on.

Rita nodded. "I'll set it up."

The officer gestured to the other people waiting in the room. "You are lucky. This one, her husband is missing for three months. Three months!" He pointed to a woman with a baby in her lap; the woman looked away, her eyes brimming. "She comes every week to ask me what I am doing to find him. But what can I tell her?" he said, continuing as if she weren't in the room—as if she couldn't understand what he was saying. "I tell her, you need to help, you need to cooperate. You need to give us more information. When there is no physical evidence, what can we do?"

"It's called *investigation*," Sabine said. Now the word felt necessary and strong.

The man shrugged. "Look around," he said. "Where shall we get the money? Where shall we get the manpower? In this room—this is everything."

He set the page of notes on a growing stack at his right hand. It was a clear dismissal.

"It's *Lily*, one *l*," Sabine said as she walked out. "*Bennett*, two *t*'s."

Outside, Rita said, "This is bullshit." Her tone, however, did not convey disbelief, and Sabine found that she too was unsurprised. She looked up as the stork on the billboard flapped once and took flight, its massive wingspan casting a cool shadow across their path.

Christmas dinner was a quiet affair. After eating, Sabine checked her e-mail, which was filled with messages from her old contacts, former colleagues now based in Singapore and Honduras and Peru. They offered plenty of concern and condolences and hardly any tangible advice or leads, besides one Senegalese aid worker who said he knew a private detective in Mombasa; he gave her a name and phone number. Others had diplomatic contacts at various U.S. embassies across the continent. She replied to each asking them to follow up as best they could, though secretly she doubted any of these tenuous connections would amount to much.

After nightfall she sat with Rita and Jochem on the balcony, looking out over the lit-up buildings of downtown. Earlier that afternoon Sabine had stood in the same place while on the phone with the duty officer at the American embassy, who finally agreed to set up a meeting with the deputy chief of mission first thing the next morning. Then, the division between land and sky had been visible, if diluted by smog. Now on the hills in the hazy distance, tiny lights flickered like dense constellations of stars. When she squinted, Sabine lost track of where the hill stopped and the night sky began. A light rain pebbled the overhang above them, and a lamp drew assorted winged creatures into its aura.

"Kampala feels different than I remember," Sabine said. "Was it always this way? Have I grown soft in Marburg?"

"It's not you," Jochem said. "We've had armed robbers break into houses on our street. A tourist was stabbed in Kabalagala last month. It feels more like Nairobi every day."

"And the north?" Sabine asked.

"Probably safer than Kampala. The LRA's based mostly out of Congo and Sudan now. Hundreds of kilometers from the Ugandan border."

"After Museveni's little shock-and-awe show, who knows where they'll go next," Rita said.

Sabine was confused. "What's this?"

"Operation Lightning Thunder," Jochem said, leaning forward. "The UPDF has been bombing the hell out of LRA camps in Congo."

"What happened to Juba? I thought the peace negotiations were going well." On the rare occasions that Uganda made the news in Germany, she always switched the channel.

"The negotiating teams reached an agreement, but when it came time for Kony to come out of the jungle to sign, he didn't show up. That was the end of November. The attack started a few weeks later."

"Have they gotten Kony?"

"He keeps slipping the net."

"I can't imagine that's playing out well in the newspapers," Sabine said.

"It's all propaganda anyway," Rita said. "Museveni's cracking down on free media. You know the police raided the offices of the *Independent* here in Kampala?"

"Three Ugandan reporters have been attacked this year," Jochem added. "One was killed. They said it was a car accident, but . . ." He looked at Sabine askance and asked carefully, "Was Lily doing any writing? Any research?"

"She didn't mention it. Why?"

He told a story about an Australian couple, good friends of theirs, who'd lived in Kampala nearly a decade; the husband was a journalist. The previous month they were stopped by the police at a checkpoint while driving home from dinner. The husband hadn't been drinking, but the police arrested him anyway, then brought him to the station and put him in a cell with a hundred other prisoners, some of whom had been there for months. By the time his wife was allowed to see him, he'd been badly beaten. She was allowed to give him some food and blankets, but that was all. When he was finally released the next morning—without explanation—the man told his wife that the violence in the cell was unreal. Another man had been murdered while he'd watched. The only reason he'd stayed safe was that he'd been able to buy protection with the few items she'd brought. He felt pretty strongly that it was a message.

"What was he investigating?" Sabine asked.

"Resource smuggling," he said. "Mainly from Congo. The Ugandan and Rwandan militaries have had a strong presence in eastern Congo since the Rwandan genocide. It's said to be a cover for illegal exploitation of gold, timber, ivory; that sort of thing. There was a UN report a few years ago that showed a significant spike in exports of gold and diamonds from Uganda and Rwanda despite zero increase in mining or production. This spike occurred during the same years as the war in Congo."

"Our friend was looking into the political connections," Rita said.

"And now?" Sabine asked.

"He's taking precautions."

"They live just down the road from here," Jochem added.

"Still?" Sabine said.

Jochem seemed surprised she would ask. "Of course."

Sabine had to remind herself that she, too, had made that choice time after time. She'd been mugged in Mozambique, faced down drunk soldiers at military checkpoints. She'd been evacuated by her organization twice, but she'd never chosen on her own to leave a post because of physical danger. Of course she understood why the couple had chosen to stay, why the journalist hadn't stopped pursuing the story. Selfish as it was to admit, it was invigorating to be mixed up in the wrongs of the world, to have a finger on the pulse of evil. Better the danger you can see and touch and beat back with sticks than the one that comes slinking through the shadows, entering your home through a hole in your heart.

Not that she'd avoided that one, either. *A dusty road . . . a dark closet . . . her grandfather's secret—*

"But you said Lily wasn't doing any research," Rita said.

Sabine nodded. "Right."

When she thought of how little she knew about Lily's Kitgum

experience, though—how brief their communications had been—she wondered. The truth was that Sabine never really pressed for details; she hadn't wanted to imagine Lily in Kitgum too vividly. Her own memories were still too close. Why hadn't she asked more questions? She thought of a photo Lily e-mailed her a few months back—her niece stood smiling in front of the rehabilitation center, surrounded by giggling children. It was so pat, so facile. The knot in Sabine's stomach twisted.

The overhead lights went out abruptly, and in the darkness she could feel her pulse drumming against her chest. She'd forgotten the uncertainty of Kampala's power grid.

Rita laughed. "Dramatic, isn't it? Sam will put on the generator in a minute." She flicked a match, and the tiny flame spun into two, then three, as she lit candles she surely kept nearby for expressly this purpose. The light sputtered and held, and the smell of sulfur reached Sabine's nose. She thought of her niece somewhere out in the vastness of land beyond and hoped that wherever she was, Lily was taking shelter from the storm.

CHAPTER 4

ROSE

December 25

Christmas Day in Kitgum was alive with song. Praise music and hymns echoed from a dozen churches and front-yard radios as Rose entered the Bomah Hotel compound and saw Christoph waiting for her outside the lobby. He wore sunglasses and was dressed in a pressed white collared shirt and jeans. Agnes's words came back to her: *With him you could really go somewhere.*

"Merry Christmas," he said, and kissed her on both cheeks.

"Eh, you are looking smart," she said.

"Well, it is a special occasion." He lifted a plastic bag, which she could see was filled with chocolate bars. "I didn't know what to bring, so I thought maybe these would be nice for the children?"

"I think they will be very happy."

When Rose had realized Christoph would be remaining in Kitgum over the holidays and would have nowhere to celebrate, she'd invited him to join her clan for their festivities. It was sad, she thought, that he couldn't be with his own family, but he insisted he was happy to be here. He said he'd be going back home in January anyway, and it was silly to make the long flight twice.

They'd skipped the church service; he wasn't religious, and Rose had avoided the scrutiny of church ever since she'd returned to Kitgum. Now they drove together to the hamlet outside town where the clan would gather. Aside from Rose's occasional directions—left at the bridge, straight past the primary school—they sat in comfortable silence. They'd worked together since April and had become something like friends. He had met Ocen a few times, and Rose was familiar with the ins and outs of Christoph's wardrobe. He saved this white shirt for the most formal of occasions, and the fact that he'd chosen it for today made her feel especially affectionate toward him.

She was nervous, though. Christoph hadn't met her family—she'd managed to keep these two parts of her life separate until now. What if Agnes carried fresh bruises? Last night Rose had stayed as long as she could after dinner, remaking samosa dough, but eventually she'd had to return home. And then there were James's words; would he be so cruel as to repeat them in front of her employer? She'd never told Christoph about her past. She felt nauseated and put the cool back of her left hand to the underside of her jaw.

"Should I slow down?" Christoph asked.

"It is nothing," she said. "Look—we are there."

She didn't have to tell him where to pull over and park: the place was obvious from the cluster of cars, *bodas*, and bicycles already along the roadside, skewed at various angles. She caught herself searching for Ocen's familiar tassels, and swallowed the sting of disappointment.

James approached as soon as they got out of the car. Rose was relieved to see that his eyes were clear and his manner respectful as he greeted Christoph.

"It is good that you are taking care for our sister," James said in his halting English.

"Rose works . . . hard," Christoph said in his correspondingly limited Acholi. Though he had some facility with the language on paper, he fumbled with it in practice. "I am the lucky."

James nodded to her then, and she saw the apology in his eyes. He turned back to Christoph and switched to Acholi. "You are very welcome today. I hope you feel at home."

Grace and Isaac came running over, Isaac slow on his short legs. Grace carried Wilborn on her back; she was the baby's *lapidi*, his guardian, until he was old enough to be independent. Though many traditions had become stretched and mutated during the war decades, certain things remained. The first time Rose mentioned the term *lapidi* to Christoph, he said he'd already read it in a book by a man named Girling. Rose had once glanced through the files Christoph showed her on his computer, marveling to see those Acholi words dissected in English. Such clinical descriptions for ordinary objects— *lot-kwon*, "the oar-like millet stirring stick"; *nye kidi*, "small grinding stone used for making millet flour; *odero*, "winnowing basket"; *pala*, "woman's small waist knife." Nowhere did this Girling describe the rich, nutty smell of cooking millet, the naughty jokes the women made while separating grain from chaff.

Grace and Isaac hugged Rose's legs, and Grace gave a tiny curtsy when Christoph handed her a chocolate bar from his bag.

"Can you share with your brother?" he said, and Grace nodded shyly.

"What do you say, Grace?" Rose said.

The girl's voice was barely a whisper. "Thank you."

"You're very welcome," Christoph said.

A group of children lurked nearby, the braver ones shouting *"Mono! Mono!"* at periodic intervals. One ventured close enough to shake Christoph's hand, then bolted away, shrieking while the others burst into raucous laughter. Christoph was a gracious object of attention and curiosity—and, upon further distribution of chocolate, an object of reverence.

Agnes was there, too, and Rose noted no visible bruising. When Rose introduced her, and Christoph said *apwoyo*, Agnes clasped a hand to her chest in surprise.

"Acholi!" Agnes said, pointing at Christoph, and he laughed and replied, "Only a little."

"Come," Agnes replied. "Food is this way." She took Christoph's elbow boldly, and with a nod from Rose, led him off into the crowd.

Rose remained at the edge of the *dye-kal*, the clean-swept circle of earth in the middle of a handful of huts. Plots of simsim and sorghum stretched off to one side, and tall grass and brush surrounded the other edges. The clearing was lined with wooden tables and plastic chairs, and there were woven mats on the ground beneath a shade tree. Fifty or so people mingled in their best dress, which meant something different for everyone. The men wore button-up shirts or suit jackets bought at the Kitgum market. Some women wore vividly colored traditional fabrics cut in elaborate patterns with giant sleeves and a tightly fitted waist; others had knee-length skirts and blouses in the Western style. It had always puzzled Rose how *mono* girls seemed to choose dirty jeans and flat sandals, when they could afford such lovely clothes. The fabric of Rose's dress was spectacular in yellow and purple; she'd had it specially made so that the sleeve closed over her stump, shrouding it from view.

Looking across the gathering, Rose felt that the carefully cultivated atmosphere of cheerfulness was both strange and necessary. Strange, because bloodshed had loomed over this land for so long; necessary, because of the same. In the two and a half years since the start of the Juba peace talks, people had begun to imagine a future without war. Now, Museveni's military action in DRC—this "Operation Lightning Thunder"—threatened to unsettle their fragile faith. It was a controversial operation. Some, like Agnes, wanted the rebel commanders to be killed; others wanted the chance to reconcile, to forgive; still others wanted international justice, for their suffering to be recognized by the world.

Fundamentally, they were torn by love. As much as they feared and hated the actions of the LRA, neither could they simply wish them all dead. The rebels were their brothers, their sisters, their fathers, their daughters, their sons. Though the rebellion had originally consisted of volunteers and Acholi defectors from the Ugandan army—people who chose to fight—the LRA had turned to abduction in the nineties as a means of recruitment. Children were taken, trained, forced to kill or be killed.

Rose had been one. Ocen's twin brother, Opiyo, was another. Rose and Opiyo were abducted on the same day, nearly ten years ago, from their village outside Kitgum. Rose was thirteen years old when she was tied with rope and marched deep into the bush. She was given a gun and called *recruit*. Then *babysitter*. Then *wife*. Five years after she was taken, she returned to Kitgum, less than whole.

At first she had nightmares every night. The faces of men. The sound of gumboots in the mud. The rocking of the earth as bombs fell near. She tried not to think of those years now.

Some said it was God's will that she survived at all. So many were still gone. Their fates might never be known. Rose understood the impossibility of hope: how could you want your child alive, knowing the acts he must have committed in order to remain so? But how could you wish for anything else? How could you support Museveni's army, when they committed atrocities of their own? When it could be your child, your lover, fleeing their bullets?

She missed Ocen with a sudden desperation. With him, she felt released. Understood. Seen.

Why had he left? Why hadn't he returned? Why was the world only full of the missing?

Christoph approached carrying a chipped plate of malakwang and millet and groundnut sauce and boo. "Hold this a second," he said. She obliged, and he dug in his pockets for the recorder he always carried with him.

"One of the elders has been telling me Acholi proverbs," he said. "I've got to record these. Wicked sense of humor, that man."

Rose saw Thomas Obita, a clan elder, come up behind Christoph and clap his hand on Christoph's shoulder. "I have one more for you. *Lapyelo inget yoo nyebe.* In English you would say . . ." He hesitated, searching, then came up triumphant: "A person who defecates at the side of the road can make it a habit."

Christoph laughed. "I give up. What does it mean?"

"It means, okay, somebody commits a crime, and it seems easy the first time, and easy again, and he can become addicted. But eventually if he repeats it, he will get caught."

"What was the one you just told me before?"

"*Cing acel pe kweko ngwiny.*"

"One hand cannot open an anus," Christoph said soberly.

Thomas grinned. "Correct! Like, some things, you cannot do them alone."

"In English, you say, two heads are better than one. In German—*vier Augen sehen mehr als zwei*. Four eyes see better than two. It's fascinating, isn't it?" Christoph turned to Rose now. "Hands, heads, eyes . . . the body part is different, but the principle is the same." He turned back to Thomas. "But as far as memorable images go, Acholi is the clear winner."

"You are an anthropologist, yes? What is your research here in Kitgum?"

"I study cultural anthropology," Christoph said.

"What is that?"

"In a word, folklore. *Tekwaro.* Stories, legends, jokes, proverbs—*carolok* in Acholi, right? The ones you've given me are very good. My academic research centers on storytelling traditions."

Thomas was listening closely, a serious look on his face. He brightened at this last word. "Traditions! If you are interested in traditions, you should come to the ceremony this Saturday. Two days from now. It is *mato oput*, the forgiveness ceremony, between our clan and another clan."

"I'd be honored," Christoph said. Rose sensed his excitement, and her heart sank. She knew he'd been waiting for such an opportunity all year. But it would not be easy to watch.

"It is settled," Thomas said. "Come, let us sit. I have thought of more proverbs already."

There were hymns, there was music, there was dancing. Dusk came and went. There was *waragi*, too, and Christoph partook, and now he was jolly and flushed. His participation in an impromptu *larakaraka* dance caused a delightful uproar; probably they'd never seen a *mono* man dancing the female role. Shrill whistles and ululations accompanied his surprisingly graceful body. *Monos* could get away with anything. Rose did not dance but observed from the side. She'd been too young to dance the *larakaraka* before she was abducted, and there had been no such courtship rituals with the rebels in the bush. Now, at twenty-two, she was too old. And her center of gravity had changed, her balance a delicate thing to maintain. She was missing six pounds of weight on her right side; every movement must be re-calibrated to compensate.

When the dancing was over, things began to wind down, and Rose took a seat in a plastic chair away from the crowd. No one approached her; she did not expect them to. When she'd returned from her life with the rebels, she'd received no warmer a welcome from her clan than she did from her brother and Agnes. Her father had died while she was away, and her mother had traveled to Kampala and had not been heard from since. Her aunts and uncles said Rose brought *cen* with her, and these vengeful spirits would spread to the entire clan so that they all became ill and infected with madness. They accused her of supporting the LRA even now. Rose discovered that many people believed that escape was easy, and that those who remained in the bush did so out of choice. *If you love them so much,* James said upon first laying eyes on her, *you should go back.* After she started earning money, he usually held his tongue. But others among her clan and in town continued to find ways to be cruel. Once she bought fabric to make a dress; when the tailor returned the package, Rose unwrapped the paper to find the fabric shredded into slender ribbons and saturated with gasoline. Another time she was sick—she thought maybe malaria—and went to the hospital, where her cousin worked as a nurse. Rose waited for hours for medication, and finally her cousin dismissed her and said, *Ask your husband in the bush for herbs, if you are feeling bad.* In the last year, relations with her clan had gotten better, and she had been seen enough around town with a *mono* at her side that people were not so outwardly vicious. Still, Rose did not feel at home with the people here. But where else should she go?

She startled at a touch on her knee; it was Grace, with baby Wilborn still tied to her back, sound asleep. Grace opened Rose's hand and pressed something into her palm.

"Merry Christmas," the girl whispered.

Rose looked down at the gift. It was a paper bird, folded perfectly with crisp edges. "It's beautiful, Grace. Where did you learn to do this?"

Grace pointed to where Christoph stood at a wooden table with a group of enthralled children crowded at his elbows. Rose watched as he folded a page of paper, torn out of a school notebook, onto itself, over and over again, in strange ways. At every point he made sure all the children could see what he'd done. After a moment, the paper was transformed into the wings, beak, and tail of a bird. Christoph handed the exquisite object to a small boy, who ran off with his treasure. The other children pressed closer, wanting to be next. Their slender hands grappled for a turn with the paper. Christoph looked up and caught Rose's eye, and smiled.

A moment later, he came to sit beside her. He had the look some men did after a long day digging in the fields, weary and satisfied.

"The lesson is over?" she said.

"I ran out of paper."

"It's a bird?"

"A crane."

"*Owalo,*" she translated.

"*Owalo,*" he repeated.

"It is the national bird of Uganda. You are a good teacher."

"Oh, it's easy."

She stretched her legs long before her. "Shall we return to town?"

"Shouldn't we help clean?"

"It is already done." And indeed it was: the pots were washed and set out to dry, and the chairs needed only to be stacked. The clearing would be swept clean in the morning, and the trash burned. The only remaining rubbish was a few empty chocolate-bar wrappers that had been blown into the brush or crushed underfoot.

"All right," he said, standing. "That dancing sobered me right up. Let's give your brother's family a ride, too."

In the backseat, Isaac fell asleep in Agnes's lap, his grubby hands clutching five paper birds. When they exited the car, James said low into Rose's ear, "I am coming soon to see you, sister." He was gone before she could determine whether he meant it as kindness or threat.

As Christoph drove her the rest of the way home, Rose asked, "What is that called, the thing you did to make the bird? The children were so pleased."

"Origami," he said. "It's a Japanese art form. I have to confess, the crane . . . *owalo* . . . is the only one I know." The car headlights caught on the bridge into town. "Do you know the story of the thousand paper cranes?"

"Tell me."

As they turned the roundabout and navigated the potholes through town, Christoph described a Japanese legend that said if you fold a thousand origami cranes, you would be granted a wish by the gods. Some versions of the story said it was eternal good luck or recovery from illness.

"My parents read a children's book to me when I was young," he said. "It was about a girl who survived the atomic bombing in Hiroshima. She developed leukemia and tried to make a thousand paper cranes so that she could make a wish to survive. But she died before she could finish. Her friends and family folded the rest and buried them with her."

Rose had heard the terms *leukemia* and *Hiroshima* and *atomic* only a few times before, but *bombing* was something she understood intimately. "I think this is not a nice story for children."

"It was supposed to help us understand the importance of peace."

She considered this a moment. "Maybe the rebels should read this one, too."

He let out a short, humorless laugh. "Maybe."

They pulled up to her building.

"Thanks for inviting me today," Christoph said.

"I'm happy you enjoyed it." She reached for the door handle.

"Rose—there's something I wanted to ask you."

She grew tense. Did James say something to him? Had he noticed how the others avoided speaking to her?

Christoph was tapping his fingers against the steering wheel. "You know my research period is almost over. I'll be going back to Switzerland. I've been thinking . . ." He hesitated. In the dim light, Rose couldn't read his expression. Her heart thrummed.

"You're a smart girl, Rose. It would be a shame if you just did transcriptions all your life. Have you thought about trying to study in Europe? I could help you fill out applications, look into scholarships . . ."

In an instant she felt relief and excitement, and then disappointment. He was waiting for her to answer, but she had difficulty finding the words. "My education was . . . interrupted here."

"I know."

She looked at him questioningly.

"About the LRA," he said. "That you were abducted. You spent a long time away."

The car grew thick with the very many things she could not say.

"I have until Primary Six," she said at last. "I did not go further."

"It will take a while," he said. "You'd have to complete your secondary school here first, I think. But I can help you with school fees. And if you went to Gulu or Kampala, you might be able to get on an accelerated track. Your English is already very good."

"I had a teacher in the bush."

Christoph nodded. "And maybe a fresh start could be good. I know it's difficult for people who have come back from the LRA. I saw you sitting apart from everyone tonight. I've heard stories of how returnees are stigmatized."

"Do you know what happens to LRA commanders when they return?" she asked.

He frowned. "What do you mean?"

She turned toward the window. "They are given positions in the government army. They are paid well." Christoph was silent. "And the women?" she went on, her voice beginning to tremble with suppressed rage. "Those who cooked their food and bore their sons and daughters? Those who were taken against our will?" *Out there we were given guns, too,* she wanted to say. *We were taught to march, taught to kill.*

"We get nothing," she said quietly. "They call us children when we return. But we are not children."

A *boda* rode by loudly, the headlights jumping on the rutted road. "I want to help you," Christoph said after a long pause. "In any way I can. Think about the idea, please?"

Ocen's face came to mind: the bronze glow of his skin, the way he closed his eyes when he lay beside her, his cheek against her breast.

"I will," she said.

CHAPTER 5

SABINE

December 26

"Welcome," said a tall woman with her hand outstretched, "I'm Kathryn Willis, deputy chief of mission. Thanks for coming in this morning. I'm very sorry to hear about Lily. The duty officer briefed me on the situation."

Sabine shook the woman's hand. "I appreciate your concern, Ms. Willis."

"Please, call me Kathryn."

The two stood in the foyer of the U.S. embassy, their voices echoing eerily in the overlarge space, empty of what Sabine assumed would have been its usual bustle. Rita and Jochem had wanted to join, but there'd been some confusion at the rental car lot when Sabine went to pick up a car—the confusion being that there were no cars—and to save time, the Stüchers offered to track down a vehicle while Sabine attempted to prod the U.S. State Department into action.

Kathryn led Sabine into a small, sterile meeting room with a glass table and a framed photograph of American President George Bush on the wall. Sabine knew it wouldn't be there much longer; Barack Obama would be sworn in soon, in January. She didn't remember the exact date. Lily would know, she thought with a pang. Her niece had been thrilled by the election results last month—she'd sent in an absentee ballot from Uganda—and told Sabine in an e-mail afterward how exhilarating it was to be in Africa for the election of the first African-American president, especially one whose African origins were so clear and near. *You start to think anything is possible,* Lily had written. *Anything at all.*

"Please, have a seat," Kathryn said. "How can I be of service?"

Sabine lowered herself into a chair. "I was hoping you would tell me."

"Yes, well." Kathryn maintained a loose smile, but her words were already tinged with apology. "I expect our duty officer explained that there's not much we can do."

"That's what the police said, too."

"I'm sure they'll be conducting a thorough investigation."

Sabine let a breath pass to make sure the woman wasn't joking. "You know as well as I do how the Ugandan police operate."

"I understand this is a distressing situation," Kathryn said, her voice smoothed with diplomatic touches. "But you have to remember that Lily came here on her own. She traveled to northern Uganda despite the travel warnings that are clearly displayed on our Web site."

Sabine sensed a distinct shift in tone. "You're saying it's her fault?"

"I'm saying she knew there was a risk." The president's portrait smiled vacuously upon them as Kathryn continued. "I can tell you that Lily hasn't been admitted to any of the hospitals in Kampala. I was also on the phone with the Peace Corps director this morning. He's going to send an alert to his volunteers."

"What about a search team?"

"I'm afraid the State Department doesn't have the budget for search-and-rescue operations. However, I'd be happy to give you a list of private investigators in the U.S. who have experience in East Africa."

Sabine wanted to laugh; she wanted to cry. "That's it? That's everything?"

"Unfortunately, we're constrained by the limits of legal authority. We can't just take over a local investigation."

"There is no local investigation. That's what I'm telling you."

Kathryn brought her hands together on the table. "Mrs. Hardt—"

"Miss."

Kathryn nodded. "Miss Hardt. If I could ask a delicate question?"

Sabine inclined her head.

"Was there any indication that Lily might be unhappy? Depressed?"

The words knocked the air from her lungs. "Absolutely not."

"She never talked about starting over?"

Sabine eyed the woman and regained her breath. Her fists were clenched beneath the table. "She didn't run away."

Kathryn pursed her lips. "I understand she lost her mother."

"That was years ago," Sabine said. "You're not listening to me. Something *happened* to her."

A three-toned chime sounded, and Kathryn pulled a phone out of her jacket pocket. The woman's jaw tightened as she read the message. She stood abruptly. "I'm sorry, Miss Hardt, but I'm afraid we can't do anything more for you at this time. Please keep us informed as the situation develops." She waited at the doorway for Sabine to exit. "You can find your way?"

Outside, Rita and Jochem were standing on the other side of Ggaba Road with a maroon SUV parked behind their car. Sabine had to wait for a handful of minibuses and *bodas* to go by before she could cross.

"And?" Rita said, shading her eyes from the sun.

Sabine shook her head.

"Nothing?" Jochem asked.

"What did we expect," Rita said. It wasn't a question.

"This is the car?" Sabine asked.

Jochem dropped the keys in her hand. "Free and clear for two weeks. Your bag's in the trunk."

She hugged them both in turn.

"Stay in touch, okay?" Rita said. "And be safe."

Sabine climbed into the driver's seat. At last. "Of course."

———

With every kilometer she put between herself and the capital, she breathed easier. No more useless embassy; no more apathetic police. After ungodly snarls of gridlock through Kampala, the traffic thinned out, and instead of one massive, continuous sprawl, the land became wide and spacious, the buildings low. This, to Sabine, was classic Uganda: rain-rutted roads under a cloudless sky, bicycles and *bodas*, fruit vendors at the roadside, round huts and green terraced fields, men whacking cows on the rump with a stick. She'd made this drive north countless times, and out here she could almost pretend she was still an aid worker, headed home after a staff meeting in Kampala or R & R in Zanzibar.

Back in Germany people viewed aid work as a necessary and noble endeavor, glamorous even, and maybe she, too, believed that once. By the time she took the post in Kitgum, she knew better. There was no suffering she hadn't documented. She'd become hardened to it; there was no other way. The job required you to transform tragedy into a quantifiable object, defined by the hours a woman had to walk to access clean water, the circumference of a baby's upper arm, the average mortality rate of children under five. Numbers were measurable: at the end of the quarter, you could prove to your donors in faraway countries that you'd used x amount of dollars to help x amount of beneficiaries by giving them x number of blankets and bags of rice. People became known by acronyms—PLWHA, person living with HIV/AIDS; CHH, child-headed household; IDP, internally displaced person. This was the great irony of humanitarian work, Sabine thought: it required you to dehumanize the very people whose lives you were trying to better. Sabine felt occasionally buoyed by the sense that she was improving the immediate prospects of people in need: a blanket kept this nursing mother warm; a bag of rice kept this family of orphans alive for a week. But such moments were brief and insufficient. Wars, floods, famines came and went; people suffered and died; and back home, bored teenagers and stressed-out soccer moms changed the channel or flipped to another page in the newspaper.

For a while, Sabine had told herself that her cynicism was just another tool in her arsenal. She was committed, efficient, effective. Aid was flawed, intervention was imperfect, but at least she was here—she hadn't turned her back.

But across this belief spread a fine tracery of hairline fractures, and all it took was a single touch to crack the whole thing open.

The month was October, the year 2006; the Juba peace talks were at a low point, but the roads in Kitgum district had been declared land mine free, and NGO vehicles could travel to the distant IDP camps without a military escort. Sabine and some colleagues were driving out to Palabek, several hours from Kitgum town; they'd gotten a late start, and they'd taken two cars so that Sabine could return to town in time to meet a friend for dinner.

David was driving, with Sabine in the passenger seat. She liked David—his bravado, his hipness. He was lanky and handsome, like so many young Ugandan men, and wore square glasses frames with the lenses removed, "for the style," he liked to say.

As they came over a hill, a camp came into view in the distance. The cluster of brown huts seemed modest, but Sabine knew there were seven thousand people living in the space of a square kilometer. The camps had been created by the government early on during the conflict with the LRA, to "protect" the Acholi people. Relocation was mandatory. But the camps themselves made easy targets for attack—everyone in one place, often without UPDF soldiers to defend them—and in the crowded quarters disease ran rampant. The year before, a UN report studying displaced people in northern Uganda found that a thousand people were dying every week of malaria, AIDS, malnutrition, and violence.

As they descended the hill toward the camp, Sabine spotted them: two women, walking slowly uphill on the road, in the direction of the oncoming car. Both were barefoot, and the one behind was bent over as if in pain. When the first woman saw the vehicles, she ran forward clutching a bundle to her chest and waving frantically. The woman behind stopped, half crouched, and rested her hands on her knees. David slowed the car to a halt, and Sabine in the passenger seat rolled down her window.

The woman was old, her face creased with wrinkles, and she spoke frantically in Acholi, which Sabine only caught snippets of, but then the woman held up what she was carrying and drew back a fold in the blanket. Beneath it Sabine glimpsed a mess of blood and limbs— she turned away in immediate revulsion. Then she forced herself to look again, closer. She saw the distinct parts now, the tiny hands, the knees, the skin covered in blood and something slimy. The little face, pinched and red. The baby began to cry.

Covering up the child, the elderly woman pointed back at the second woman, who had sunk to her knees, unable to go farther. She was the mother, Sabine realized. David began to translate, but Sabine had already grasped the situation. There was something wrong with the birth, and the two women were going to the hospital in Kitgum. They couldn't afford the *boda* fare, so they walked. Town was still twenty-five kilometers away.

Sabine knew it wasn't an uncommon situation. Medical care in the outer camps was primitive, at best. Mother and infant mortality rates were extremely high. She'd read the statistic just last week, but now, staring at the wildly gesticulating grandmother, Sabine found she could no longer recall the numbers.

And in the next moment, she wondered whether the borehole they'd drilled last week in Ogili was operating at capacity, and she shouldn't forget to include maintenance training for the water pump they were planning for Matidi. And—why was the car still stopped? Didn't they have an appointment in Palabek?

"Let me take them," David said quietly.

Them? she thought—and the understanding struck her down.

"I know it's against policy," he continued. "If you want, you can fire me. But wait until I have brought them to the hospital. Let me do that much. There is space for you in the other car." Without waiting for Sabine's response, he said something to the woman in Acholi, and the woman turned back to her daughter with her hand raised, shaking it in relief or praise or *hurry up before they change their minds*. Sabine undid her seat belt as if in a daze. In a moment she was sitting in the backseat of the second vehicle, squeezed in next to three others, watching David's car disappear over the hill in the direction of town.

That night when she'd finally gotten back to her house in Kitgum, behind tall walls and pink bougainvillea and a guard with a gun, Sabine cried for a long time. It was the banality of her apathy that horrified her; how she'd sat there, inches away, and it hadn't even occurred to her that she might act—that she could make a choice to save a life. She felt as though she'd spent her entire life looking at an image she thought was her own reflection, but it turned out to be a picture of a stranger. Now, finally, she was standing in front of a mirror, exposed to the coldness of her heart for the first time.

The next morning, she handed in her notice. Two weeks later she was on a plane to Germany.

Now, two years later, she'd returned.

As the equatorial sun sank toward the western horizon, scattering its light upon the calm ripples of a river leading away from the road, Sabine reminded herself that this wasn't about her—it was about Lily. But she felt, too, that the mirror was angling once more into place, and she feared stepping forward into its picture. She feared that this time, she would be exposed for all the world to see. And the person who would bear the consequences was her own niece, her own blood.

Evening was falling as she crossed the Nile River at Karuma, the unofficial border between southern and northern Uganda. She stayed alert for goats and baboons, as well as erratic cars and buses. As one big blue Homeland bus passed her recklessly on a blind curve, she noted the motto painted along the side: RELAX, JESUS IS IN CONTROL. Notwithstanding, she gave the vehicle a wide berth.

It was dark by the time she reached Kitgum. Storefronts were closed—the holiday, she remembered—and pedestrians walked in blackness without the help of streetlights. Here and there, half-remembered shapes lurched out at her: the hulk of a building, the silhouette of a tree stump. She drove past quickly with her windows up, as if the menace of her memories might sneak in through the smallest of openings.

When she pulled into the Bomah gates, she saw a few people sitting at the tables outside the hotel bar. Under the dim lights she counted three African men and two *mzungus,* one a heavyset woman with red hair and the other a broad-shouldered blond man with his back to her—no one she recognized. As she parked, the blond man turned slightly, and she caught a glimpse of his profile: he seemed instantly familiar, though she was sure she'd never met him. She wondered if he was one of the expats Lily had mentioned in her e-mails. She decided to drop off her things first, maybe take a quick shower, and then come back out to make some inquiries.

In the lobby, two musty couches sat uninvitingly in a dark corner, with a fake plant between—just as she remembered. There were several hotels in Kitgum, most of which were dingy affairs with shared drop toilets and cramped quarters. The Bomah offered relative luxury: private bathrooms, mosquito nets without holes, warm water most mornings, and its own generator so that they could show English Premier League soccer games in the bar even when the power was out, which in Sabine's days had been a regular occurrence. She'd never stayed here herself—she'd had a house across town—but she'd eaten often at the restaurant. She wondered if they still served their famous chicken fricassée, or as the expats called it after countless nights of the same, chicken freaking chicken.

A gawky Ugandan boy showed her down a dark hallway to a basic but clean room, furnished with a bed and mosquito net, a wooden dresser with one door that didn't quite close, a table and two chairs, and an attached bathroom that had a shower but no curtain.

"Is there hot water?" she asked.

"Tomorrow, maybe," he said.

A shower could wait.

Steve called just after the boy left. His updates were as inconclusive as hers.

"Did Lily mention anything about research to you?" Sabine asked. "Maybe an article she wanted to write?"

"She kept a journal," Steve said. "She bought a new one for this trip, I remember. But formal writing? I don't think so. She's always been more of an artist."

"That's right. I remember now." Sabine recalled a project Lily had done in high school, when Hannah was still alive—an assignment for her art class that involved maps. Lily had brought her sketchbook to Germany for Christmas, proud of her painstaking pencil-sketched versions of world maps from medieval Europe, with the thrilling words *terra incognita* across places yet unexplored. She'd showed Sabine copies of her favorite maps: the Babylonian Imago Mundi, depicting the known world in the sixth century B.C. as a seven-pointed star, and a view of sixteenth-century Florence, Italy, where, in the lower right-hand corner of the map, a man in a red coat sat on a small hill over-looking the city, pen and paper in his hand—the cartographer, drawn into his own illustration. Sabine remembered that Lily was especially fascinated by this human flourish. It made her feel connected to the mapmakers of old.

"Why do you ask?" Steve said. "Is there a lead?"

"It's nothing," she said. It made no sense to worry Steve with tales of journalists thrown into jail. She watched a gecko scurry across the ceiling. "The woman at the embassy asked me something this morning. About whether Lily was depressed."

After a pause, Steve said, "My police contact said sometimes it's the people you least expect who . . ." He took a breath. "He asked if Lily had ever had suicidal thoughts."

She shook her head, even though she knew he couldn't see it. "No. Never."

"I told him that she saw a grief counselor for a while after Hannah died."

That was news to Sabine. A grief counselor? Had Lily been so in need, and Sabine never saw it?

"But these last few years," Steve went on, "she's been in a good place, emotionally, I think. And in Uganda, you know, she saw some hard stuff. But she was always so positive. She wrote to me and said Kitgum was really helping her to put things into perspective."

Sabine thought of Hannah's memorial service: Lily at sixteen in a black dress that hung a little too loose, her straight dark hair falling across her forehead as she clung to Sabine's embrace, racked with sobs. That whole week Sabine had been frantic; grappling at once with the loss of her sister and the gain of a suddenly motherless niece. *She'll need you*, Hannah had said when Sabine visited her in hospice for the last time. *She's more fragile than she knows. She'll need you to be there for her, after I'm gone.* But Sabine didn't know the first thing about comforting teenage girls, let alone cultivating a relationship from a world away. And in the end, it had been Lily who pulled away from Sabine's embrace, her eyes swollen but her face composed, and said, *We'll be okay. It's going to be okay.*

Sabine flew back to Tanzania three days after the memorial, back to azure beaches and glossy fishermen, back to honking buses and sporadic electricity, acacia trees and the endless savanna, grant proposals and emergency funding and donor reports. A world still thrumming and hungry and alive. She welcomed the way the light seared her to the bone. She didn't explain her absence to anyone, and the gentle laughter of her Tanzanian colleagues, their earnest focus on the tasks at hand, soothed her. It was easy, then, to respond to Lily's e-mails with magnanimity, missives of encouragement. *Working as a camp counselor sounds wonderful, I'm sure the children adore you,* she wrote. *Did you know Hannah was studying to be an elementary schoolteacher in Germany before she met your father?* When Lily wrote saying that she'd finally chosen a college major, Sabine had just transferred to Uganda. *A degree in psychology would be challenging,* she wrote, *but a worthwhile endeavor, certainly.* Whenever they spoke on the phone, Lily seemed cheerful and optimistic, brightly American. What shadows had she hidden behind that façade?

In her room at the Bomah, Sabine and Steve hung up, and she sat on the bed to gather her thoughts. She was tired; the drive had drained her, and now the possibility that Lily had wanted to disappear . . . She meant to go out to the courtyard, but the moment she closed her eyes and lay back, exhaustion overcame her, and the last thing she heard was the gecko's chirrup before she was fast asleep, far from herself, in a town she'd once called home.

CHAPTER 6

ROSE

December 26

Rose woke with the sense of someone in her bed. With her eyes still closed, she drifted in and out of consciousness, and the warm figure at her side grew and changed. First it was her son, now grown the size of Grace; then it became Ocen, fondling a breast; then it was Christoph, who touched her shoulder and whispered, *"Tak tak tak, tak tak. Tak tak."*

When she roused at last and opened her eyes, she was alone. Through the thin walls she could hear the sound of someone hammering a tin sheet, and through the window a slant of sun striped her body with a band of warmth across her chest and shoulders. She rolled over to blink away the painful brightness.

Christoph's offer was on her mind. She'd stayed awake late into the night thinking of his words and what they could mean. She had considered the possibility, but had never truly believed that it would happen for her. It frightened her a little. Imagining the sparkling cities of Europe; the clean, tall buildings; the well-dressed strangers; the cold that she'd heard others speak of as if it were an animal, nipping at every place of your skin. In Europe, there would be no one who knew who she was, what she had been through, what she had lost. Was it possible to leave this self behind, if she left this town?

At the edge of the bed, she dressed in her skirt and a blouse and slipped on her sandals. Her room, for which she paid thirty-five thousand shillings a month, consisted of four walls, one door, and one window. The floor was concrete and easily swept; a short thatch broom stood in the far corner. She had a bed frame and a mattress and one set of sheets, which she paid the woman of the house to wash every Sunday, along with Rose's clothes. Laundry was a task best suited to those with two hands, Rose had found. The only other items of furniture were a small dresser for clothes and a nightstand with a locked drawer, where she kept some cash, her identification papers, and Christoph's equipment when she was doing transcriptions. She had no desk and so she worked on the bed.

She locked the door behind her and, carrying a small towel over her left shoulder, shuffled across the dirt courtyard to the shared toilets. There were eight people in the house. Rose was the only renter, and the only one not related by blood. The rehabilitation center had organized the room for her when Agnes and James said they could not take her in. The family she stayed with asked no questions, but neither did they invite her to their table. At first, the mother would pull her children closer whenever Rose passed near; she once heard the husband and wife arguing in the next room—so thin, these walls—over whether to let her stay. *She is a threat to the children,* the woman said. *These rebels, they come back from the bush with terrible thoughts.* The husband calmed her: *The* mono *would not hire her if she were bad. And the money, it will pay for medicine for the baby.* Now, after three years of polite behavior and paying rent on time, the adults in the family paid her as little attention as they did the chickens that clucked freely around the yard.

She splashed her hand in a plastic bucket of water and wet her face, then patted it dry with the towel. One of the chickens ventured toward her feet, and when she turned back to her room, it raced away on strong little legs, then slowed and resumed its pecking near a rusty metal wheelbarrow.

In her room, Rose opened the locked drawer of the nightstand and touched her fingers to the small purse of emergency cash, and then the stiff blue passport that lay next to it. The crest of Uganda, etched in gold paint, showed a shield with two spears behind, an antelope-like kob on its hind legs on the left, and a crested crane on the right; beneath was a banner that read, FOR GOD AND MY COUNTRY. The last *mono* Rose had worked for—a petty, mean-spirited British woman—had wanted Rose to come with her to South Africa for something or other, and so she'd helped Rose gather all of the necessary materials to apply for a passport. She even brought Rose to Gulu to show her support—and pay a bribe—at the Ministry of Internal Affairs's regional office for northern Uganda. The trip to South Africa didn't work out in the end, and the *mono* woman had in fact left Uganda without paying Rose her final balance, but the passport itself was such an object of beauty that Rose almost didn't mind.

She took it from its place in the drawer and held it in the palm of her hand. So light! She fingered the edges and then opened it to examine her serious, unsmiling face in the photo. There was her name, Rose Akulu, and her birthday, May 17, 1986, though the exact date was just a guess. She didn't feel twenty-two; she felt a hundred years old, a wizened crone, shriveled up on the inside.

Ocen made her feel young again. When he lay with her, when he traced his fingers along her left arm from shoulder to wrist—when he cupped her stump with infinite tenderness, unspeaking—she could imagine better things for herself, for her life. The first Christmas they spent together after she returned from the bush, she gave him a hammered metal cuff bracelet she'd found in the marketplace; the saleswoman told her it came from Kenya, and its interlinking iron, brass, and copper strands were made from old train tracks and wires and melted bullets. It was traditionally a wedding gift, she said—but Rose told Ocen none of that. She simply told him that it was beautiful, and that she'd thought of him when she saw it. He'd received it in reverent silence and slipped it on then and there. She'd never seen him take it off. That was the loyalty he'd shown, the gift he'd given her every day in return.

The laptop and earphones beckoned, but Rose put her passport back and shut the drawer and locked it. The loneliness she'd felt these few weeks without Ocen made their argument seem trifling and small. Every night she spent alone, she sensed the specter of the commander who'd named her *wife*. His looming face, his body, his threat. She hadn't looked for Ocen both out of pride and out of fear, in case what Agnes said was true, that he had found another woman, or had been keeping another all along. But now she feared the specter would manifest—he would become too real in her dreams, and stalk her when she woke. Only Ocen kept the ghosts at bay.

The day was warm and still as she made her way to the corner in town where Ocen sometimes waited for passengers with his *boda*, the place where she'd seen the three napping men two days before. Ocen had paid a onetime fee of fifteen thousand shillings for the right to work this stage; he'd done the same at three other stages around town. Having a *boda* was a straightforward business but not very lucrative. A permit cost two hundred and fifty thousand shillings, and renting a motorcycle was sixty thousand shillings a week. Depending on how aggressively a driver pursued passengers, he could make anywhere from fifteen to thirty thousand shillings a day, minus fuel. A man had to work hard to pay for his necessities with what he earned, let alone accumulate enough to pay a dowry. Ocen had told Rose from the beginning that he needed to save first to buy his own motorcycle, so that his business could be more secure. But Rose had felt that he wasn't trying hard enough, or saving fast enough; she'd offered to buy the bike on his behalf with the money she'd saved from her own work. Ocen lashed out at this offer with unexpected vitriol. She'd called him a coward, among other things. She regretted those words now.

That was the end of November. It had been a strange month anyway, with Rose sensing a growing distance between them. She could understand if he needed to take some space. But surely he wouldn't leave Kitgum forever without telling her?

At the first *boda* stage, the two drivers were new in town and didn't know Ocen at all. Rose continued to another stage outside the mosque. Four bikes stood along the side of the street, and their respective drivers sat in the shade beneath a tree. Rose recognized a few of their faces.

"*Boda?*" one man asked, snapping to attention as she approached.

"I am looking for Simon Ocen. He works this stage sometimes."

"Eh, Ocen. He is not around for some weeks," the man said.

"You have not seen him?"

"No," a second man said. "Not since . . ." He thought a moment. "Not since last month."

"He was here in December," a third said.

"He was gone."

"He was here," the man insisted. "I had to take my sister to hospital, and Ocen took my regular passengers that day."

"What date was that?" Rose asked.

"December first."

"You are sure?"

"I am sure."

"And he did not call or write since then?"

"We are not his friends. We pay to sit here the same as he does. If he pays and does not come, that is his choice."

The fourth man finally came forward. "And if he does not come anymore, he does not get his money returned. That payment is gone."

Rose felt a slight shift in atmosphere, a darkening of the tone. The other three men turned away. So this fourth man was the leader, then.

"He will not ask for the money," she said carefully, addressing him. "I am only here because I am concerned. Have you heard anything about him?"

"He has some regular clients," the leader said. "He takes some children from Matidi to school in the morning and takes them back in the afternoon."

"Brody takes those children now," the second man volunteered. "I saw him last week."

"And there was a *mono* girl," the leader said. "She lived at the Mission. He brought her to the rehabilitation center, and around town."

"He was lucky," another said, grumbling. "She paid too much."

Rose had a flash of memory—yes, the *mono* girl. Lily. She'd seen Lily and Christoph together at the Bomah on several occasions, had even spoken with the girl once. She remembered Ocen receiving Lily's calls in the evening when she wanted to be taken home late; Rose had never minded him answering, because it meant he would earn a little extra, though she was annoyed when he left her bed to do it. "And who takes the *mono* girl now?"

A woman shouted out to the *bodas* from across the street, and one of the men moved swiftly to his bike and started the engine. He pulled the bike out and waited while she sat, her legs to one side, her hands gripping the cushion. They murmured a quick negotiation and then took off.

"The girl? Who takes her?" Rose asked again to the three who remained.

"No one," the leader said. "She is gone."

These foreigners, Rose thought—coming for a few months and then leaving again like it was nothing.

"You should talk to his cousin," the third man said. "Paddy."

"He knows where Ocen is?"

"Ocen met with him the day before my sister went in the hospital."

Rose thought a moment. Paddy lived far from town. A few months ago Ocen told her that Paddy and his wife were planning to leave the government camp and return to their ancestral land in Palabek. Such a choice was becoming more common now that the LRA was less of a threat within the Ugandan borders.

"Can you take me to Palabek?" she asked the driver.

"Palabek?" The man shook his head. "The man is not in that place."

"Where is he, then?"

"You didn't know?"

"Know what?"

The man shielded his eyes from the sun as it peeked above the mosque. "Paddy is in prison. You can find him there."

At the suggestion of the *boda* driver, who spoke in graphic terms of the unpleasant conditions in which prisoners were kept, Rose stopped by the A-One Supermarket to pick up a few things for Paddy before her visit. Power in town had gone off sometime in the morning, and the noise of generators had begun to fill the streets. As she climbed the steps to the store, she tried not to look at the madwoman laid out, asleep, on her woven mat on the concrete next to the shop entranceway. Her limbs were skinny, and her clothes ragged with holes. Everyone knew her tale. For a long time it was merely sad— homeless, mentally unfit. Two years ago the story became a tragic one when she was raped one night by a drunk UPDF soldier and became pregnant. When she had the baby, she couldn't care for it—she was no more than a child herself—so a local government employee came to take the little girl away.

The madwoman had shifted to various places in town over the years; Rose remembered when she stayed next to the gas station close to the bridge, and also when she slept up on the hill where an unfinished hotel had gone to ruin. She wondered whether the woman was coherent enough to appreciate when people left plates of food for her to eat. And did she know about the baby they'd taken away from her? Did she understand that act as a kindness, too? Did she feel the loss like a fishing hook caught in her heart, tugging? Or was it only part of the disconnected, perpetual dream of her life?

Inside the shop, the aisles were dim and dusty. The Pakistani man behind the counter read the *Daily Monitor* while a young Ugandan girl with pronounced buckteeth swept the floor. Rose took bread, tea, sugar, and toothpaste one by one to the counter—she couldn't carry them all in one hand—and paid.

"And this," she said suddenly, reaching for a second bag of bread

rolls. The man added it to the total without remark and put everything in a plastic bag.

When she left, she placed the bag of rolls on the ground so that
the woman would see it when she woke.

The Kitgum prison—which housed the police station as well—
stood almost across the street from the Bomah, but Rose took the
long way around to ensure that Christoph would not catch a glimpse
of her through the gates. She did not want company on this mission.

The building was white with a blue wooden door; hand-painted
on the wall was a sign that read, A CENTRE FOR EXCELLENCE IN HUMAN
RIGHTS BASED CORRECTIONAL OPPORTUNITIES IN AFRICA.

The guard who greeted her at the door was friendly—enthusiasti-
cally so. He wore a maroon police uniform and a red beret.

"Ah, my sister, come in, come in," he said, and gestured her inside,
into a hallway so narrow there was barely space for them to stand side
by side. "How may I be of service?"

"I would like to see a prisoner," Rose said. "Paddy Okech."

"Of course." He ducked into a side room and brought out a visitor's book. "I only need your information. These are gifts?" He looked
toward her bag of groceries, and she nodded. "That is fine. Now, your
name please, and nationality . . ."

After he'd finished writing everything down, he went to the other
end of the hallway, just fifteen feet away; there was a square cut into
the wall with vertical bars and no glass. Through the opening Rose
could see into the prison yard, where men in bright yellow uniforms—
T-shirts and long shorts—were gathered in small knots of two and
three. The guard called out to the nearest prisoner and told him to
find Paddy, and the man trotted off.

The guard turned back to her. "You may leave your purse there,"
he said, pointing to a narrow wooden bench along the side of the
hallway. She did so and brought the bag of foodstuff to him to examine. He looked through the items and then smiled. "Now you may
wait."

Rose took a seat in a chair a few feet away from the window. She could see through an open door into a room off the hallway, where a desk stood piled with files and papers and some old computer equipment. She was apprehensive. Why was Paddy in prison? Did it have something to do with Ocen's leaving town?

"Rose?"

She turned to the window and saw Paddy's face, his hands gripping two of the steel bars. She stood and took a step closer. His expression was tired and a little confused.

"*Apwoyo*," she said. "Here, I have brought you some things."

"*Apwoyo*." He took the bag through the bars and kept hold of it at his side. "I thank you for your visit."

"Why are you in here?" she asked.

"Eh, it is these people from Kampala . . ." He seemed almost embarrassed, but Rose could see concealed anger. "You remember I took my family back to our homestead. The camp was very bad surroundings. We needed to be on our own land, digging in our fields . . ."

"Ocen told me your plans."

"Yes. We returned in September to rebuild the old huts. In October we moved with all of our belongings. In November, two men appeared with papers. They were from Kampala, and their papers said they were the owners of this land. *My* land." His rage bubbled to the surface. "They said I could buy the land back. Otherwise we must leave in three days, or they would send the police." His hand gripped the bar so tightly that his knuckles grew white. "I went to the local chief, even to the police. But they have all been paid by those men. They said there was nothing to be done."

Paddy was not the type to be false, and Rose felt sorry for his state. But she'd heard about other cases of land-grabbing and knew there was little Paddy could do without formal paperwork, which few families in northern Uganda possessed. The police could hold him for four months without a trial. "How much do they want?"

"Three million," he said, flushed with frustration. "But I have nothing. My wife can't pay our children's school fees as it is."

"I'm very sorry," she said.

"Yes." He turned and spat on the ground. "But I think this is not why you have come."

"I am looking for Ocen," she conceded. "He left some weeks ago and has not returned."

Paddy looked away but said nothing.

"One of the *bodas* said you met with him before he left. He didn't say anything to you? He didn't tell you where he was going?"

"No," Paddy said.

"Why did he come see you here?"

"My wife asked him to come. He wanted to help me in this situation. But the only thing that will help is money, and Ocen didn't have any." Paddy looked as though he were about to continue, then stopped.

"What is it?" Rose said. "What else was there?"

"He . . . said he had some ideas about money. He thought he could get some."

"How?"

"He wouldn't tell me."

"Paddy, please."

Paddy bit his lip and turned his face away again. Rose sensed the looming presence of the guard behind her and understood that Paddy would not speak where the guard could hear. Past Paddy in the yard she noticed some of the other prisoners looking their way. It was the day after Christmas and she was the only visitor; this struck her suddenly as deeply sad.

"When Ocen returns," Paddy said at last, "you will ask him not to forget my wife and children, yes?"

She softened. "I will take them something, if I can."

"Thank you," he said. His hand slipped from the bar. "Go well."

CHAPTER 7

SABINE

December 27

A rooster crowed, a water pump groaned, and Sabine woke with a disorientating rush. When she remembered where she was and why, her heart twisted and she lost her breath for a quick moment. Then she gathered herself together. To let herself slip into the gray sea of doubt and despair would serve no one.

The hot water still wasn't on, but a cold shower made her quick and alert. She chided herself for falling asleep last night before she could talk to the expats at the restaurant. She saw a text message from Steve—he said he'd e-mailed her a flyer with Lily's photo and information for her to distribute around town—and she replied that she'd take care of it as soon as she found an Internet café with a printer. She hurried to dress and pack a small bag for the day, then checked her watch: just before seven. She decided not to wait for breakfast to open at eight—she'd pick up chapati or samosas somewhere in town.

When she exited the front lobby, though, she saw someone sitting at one of the tables outside the restaurant. It was the blond man from the night before, reading a newspaper, a canvas shoulder bag at his feet. In the bluish haze of dawn, his features were soft and handsome. She guessed him to be in his midthirties. Under other circumstances, Sabine thought, she might want to make his acquaintance for a very different reason. He looked up at her approach, and his expression was friendly and curious.

"I'm sorry to interrupt," she said. "Do you mind if I ask you something?"

He gestured to an empty chair. "Please. Join me." When he set aside his newspaper, Sabine caught a glimpse of the headline: OPERATION LIGHTNING THUNDER SET TO CONTINUE THROUGH NEW YEAR'S, and the subhead: MUSEVENI VOWS HE WILL NOT REST UNTIL REBELS ARE DESTROYED.

"I won't be long," she said, but she took a seat nonetheless.

The man offered his hand. "Christoph."

She accepted. "Sabine." The touch of his skin was cool and dry. He wore no wedding ring.

"Sabine," he repeated, as if weighing the name in his palm. Americans often pronounced her name with a sibilant *s* and only two syllables, *Suh-been,* but Christoph's pronunciation was crisp and perfect, *Za-been-ah.* On his tongue, the name zinged. "Germany?" he asked.

"Indeed."

"Ah! We're neighbors," he said, pleased. He switched to German. "I'm from Geneva originally, but I studied in Heidelberg. Beautiful city."

"It is," she agreed.

"Lousy with tourists, though. Kitgum, on the other hand . . ." He smiled.

For a second she felt seduced by the promise of small talk with this man; she could imagine lingering over breakfast, circling at the edge of flirtation. He smelled clean, with a touch of mint. She wanted to reach over and touch the tuft of hair that had escaped from behind his ear. When was the last time she'd felt this ease of connection? Not Marburg, where the men were nice but somehow unimaginative, and she had the sense that they never quite knew what to do with her, a woman who spoke fluently of floods and famines and places they'd only ever seen on TV. Her love life in Africa, on the other hand, had been a series of affairs with other aid workers or journalists or professors, with Bangladeshis or Ecuadorians or Ghanaians or Brits—fervent flings, bodies thrown together by proximity and circumstance. She told herself it was the nature of her profession not to form real attachments, because her assignments lasted only two or three years in each location. She was an aid worker first, a woman second.

"You wanted to ask me something?" Christoph said.

Sabine snapped back to the present. "It's—a bit difficult." She leaned forward. "Do you know Lily Bennett? She was a volunteer with Children In Need."

"Lily? Of course. She left a few weeks back."

"She was supposed to be backpacking. But she never showed up for her flight home."

Christoph frowned. "I don't understand."

As she explained, his shock became apparent, and his questions showed deep concern. When Sabine asked whether he knew anything that might help, he shook his head, his expression grave.

"She had dinner here the night before she left," he said. "It was December first. I remember because there was a triple conjunction that night—the moon with Venus and Jupiter . . ." He trailed off, discomposed.

She latched on to the fact that he'd seen her, he'd spoken with her—maybe right here, right at this table. She started to feel dizzy and squeezed her hand between her legs to steady herself. "Was anyone else there?"

"There were a few others with us. They're mostly gone now, back home for Christmas. But it was just like you said: she told us she was leaving in the morning, that she'd be traveling for a few weeks, and she wouldn't be back to Kitgum, so this was good-bye."

"Did she say where her first stop would be? Was she traveling with anyone?"

"No, she never mentioned anything."

Sabine felt her heart deflate. Christoph rubbed a hand on his neck. "Christ. Where do you even begin?"

"That's why I'm here."

"Are you a detective?"

She almost laughed. "Lily's my niece."

Christoph looked at her anew. "I do see the resemblance. You have the same cheekbones. And . . . something about the mouth."

Sabine could feel herself blushing. She quickly jotted down her phone number and stood up. "If you remember anything, or if you talk to anyone who has a lead, please call. I'm staying in Kitgum for a few days at least."

He gave her his number in return. "I'll do whatever I can to help. Today I'm in the field, but I usually have dinner here. Where are you headed now?"

"Bus station, her house at the Mission, her office at the NGO. Do you know when the closest Internet café opens?"

"There's one across from the mosque—I think it opens around nine."

"I'll need to get there, too. I'll check in with the police, for what good it'll do."

He glanced over to the Bomah gates, where a Ugandan woman had just arrived and was standing at the entrance. There was something odd about her, Sabine thought—and in another instant she realized: the woman only had one arm.

Christoph rose and picked up his shoulder bag. "Sorry—that's my cue. I can't be late. Will you be all right getting around town by yourself?"

This time she did laugh. "I lived here for three years. I think I'll manage."

As she drove out of the Bomah, Sabine chided herself for the school-girlish satisfaction she derived from Christoph's surprise at her last words. She'd given what she intended to be a mysterious smile before walking off. She could smack her head on the steering wheel. *You're forty-two*, she told herself, *not fourteen*.

She stopped at the bus station, a dirt lot surrounded by wooden stalls and concrete shops, and found several people who not only worked for the bus companies but also claimed to have been here the morning Lily supposedly left town. No one remembered seeing her, or any other foreign girl, get on a bus that day or the next. They even showed Sabine the booking receipts from November 30 through December 3, and Lily's name wasn't there. But it didn't mean much: Lily could have bought a ticket on the bus or even taken a minibus. Not quite a dead end, Sabine thought, but not an open door, either.

Driving through town felt strange and dislocating. Kitgum had the same geographical layout and landmarks as she remembered— the Bomah, the bus station, the mosque, the enormous uprooted tree with blanched-white bark that doubled as bleachers next to the sports field—but the atmosphere was palpably different. The war years had felt electric, humming; now the town seemed subdued, as if the streets themselves were eager to sweep their history into the trenches at the side of the roads. She noted far fewer NGO signs than she remembered, evidence that organizations had already started to pull out; after two years of relative peace, "crisis" funding was probably harder to come by, she guessed. She'd heard through Rita that her old NGO had closed its Kitgum office earlier this year. She hadn't yet recognized any aid workers, foreign or national. She thought of the house she'd lived in—just over that hill, below the radio tower—and wondered who lived there now.

A few kilometers out of town, at the end of a wide red-dirt road flanked by tall avocado trees, the Mission came into view: its spectacular white-and-tan façade, the clean lines and spotless paint. Founded a hundred years ago by Comboni fathers from Italy, the Mission was easily the most picturesque building in Kitgum, possibly in all of northern Uganda. She drove around the side of the church and stopped at the gate to the housing compound just beyond, honked once, and waited for the doors to open. A few minutes later, the gate swung slowly inward, and Sabine pulled into the courtyard and parked near a hedge that separated low grass from a plot of vegetables.

She took in the shed, the chickens, the fire-orange blossoms of the trees in the middle. A jackal-looking dog trotted toward her, wagging its tail excitedly. This must be Blue, Sabine thought; she remembered the name from Lily's e-mails. Here was where Lily had bent down to scratch Blue's chin; there was the view she looked out upon every day when she crossed the yard on her way to work. The glossy, gregarious starling perched in the tree overhead, the children shouting on the other side of the wall, the sound of a scythe cutting through wet grass—these were Lily's sights, Lily's sounds. Sabine felt suddenly as though it would be the most rational thing in the world to see Lily herself step out from one of the huts, smiling, raising a hand to her brow to shield her eyes from the morning sun. She'd look exactly like Hannah did after her elopement, when Sabine visited her before she left for the States: Hannah, nineteen years old, in jeans and a cream-colored blouse and her hair tied up in a blue handkerchief, standing shyly in the doorway of her little apartment with one hand acting as a visor, smiling and saying, *Can you ever forgive me?* The vision nearly knocked the breath right out of her.

"*Apwoyo?*" the guard said as he approached, his tone raised in a question. He wore black gumboots splattered with mud and carried a hoe. "I am Kenneth."

"*Apwoyo,*" Sabine replied. "My name is Sabine Hardt. I'm Lily Bennett's aunt. Lily rented a room here, didn't she?" Her eyes darted about to each of the doorways.

Kenneth broke into a brilliant smile. "Eh, Lily! You are her mother?"

"Her aunt," she repeated. "Lily is my niece. My sister's daughter." She paused. "Lily isn't here, is she?" The second she asked it, she felt how absurd the question was. The vision vanished, and the loss was acute.

"Lily, Lily," Kenneth said, still smiling. "She is gone since weeks. Eh, we are really missing her."

"Were you here when she left?"

"Me? I am asleep. She is leaving very early. Very early! Still when everything was dark. She is so quiet, even I do not wake."

"What about the night before? Did she tell you where she was going? Was she catching a bus? Anything you can remember is impor-tant." She paused. "Lily's lost, Kenneth. We can't find her. Something bad might have happened."

"Lost!" His face fell, and he stood very still, very solemn. "Sorry, sorry."

"I just need to know if you saw anything. Was she traveling with anyone? Was there anyone—" Her voice caught, and she forced her-self to go on. "Was there anyone who wanted to hurt her?"

"No, no," he said, stricken. "Lily, she's very nice. Everyone is happy to see her."

"Can I see where she stayed?"

He led her to Lily's hut—round with a conical top, concrete walls instead of mud, and a tin roof instead of thatch—and opened the door. Sabine saw right away that she was unlikely to find any clues here. The space was clearly unlived in: spare and tidy, with just a few Ugandan crafts as decoration on the coffee table and some books on the shelves—no journal or sketchbook, Sabine noted. But Lily would have brought that with her. She recognized a few books, among them Giles Foden's *The Last King of Scotland*—a fictional account of a Scottish doctor serving Idi Amin during his reign of terror—and Els De Temmerman's *Aboke Girls*. The latter told the true story of 139 secondary schoolgirls who were abducted by the LRA from their dorm rooms at St. Mary's College in 1996. An Italian nun and a Ugandan schoolteacher—unarmed and unaccompanied—pursued the rebels into the wilderness and persuaded the LRA to release all but thirty of the abducted girls. Sabine had read the book during her first year in Kitgum; it was, at the time, one of just a handful of pub-lished volumes about the northern Ugandan conflict, and she wasn't surprised to see it on Lily's shelf. A dozen or so novels rounded out the collection. Sabine opened the drawers in the bedroom but found only an extra set of sheets, a stack of folded towels, and three partially used candles next to a box of matches.

She turned back to Kenneth, who lingered at the doorway. "Did she have any friends over? Is there anyone else who might know something?"

He turned to the side and yelled something quick in Acholi, and a moment later a tall Ugandan woman appeared next to him, their bodies silhouetted by the morning light. They engaged in a muted but rapid-fire conversation.

"Esther says Lily has no friends coming," Kenneth said, turning back to Sabine. "Lily is only going into town sometimes for dinner. This is also what I can say."

She heard the sound of a baby crying, and Esther disappeared.

Sabine exhaled. "Thank you, Kenneth. If you think of anything else . . ." She gave him her phone number and got back in the car. After she'd driven out she could still see him in her rearview mirror, closing the gate behind her, shaking his head.

As she parked outside the Children In Need rehabilitation center, a tired-looking Ugandan man approached the front and put a key in the cutout door in the gate. Sabine hurried to get out of the car and catch his attention, calling out, "Excuse me! *Apwoyo.*"

He turned. "Can I help you?"

"I hope so," she said. "It's about Lily Bennett?"

He gestured for her to follow him inside. The outer gate surrounded a dirt yard and three long, low buildings. A group of children played soccer in the far corner of the yard.

"I'm Sabine Hardt. Lily's aunt."

"I'm Francis," he said.

"Lily told me about you."

"Likewise," Francis said. "I thought you were in Germany?"

"I was."

"Germany is a long way," he said. "I'm sorry to be the one to tell you . . ." He paused to shout something in Acholi to the children, who stopped their game while one answered back. Francis chuckled and waved for them to carry on. Meanwhile Sabine's heart had ratcheted up to a racehorse pace.

"Tell me what?" she said.

He stepped into the nearest building and set his briefcase on the floor next to a desk. "I'm afraid you're too late to visit your niece. Lily left at the beginning of December."

She exhaled, then explained why she was there. As with Christoph and Kenneth, Francis's surprise and sadness came through clearly.

"So you haven't heard anything from her, either?" she said.

He shook his head. "I wish I could tell you otherwise." He sat heavily at his desk and gestured to an open chair for her. She sat; she didn't know what else to do. She felt like she should be asking more questions—*investigating*. But how?

She noticed the blocky computer and its yellowing keyboard. "Old Reliable," she murmured.

Francis smiled and tapped a finger against the blank screen. "Lily was always complaining about this thing. She tried to sneak in the funding for a new one into a few grant proposals, but it never stuck." They sat a long moment in silence before he spoke again. "You also worked in Kitgum, didn't you?"

"From 2003 to 2006," she said.

"Those were difficult years."

"They were."

"I was in Gulu then," he said. "At the reception center for World Vision. I remember some months we had more than two hundred children arrive. Two hundred children a month, escaping from the rebels. And for every child that escaped, the LRA would abduct another to fill the place."

"And now?"

"Things have been slower, especially here in Kitgum. We had a group of returnees in October—they were with the LRA in Congo and they escaped together. They turned themselves in at the army barracks in Arua, just on the Ugandan side of the border. The UPDF soldiers kept them for weeks, first, to make sure they weren't spies." He clicked his teeth. "Some of these kids were abducted ten years ago. Can you imagine? And now this military action in Congo . . ."

"Operation Lightning Thunder?"

"It won't succeed," Francis said. "But we already have reports from the UPDF that they have rescued some children and will send them to us next month, or the month after. So we continue. Our work never ends." He let out a humorless laugh. "You know, when rebels are killed by the UPDF, they are 'enemy combatants.' When they are captured, they are 'rescued children.'"

Sabine's heart squeezed. "Lily was grateful to be working here."

"She cared a lot about the children—she spent so many hours in counseling sessions, just listening."

Sometimes after they tell me their stories, Lily had written to Sabine that summer, *I have to go sit in the bathroom and lock the door so they can't hear me cry.*

"I remember the first time I met a former child soldier in Kitgum," Sabine said softly. "He was twelve. Skinny as a flute. My coworker asked him what was the hardest thing he'd done in the LRA. You know what he said? *Forced to kill.*"

Francis nodded. "Not just in battle, but other children, the ones who fall behind or try to run away. Friends. Some were forced to kill their own parents. Or they're told that if they try to escape, the rebels will kill their entire family."

The room got very small.

"And when they do escape and come home, everything is different," he continued. "Sometimes the family doesn't accept them. There's a real stigma. People call them names—*rebel, killer.* And the kids themselves, they want to integrate, but they've been normalized to survive in a brutal environment. They have dangerous, powerful feelings. They don't always know how to control their anger."

"And you help?"

"We try."

"Psychosocial support?"

"That's the term donors like, isn't it?" He grimaced. "I don't mean to be negative."

"You'd be preaching to the choir."

Sabine's eyes drifted past him to the wall behind, where a dozen or so drawings were pinned. Most showed sticklike figures in various family settings, with huts and livestock and green grass and blue skies. And then: a body on its side, spilling open with bright red scribbles; a line of smaller bodies marching behind one large, dark figure with a black rifle pointed forward. She caught a glimpse of three pencil sketches at the far left: an exquisitely lifelike portrait of a young African woman, a bird's-eye view of Kitgum town, and a map of the entire district of Kitgum, up to the Sudanese border. Looking at the maps she had a strong sense of déjà vu.

She asked, "Are those . . . ?"

Francis turned and followed her eyes, then nodded. "Lily's work," he said. "That was her favorite activity. The kids loved having their portraits drawn."

"Who's that on the wall?" she asked.

"That's Miriam." He leaned forward suddenly. "You know what? You should talk to her. She's one of the girls who came in October. She and Lily were very close."

"I'd like that."

He stood up and gestured for her to follow.

In the yard, the boys kicked the soccer ball in their direction, and Francis volleyed it back and said something in Acholi that made all the kids laugh. Sabine could see how well suited Francis was for this job: as serious as he was in the office, among the kids he seemed relaxed and carefree.

"What did you say to them?" she asked.

"I said, if they focus as hard on their studies as they do on their footwork, they'd already be running the country. They laughed because everyone knows Museveni would never allow an Acholi to be president." His face took on that serious look again. "That's what the rebels are fighting for, in theory," he said. "To liberate northern Uganda from Museveni's oppression."

Sabine remembered how the journalists all used the same line, making the LRA out to be some kind of extremist religious cult, calling Kony a self-styled messiah, a madman, a warlord, saying he wanted to rule the country by the Ten Commandments. They said the violence was senseless. But she knew there were political aims, too, that the media overlooked. Or there had been at the beginning.

"Doesn't Kony claim to commune with spirits?" she said.

He gave her a sideways glance. "There are many stories about him. Myself, I cannot say what is true."

They found Miriam with two other girls in an empty classroom, leaning against the desks, chatting. Francis explained who Sabine was, then asked the two girls to help him do inventory in the kitchen, leaving Sabine alone with Miriam.

The girl was visibly pregnant—Sabine guessed six or seven months. She couldn't be more than seventeen. Her hair was shorn close to the skin, and her eyelashes were dark and curled at the tips. She had a delicate loveliness about her features and mannerisms. Sabine could see why Lily would be drawn to her.

"*Apwoyo*, Miriam," Sabine said. "Is it okay if I ask you some questions?" Miriam's nod in response was so subtle Sabine thought she might have imagined it. "I'm worried about my niece, Lily. Francis said you were friends, that you spent a lot of time talking. Can you tell me what you talked about?"

Miriam's eyes rested somewhere to Sabine's left, and with her right hand she rolled a pencil back and forth on the table. She said nothing for several long minutes. Sabine understood her reticence—why should she share the pain of her life with a stranger? *Please*, she begged silently.

"We were friends," Miriam said at last. "But I don't know where she is now. She never wrote to me after she left." She made a small movement with her left hand, a sort of throwing away. "She forgot us already."

"I don't think she's forgotten you," Sabine said. "It's just—we don't know where she is. She could be in danger. That's why I'm here."

Miriam lowered her eyes. "She told me about her mother. I was sad because when I came home from the rebels, my mother was gone. Lily shared my sadness."

"Lily's mother was my sister. Did Lily tell you how she died?"

"Cancer."

Sabine nodded, choking back sudden tears.

Miriam rolled the pencil back and forth, to and fro. The clicking of wood against wood reverberated lightly; through the window came the energetic shouts of the boys at their sport. Sabine took in the unswept corners of the room, the cracked chalkboard.

"I told Lily about life with the rebels," Miriam said at last. "The names of our people, the rivers, how we traveled, where we stayed . . . Sometimes we drew pictures together."

Sabine could imagine it easily: the two girls side by side, pencils in hand.

"It helped me to tell her," Miriam said. "I could just talk and talk. She always listened." For the first time in the conversation, she met Sabine's eyes. "I told her about the ivory."

"Ivory?" The back of Sabine's neck tingled. What had Jochem said? *Resource smuggling. Illegal exploitation of minerals, timber . . . ivory.* "What about ivory?"

"In the camp."

"With the rebels?"

She nodded.

Sabine's throat went dry. "Does anyone else know?"

"The others weren't there. They didn't see."

"The UPDF? Do they know?"

Miriam shook her head.

"Did Lily tell anyone?" Her veins were thrumming with adrenaline. She could feel a wave of desperation begin to swell.

"I don't know," Miriam whispered. Her eyes darted to the door just as Francis's shadow fell across it, and he leaned in.

"Everything okay in here?" he asked.

"Fine," Sabine said, too fast. "Thanks."

"We are almost finished," Miriam said, loud enough for Francis to hear. He gave a thumbs-up and disappeared.

Sabine raised her eyebrows questioningly in the direction Francis left.

"I told Lily not to trust anyone," Miriam said. "Some things are dangerous to know." Her expression broke into worry, and she put a hand on her round belly. "Is it my fault that she's gone?"

"Of course not," Sabine said. Her mind was spinning. She'd planned to go to the police next, but now she wasn't sure. The dead end had suddenly opened up like a sinkhole, and she was falling into the deep.

CHAPTER 8

ROSE

December 27

The two clans sat in half moons facing one another, the men in plastic chairs, the women and children on mats on the ground. Rose felt sweat beading at her temples; the sun was hot and getting hotter, and there wasn't shade enough. She'd been granted a chair so that she could sit next to Christoph—he'd tried to insist that he was fine sitting on the ground, but such impropriety would not be allowed, and as his translator, Rose must be close enough to whisper in his ear without disturbing the other parties present.

"Now they are discussing compensation," she told him. "This man is saying that the compensation is too high. They cannot afford to pay."

The negotiations occurred in even tones, without raised voices. The perpetrator of the crime—a boy of twenty-six—sat quietly among his clan. Rose had already explained to Christoph the backstory: how this boy had been abducted by the LRA twelve years ago, and had, at some point during his captivity-turned-deployment, killed a child from Rose's clan; now, after returning from the bush, the boy wanted to cleanse himself of bad *cen* and thus pursued reconciliation through *mato oput*, drinking the bitter root. He'd had many victims, but they were unknown to him—how could one ask forgiveness from an unnamed ghost? He went to a great deal of trouble to learn the identity of one of his victims and track down the family members so that a ceremony might be conducted. The planning and preparation had taken weeks. First the boy made a request to Rose's clan that they would hear his confession; then came the confession itself, with details that were painful—but vital—for all to hear. "I confess to the killing; must I say more?" the boy had said weakly. In response, the victim's grandfather, with knobby knees and half blind, replied: "I am an old man. I want to hear the truth before I die."

After the confession, the boy grew paranoid and concerned for his safety—for good reason. James wasn't here today, but Rose remembered him saying last week that he would go personally to the boy's home if compensation was not agreed upon; other men in the clan had said the same. For all of the emotional aspects of a reconciliation ceremony, compensation was the one truly indispensable element of *mato oput*; without compensation, the ceremony could not be performed.

"How much is your clan asking?" Christoph said.

"Three hundred thousand shillings," she said. "But the other clan can only pay two hundred thousand."

"The difference is less than fifty euros."

"Yes." A pause, while the others spoke. "But now my clan is asking for two million for funeral rites."

Christoph's phone buzzed in his pocket; he hushed it with a flick of his hand. The mother of the victim spoke up, and Rose leaned in to listen.

"What's she saying?" Christoph whispered.

"She says, 'If the killer is feeling pain, let him suffer. I've lost my family, and I am alone.'"

More discussion; more negotiation. Compensation was raised and whittled down. Payment plans were offered. Strangely, though Christoph asked questions and kept his voice recorder on, Rose had the sense that he was distracted—his academic intellect was here, but his thoughts were elsewhere. They had not spoken of his offer to help her further her studies since the day before yesterday, and she wondered whether he would change his mind. Finally compensation was settled. The money was brought out.

"Now they will begin the ritual," Rose said.

The perpetrator had purchased the necessary items at the market that morning: two knives, a spear, a large calabash gourd, and a clay bowl. Earlier his clan had dug up a piece of the root of the *oput* tree, dried it, and ground it into a powder; this was mixed with local beer—*kwete*—in the calabash.

Dialogue:

Why have you come here?

I have committed a crime here and have come to compensate you.

The sheep were brought out—two: one black, one red.

"Are these for exchange?" Christoph asked.

"No," Rose said.

The elder of her clan took the black sheep and laid it down, facing north toward them, the victim's family. The elder of the boy's clan laid the red sheep facing south, toward their own members.

Then the knives, sleek and quick, glinting in the sun—and the blood, crimson, glugged freely across the dusty earth; the blood, thick; the blood, mingling.

It smelled warm, metallic, and sweet. Rose's vision went blotchy and strange.

Suddenly she was somewhere else.

It was the morning after her abduction. Many had been killed in the night, but it was dark, and she was young and cowering and covering her face when the rebels found her, bound her, made her march. By dawn they were deep in the bush, tired and thirsty. Their feet were blistered, their tongues the size of rodents in their mouths.

There was a girl who was too slow. Rose did not know her name. The girl was older than herself, and stubborn. She sat and refused to rise.

The rebels gave them machetes. A lesson, they said.

The sweat rolled down her jaw.

She remembered holding the weapon; had she brought it down? She had both arms, and she was small but strong.

The rebels at their backs, punishing those who did not punish the girl. The girl cried out, begged, but Rose did not stop. The smell of blood. Blade on flesh. It was the weapon, not the bearer, with the will; this was what you had to believe. Rose closed her eyes. They were many; the girl was only one.

Christoph coughed lightly. She blinked, returned. Her heart raced; her body trembled. A thousand needles shot through her missing arm, filling out where her bone and muscle should have been, setting the ghostly space ablaze with pain. She looked at the empty air, terrified and confused: her arm was on fire, how could it not be real?

"Are you okay? Do you need to leave?" Christoph whispered.

"It is only . . ." She winced as another jolt stabbed.

"Let me take you home," Christoph said.

"No," she insisted. "I am fine." She gestured with her left hand to her right shoulder. "It shall pass."

Before them, two people kneeled on the earth, facing each other: one, the killer; the other, the victim's father. Their hands were clasped behind their backs.

Rose took a deep breath.

"Heads together," said the elder who stood over them, guiding their foreheads to touch: "One. Two. Three." A kiss of skin for each count. "Now, take three sips of the bitter root."

As each person dipped down in turn—mouth to calabash shell, like antelopes bending to drink from a pool—Rose wondered: and what of the crimes that were never recorded? The transgressions that flowed beneath the skin like groundwater, undiscovered; a dormant disease in the blood?

And what did it taste like, the bitter root? What was the sense that lingered on the tongue? Did it taste of death? Did it taste of release?

The body—left behind. Unburied. Open to animals, the rain, the sky. *Not the girl's body, no: the body of another. Small. With hands like blossoms. Opening—grasping—*

Gone.

The ceremony lasted all day. Late in the afternoon, the clans shared food and drink, a ritual to complete the return of unity between them. When it was finished, the perpetrator looked relieved, but Rose saw that the victim's mother was pained, as if carrying a fresh wound on an old scar.

On the drive back to town, Christoph was quiet, his expression troubled. Usually after a day in the field—an event, such as today, or an interview—he liked to "debrief," as he called it. He would ask her opinion of certain things he couldn't ask in the presence of others, or he'd want her to clarify something he didn't quite understand. This evening, though, he seemed detached. He'd hardly spoken with Thomas, the elder who'd invited him to the ceremony. Rose saw him check his missed call before they got in the car, but he hadn't called whoever it was back. Rose would not pry. Finally he broke the silence himself:

"Did you ever meet Lily?" he asked.

"Mm," Rose said noncommittally. "Lily. Let me remember."

"American girl, dark hair?"

But the name had already clicked into memory: the *mono* girl, Ocen's customer. Funny that she'd just been reminded yesterday. "She was working at the rehabilitation center."

"That's the one," he said. "She's missing. That woman I was talking to this morning at the Bomah? That's her aunt. She came out to look for her."

"Missing? From Kitgum?"

"No one knows. She was traveling all over the country, so if something happened, it could have been anywhere along the way." He turned to her. "Have you heard of anything happening here? Any . . . trouble? It would have been a few weeks ago. The beginning of December."

If there was trouble in town, Ocen would know; *bodas* always knew. They went everywhere, listened to everything. If there had been a half-whispered word of a crime against a *mono* girl—a robbery gone wrong, kidnapping, worse—Ocen would have snatched its echo from the air. But Rose, alone: what did she hear? Only the hush of curses: *LRA. Killer. Rebel whore.*

"I am sorry," she said to Christoph. "I don't know anything."

"I feel gutted, like I should have known. She's been missing for weeks." He shook his head. "It's so sad. Just horrible, isn't it? It makes you think."

About what? she wondered, but didn't ask.

He cleared his throat. "Anyway, I'm glad we got to witness the ceremony today. I've read a lot about it—about the variations from clan to clan, what the rituals mean. But seeing in person . . . it's powerful. You get the sense that this could be the path toward real peace. Imagine Joseph Kony kneeling on the ground before all those people, asking for forgiveness."

Rose felt a bloom of nausea and anger rise. "So he should not go to The Hague?"

Christoph downshifted to make a right-hand turn toward town. "Why should the rest of the world impose our version of justice on the Acholi people? Why should we rob you of your traditions?"

"Is your justice too good for us?" she said, her tone cutting. "Are Kony's crimes against the Acholi not also crimes against humanity?" *Are they not also,* she willed him to hear, *crimes against me?*

Christoph looked at her in surprise. He seemed about to respond when they turned the corner and a crowd of people appeared in the road directly in front of them.

Christoph slammed on the brakes, and Rose's seat belt snapped hard against her chest. Then the sound of the engine rumbling idly and the muted shouting from the crowd ahead. Yellow dust darkened the air in front of the windshield.

"What's happening?" Christoph said, craning his neck. "Rose, can you see what's going on?"

The question was answered without her as the dust settled and the crowd shifted—opened—and they saw a man: kneeling. Shirtless, his pants torn and dirty. His arms were tied behind his back, and his upper body swayed slightly. There was something dark and wet on his face, running down his neck, across his chest.

"It's a mob," Christoph said, understanding.

For a moment the man just swayed there. The scene seemed stalled, suspended; an act on a stage. Then a man from the crowd stepped forward and swung the long wooden handle of a hoe in an arc over his head, swift—*whhifft* came the noise, distantly, and then *crack!*—across the kneeling man's back.

Christoph began to frantically work his seat belt buckle.

Rose reached out to grab him—*only air; why couldn't she feel him?*—and realized she was reaching with her right arm, the non-arm, the gone arm.

She found her voice instead. "Stop. Don't."

His hand was on the door handle. Rose could see a few people in the crowd looking their way.

"We have to do something. They're going to kill him." His voice trembled but his body was rigid, frozen, hand on handle, as if her invisible arm held him there.

"If you try to stop them, they'll beat you," she said, low and even. "They won't care that you're a *mono.*"

Another man broke from the crowd and punched the kneeling man in the mouth. Rose flinched; Christoph jolted as if he'd been hit himself.

"No," Christoph said. That was all. Before she could say another word, he swung the door open and got out, shutting it behind him.

She took a breath. The air was heavy and close. The scene before her seemed to happen in slow motion: the three men who splintered from the crowd when they saw Christoph get out of the car; Christoph striding forward, his whiteness no shield; the limb-locked collision. He tried to shoulder past—there was yelling—and the three men held him back, pushed him down to the ground; the struggle brutal and fast—

—and release, a parting: the crowd thinned and dispersed, like oil separating on a hot pan. From the direction of town, the police had arrived, a pickup truck that now spilled out two officers in khaki uniforms with red berets and black batons. They grabbed the kneeling man—an elbow each—and jerked him to standing, then pushed him forward, though the man's feet stumbled and dragged. Roughly they shoved him toward the back of the pickup, where two more officers hauled him chest over tailgate, letting the man fall hard, face-first, onto the metal truck bed. Meanwhile Christoph had picked himself up and was brushing the dirt from his palms.

Rose opened her door and stepped down. To a person passing, she asked, "What is the man accused of?"

"He is a thief," the man said before trotting onward, unwilling to linger.

When Christoph returned to the car, Rose could see he was shaking. He had a small rip in the shoulder seam of his T-shirt—nothing large, the size of a silver two-hundred-shilling coin, through which his pale skin was visible. He wiped his mouth with his hand.

"My God," he said.

"Are you all right?" she asked. "Are you hurt?"

"I'm fine." He brought his hand to his forehead. "That man—"

"He was a thief. Someone told me just now."

"But it's barbaric! It's . . . inhuman! If the police hadn't come . . ."

She met his eyes, his wild, horrified eyes. Her gaze was level. She said: "You believe in traditional justice? This is traditional justice, too."

He dropped her off half an hour later at the corner near her house. In the car they'd hardly spoken. Christoph was shaken, that much was clear; Rose felt unsympathetic to his distress. She said good night and got out. Through the rolled-down passenger window he spoke in a monotone, "See you Monday." His eyes stayed straight ahead, and seconds later he was already driving away, back to the safety of the Bomah compound, the comfort of cold beers, *mono* conversation— probably to "debrief" the day's excitement and the evening's brutality, she thought as she watched the red rear lights of the car turn the corner and disappear.

As she turned toward the house, a shadow came out from behind a tree—a figure, tall, looming. Instinctively, her body sprang to flee, so fast that her mind hadn't even formed the thought. Not fast enough. The figure grasped her good arm and held her tight.

"Shh, sister," a familiar voice said. "I am not here to hurt you."

James. Her pulse slowed but her mind quickened. He was smiling, a sort of half grin; was it embarrassment she saw there?

He let go of her arm. "I told you I would come see you, didn't I?"

"What do you want?" she said, wary.

"You should not walk alone at night. Kitgum is not safe."

"I am not walking. I am already home. And now I am not alone."

"True, true," he said, chuckling.

"Why are you here?"

She sensed him weighing his words.

"Agnes is pregnant," he said at last. "She is carrying my child." In his tone Rose heard wonder, and joy, and perhaps a hint of fear—good fear, she thought. The kind that makes a man see himself anew.

"A blessing," Rose said. "I am happy for you."

"I know I've done wrong. Too much." He was shaking his head. "I have been a poor husband, a loiterer, a drunk. I have not cared for the children God sent to me. I have done you wrong, too, my sister."

A warm flush came up her neck. Had anyone ever said this to her?

"I want to change," he continued softly. "It is time. I am ready to work hard. I will do anything. I will humble myself before the miracle of my child." Fiercely, he gripped her arm once more. "You can help me, can't you? Your *mono* friend? Maybe he knows some work I can do. Or I can drive a *boda*, like Ocen. He can help me get started."

Unease loosened the knot, and she spoke, though with sadness: "Ocen is gone. And Christoph . . ." She thought of the shock in his expression when she'd thrown his outrage back in his face. *This is traditional justice, too.* Surely he would never help her study now; to think he might help her brother was almost laughable.

Yet James's presence before her, his earnest face—how young he was! Only twenty-four, with three orphans under his roof and a baby coming soon. This was the future she must invest in, she thought: this was her family.

"I will ask," she said finally. "We will find something for you."

He clasped her single hand in his two large ones. "Bless you, my sister. Bless you."

CHAPTER 9

SABINE

December 27

She'd forgotten how night fell in Kitgum: the sensuality of a yellow-gray sunset seducing her into believing it might be like this always—the sweet trill of birdsong, somewhere a radio playing Ugandan reggae songs, a refreshing coolness sweeping away the heat—until the swift curtain of night dropped and she was left spinning, startled, blind.

In her room at the Bomah, Sabine washed the day's sweat and grime from her face. She had only a candle for light; power had gone off in town that afternoon, and the hotel hadn't turned on its generator. She hadn't stayed much longer with Miriam that morning. The girl was reluctant to share too many details, and Sabine didn't need specifics to understand what was happening: the rebels were trafficking in illegal ivory as a way to fund their cause. It seemed so obvious—yet even obvious knowledge could be dangerous to the knower.

After she'd left the Children In Need center, instead of going to the police she found an Internet café. The connection was slow but functional, and the screen was angled away from the other tables so that no one could see what she was reading. For hours she scoured news sites, UN reports, NGO newsletters; there was nothing that connected the LRA to ivory, but plenty about the illegal ivory trade in Africa as a whole.

As she read, a narrative began to emerge. Demand for elephant tusks and rhino horns skyrocketed in the 1970s, causing a massive decline in animal populations across the continent; a 1990 ban on the ivory trade temporarily slowed the slaughter of rhinos and elephants, but in the past decade, there'd been a resurgence of demand in Asia and, subsequently, of illegal activities in Africa to meet the market's desires. Criminals became organized and brutally effective. More often than not, the people doing the killing were better armed than the rangers trying to stop them. It was more than scattered violence; it was a war. The illegal ivory trade was spreading deeper and wider, with vast interlinking networks of poachers, smugglers, distributors, and corrupt officials at every point along the way.

Sabine knew many of these things already, of course. But it was the scale of the slaughter that astounded her. And the photographs: the ragged carcasses, the stacks of curved tusks as tall as a man. Tens of thousands of elephants were being killed every year.

She learned other things, too, of elephant intelligence and empathy. They mourned their dead and nursed their wounded. They could distinguish between languages, between genders, between faces: they could recognize the humans who had helped them in the past, and those that posed a threat.

Her heart broke at the thought of those splendid creatures dropping to the ground, never to rise. She recalled a game drive she did years ago on a weekend R & R in Kenya: it was the off season in the Maasai Mara, so she had a safari Jeep and a driver all to herself. At midday they'd come across a small herd of elephants at a watering hole. For a drowsy half hour, with the Jeep parked under the shade of a Kigelia tree, Sabine watched, entranced, as the calves wove unsteadily between their mothers' legs, and the adults' trunks prodded and splashed and swung as if they were separate creatures altogether. Then the wind shifted, and the elephants caught the scent of some predator in the bush. The herd began to move as one, gaining momentum as they climbed the slope away from the pond—directly toward the Jeep. The driver scrambled to turn the ignition and put it into gear. But Sabine was enthralled: the earth literally rumbled beneath them as the herd came closer, ears wide and flapping, long muscular legs pumping, trunks aloft and trumpeting. The noise was stupefying. Such magnificence! The driver had gotten them out of the herd's path just in time, and with the windows open, Sabine felt the exhilarating rush of air as they stampeded past. She'd believed it was a force beyond man's reach—a tsunami, an earthquake—but of course that was foolish. Anything that drew breath, man could bring down.

Sometime around two o'clock, the computer screen winked abruptly and went black.

"Eh, sorry," the woman at the counter said. "No generator."

Probably for the best, Sabine thought. She was exhausted and defeated and hungry to boot. She emerged from the Internet café dazed, blinking into the harsh daylight. At the corner was a woman in a headscarf selling samosas, and Sabine bought four little potato-filled triangles, then a bottle of water from the kiosk across the street. The kiosk had two plastic chairs set out under the overhang, and Sabine sat and ate.

So Lily knew that the LRA had ivory. Miriam said she'd first told Lily in mid-November. Two weeks later, Lily left Kitgum and fell out of touch. Three weeks after that, she failed to show up for her flight home. It could be a coincidence, Sabine thought. Simple happenstance. She reiterated in her mind what she'd told Rita back in Kampala: Lily never mentioned being interested in research or writing or journalism of any kind. But it would have been easy for Sabine not to know. Those buoyant e-mails, the smiling photographs: how much had Lily been curating her experience in Uganda, selecting only the pieces she wanted Steve and Sabine to see?

She remembered an e-mail Lily had sent in November. There were lines she recalled now with vivid clarity; they came at the end of a paragraph where Lily talked about how much she'd learned at the rehabilitation center, how she finally understood the limits of charity. *For a while I just felt helpless,* she'd written, *like no matter what I did here, there was no way to make a difference. But now I think I've found a way. It's about finding something that's bigger than yourself, and being brave enough to commit to it.* At the time Sabine had been preoccupied with some minor crisis at the animal shelter; she'd read the message quickly and thought nothing of it—a surge of optimism stemming from a complex brew of emotions Lily was experiencing as her time in Uganda came to a close. But now Lily's words cast a long, dark shadow.

Speculation would get her nowhere. What she needed was evidence, hard proof. If Lily *had* been investigating the illegal ivory trade, she couldn't have been working alone. Lily would have needed allies, people who could ask probing questions, who had access to information and to the possessors of that information.

Christoph? She dismissed him almost at once; he'd seemed genuinely shocked at Lily's disappearance, and he hadn't said anything about Lily being privy to sensitive information. But at least he might know who else she'd talked to, who she spent her time with.

Sabine called his phone but he didn't pick up, and, with newfound caution, she decided against leaving a voice mail. She sat a little longer in the chair outside the kiosk, watching the street, still quiet on this Saturday after Christmas. Two children passed, giggling and whispering with their eyes on her; then a man pushing a bicycle to which a dozen yellow jerry cans had been tied with rope. Sabine remembered suddenly that she'd promised Steve she would print out his flyer and post it around town; she hadn't even checked her e-mail, she was so fixated on ivory. Now she'd have to wait until the power was back on. The low-bellied growl of an engine announced an incoming *boda,* and Sabine caught a glimpse of the gaudily decorated motorcycle as it rumbled past, the driver wearing oversized sunglasses, his passenger—a woman in a gray skirt and white blouse—sitting sidesaddle on the cushion behind him, legs crossed at the ankles.

As clear as a chime, a question rang through her mind: how did Lily leave the Mission the morning of December second? If she met a friend or an informant, whoever it was could have picked her up in a car; there was no way of knowing. But if Lily was backpacking and planning to take a bus, she wouldn't have walked all that way in the dark—the Mission was nearly three miles from the station in town. Taxis didn't exist in Kitgum as far as Sabine knew. Lily would almost certainly have organized a *boda*. In fact, she probably had a regular driver, someone who brought her to and from the office, someone she could trust to drive safely.

Again, Sabine thought of Christoph: he must have seen Lily get dropped off or picked up at the Bomah; he might even know the driver's name. It didn't seem like much of a lead, but right now, it was the best she had.

That had been hours ago. Now Sabine patted her face dry with a towel, the candlelight flickering in the foggy mirror—foggy by age and uncleanliness, not by steam, as the hot water still wasn't on. The blurriness softened her features, took away the years. She considered her reflection: not pretty, like Hannah; handsome, maybe. As a girl she'd been jealous of her older sister's effortless charm and the rewards it garnered—extra sweets from visiting aunts and uncles, attention from boys, a natural likeability. Hannah's prettiness wasn't so extreme as to be intimidating, and she was too shy to be mistaken for haughty in the way of other women who were aware of their own allure. Sabine had recognized quickly that she would never be Hannah's equal in looks, and so she pursued excellence in other endeavors: school, sports, service. The longer she told herself it didn't matter, the truer it became. She was so focused on her work that things like makeup and hairstyles became extraneous. Fashion was irrelevant; what would she do with high heels in a refugee camp? And spending most of her life in countries across Africa meant that she was viewed, even by other expats, as a white woman first, and only after that as a woman, period: someone whose features might be evaluated individually and as a whole for qualities of attractiveness.

Now, at forty-two, she examined her cheekbones, the arc of her eyebrows, the line of her jaw. What did Christoph think of this face? When he'd commented on the shape of her mouth—had he imagined kissing her? That schoolgirlish flutter she'd felt ruffled through her chest again. The men she'd dated in Marburg told her she was "hard to read," as if the wrinkles around her eyes ought to spell out *happy* or *sad* or *bored* or *aroused*. She'd told them, *If you want to know what I'm thinking, just ask*. But when they did, they never seemed to like the answer.

In the courtyard, Christoph was sitting at the same table where she'd found him that morning, but with a beer instead of a newspaper. He saw her and waved her over. He seemed distressed; she felt an instinct to comfort him, to place her hand upon his knee.

"Sorry I missed your call earlier," he said. "Did you find out anything about Lily?"

Circumspect, she said, "I'm not sure yet." She took a seat just as the waitress came by to take their orders.

After the waitress left, Christoph leaned forward. "I have to admit, when you said this morning that you were here during the war, I was impressed."

She fanned away a blush. "Kitgum was my last assignment. I lived in Africa eighteen years altogether."

"Long time. Why did you leave? Burnout?"

"In a manner of speaking."

"It gets to you, doesn't it? Just today . . ." He pressed the heels of his palms against his eyes, and Sabine noticed a slit in his shirt, near the shoulder. "You know about mob justice, I'm sure," he said. "There was a crowd in the road when we were driving back from Ogili. Christ, I thought they were going to kill the guy. I tried to break it up, but . . ."

He paused, and Sabine's breath hitched. "You tried?" she said. He'd said it like it was nothing, like anyone would have done the same.

"Didn't matter. The police came and took the guy away." He shook his head as if to throw off the memory. "Anyway—you said you might have a lead about Lily? Did someone hear from her?"

Sabine's beer arrived, and she waited until the waitress had left before continuing. "Nothing so tangible. I was hoping you'd know whether she had a regular *boda* driver—maybe the person she would have called to take her to the bus station that morning."

Christoph blanched. "Of course."

"You know him?" Her heart leaped.

"My assistant, Rose—the woman you saw this morning. Her . . . boyfriend, fiancé, I don't know. His name's Ocen. He was Lily's driver. I didn't even think of it until now." His expression turned puzzled. "Strange, I asked Rose about Lily, and she didn't say anything, either."

"Could you ask again?" She tried to temper her eagerness; it might come to nothing. "If I could talk to him, it would be a huge help."

He hesitated, then evidently came to a decision and tapped out a short message on his phone. "She usually answers pretty fast."

There was something odd in his tone, Sabine thought, but she said, "I appreciate it."

A woman approached their table—a *mzungu,* Sabine saw, perhaps fifty years old, with red hair and a hefty shoulder bag. Sabine had a flash of recognition and remembered seeing the woman last night when she arrived.

"Hello," the woman said cheerfully as she flopped her bag on the dirt and stuck out her hand. "I'm Linda."

"Sabine," she said.

"Lily's aunt," Christoph added.

"Oh?" Linda said, sitting. Her smile was wide and easy, and her ebullience extended outward, along with her girth. "Did Lily have a good time in Bunyonyi?"

Sabine's heart raced. "Is that where she went?"

"I thought . . ." Linda looked between them, still smiling, though doubt tugged at the edges of her mouth. "Or was it Murchison?"

When Christoph spoke, his voice was low. "She never showed up for her flight home."

It took a few seconds for the implication to sink in. Linda inhaled sharply. "Oh!"

Christoph's phone buzzed and he checked the message. "Rose says she'll ask him tomorrow."

"Ask who what?" Linda said.

"Lily's *boda* driver," Sabine said. "I'm hoping he'll know which bus she took."

Linda was nodding, a bit dazed. Her eyes wandered, and abruptly she sobered. "Look—do you see that guy?"

Christoph turned his head. "Where?"

"At the gate." Linda fixed her gaze on Sabine and said, "I'm being followed."

Sabine looked toward the Bomah gates and noticed a figure there: a man, hands in pockets. He turned away and disappeared. "He left," she said.

"He'll be back." Linda seemed confident.

Sabine's doubtful look caused Linda to purse her lips. "Let me tell you: I was in Sudan for two years before here, off and on. It's chaos up there, you know?" Her voice suggested a trace of Nordic heritage— Swedish, perhaps? She leaned forward conspiratorially. "Kitgum is chaos, too, but they *watch* you. I've never experienced surveillance like I have here. I only crossed the border to document the cases that have been reported here, but . . ." She glanced toward the gate.

Sabine and Christoph exchanged a look; Christoph's face clearly said, *Don't encourage her.* But with illegal ivory still on her mind, Sabine wasn't so ready to brush the woman off. "You knew Lily, Linda?"

"Lily!" Linda sighed. "A bright girl, really."

"Do you remember anything that might help?"

While Linda thought, the waitress brought two dishes of chicken stew with rice. Sabine ate rapidly while Christoph merely pushed the food around on his plate.

"*Disillusioned*," Linda said at last, her tone triumphant. "That's the word. Lily seemed disillusioned."

"With aid, you mean?" Sabine said between bites.

"With the world," Linda said grandly. "Poor girl. Father gone, no mother, no family . . ."

"I'm family." Sabine's tone was cutting.

"Yes, dear, but you were in Germany! There was an entire ocean between you."

Sabine couldn't remember the last time someone had called her *dear*. She resented Linda's blunt evaluation of Lily's de facto orphanhood, but beneath the pique, she saw the truth in the description.

"Something changed, though," Linda mused. "At the end of October. Didn't you notice?" she asked Christoph.

"Notice what?" Christoph said.

"*Lily*. Something changed with her. She became secretive. But not depressed, you know. Purposeful. Determined."

Sabine perked up. The end of October: *before* Miriam told Lily about the ivory? Miriam could have gotten the timing wrong.

"At first I thought she'd taken a lover," Linda continued. "She had that look about her, you know." Her tone was so matter-of-fact that Sabine nearly dropped her beer. She couldn't help but glance at Christoph, who was—could it be?—*blushing*. A strange feeling coiled in her stomach.

"Did you see her with anyone?" Sabine asked, sensing a new lead. She could deal with the strange feeling later.

"No," Linda said. "But that doesn't mean much. She didn't always come to the Bomah for dinner. She was here, though, the night before she left."

"What did you talk about that night?"

Linda inhaled deeply, as if the past was something she could suck up out of the air. "Mister Mythology over here was going on about the triple conjecture."

"Conjunction," Christoph grumbled.

Sabine caught his gaze and he smiled, fleetingly, and looked away; the twinge in her stomach returned. Lily was young and attractive; Christoph, the handsome older man. Sabine knew how easy it would have been, how inevitable even, for the two to come together in a town as small and remote as Kitgum. At once she was filled with shame. It fanned hotly across her chest and up the back of her neck. She took a long draft of her beer to help swallow the knot forming in her throat.

"Oh!" Linda said, eyes widening. "Aboke." She tapped a finger to her nose. "Lily was asking if we'd heard the story."

"Right, I remember," Christoph said. "The LRA abducted all those girls—over a hundred, weren't there?—and then one of the Italian nuns tracked them for days into the bush. She ended up rescuing most of them if I recall."

"What courage!" Linda said. "Can you imagine?"

"Lily had the book on her shelf," Sabine said. "I saw it this morning."

"My favorite part was the way they found the rebels," Linda said. "Following the trail of candy-bar wrappers through the bush."

"I just thought of something else," Christoph said. "The National Memory and Peace Documentation Centre—it's run by the Refugee Law Project out of Makerere University in Kampala. They opened this spring. The building is just down the road from here, across the soccer field."

"It's a museum?" Sabine asked.

"They have a library and exhibitions. They also run workshops and events. I use the desks there when I need a change of scenery. I ran into Lily a few times."

"Did she say what she was there for?"

"She never said." Doubtfully, he added, "Doesn't sound very promising, does it?"

"She might have checked out a guidebook. It could be a hint about where she was planning to travel."

"They'll be closed tomorrow," Linda said, "but you could go by Monday morning."

"I'll do that."

The waitress came by to clear their plates. Christoph ordered another beer and turned to Sabine. "You, too? It's on me."

Sabine flushed under his gaze. "No, thanks. I should get to bed pretty soon. Long day."

"Of course," Linda said.

When the waitress brought Christoph's beer a minute later, Sabine paid her bill and rose from the table. "Thanks again for all your help," she said, avoiding Christoph's eyes. "It means a lot."

"Anything we can do," Christoph said. "Just say the word."

CHAPTER 10

ROSE

December 28

Rose sat with her hand in her lap, conscious of a desire to fidget and trying to fight it. The plastic chair was no more or less comfortable than any other she'd sat in; it was the location that made her edgy. When was the last time she'd come to church? From her pre-abduction years she had hazy memories of long, hot Sunday mornings, secret looks and hand signals between friends, sneaking outside to gossip under the shade of some trees out back. Afterward, life with the rebels had demanded its own kind of religion, and when she returned to Kitgum, she'd been repelled by the idea of a God who could have stood by in silence all those years.

But last night, before she and James had parted ways, he'd asked her to join them this morning, and despite her reluctance, Rose had agreed. Now she regretted her decision. Already she felt awkward in the large but strangely vacant room built of concrete and void of decoration—a community center from Monday to Saturday and home of the Awesome Glory Pentecostal Church on Sunday. She felt unwelcome among the women who'd greeted each other so warmly then snubbed their noses at her. One woman spat at Rose's feet when Rose passed her on the way inside. Rose maintained her poise, determined not to let them see her waver. When she sat on the bench, she discretely wiped the saliva from her ankle, where it had landed.

Agnes was singing with the choir, and it was so strange to see her sister-in-law standing, swaying, praising Him with such enthusiasm, so altered from her pedestrian domestic self. James sat to Rose's left, leaning forward, his hands clasped in the wide space between his knees. Grace was to her right, with Wilborn in her lap. Isaac was at an age where he could wander with the other children in the yard outside—too old to sit in anyone's lap, too young to sit politely during worship.

She wondered what Grace thought of God. The girl was so quiet. Rose noticed a piece of paper sticking out of her pocket: a paper crane. Rose thought of Christoph, and her heart squeezed with the sense of a missed opportunity. She believed that Christoph was a man of his word, but he'd said nothing more about his offer to help her study in Europe since that first conversation in the car. And last night, when he'd sent her the text message about Ocen, she couldn't bring herself to tell him that Ocen wasn't around. She didn't mean to lie; she needed time to evaluate. His message had sparked a swift and dangerous train of thought. Ocen wanted money, after all, and Lily had it. Paddy said that Ocen had come up with a plan. What was he capable of, the man she loved?

During the weeks of Ocen's absence, Rose had thought only of the last fight, the argument over her dowry—but when she was honest with herself, she knew that things had been strained for a month before that. At the end of October there had been a day when he invited her to his hut to spend the night, but when she arrived there was no sign of him; she waited alone until dawn, when he finally arrived, nearly falling off his *boda* and stinking of *waragi*. He wouldn't even look at her. After that Ocen had been moody and distant. She'd taken his sulking for a phase; she knew such things well enough from James. If Ocen needed his privacy, who was she to judge? She herself had secrets she'd never shared with him, truths that would have gouged a rift between them that could never heal. It was only fair that she afford him the same courtesy. Now she wondered: had she chosen wrongly? Were the consequences of Ocen's covertness more serious than she could have imagined?

Agnes and the other singers concluded their performance and sat in their designated seats in the front row. The preacher walked slowly to the front of the room where a microphone rested on a crudely built wooden pulpit. Rose was skeptical; she knew this man from town, and he was ordinary and even a little inept. When he stood a moment at the pulpit, however—his two hands resting on the edges, his eyes closed in concentration—he seemed to be gathering some force from the air around him, from the lingering echoes of the choir's song in the corners of the room. When he opened his mouth to speak, he was transformed.

"'We are hard pressed on every side,'" he bellowed, "'but not crushed; perplexed, but not in despair.'" The preacher opened his eyes and gazed upon his congregation of fifty or so people. "'Persecuted'"— he raised his voice—"'but not abandoned; struck down, but not destroyed.'" He stopped to let the vibrations of his words ricochet off the back walls and escape through the cut-open squares of windows. "That is what Paul the apostle wrote in Second Corinthians. Is it not what we, the Acholi people, might also say?" He raised his hands from the pulpit and spread them wide. "We have *suffered*," he said. "We have lost our brothers and sisters, our mothers and fathers. We have lost our children." Now his right hand came up, alone: "But we have not lost our hope."

James was nodding beside her, but Rose had already lost interest. Suffering, yes: who here had not suffered? But if they had not yet lost hope, perhaps their suffering had not been enough. The men might know the pain of hard labor, fine, but how many knew what it was to travel from here to Sudan on foot, crossing rivers at night with only a rope to guide your chafing hands, and nothing to eat but plants you found along the way? The women knew the pain of childbirth, but who among them had been cut open right there in the dirt, sewed up a minute afterward so that she could flee a UPDF bomb strike, without even water to wash herself and her newborn child? She wanted to scoff: hope, indeed.

Then she felt it: a tickling on her fingers. She looked down and saw Grace's arm extended lightly across her lap, the girl's hand brushing Rose's. That was all: not an embrace, not a squeeze; Grace didn't even look her way or turn her head. But her touch—as slight as a stalk of grass, or a bird's feather traced across the skin. Rose found herself blinking back tears. Grace's existence was almost as precarious as Rose's own, and yet here was this small, wise being, hopeful, unafraid.

Rose stopped listening to the sermon; she felt it more soothing to let it roll over her, the surge and drop of the preacher's cadence like the swells of a storm in the rainy season, his words like tiny droplets pelleting the walls and ceiling while she, inside, surrendered.

Afterward, when the sermon and the singing were finished, every-one stood, and Agnes left her place at the front to join Rose and James and the children. Agnes's green cross lay neatly against her collar-bone above her blouse, and she had a radiant look about her.

Rose kissed her on one cheek. "You sing beautifully."

"My wife does everything beautifully," James said. Agnes put a hand on her belly, beaming.

Agnes's sister, Beatrice, approached with the four children under her care, who mingled with Grace.

"*Apwoyo*," Rose offered, but Beatrice didn't even spare her a glance. It was as if she were invisible; no one worth noticing.

"Eh, sister," Beatrice said to Agnes, "the light of God shines upon you. Today He is smiling on your unborn baby."

"This is true, Agnes," said the preacher, who had come up behind Beatrice. "The Lord has blessed you with this gift."

"I have sung His praises in thanks," Agnes said.

The preacher turned to Rose. "And you, my sister," he said, the whites of his eyes glittering. "You are *most* welcome here." He took her hand and enclosed it in his two warm, soft palms. "We are pray-ing for you to find salvation in Jesus. In the Lord you will find for-giveness for your sins."

"Yes," she said, though she knew what he said was a lie. Who would forgive her if they knew everything? Not Christoph, not Ocen, not God. She released her hand from his grasp.

Rose wandered outside to find Isaac and discovered that he'd been caught throwing stones at the chickens and had been made to sit with the women cooking millet around the back of the church until the service was over (*He is too stubborn,* the women chided)—and Rose took advantage of the moment to steal away. After the unkindness of the congregation, she wanted to be somewhere she felt safe. Up the road a little ways from the church she waved for a *boda,* who agreed to take her to the cluster of huts past the airstrip where Ocen had his hut. She'd slept there many times, grateful for the relative privacy it offered compared to her rented room, whose walls were thin. She thought of the way Ocen would drive her on his *boda* late at night, her arm around his chest, her cheek against his back, the wind whipping her face, bones jarred by potholes; he'd take the turns gently, careful of her, his precious cargo. Riding there now without Ocen's familiar body in front of her made her disoriented and sad. When the *boda* dropped her off, she paid him and told him not to wait. She wasn't sure what she would find here—if anything—but she wanted the luxury of time.

Ocen's hut was one of several standing in a scattered group at the southern edge of town. Beyond the circle was the old airport, surrounded by a fence to keep out goats and children. The dirt runway was out of use now, apart from private planes and missionary landings. It had seen its peak during the last of the war years, when humanitarian activity increased to such an extent that Eagle Air offered regularly scheduled flights to Gulu and Kitgum for those who were willing to pay extra to avoid the long, bumpy drive from Kampala. Rose had never been on a plane, but she remembered watching them take off. The instant of liftoff always seemed impossible to her— *surely this time physics will fail*—until the plane was afloat, high above, a speck that appeared to be hardly moving at all, and she would long for that escape. Then Ocen would slip a hand around her waist—the hand with the braided metal bracelet she'd given him, always that hand—and she would feel tethered and content.

Besides a stray dog sleeping on its side in the shade of a neighbor's hut, the clearing was deserted. The other families were at church, Rose knew; she recalled those delicious Sunday mornings with Ocen in his bed, undisturbed, engaged in their own acts of worship.

The door on his hut—a thick slab of wood—was closed tight but not locked. It could only be locked from the inside. He kept no money at home; with her help he'd opened a bank account at the Stanbic branch in town, where she also kept her savings. His cell phone was cheap and he carried it with him always, and the other objects he owned would be of little value to thieves. She ducked beneath the low thatch roof and leaned against the door hard with her good shoulder, and it swung open with a creak.

Inside, the ceiling was angled so steep that she could not stand up straight except in the very center. The atmosphere was dim, and the dark outlines of the shapes were sweetly, heartbreakingly familiar. There was the small pile of folded clothes; the bowl and spoon for when he joined the neighbors for a meal; the thin mattress beneath a haphazardly draped mosquito net. Here, a calendar from 2007 stuck to the mud wall with rusty nails; a dented yellow jerry can; the slant of light angling in from a tiny square window onto a pen and the school notebook he used to track his earnings and expenses as a *boda* driver. He'd probably started a new one when he left, she thought. The air was stale and dry. She tried to find any trace of Ocen's scent—a distinctive combination of soap and clean sweat—but there was only a touch of mustiness, a hint of earth. The space felt close and empty.

Had Lily come here? she wondered suddenly. *Was the* mono *girl not just a source of money but something more, too?* It happened, sure: foreign girls relishing in the adventure of a Ugandan lover, swayed by sweet talk and the heady proximity of a war they hadn't experienced and couldn't understand. Rose's breath became short; she couldn't stay longer. What did she think she would find here, anyway?

She picked up Ocen's notebook on her way out—a token, something tangible that she could weigh in her palm, put to her skin—and in the bright sunlight of the clearing, she sat on a wooden stool, set the notebook on her knee, and with her one good hand flipped slowly through its pages, hoping to calm her mind.

But the neat, tidy columns of numbers tugged at her, the dates, the distances, the fares—such meager makings! A thousand shillings, five hundred, one seven; Rose earned twenty thousand a day, on the days that she worked. And at the bottom of every page, the subtraction of his weekly cost of fuel and rentals and personal expenses—a disheartening tally. The total grew over the course of the notebook, but by such agonizingly minute increments. How had she been so blind to his poverty? He'd worked so *hard*, said nothing. Perhaps she'd willed herself to be deceived.

Stop. The thought reached her brain a moment too late, and she had to flip back a few pages to see what had caught her eye. She found it again—three words written at the very top of a page, above the columns; a strange incongruity—and pressed the notebook open to the spot. Ocen's handwriting was clear and deliberate, as if he were copying the letters from somewhere else:

Patrick Flynn Lakwali

She read the words several times. *Patrick* she recognized as a Christian name, and *Lakwali* had the right consonants and vowels to be East African, but in combination with this mysterious *Flynn*, the phrase meant nothing.

But it must mean *something*.

Patrick Flynn Lakwali.

The sleeping dog rose abruptly and shook itself, stood a moment panting, then trotted off down the road.

———

"Visiting hours are strictly Monday, Wednesday, and Friday," the maroon-uniformed officer said in a monotone. It was a different officer than the last time she'd been here. "You must return tomorrow."

Rose stood at the door of the prison, which the officer had opened a crack at her insistent knocking. "It's important. I have to speak with him. It can't wait."

"I cannot help you." His eyes lowered lazily to her breasts.

Her heart beat hard against her rib cage. Instinctively she began to cross her arms, but with only one, the movement felt futile. She let her arm fall again to her side. "Is there . . . an extra charge, perhaps? A special weekend fee?"

The officer nodded to her to come inside. "It is possible."

The narrow hallway of the entrance felt tighter than she remembered. The officer on Friday had been courteous, at least. This man had an aura of apathy to him that frightened her. There was no one else in the hallway or in the side room that she could see, and from here the window that looked out onto the courtyard showed only the roof of the barracks and the sky above. The officer looked her up and down. It took great effort not to tremble.

"Here," she said, thrusting a light-purple-and-green twenty-thousand-shilling bill toward him. It was not a subtle gesture, but at least it put an arm's length—and cash—between them.

He took the bill delicately and flicked it with a finger.

Rose stepped back. Without this thinnest line of defense, she felt naked, but this was for Ocen, she reminded herself. What would Ocen have done for her? What had he done for her already? She pressed forward again, taking a second bill from her pocket.

"And this, for the holiday," she said. Her voice would not stay steady.

The officer laughed, his white teeth large in the hazy light. "You amuse me," he said. "I would have settled for a kiss. What is the name of the prisoner? You can have five minutes."

A moment later, Paddy stood again at the window, his hands on the bars. He seemed warier this time than before.

"You have seen my family?" he asked.

"I will go this evening," she promised. "I can give them a little something to help."

He breathed more freely. "Thank you."

"Paddy," she said, leaning in, "do you know the words *Patrick Flynn Lakwali?*"

Paddy frowned. "Say it again?" But her repetition sparked no greater recognition in his expression. "It is a name?"

"I'm not sure."

"I never heard it."

A second prisoner appeared at the periphery of the window. "*Lakwali*," the man repeated. "Eh, I know this place."

"What is it?" Rose asked.

The man came into full view. His face was batlike, small and squished. "It is the name of a gold mine."

"Kitgum has no gold mines," she said.

"Eh, the place is in Congo. My cousin went there to work."

"Congo?" Rose's vision began to tilt. "What do you mean, Congo?"

A shrill whistle cut through the air, and the man flinched and looked toward the barracks across the courtyard. Already the other prisoners that had been outside began to move reluctantly toward the officer with the whistle in his mouth, standing in the barracks' doorway. Paddy released his hands.

"What's happening?" Rose asked. "Where are you going?"

"Labor duty," Paddy said. "They sell us like oxen."

She gripped the bar. "Why would Ocen know the name of a gold mine? Who is Patrick? What is Flynn?"

But Paddy only shook his head. "Please," he said, turning away. "Tell my wife I am well."

––––––––

Outside, the noon sun twisted cruelly overhead. The light turned to white then turned to yellow while she stood at the roadside, unsure where to direct her body next.

A gold mine? It didn't make any sense. What was his interest there? Had he gone for work, like the man's cousin?

Or was it more subversive? She thought of Ocen's uncle Franklin in Arua, far in the west, just a few kilometers from the Congolese border. She'd met Franklin several times and had no liking for him. He owned several successful shops, but Ocen had spoken of Franklin's involvement in a loose band of small-time thugs in Arua who called themselves the Opec Boys—smugglers, mostly, taking fuel and cigarettes from Congo into Uganda. Ocen had always disdained such dishonesty, but Rose knew there was good money to be made. Had Ocen come under his uncle's sway in order to earn her dowry?

Who was *Patrick*? What was *Flynn*?

And Lily: where did she fit?

The shadows tightened; the questions spun; the sun beat down.

CHAPTER 11

SABINE

December 28

It was midday Sunday before Sabine left the Bomah to visit the police station down the street. She'd spent the morning on the phone, first with Kathryn in Kampala, who wanted to set up face-to-face meetings with Ugandan officials for her the following week. Sabine explained that she wasn't ready to leave Kitgum, but she'd appreciate any direct assistance they could offer. Kathryn prevaricated for ten minutes before Sabine finally got fed up and claimed a previous engagement. Then Steve called to update her on media coverage while she snacked on a plate of chapati she'd asked the restaurant to bring to her room. Lily's story had been reported by Denver-area TV stations and newspapers but hadn't been picked up nationally, and after Saturday's air strikes in Gaza, everyone's eyes were on the Middle East.

"I'm still pushing for more coverage," Steve said wearily. "Any luck on your end?"

Sabine summarized her encounters in Kitgum so far, carefully excising any hint of ivory. Steve agreed that tracking down Lily's *boda* driver sounded promising.

"By the way," Steve said, "remember that guy who was hacking into Lily's e-mails?"

"Did anything come of it?"

"Yes and no. There's been no activity since her last night in Kitgum—since the message she sent to us."

Sabine thought of the words, those three exclamation marks: *Wrapping up things in Kitgum . . . don't freak out if you guys don't hear from me before my flight!!!*

"But there was something else?" she asked.

"Apparently Lily opened another e-mail account a few months ago. There was a blank message sent to her main address in early November. My guy said it's probably nothing—lots of people have secondary accounts they use for online stuff."

Or for conducting secret investigations into illegal activities, Sabine thought.

"The weird thing is," Steve said, "she used Hannah's maiden name—your last name—instead of Bennett."

"Lily Hardt?"

"Strange, huh?"

"Very."

"In any case, he couldn't access that account yet. Hopefully soon. What about the Kitgum police?"

"I'm headed there next."

But before she could leave, her phone rang for a third time that morning: Rita, wanting to catch her up on the news in Kampala.

"The radio ads have been playing on Simba and Radio One since Friday," Rita said. "I went by the missing persons' desk yesterday and it sounded like they've had some calls. Mostly inquiries about whether there's a reward. The police are supposed to be following up on substantial leads. They have your number if they find anything."

"I won't hold my breath," Sabine said.

"Also, Jochem posted Lily's picture on some kind of expat forum online. They've got people all over Uganda, so there's a good chance that if Lily passed through one of these places, we'll hear about it."

She appreciated these updates from Rita and Steve; she knew the importance of coordination and organization. Still, the time she spent on the phone felt cumbersomely administrative—too much like aid work, where every hour in the field corresponded to a hundred hours in the office wading through paperwork, proposals, permissions, contracts, reports. Even though she'd specifically taken postings in smaller field offices rather than capital-city headquarters, she'd nevertheless spent most of her working hours behind a desk. The little round table in her room at the Bomah was starting to feel too familiar, and she was grateful when she finally closed the door behind her and crossed the courtyard in the warm sunshine, headed for the police station across the street.

As soon as she exited the Bomah gates, she saw a woman emerge from the yellow police building—Christoph's assistant, Sabine knew immediately. The woman's one arm made her unmistakable. Sabine hurried to catch her. If Rose—that was her name, wasn't it?—if Rose could put her directly in touch with Lily's *boda* driver, it would spare Sabine from searching out Christoph, whom she hadn't seen this morning, and whom she hoped to avoid the rest of the day after last night's awkwardness.

Sabine expected Rose to stride purposefully onward, but the woman stopped at the roadside, as if uncertain. As Sabine got closer, she could see that Rose's expression was some mixture of confusion and concern. What was her interest at the prison? Not that it mattered, Sabine thought. It was none of her business. She approached slowly.

"Rose?"

The woman looked up, startled out of her reverie. Her eyes focused, and Sabine saw that Rose recognized her. Sabine thought she noticed a flicker of wariness in Rose's gaze. "You are Lily's aunt," Rose said.

"Yes. Sabine. And you're Christoph's assistant, is that right?"

Rose gave a slight nod.

"Christoph said you know Lily's *boda* driver," Sabine pressed. "I need to talk to him—he might be able to help find her."

Rose was quiet, and Sabine sensed her deliberating.

"Rose, if you know anything—"

"Ocen is not around," she said. "He left Kitgum."

Sabine's hopes sunk. "Can you call him?"

"He does not answer." Rose looked away. "We had a fight."

"Maybe if I tried?"

Rose shared his number—reluctantly, Sabine thought, though Rose watched closely as Sabine dialed and held her phone to her ear. It clicked straight to the automated no-answer message.

Sabine shook her head. "He must be out of range, or his phone is off. I'll try again later." Rose seemed disappointed, too, and Sabine felt sorry for her. After an awkward pause, she said, "I'm sure you and Ocen will work things out."

Rose tilted her head and met Sabine's eyes. "If you find her, please tell me?"

"Of course."

When Sabine knocked at the police building a moment later, she was still thinking of the strange look in Rose's eyes as they'd parted ways—was it defiance? Entreaty? Or had Sabine simply imagined it, wanting to see a message where there was none?

The officer who answered the door—but did not invite her inside—listened to her queries with a bored expression and offered distinctly unhelpful single-word answers in response. Did they know Lily was missing? (Yes.) Were they coordinating with the police in Kampala? (Yes.) Was there a local investigation under way? (Yes.) Were there any leads? (No.) The man scratched his chest absentmindedly throughout. After five minutes Sabine gave up, and he closed the door without saying good-bye.

Now it was her turn to stand at the roadside uncertainly. Back to the Bomah? The Mission again? As she mulled it over, a large truck rattled out from behind the prison; its long bed had tall walls and metal bars arching over—usually for transporting livestock or goods for market. But now the back was filled with prisoners in yellow T-shirts and shorts, standing up, holding onto the bars or each other to keep from toppling over. Cheap labor, she thought—and a shame, too, when there were probably plenty of young Ugandan men who couldn't find work themselves, who turned to drinking instead.

"Sabine!" a woman's voice called from the direction of the Bomah. Sabine saw Linda at the gates. "Where are you headed?"

"Nowhere," Sabine said honestly.

Linda waved her over. "Walk with me. I'm going for lunch."

It didn't take a moment for Sabine to catch up.

"We missed you at breakfast," Linda said.

"I was on the phone all morning." Sabine felt her feet begin to drag. "Trying to coordinate the search has been a nightmare. There are a hundred things to think of, and no one has really been able to tell us what we should and shouldn't be doing. The State Department wants me to come back to Kampala to shake hands with the chief of police or something, so they can pat themselves on the back and feel good about their 'contribution to the investigation.' And the police, my God . . ." She threw up her hands in frustration.

Linda smiled sadly. "It sounds like you're doing everything you can."

"Am I?" Sabine stopped midstride. Why couldn't she catch her breath? She buckled over; her hands were on her knees, and she was laughing. Why was she laughing? No—she was crying. But her cheeks were dry.

"Sabine?" Linda's voice echoed distantly. "Are you all right?"

"I'm fine. It's okay." Was it? She took a deep breath and stood up straight, her throat catching. They'd stopped in the middle of the road. Somewhere distantly she could hear praise music playing, and the sound of clapping hands. Sabine brought a hand to her forehead to shield her eyes from the bright sun. "It just—feels so useless sometimes."

"What feels useless?" Linda asked gently.

"All of it."

The war. The world. The mother and baby at the side of the road, her grandfather's secret, the hatbox with his handwriting . . . all the burdens of the past, living inside her.

"It will be four weeks tomorrow," she said. "Four weeks without a word." She closed her eyes and breathed in the dust. "I'm not sure what to hope for anymore."

Linda was silent, and Sabine turned to face her, dropping her voice. "I think she was in trouble before she left Kitgum, Linda. She had access to—sensitive information. If someone found out . . ."

Linda touched her shoulder. "Let's keep walking a bit, shall we?" Her tone was light and jaunty, but Sabine followed a flick of her eyes toward a man who stood loitering in the shade of a tree across the street.

Sabine nodded. "What's for lunch?"

Ten minutes later, the two women were comfortably seated at a table in an otherwise mostly empty courtyard, with two cold Cokes in front of them and food on the way.

"They never follow me in here," Linda said. "I know the owners. And our voices won't carry. It's safe to talk."

"Why are they watching you, anyway? Are you a journalist?"

"I'm studying nodding syndrome—it's mostly been recorded in southern Sudan, but cases have started popping up in northern Uganda."

"So you're a doctor?"

"A medical anthropologist."

"I never imagined anthropology to be so risky."

"It shouldn't be," Linda said. "But with nodding syndrome, no one knows what causes it or how it spreads. There's the possibility of it becoming a political issue, especially in a place like northern Uganda, which is already so marginalized. Museveni probably doesn't want the international community to accuse him of sitting on his hands."

"If there's one thing I learned from three years here," Sabine said, "it's that everything in northern Uganda can become a political issue."

Linda clinked her glass Coke bottle. "Amen. Now, what do you think Lily was into?"

Sabine told her about Miriam and the Australian reporter in Kampala who'd been thrown in prison to deter him from his research into mineral smuggling.

"I'm worried that before she left, Lily was investigating the illegal ivory trade," she concluded. "She's not a journalist. She might not have known how dangerous it was."

"If so, she was extremely discreet," Linda said. "I certainly never suspected. And I'm alert to these sorts of things, you know. Do you think the backpacking plan was a ruse?"

"I don't know. No one at the bus station saw her the morning she left. She might have been meeting someone—an informant, maybe. Or she could have decided to give up her research since she was leaving the country in a few weeks."

"But she was intercepted on her way to the bus."

Sabine nodded.

Neither woman spoke.

The food arrived, two hot plates of rice and beans and boo. The rich, earthy scent of the cooked greens should have been appealing, but Sabine had no appetite. Linda didn't seem to be much interested in eating, either, as she tapped her fork absently against the side of her plate.

"Christoph mentioned seeing Lily outside some kind of museum," Sabine said.

"The National Memory and Peace Documentation Centre."

"Does it mean anything?"

"Their library isn't huge, but they have a collection of UN reports she might have looked at. They also have computers where you can use the Internet for free. I suppose if I didn't want to be linked to a particular search history, that's where I'd go. It wouldn't hurt for you to ask the staff tomorrow morning."

Sabine sighed. "I don't know why I'm still here. In Kitgum, I mean."

"You only just arrived."

"But every day counts. Every *hour.* She could be out there somewhere. Scared, in pain."

"I don't think it's helpful to think about that."

"I just feel stupid sitting around in one place."

Linda gave a short laugh.

"What?" Sabine said.

"It's funny," Linda said, taking a forkful of boo. "Lily said the same damn thing."

After lunch Sabine found an Internet café where she could print Steve's flyer, and she spent the afternoon distributing copies in town. *Sorry, sorry,* people would say when they looked at Lily's photo underneath the headline DISAPPEARED!! They'd cluck and shake their heads. *We are praying for you, really.* Some recognized Lily's image, and in this way Sabine could trace her niece's footsteps through town, from the fruit stall where Lily bought a pineapple once a week, to her preferred grocery store, to the kiosk where she bought pay-as-you-go airtime for her phone. People knew Lily in the oddest places: a woman in a fabric shop who'd taken Lily's measurements for an Acholi-style skirt; a furniture maker who remembered Lily getting on the back of a *boda* outside his shop; a waiter in a bar who'd watched her play a round of pool with Christoph. Each detail accumulated in Sabine's mind, filling in her picture of Lily's experience, her interests, her life. Sabine hadn't realized how limited her own time in Kitgum had been; she'd spent so many hours either at the office or at home, or at the Bomah for dinner or drinks—was it possible she'd never walked this side street, never looked down this row of market stalls, never thought to glance past what you could see from behind the windshield of her company car?

By the time dusk grayed the sky, Sabine still had no new leads, and her back ached. At the Bomah, dinner was subdued. Christoph and Linda were shaking their heads over the latest news from northeastern Congo, where the LRA was responding to Operation Lightning Thunder as expected—that is, with swift, brutal attacks on local people. The Ugandan newspapers reported a massacre of a hundred and fifty Congolese on Christmas Day in a place called Faradje, which Sabine had never heard of until now, and which would probably never be reported outside East Africa. This was a conversation she remembered well: one she'd had a thousand times before. Her heart couldn't take it. After eating, she begged off, claiming administrative necessities. As she rose from the table, Christoph stood too and gave her an awkward hug—a gesture of comfort? Her forehead fit perfectly against the underside of his jaw, and the warmth of his skin made her pulse skip. She broke it off with a mumbled excuse and retired to her room.

She lay awake in bed trying to find any thread of hope that remained in the search for Lily. This ivory thing: it was a stretch, wasn't it? Aside from Linda's general paranoia—which, from what Sabine remembered of her time in Kitgum, was not entirely off base—there was no real evidence of foul play. And in the meantime, there was an entire country to search, and she couldn't be in every place at once. Maybe it was time to try Steve's way, head back to the capital, meet with the people in suits, follow the rules. Maybe that was what she should have done from the start.

One last chance, she told herself. The National Memory and Peace Documentation Centre opened at nine o'clock tomorrow morning. If she walked out of that building empty-handed, she could be back at Rita's house in Kololo by sundown.

Monday dawned darkly, the air chilled with the promise of rain. The gloom seemed appropriate. Sabine had woken to thunder several times in the night, and in the morning there lingered a disorientating sense of having been spoken to, a feeling that Kitgum was telling her in no uncertain terms: go on. Get out. There's nothing left for you here.

She packed her bag—she'd hardly unpacked in the first place—and tossed it in the back of her rental car, then went back inside and dropped her key at the small reception desk with the young man who'd checked her in the first night. The tables outside the restaurant were empty; all the better, she thought. Sabine was not skilled in the art of good-byes. At social events she invariably tried to duck away unnoticed rather than make the obligatory round of farewells.

Here was no different: she had Linda's and Christoph's contact information, and they, hers. What useful words of parting could there be?

For the first time since Sabine arrived, the main road seemed to
display normal traffic and signs of commerce. Bicyclists, *bodas,* NGO
vehicles, and a steady flow of pedestrians carrying all form of
cargo from chickens to jerry cans to firewood. Sabine missed seeing
the flocks of schoolchildren in their crisply colored uniforms, but of
course school was out for the holiday. Two raindrops fell in quick
succession against her windshield, and then nothing.

She pulled past the drab local government buildings and parked
outside the newly constructed, cleanly painted two-story documentation center. Three men stood in the door frame of the nearest government building, chatting. She sensed them watching as she walked
to the center and tried the front door. They didn't seem suspicious;
their conversation was buoyant and hearty.

The door was locked. She checked her watch: five minutes after
nine. She knocked and waited. Still nothing.

"He is there," one of the men called. He pointed to a car approaching from down the road.

"Thanks," Sabine called back.

When the driver came into view, Sabine lost her breath.

"David?" she said incredulously the moment he stepped out of
the car.

The lanky Ugandan took a second to recognize her, then broke
into an enormous smile. "Ehhh!" He clasped her hands in his. "Sabine, my friend. You have returned. It has been a long time."

Sabine felt overcome. She hadn't stayed in touch with anyone from
her old NGO once she moved to Marburg. Now that the NGO had
pulled out of Kitgum, she'd assumed that the Ugandan staff would
scatter as well. But it made sense for David to stay; his family was
here, she remembered—a wife and two children.

"You haven't changed a bit," she said, grappling for solid ground.

"You are very different," he said.

"How so?"

He cocked his head, examining her. She expected him to comment on her haggard look, the worry and resignation that must certainly be showing under her eyes. He pursed his lips. "Your face is somehow fat."

She laughed. It wasn't meant as an insult, she knew; her Ugandan colleagues had sometimes greeted her by saying, *You are looking big today*.

"I eat better in Germany," she conceded. "My life is more relaxed there."

"That is good," he said, nodding. "You worked too hard before."

Guilt pinged through her chest, but before she could say anything, he put a hand on her elbow. "Come. Tell me why you have returned."

She glanced up at the thunderclouds. "Shall we go in?"

It began to sprinkle while David was unlocking the door, and once inside, Sabine brushed off the drops that peppered her shoulders while David turned on the lights in the reception room. The walls were covered with photographs, posters, newspaper articles, and tools of war on display with captions beneath. As David put his briefcase behind the desk, she walked closer to the exhibition. A long collage of newspaper clippings caught her eye: REBELS KILL 23 IN KITGUM CAMP. HUNDREDS SLAUGHTERED IN BARLONYO. UNICEF ESTIMATES 25,000 CHILDREN ABDUCTED SINCE START OF CONFLICT. NORTHERN UGANDA REACHES 1.8 MILLION DISPLACED. IDP CAMPS: FROM MILITARY TACTIC TO POLITICAL NIGHTMARE. Farther on: ANGRY LRA REBELS WALK OUT OF JUBA PEACE TALKS. KONY REFUSES TO SIGN CEASEFIRE. MUSEVENI TO KONY: SIGN, OR ELSE.

At the end of the collage, an Acholi proverb was painted on the wall: KA LYEC ARIYO TYE KA LWENY LUM AYEE DENO CAN. "When two elephants fight, it is the grass that suffers."

Then came a series of photographs of the top LRA commanders, with the unmistakable face of Joseph Kony at the top. In the picture he wore a green military uniform with red and gold shoulder patches and a matching cap; his goatee was scruffy and his eyebrows furrowed. His expression seemed confused, she thought. Not malicious or bloodthirsty. Yet the LRA operated almost completely under the sway of his command, the brutal tactics ordered by the "spirits" that spoke through him. He was said to have sixty wives or more. How could one person do so much harm?

"It's still a work in progress," David said behind her. "This is all temporary. We're trying to put together a permanent exhibition."

"It's remarkable," she said.

"Is there something you're looking for in particular?"

She turned back. "Yes. It's about Lily. My niece."

Again, the explanations; the sorrow, the murmured consolations. Sabine probed further before the weight became too much.

"Christoph said that Lily used to come here," Sabine said. "Do you remember seeing her? Do you know what she was looking at?"

"I remember very well." He gestured for her to follow, and they went into the next room—the library Christoph mentioned, with books lining the shelves on the walls, three long desks in the middle, and six computers at the far end. David stopped in front of a shelf and pulled down an enormous, heavy volume.

"*National Geographic Atlas of the World*," he said. "It's an old edition—1996, I think." He set it on the nearest table and opened to the spread of East Africa—Kenya, Tanzania, Uganda, and Rwanda, with the large blue splotch of Lake Victoria in the middle, and extensive coverage of eastern DRC to the left and southern Sudan at the top edge. "She liked to copy from this page," David said. Sabine recalled Lily's hand-drawn maps in her sketchbook in Stuttgart—the cartographer drawn into the landscape—and the map of Kitgum that hung on the wall at the rehabilitation center. A familiar creative habit, to ground herself in unfamiliar territory. Sabine felt her disappointment threaten to brim out from behind her eyes.

David leaned back, crossing his arms. "She showed me her drawings of Kitgum, too, even the woman who sleeps outside A-One Supermarket. Eh! She has talent, this one."

Sabine sighed. "It doesn't really help, though, does it? If she had circled the name of a town or something . . ."

David said nothing, keeping his hand on the open page.

"How do you keep hoping?" she said suddenly, desperately. "She's been gone for nearly a month, David. There's no trace of her, nothing. I'm not getting anywhere. I don't even know if she's still alive." Emotion choked her voice. Light-headed, she put a hand to her forehead. "What if it never gets easier? What if we never find out what happened?"

David closed the atlas and returned it to the shelf. "Let me show you something."

He led her back out into the lobby and stopped in front of a long banner on the wall opposite the newspaper collage. It was a list of names and dates. *Okello Martin 1989/2000. Okema Nancy 1981/1996. Okwera Emmanuel 1993/2005.* The names went on and on. There must have been hundreds. *Onen Francis 1991/2004. Opiyo Jeremiah 1984/1999.* Sabine couldn't read them all. Her eyes moved to the caption beneath.

During two decades of war, tens of thousands of people were abducted by the LRA, most of them children. Many are still missing. If you know anyone who is missing, please add their name, birth year, and date of abduction here.

"These are just the ones from Kitgum," he said. "The ones we've been able to collect. There are thousands more." He traced a finger along the list and paused at a name: *Odong Fiona 1998/2002.* "This is my niece." He ran a line to another, *Oyet Denis 1984/1997.* "My cousin." When he stopped at a third name, his finger trembled ever so slightly. *Otim Gilbert 1981/2003.* "My brother."

Sabine read the names in silence. She thought of her own banner of loss: her father's parents, before she was born; her mother's parents, before she graduated *Gymnasium*; her parents, in a sailing accident; her sister, to cancer. No grief was easy. But the missing—this was something else entirely. You couldn't grieve, but neither could you hope. Both were too painful to bear. "How do you manage?"

"Everyone has to find their own way. For me . . ." He paused. "I put my faith in God, that He has a plan. I am praying to Him every day."

"And if God and I are not on speaking terms?"

"There must be something you believe in, above all else. Pray to that."

The sound of rain outside grew louder. Sabine hesitated. "Do you remember the woman you took to the hospital? The one with the baby."

"Eh, I remember."

Her throat clenched. "I'm glad you broke the rules. If it had been me alone, I wouldn't have helped."

He looked away. "It was a small thing."

"It was brave."

David seemed uncomfortable, and she pressed forward—he needed to understand the good he had done, the good she had failed to do. "Everything we did at the NGO, that was just numbers, it was our job. But you didn't let it blind you, like I did."

Still he was quiet.

"It was a life," she insisted. "Two lives. You saved them."

Now he was shaking his head. "Only God can save."

"But you were there. You put them in the car. You made that call."

"Sabine," he said, "I did not save them. The baby died."

Outside, behind the wheel of the parked car, Sabine sat and watched the storm roil. Her hair and shoulders were soaked just from the short run from the building. The change in weather was spectacular: the sheer force of it. Trees danced violently in the sudden wind. A *boda* driver skidded in the slick mud and recovered; two women with yellow jerry cans took shelter under the overhang of the government buildings nearby as a rush of running water surged off the sloping tin roof and broke the stalk of a green plant beneath.

If she believed in anything "above all else," she thought, it was this—the apathy of the universe to the individual desire, the personal plight. There was birth and there was destruction. The fairy tales she grew up with were filled with signs and circles, questions that never went unanswered, riddles that never went unsolved. But in life, the world kept turning and the mysteries only deepened, chasms never bridged.

As she drove out of town, she turned on a whim down the road that led to her old house. It felt appropriate: a final farewell to Kitgum. The street was acutely familiar, even in the storm: an unfinished brick wall; a hand-painted advertisement for Omo laundry soap; a *boda* stage; and then, just around this corner, behind the next red gate, with tall walls and pink bougainvillea and a guard with a gun, her house—

The car judded to a stop. She turned off the engine. She looked, kept looking, as if waiting for the punch line.

The house was gone. The perimeter walls were only partially dismantled, but the building inside had completely vanished; only the concrete foundation remained, now wet and pooling in the rain. Three years of her life, a thousand mornings, a thousand nights. No evidence remained. She felt the house's absence like an empty space in her chest.

The rain on the windshield and roof grew more urgent, and in the cacophony of noise, she turned on the engine and shifted into first gear. It was time to go.

CHAPTER 12

ROSE

December 29

Rain threatened overhead as Rose made her morning trek across the yard to shower. She'd slept poorly, her dreams ragged and weighty: the face of an LRA commander, the thunder of bombs. Her encounter with Lily's aunt yesterday outside the prison unsettled her, and throughout the afternoon and evening—when she took a *boda* to the IDP camp in Palabek to take some money to Paddy's family then stayed for dinner—her thoughts were elsewhere. She kept playing back conversations with Ocen, picking through every remembered phrase for references to *Patrick* or *Flynn* or *Lakwali* or *Congo* or even *gold*. She thought of his growing distance that last month, his jumpiness; what was his secret?

Lily was a part of it. She couldn't say why she felt so certain. But where the connection was exactly, she couldn't say. Did Lily know someone at the gold mine? Would she help Ocen get a job there? Or were the words in Ocen's notebook just words, unimportant; was it the girl herself—her whiteness, her bank account—Ocen's idea about money? If Christoph was Rose's "opportunity," why would Lily be any different for Ocen?

Rose soaped her body with cold water, her arm terse and quick. Had Ocen left her for the *mono* girl? Had they run away together?

She thought of the way his face would change when he saw it was Lily calling. Was it more than money?

Was it—love?

She rinsed and dried. Her skin prickled with goose bumps; the weather was shifting. And if it was love, what right did she have to be jealous? *None,* she told herself. She had no claim to Ocen, just as she'd had no claim to Opiyo all those years ago, when they were all young, on the cusp of young adulthood—Rose and the twins, a perfect trio of playmates. Opiyo was the smiling twin, charming and boisterous, while Ocen lingered shyly behind. So different, the two, and yet they were more than brothers: blessed by *jogi,* two halves of one whole. Opiyo would sneak away to engage in some mischief or another, and Ocen would reluctantly follow, unwilling to endure the humiliation of Opiyo's creative taunts if he stayed behind, usually involving dog vomit and elephant piss. When Rose watched the two together, she passed over Ocen's hesitancy in favor of Opiyo's confident, feline motions.

The first time Opiyo kissed her in the brush at the edge of the river, her insides tightened and moved like snakes, and she wanted more, always more. Miraculously, Opiyo wanted the same, and they became sweethearts, Rose and the smiling twin, sharing the heady promise of a marriage someday, and children—a shared life.

Then, Rose and Opiyo were abducted together; Ocen, left behind, remained in Kitgum. During her years in the bush, Rose couldn't think of the people at home, couldn't bear to wonder how they had changed, what they dreamed, if they were alive to dream at all. She became a wife and a mother, though it was nothing like she'd imagined.

And then she was neither. That was what it meant to return.

After she left the rehabilitation center in Kitgum, Ocen appeared on the street like a ghost: his face, Opiyo's face. His body no longer hesitant but graceful and strong. The war years made a man of the boy. The first time she saw him she gasped—it wasn't possible, Opiyo, here—and Ocen stopped, and she saw him with new eyes. She was terrified and overjoyed, and he was gentle, so gentle when he traced his fingers along the bandages where her right arm had been, when they embraced. *It is you,* he said, over and over again. *You.* And then: *Where is my brother? Where is Opiyo?*

Her cheek was pressed into the hollow between his chest and shoulder, and she meant to tell him everything—the truth from the beginning, the countless small ways Opiyo had saved her, and the one large, impossible to repay, but then she wouldn't be able to stop, the river would gush forth, and Ocen would have to know not just what his brother had been but what he had become. The lie slipped out before she could stop it: *he is at peace.*

Later she told herself it was a kindness, this gift of closure. Ocen would not have to wonder what choices his brother was making in order to stay alive.

Ocen never asked again. Not about Opiyo, nor her missing arm, nor the signs of childbirth that still showed in the places where she'd been cut open and sewed together again. When he touched her scars, he was quiet, as if saying: *I see you as you are, and it is enough.*

In her room, she dressed in comfortable clothes—jeans and a loose blouse; she had a special bra without a clasp that slid over her head and needed no fastening—and put out the transcription equipment on her bed. A bare lightbulb cast some brightness against the darkening sky outside. She hadn't spoken to Christoph since Saturday evening after *mato oput,* but he'd given her the USB stick with the recordings from the ceremony before they got in the car—before the mob—and she would remain professional, whatever he decided next. She toyed with the earphones as the laptop was booting up, her heart aching. She didn't care about the payment anymore; she was not like so many other hungry, grasping people. She hadn't thought Ocen was that way, either. Perhaps his uncle had a greater impact on him than Rose imagined. This saddened her, because from what she knew of Franklin, he would sell his own child for the right sum.

An idea struck her. She took her phone and began to type a message to Franklin's number.

I have a payment for Ocen, she wrote, *1.5 million shillings. It is from a special job he did before he left Kitgum. It must be given to him personally. If you know how I can reach him, there may also be a reward for you.*

She hit send and settled in to wait. It was still early; she knew that "big men" like him slept late so that they could rise when everyone else was already hard at work, while they yawned and stretched and spent half an hour scratching their bellies and feeling manifestly superior in their sloth.

So she was surprised when her phone began to ring within a minute. When she looked at the caller ID, though, her excitement was curbed.

"*Apwoyo,* James," she answered. "Is all well?"

On the other end of the line, she heard muffled scratching. A rooster crowed faintly. Someone breathed into the mouthpiece.

"Brother?" she said. "Are you there?"

A sound like howling—horrible, unnatural—filtered through, as if from a distance. The fine hairs on the back of her scalp tingled.

Then a whisper: "Auntie?"

"Grace," Rose said, relief rushing through her. "What is it?" The eerie howl came again, and Rose understood it was not coming from Grace. It hardly sounded human. "*Grace?*"

"You must come," the girl said, her voice quick and fragile and hushed. "Please."

Rose's heart was in her throat. "You are at home?"

More muffled scratching; the howl, rising in pitch. Then Grace again, a plea: "Hurry."

A click: silence.

Rose moved to action, shutting the laptop and fumbling to put it away. With the drawer open she caught a glimpse of her passport and little purse, and she grabbed them on an impulse. In a matter of seconds she had slipped on her only pair of tennis shoes and was running down the road in search of a *boda*. She found one leaning lazily outside the Bomah and gave him directions without negotiating a fare first. With the chilly wind rushing past, her thoughts were jumbled and racked with guilt: she should have known James hadn't changed, she should have pushed Agnes harder to leave him; had he finally gone too far? Had he hurt one of the children? That howling— *what was it?*

The *boda* dropped her off at the roadside, and she put three thousand shillings in his hand, more than enough to preclude an argument. As she hurried down the narrow footpath to her brother's home, the grass whipping her calves, she heard the driver rev the engine and pull away. The brisk, rain-ready air bit at her bare skin. *Please let the children be fine,* she said to herself, the words beating in time with her footfalls: *please, please, please let the children be fine.*

The *dye-kal* was empty when she came to it. She saw the hut, door swung slightly open; a thin rope of smoke rose over the top of the roof from the cooking fire on the other side. Three chickens pecked unobtrusively at the far edge of the brush. Aside from the cluck and burble of the hens, all was quiet.

"Grace?" she said. "Agnes? Are you here?"

She approached the hut and pushed the door farther in. The space was dark compared to the gray morning light outside, and for a few seconds she saw nothing but blackness. Then the blackness moved.

"Auntie?"

Rose's eyes adjusted, and now she could make out Grace, with Wilborn in her lap and James's phone clutched in her tiny hand. Rose leaned in and saw Isaac on the mattress, methodically tearing up a piece of paper. She looked closer: the paper shape still retained one folded wing, a long, slender beak.

"What happened?" she said. "Are you all right? Where is Agnes?"

From outside came the sound of crying.

Grace pulled Wilborn closer. "Auntie," she whispered, "please. I'm scared."

"Stay here," Rose said as she backed out of the dim doorway. She came around the side of the hut slowly, her left hand touching the low edge of the thatch roof. With each step the scene revealed itself in pieces: an overturned pot; a stray spoon next to a small sharp stone; a yellow jerry can on its side; the fire—and two bare feet, the soles pointed toward Rose, too still.

One more step and Rose saw it all: Agnes on the ground, limbs limp, her legs in a fetal position and her chest twisted skyward, head resting in James's lap, and James, hands cradling his wife's face, his body racked with sobs—and the blood, everywhere, wet and dark on James's hands, his clothes, Agnes's throat and dress. James didn't even seem to notice Rose's approach, his mouth pulled back in a grimace. His crying heaved into a keening—the howl she'd heard in the background of Grace's call. A glance at Agnes's slack face made it clear she was gone.

It had been four years since Rose escaped the rebels, but it took only an instant for something inside her to shift—for her to become swift and hard, to look past the blood and shut her ears to the anguish. She strode to her brother—skirting the congealed blood in the dirt around his legs, where it had pooled from the gash in Agnes's throat—and crouched next to him, set her hand on his shoulder. "Hush now," she shushed. The howl faded to a whimper. "James, look at me. *Look at me.*"

His face turned groggily toward her. She expected to see the signs of *waragi*, but his eyes were clear. His mouth opened but nothing came out.

"James, you have to concentrate. Tell me what happened." But it didn't matter, did it, if it was a fit of rage, an argument gone wrong. Agnes was dead—killed—and her unborn child. That was the only part of the story that mattered.

In the bush she'd learned many things about survival, but the most important act was instinctual: *flee.* Was that why she'd brought her passport and purse? Had the knowledge been there all along? *Flee.*

If a mob found them, it would be the end.

James, the wife killer; Rose, rebel whore.

"The boy," James croaked.

"Eh?"

She heard a noise at the hut and whipped around to look. Grace stood there, half hidden.

"Grace! Stay back. Turn your head!"

Grace shrank into the shadow.

"What boy?" Rose asked James. "What do you mean?"

"Ehhhh, the boy . . ." He began to rock back and forth.

From behind her, Rose heard Grace whisper: "It was Isaac. He threw the stone."

The stone.

She thought of Isaac at church, with the chickens; on Christmas Eve with the goat. The strength in those tiny arms. She turned to the small rock she'd noticed next to the spoon: flat and jagged at the edge . . . Rose had once seen a woman get nicked in the neck with a piece of shrapnel; for a half second it looked like nothing, a crease or a wrinkle on the skin, but then it bloomed reddish-black and gurgled forth, and the woman fell to her knees, choking. It took less than a minute for her to die.

"Eh," called a voice from beyond the edge of the clearing. "*Apwoyo*, Agnes?"

Rose stood swiftly. Grace pressed herself against the hut as Rose came around the side and saw a man approaching from the footpath that led to the road. It was the preacher from Agnes's church. From his vantage point, the hut concealed the gruesome scene.

She stepped forward to intercept him, and he smiled when he recognized her. "Ah, Rose," he said. "I've come to give Agnes a blessing." He took in the look on her face and his smile fell. "Are you all right?"

"There's been an accident," she said. "Can you get someone from Saint Joseph's?"

He hesitated, bringing a hand to the back of his neck as he craned to look past her. "I . . ."

"It's an emergency. Go!"

She watched him scramble back through the undergrowth. Agnes was past help, but now they had time. Ten minutes, maybe.

There was one thing she understood above all else: there was no way to hide what was done.

And glinting behind that knowledge was a question—*would a thirsty mob spare a child?*—whose answer she did not want to have to learn.

She turned to Grace. "Take Isaac and Wilborn. Leave everything else. Come." Grace disappeared inside and Rose went to her brother and touched his shoulder again. He was stroking Agnes's cheek with a bloodied hand.

"James, we must go."

He looked up at her with blinking eyes, making no sound. Tears rolled down his cheeks.

Thunder erupted all around them. The first raindrops began to fall.

"We need to leave, James. Now."

She heard Grace inside the hut, coaxing Isaac to leave the paper bird and take her hand. Rose's calm—the hardness of the bush—began to crack.

"Think of Isaac," she pleaded. "Think of what they would do to him."

"Isaac," James repeated dumbly. Agnes's head lolled in his lap, her mouth slightly open. The rain grew steadily stronger, making patterns of pockmarks in the dust, thickly crimson.

Voices carried from the direction of the road. So soon? She tried to wrench James up by his elbow, but his body was slack and heavy. She heard Isaac resisting Grace in the hut.

"Brother, please," she begged.

"No," James said at last, his voice raw. He met her eyes. "I will stay."

"But Isaac," Rose said. The voices were getting nearer. She could recognize the shrill tone of the preacher; several other men had joined.

James turned again to Agnes's face. "Yes. Isaac." Without looking again at Rose, he said, "Take the children to Beatrice. It is not safe for you here."

She gripped his arm tighter. "What good can you do? She's gone."

His eyes flickered up, past her, and Rose turned: Isaac had come out of the hut and wrestled free of Grace's grasp, and was standing, belly out, looking at them, uncomprehending. Thunder cracked open the sky.

"I have done enough wrong in my life," James said quietly. His eyes never strayed from Isaac. "Let me do this one good."

A moment later Rose had Isaac in her arm—he was heavy but calm, at least, wrapped around her neck—and Grace at her side, Wilborn tied to the girl's back, as they followed the path away from the hut toward the river. From there they could walk upstream to another path that would take them to Beatrice's home. They moved cautiously, careful not to draw attention; from behind, Rose could still hear men's voices escalating quickly into anger, though the noise was quickly drowned out by the storm. The men had stopped at the hut, as James knew they would; too preoccupied with the scene, they wouldn't think to pursue any possible fugitives. The preacher would try to soothe them, she expected, but the shouting would attract others, and in this way the mob would grow, seething, until it was beyond control. But she couldn't think of that. The children were safe. Even Isaac. No one would ever have to know.

They paused when they reached the river, Rose breathing heavily. Her arm shook from the weight of the boy; she was out of practice carrying a child, and even in the bush she'd had both arms. Now she felt always off-balance, no way to steady herself. The rain was becoming more intense, pebbling the muddy, slow-moving creek water, where bits of flotsam drifted. Aside from a Marabou stork stalking augustly among the reeds, the place was empty.

She set Isaac down and pulled the phone out of her purse to dial the police. They could stop this thing; they could intervene. She knew that she must report it anonymously lest they come after her, too.

The police didn't answer. The line rang and rang.

"You should not come to Beatrice's place, auntie," Grace said.

Rose turned, wiped the rainwater where it was gathering at her temples. "I have to make sure you're safe."

Grace turned to her, and it seemed in that moment that the girl was older than her years. "They do not love you there."

For a second Rose was dizzy. When she looked up, Grace already had Isaac in her small hand. The girl's eyes were bright and fierce. The rain had no care for them; it pounded harder and harder, as if searching for a way through her very skin.

"*Apwoyo,* auntie," Grace said—and without waiting for a reply, took Isaac and trotted onward, three little souls into the storm.

Rose watched their departing figures until they turned a corner and disappeared behind the brush, the leaves battered by the storm and wind. The river was growing in strength. She felt that her feet had grown long and deep into the soil. Her body was a broken thing.

When her phone began to ring, at first she didn't understand the source of the noise. The melody was so artificial and bright, it made no sense at the riverbank by the garbage with the stork, and therefore it couldn't belong to reality.

She answered in a daze. "Hello?"

Franklin's voice carried heartily through the torrent of rain. "Rose, *apwoyo,* eh? You are fine in Kitgum? I have received your message, Ocen will be happy to hear this news."

She had to sort his words for sense. Ah: the lie, Ocen's "payment."

"I must return your call later," she said.

"But he is here!"

The drumming in her ears drowned out all else. "He is there? Ocen?"

"Yeah, that is what I said."

"Since when?"

"Three weeks . . . maybe four."

Her vision became blurry, crowded. "I called before. You said he never came."

"Ach," he dismissed. "I never said."

It didn't matter.

"Can I talk to him?"

He coughed. "I mean to say, he is not here at this moment. He went for a short trip. But he is returning soon."

"Today?"

"Yes. Perhaps."

Her pulse slowed. The man told tales. He didn't know anything about Ocen. He only cared about the money.

But was there some truth here? She had to think. "And the *mono* girl?"

"Eh, Lily. I know her. That one, her backpack is bigger than herself."

"They are together?" she asked.

"Sure."

"She is with him now? She's returning with him?"

Hesitation. "Why are you asking me? Does she have something to do with the money?"

The stork hunched down against the wind, and the muddy water swirled and pushed loose a pile of plastic bags and debris.

Deliberately, carefully, she lowered her voice and said, "*Lakwali.*"

The silence on the other end of the line was palpable. She did not repeat the word. Finally he spoke. "What do you know about that place?" In the forced casualness of his tone, she heard everything. She hit the end button without responding.

The world tilted. Her hands trembled with cold and confusion as she scrolled through her contacts to find Christoph's number. She dialed, waited.

"Rose?" he answered. "Did we have something scheduled for today?"

"I need you to pick me up," she said. "We must leave Kitgum. Immediately."

"What are you talking about? Is everything all right?"

"I know where they went," she said. "Lily and Ocen. I know."

OCEN

December 2, 2008
Kitgum, Uganda

Running. Screams. Silence. Stars.

For a few seconds after he jolts abruptly to consciousness, Ocen lies blinking into the blackness, willing his pulse to slow, his breath to return. A dream, he reminds himself, as he's done so many nights before. It was just a dream.

Running. Screams. Silence. Stars.

Awake, though, the memory is sharper, more potent than the nightmare, and he struggles to push it away. The shouts, the confusion, the *pop!pop!pop!pop!* of guns going off in the dark, the red flares. Nearly ten years have passed since that night, but he can still smell the beginnings of smoke from a hut on fire, still feel the pressure of his mother's hands pushing him out the door in a panic, her voice choked with worry over Opiyo, who'd snuck out to meet Rose and not returned. He can still hear his mother's urgent whisper: *Find him and flee, find him and flee.*

But the rebels were already upon them, among them, and in his terror Ocen could not search—he could only run. He heard the screaming behind him until he wasn't sure whether it remained in life, or if it was only in his head. The earth was cool and damp beneath him, the touch of brush rough on his skin.

Night passed for a million years.

When he returned to the camp in the yellow-bluish dawn, he saw them there: his parents, unmoving. The dark earth. The hazy sky. Trails of smoke, bridging the space between.

There were other bodies, too. Too many. But not Opiyo.

Ocen checks the time on his cell phone. Just before four; he should have been awake already. He rushes to dress, to prepare his few belongings, placing an extra shirt, a pair of socks, and his toothbrush into a black plastic bag, then slipping his identification documents along with his small savings and cell phone into the zippered pocket of the jacket he's wearing. Everything else in the hut remains: the bowl and spoon, the mattress and sheets, the leaky jerry can, his logbook, last year's calendar on the wall. He won't need any of it where he's going. Around his wrist is the bracelet he always wears, the one Rose gave him: three different metals, silvery iron and reddish copper and golden brass, wired and braided and linked for all time. It comforts him to feel the cool metal against his skin, to be touched by a thing that has been touched by her.

Before he closes the door behind him, he glances around the tight, spare space one last time. If Rose comes to look for him here, what will she see? What conclusions will she draw?

It pains him to imagine her after he leaves. How long will it take her to know that he's gone? There were so many times in the past weeks when he was a breath away from telling her everything: the revelation, the impossibility, the meticulous preparations. But he was so *angry*. It shames him, this anger; yet it's the force that thrusts him forward, that he hopes will carry him through the coming weeks. The fight he picked with Rose the other night had been fabricated— he needed to cloud the circumstances of his absence, and driving a wedge between them was the safest approach—but the emotion was true. He hadn't been certain until then that he would follow through with Lily's plan, but after Rose hurled that word at him—*coward*, she'd said, an insult that pierced him to the very core—his resolve became firm, and he knew he would go.

Now the early morning stars shine high overhead, quietly dazzling in their distant shrouds. A crescent moon glints seductively on the shiny metal of his *boda* where it leans on its kickstand at the edge of the brush. When he grabs the handlebars and pulls it upright, the movement startles a stray dog, which trots off, pausing to scratch an ear before disappearing behind the neighbor's hut.

It feels different to touch the motorcycle now that it belongs to him. When Lily gave him the money last week, he was embarrassed—he never wanted to beg—but she'd convinced him so thoroughly of the necessity. This way they won't be dependent on public transportation; they can travel unnoticed, unremembered: just another *mono* on a *boda*. *You can pay me back afterward, if you like,* she said. *After we return.*

She believes this, he knows: that their return is not a matter of *if.*

She's already said she won't come back to Kitgum with him—she'll travel straight to Kampala to catch her flight out of Entebbe. *You wouldn't believe how beautiful a white Christmas in Colorado can be,* she said. *The snow makes everything clean and new.*

When he returns to Kitgum—if he returns—all will be new here. But clean? What in this place can ever be clean again? Nothing that he knows. Nothing that he's seen.

He takes the side roads through town, avoiding the bus station where the overnight bus from Kampala would be arriving sometime soon. *No one can see us leave together,* Lily said again and again, and so he is careful to skirt the streets with the bars, too, where other *bodas* will be waiting for the stumbling drunks after last call. He understands Lily's caution, though as he passes the street that leads to Rose's house, he has to make a concerted effort not to turn.

He crosses the bridge and heads down the road toward St. Joseph's. Finally, far in the distance, his headlights catch on the white façade of the Mission—and there she is, standing on the steps with an enormous backpack. His chest constricts and releases, constricts and releases.

As he slows to a stop in front of her, she smiles.

"*Apwoyo,*" Lily says, almost shyly.

"*Apwoyo.*" The low gurgle of the idling engine rises to envelop them, and for a second he wants to laugh: what are they doing? What nonsense has brought them to this point? *Let us remain,* he wants to say; *let us forget.*

But she's already climbing onto the seat behind him, her slight body burdened by the weight of her pack. She straddles the bike like a man, and he can't help but think of Rose, seated gracefully with both legs on one side—the way she'd lean her cheek against his back, wrap her arm around his belly, and he could feel her warmth through his shirt. But now it's Lily's heat, and the sense is altogether different.

"Are you ready?" she whispers.

His toes still touch the earth, but barely, as he steadies the bike while revving the engine, and then they are moving, and his shoes are on the footrests, and the ground is falling away beneath them. He turns his head and says into the wind, "Let us begin."

PART II
THE RESURRECTED

CHAPTER 13

SABINE

December 29

The SUV splattered mud as it barreled forward, rumbling through puddles and over bumps at a bone-jarring speed, the windshield wipers working relentlessly while Sabine, behind the wheel, squinted to see through the storm. Christoph sat in the passenger seat; Rose was in the back. Nobody spoke. The dirt road unfurled straight ahead, flanked by mango trees and low brush, everything blurred in the rain. Sabine knew she was driving too fast—how many times had she told David to slow down when the road was wet?—but every time she lifted her foot slightly from the gas pedal she was overcome by restlessness, by the sense that every second was precious, and her foot pressed back down and the speedometer crept higher.

She'd insisted both on taking her rental car and on driving, despite Christoph's protestations particularly toward the latter; she reminded him that she had significantly more at-the-wheel experience in Uganda than he did, and Lily was her family, not his. The statement— spoken perhaps with more force than she'd intended—had the desired effect, and he'd climbed into the passenger seat without further complaint. In the rearview mirror Sabine could see Rose in the backseat, still wrapped in the towel she'd been wearing when Sabine met them at the Bomah half an hour before. Rose and Christoph had been sitting on the musty couches in the lobby when she arrived, panicked, after getting Christoph's phone call outside the library. The exchange was brief—only the essentials: Rose had reason to believe Ocen and Lily left Kitgum together, that they'd traveled to Arua, and that Ocen's uncle would know more. *Arua?* Sabine thought wildly. *What's in Arua?* But she didn't even ask the question; she would find out when she got there. Her luggage was already packed and in the car. Rose said she had everything she needed, too. It took Christoph five minutes to put together an overnight bag, and then they were on their way.

The farther they drove from the center of Kitgum, the fewer pedestrians were on the road. Despite the approximate peace, people remained instinctually afraid of wandering from the relative security of town. Occasionally Sabine saw a bicycle lying at the side of the road, marking where a brave—or desperate—farmer had returned to his fields, and any time they approached a camp or village there would be more people coming and going, even in the rain, but in the long stretches in between, the roads were empty, the fields lay fallow, and the landscape that rolled by was vast and green and wet.

They'd just passed the junction at Acholibur—Sabine took the right fork, southwest toward Gulu—when Christoph cleared his throat and said, "We should call the police."

Sabine was quiet; Rose, too. When no one replied, he pulled out his phone from his pocket. Sabine reached across and put a hand on his elbow.

"Wait," she said.

"They can help us."

Sabine glanced in the mirror at Rose, whose face was turned toward the window. She seemed to be somewhere else. It was strange; being near Rose heightened Sabine's awareness of her own body, the symmetry of her two arms, two wrists, two hands—how suddenly superfluous the doubling seemed. Sabine thought of their encounter yesterday outside the prison, Rose's evasive demeanor. Had she known then that Lily and Ocen were together? What else was she hiding now? Could Sabine trust her?

"I'm calling," Christoph said.

"Don't," Sabine said.

"Why the hell not?"

Sabine downshifted as they approached a particularly bad stretch of road. The car shuddered and shook as she coaxed it through puddles deep enough to swallow the tires. When they were past the worst of it, she said, "There are things you don't know about Lily. Things I didn't learn until I got to Kitgum."

"What are you talking about?"

She looked at Rose again. This time the woman's eyes met hers. In her gaze Sabine saw an interest that bordered on wariness. Maybe if Sabine opened up first—if she laid all her cards out on the table— Rose would do the same.

"You remember how Linda said that Lily was acting strangely?" Sabine said. "That she'd been distant? I think I know what it was."

Christoph tensed, and she felt a sinking sense of loss. She pushed on. "Through her work at the rehabilitation center, Lily learned that the LRA was involved in the illegal ivory trade. I believe she spent her last month in Kitgum doing research. It's possible she uncovered sensitive information tracing back to local officials." She repeated Jochem's story about the journalist in Kampala. "I have no way of knowing what's true or who to trust. The police have shut me out of their investigation. It could be incompetence or apathy, but I'm not willing to take the risk."

Christoph's face was pale. So he hadn't known. Sabine had been watching Rose's expression carefully, too, as it transformed subtly from caution to confusion and—was she reading that right?—relief. It occurred to Sabine that Rose might have seen Lily and Ocen's leaving together as a sign of romantic involvement; she remembered the fight Rose mentioned. A lover's spat. It made sense that Rose would feel comforted by an alternate explanation. On the other hand, Sabine thought, was romance so far a stretch? As uncomfortable as it made her to imagine, Lily could very well have had more than one fling in Kitgum.

Finally Christoph spoke, bewilderment in his voice. "She never said a word to me."

Sabine was sorry for him: Lily's secret would feel like betrayal, a sign of distrust. She wanted to say, *She never told me, either. If anyone should have known, it was me.* But she stayed silent, and the pity passed.

"What about Ocen?" Christoph asked. "Why would they be together?"

"Transportation. Or he could have been helping her with the investigation." The latter seemed unlikely, though. Sabine flicked her eyes to the mirror. "Rose, did Ocen's uncle tell you when exactly they came to Arua? Or how long they stayed?"

"He did not say."

"But they were supposed to come back to his place?"

"That is what he said."

"Anyway," Christoph said, "it's the best lead we've got."

He used the term so casually, so unconsciously—*we,* as in *us,* as in the three of them together—and Sabine wasn't sure she liked it. She was grateful for the information Rose had brought, and she even felt appreciative of Christoph's presence as a bridge between them, but when her and Rose's interests took separate paths, she hoped Christoph would choose his assistant. Sabine expected their trio to break up in Arua once Ocen had been located and had given whatever information he could about Lily's whereabouts, her contacts, or her plans. At that point Sabine would continue on her own, without the attraction and embarrassment that kept her stiffly at arm's length from Christoph.

They rode the rest of the way to Gulu without further conversation. Sabine was glad to concentrate on driving, and both Rose and Christoph seemed lost in private contemplations. The rain stopped soon after Gulu, and the sky turned a terrific blue. Sabine's thoughts drifted, strangely, to Marburg. A week ago her life fit tidily within the parameters of *ordinary*: she'd woken to heavy snow, put a dollop of fresh cream in her coffee, driven to the animal shelter in predawn darkness for her early morning shift. It was easy to conjure the sensual details of that life in discrete fragments—the warm, doggy smell of the kennels; the shrill chorus of barking and the clamor of opening gates; the squeaky crush of snow beneath her winter boots; the crisp, skeletal branches of trees; the way the sun would catch on the frozen river and scatter into a thousand shards. But in imagining these things, Sabine felt she was observing someone else's memories—precious, delicate, contained in a snow globe. As hard as she looked, she couldn't find herself inside. Here—beneath the sweeping sky, with the low green landscape rolling past—Sabine felt full and alive and present. A part of the world, not separate from it.

"Palenga," Christoph said as they passed through the outskirts of a village. "Rose, don't you have family from around here?"

"My mother's father."

"Did you visit often?"

"Sometimes, when I was very young." A smile crossed her face. "My cousins and I would sneak away to the house of a very rich man and look through his trash pit for things we could eat. Eh, he threw away such treats! Jam and biscuits and fancy tea . . . The first chocolate I ever tasted was from licking the wrapper of a candy bar."

"Does your grandfather still live there?"

"He died when I was in primary school."

Christoph tapped a finger on the armrest. "My mother's parents died when I was young, but my father's parents are still alive. As a kid I spent summers on their farm near the French border." He twisted in his seat to face Rose. "I used to sneak away with my cousins, too. We'd go picking apples in the neighbor's orchard. My grandparents had the same kind of tree on their land, but the ones we stole always tasted sweeter." Smiling, he cast a glance at Sabine. "Your turn."

"My turn?"

"Arua's still a long ways off."

"You want to play car games?"

He put up his palms. "We have to pass the time somehow."

After a pause, she said reluctantly, "I never met my maternal grand-parents. They died before I was born."

"What about your father's side?"

"My grandmother was a schoolteacher."

"And your grandfather?"

Her *opa*'s face came immediately to mind: the stiff bristles of his closely trimmed white beard, the blue eyes that always seemed un-quiet, both kindly and sad.

"He was an engineer by profession," she said. "But his passion was Rhinelanders."

"What's that? People who live around the Rhine?"

She laughed despite herself. "Rabbits. He bred them for years."

"Breeding rabbits is a skill?" Out of the corner of her eye, she could see the hint of his smirk.

"Have you ever seen a Rhinelander?" she said. "They're beautiful—such distinctive markings. White with black-and-yellow checkers. I remember him in the yard, going from hutch to hutch with feed, speaking to the does." She told a story about one Christmas morning, when her grandfather woke her at dawn to see a litter of newborn kits. She'd been proud because *Opa* didn't wake Hannah, only her; it made her feel special and chosen. Sabine recalled the pale blooms of breath before her as she followed him across the snowy lawn. At the hutch he coaxed the dam away with a handful of oats then pushed aside tufts of warm, loose fur on the nest box to reveal six tiny, hair-less babies, their minuscule pink ears laid flat against their skin. It was the doe's first litter; she was eight months old when she kindled. Sabine's grandfather pointed to the kits' round little bellies and said the dam had already nursed, and she'd be a fine mother indeed. Then he tenderly replaced the fur over the babies' bodies and led Sabine back to the house, where she crawled back under a layer of quilts and fell back asleep.

"He sounds like a gentle man," Christoph said.

"Yes."

"That generation saw a lot of hard things."

Her throat caught. "They did."

He turned to Rose again. "You learned about World War Two, didn't you? In school, I mean?"

Sabine thought it odd that he would ask; Rose's command of English and her position as Christoph's assistant suggested that she'd had a good education. But Rose's answer—"A bit"—left Sabine wondering.

"Switzerland was neutral," Christoph continued, "but my grandparents' farm was right next door to German-occupied France. They worked with the village mayor on the French side to help Jews escape across the border." His voice turned wistful. "I remember meeting the children and grandchildren of some of the people they rescued. They stayed in touch after all these years. It was humbling."

He cast a glance at Sabine. She willed him to look away. *Not my turn*, she thought. He seemed to get the message. In a brighter tone, he said, "Rose, did you know Sabine lived in Africa for eighteen years?" He glanced at Sabine. "Eighteen, wasn't it?"

Sabine nodded.

"That is a long time," Rose said. "Almost as long as me." Sabine caught her eye in the mirror and saw her smile.

"How old are you, Rose?" she asked.

"Twenty-two."

The same age as Lily. Sabine's heart twisted. "I was twenty-two when I came to Africa," she said. "My first job was in Ethiopia. I was based in Addis for a year and a half. After that I went to Ghana, then Mozambique, then Zambia."

"So many places," Rose said.

"That was only the first five years. Crisis postings tend to be fairly short—anything from a couple months to a year or two. At first I tried to spread my focus, working in different sectors: food security, livelihood, water and sanitation, health education . . . Eventually I focused on refugees and displacement. That's how I ended up in Kitgum."

Christoph was looking at her closely. "I find it interesting that someone who spent her life running away from the idea of home would try so hard to help other people return to theirs."

"Who said I was running away?"

He shrugged.

"I wanted experience. Staying in one place would have pigeon-holed me."

"You're right. I'm sorry."

"I'm settled now," she insisted. "I own my apartment in Marburg." Her tone flared with offense, but beneath it she felt a kind of relief: the relief of being recognized, of having a stranger's astute gaze pierce you right to the marrow. *I see you,* he was saying. *I see through you.*

"Why did you leave Uganda?" Rose asked. "Did you get another job?"

Sabine kept her eyes ahead. "No. I moved back to Germany."

"You said it was burnout, didn't you?" Christoph said, and again she tingled under the spotlight of his study. He'd listened; he'd paid attention. He'd remembered.

"I said that, yes."

The road became ribbed, and they rattled over the ruts in jerky silence. Each bump sent her heart jouncing in her rib cage. By the end Sabine's entire body felt untethered, like something inside had been shaken loose. Before she knew what she was saying, the words came out, spilling off her tongue like paper banners tossed from an upper-story window, unrolling all the way to the ground: the story of the two women and the baby on the side of the road, the small, pinched face, David's intervention, her own awful apathy.

When she was through, she felt emptied of something; she was a wet towel, wrung out and wrinkled.

"What happened after?" Rose asked.

Sabine shifted uncomfortably. "I put in my notice."

"No," Rose said. "I mean, what happened to them? The woman and the baby."

Sabine sobered at the memory of her conversation with David that morning. "The baby died."

"And the mother?" Christoph asked.

"She survived."

"That is no life," Rose said quietly.

They reached Arua when the late-afternoon light was gentling toward evening. Rose guided Sabine to Ocen's uncle's compound with the briefest of words. Sabine's heart beat faster when a low brick house and cluster of huts came into view.

"Eh," Rose said, the towel falling from her shoulders and revealing the space where her arm should have been. "We are here."

CHAPTER 14

ROSE

December 29

Rose felt the world expand and contract around her as she stepped out of the car outside Franklin's house and waited for someone to appear. Her legs were stiff from the long drive—they'd only taken a single short break—and there lingered in her veins a simmering edginess. In the car, with the towel absorbing the rain from her clothes and skin, she'd kept her hand gripped tightly around her phone, both hoping and dreading that it would ring with news of James. The phone's continued silence seemed almost willful. When Christoph had wanted to call the police, Rose's mind raced with the possible consequences—not just for Ocen, who might have committed crimes himself, but for her own security, so blatantly fleeing the scene of a crime. Rose had been about to interject when Sabine began to explain Lily's secret investigation into ivory. Rose struggled to comprehend this new development: so Ocen had not been looking for trouble alone? If he was assisting Lily in her research, this could very well be the "ideas about money" he'd mentioned to Paddy. Surely he would be earning as Lily's assistant, just as Rose earned as Christoph's. Except Christoph's research was tame; Lily's was a wild animal, a predator stalking in the night. Could it be that Ocen's reticence the previous month was for Rose's safety? At this possibility she felt a surge of love, along with shame for having doubted him, her good, noble Ocen.

Still, nothing was certain, and it concerned her that in the wide compound there was no sign of Ocen: no familiar T-shirt drying on the clothesline, no *boda*. No man.

Sabine and Christoph had come up behind her.

"Is anyone home?" Sabine called out, striding forward. "Hello?"

A goat bleated from somewhere in the brush, and a moment later a woman emerged from the dark doorway of one of the huts, a bright handkerchief around her head. She stood and wiped her hands on her skirt, eyeing the group skeptically. Rose recognized her as Ocen's uncle's second wife; Ocen had brought Rose to Arua for the wedding last year.

"Where's Lily?" Sabine said. "And Ocen? Where are they?"

Christoph took her gently by the arm. "Let Rose talk to them."

Rose appreciated his intervention. Things between them were normal again, as much as they could be. When he'd met her at the Bomah, he'd taken one look at her—shaking, soaking wet—and dashed to reception for a towel. As he wrapped it around her shoulders, he said, *I'm sorry, Rose, for what happened before. I was foolish. You have every right to be angry with me.* She thought of the violent scene she'd just fled, how unfair and skewed the world was, and here was a man striving to put things right, however clumsily. And now he was—she realized with a start—her only friend in Kitgum, aside from the children. She took his hand. *Come with us to Arua,* she said. *I would like to have you there.*

"We are looking for our friends," Rose said to Franklin's wife. "Lily and Ocen. Your husband told me they passed through here some weeks ago."

The woman raised her eyebrows in a slight affirmation but said nothing.

"Can you tell us where they are?" Rose asked.

A portly man appeared from behind the brick house—Ocen's uncle Franklin. He was short and thick as a tree stump.

"Rose," Franklin said in surprise.

"*Apwoyo,* Franklin."

"I did not expect you to come." He glanced at Sabine and Christoph, then lowered his voice and addressed Rose. "Is this about the payment?"

"Where's Lily?" Sabine interjected. "I know she was here."

Franklin's cheek twitched as he took a step toward the door of the house. "Please, you are welcome to come inside."

"I don't want to come inside, goddammit," Sabine said. "I want to know where she is."

Franklin looked at Rose as if she might offer him a way out, but she kept her eyes hard.

"I'll call the police," Sabine threatened.

"Eh," Franklin said with a half laugh. "No need, no need. Lily was here. She came with Ocen weeks ago."

"The date?" Sabine said.

"December second. They left the next morning."

"You told me they were coming back here soon," Rose said.

"Ocen said he would return some days ago. But he is still away."

"Where did they go?"

"I don't know."

"They must have said something," Sabine cut in. "A word. A hint. Anything."

He opened his palms. "I wish I could help, truly."

"What do you want, money?" Sabine asked.

Franklin turned to Rose and said in Acholi, "I don't like these *monos* here. They should not be involved. Where is my protection in this situation?"

"No one wants to get you in trouble," Rose said. "We only want to find them."

Behind her, Sabine asked Christoph, "What are they saying?" Rose turned just enough to glimpse Christoph put a finger to his lips and shake his head subtly. *Let them talk.*

Rose continued in Acholi. "Where did they go?"

"You know where they went."

She met his eyes. "Lakwali." The word felt dark in her mouth.

He nodded. "They came here to cross the border."

"Ocen had no papers," she said doubtfully. She could sense Sabine and Christoph's close attention, though they remained silent. Christoph was accustomed to letting her converse freely in Acholi and trusting that she would translate everything afterward, but Sabine was restless and fidgety. For the moment, Rose was glad she was cut out of the discussion. Her single-mindedness might shut Franklin down completely.

"I have friends," Franklin said.

"Smugglers?"

"Contacts. A network."

"The Opec Boys."

"Among others."

"To get him travel documents?"

"The way we travel, documents are not necessary."

There were hundreds of smuggling routes along the border, he said—dirt roads and paths through the brush where the police couldn't patrol. Rose imagined Lily riding Ocen's *boda* at night, headlights off: the chilly air, the scratch of branches, the girl's thudding heart, her chest pressed against Ocen's strong back.

"But they were not on a mission for you?" she said.

"Do you think I would be so foolish? A nosy *mono* girl, working for me?" He scoffed. "I take greater care than that."

"But the risk—"

He waved her off. "There was no risk. They carried nothing of value. Along those roads I have people everywhere—farmers, wives, even very young children. They keep their eyes open and sound the alert at the slightest suspicion." He patted the cell phone in his front shirt pocket. "Modern technology is a beautiful thing."

"If they were caught?"

He shrugged. "The *mono* girl wanted a bit of adventure. The *boda* got lost. 'Thank you, officers, for helping us find our way back to safety.'"

She clicked her tongue. "Why Lakwali? What did they want there?"

"They wouldn't say."

"Why do you keep their secrets?"

"I am telling you I don't know. That is the truth."

"You're touchy," she said. "You behave as if you have things to hide."

He wiped away the sweat that had begun to form at his temples. "I have many things to hide, Rose. You know my business."

"But you're not hiding anything about Ocen?"

"I promised him I would. But that vow is broken now. I've told you everything."

"Do you know Patrick? Or Flynn? Did they mention these names?"

Franklin's expression showed genuine blankness. "No, I never heard these words before."

"And Ocen said they intended to return before Christmas?"

"Eh, they are only a few days late."

Normally, Rose would share his unconcern; she *had* shared his unconcern, hadn't she, these past weeks? Not apathy, but a recognition of the things beyond one's control, a capacity for patience. Christoph called it "African time": a certain malleability about calendars, a flexible sense of hours and days. When she entered primary school Rose had learned to align her movements to the clock; she'd unlearned these lessons during her years among the rebels, who aligned their movements to the position of enemy soldiers, the availability of food and water, and the possibility of safe passage. Back in Kitgum, working for *mono* researchers, she'd slid back into Western notions of timetables in order to please her employers. Still, when unexpected delays occurred or plans changed, she accepted it with a dispassionate calmness that drove Christoph crazy. Now it was different. Silence was a signal.

"Lily missed her flight home," Rose said to Franklin. "They are not merely delayed. They are missing."

"I don't know what you expect me to do."

"Help us find them," she pressed. "Call your contacts."

Franklin laughed humorlessly. "You must think me very powerful, that my network could extend so far. Lakwali is beyond my reach, Rose. Two hundred kilometers inside Congo, and operated by foreigners. White people." He brought his face very close to hers. "You should ask your *mono* friends what the girl wanted there, and why she would take my nephew into her troubles."

He turned to Sabine and Christoph and switched to English. "Please, I told Rose everything I know."

Rose met Christoph's eyes and raised an eyebrow. He spoke into Sabine's ear, and she tightened her lips but didn't say anything as Christoph stepped forward to shake Franklin's hand. "Thank you for your help," he said.

Franklin nodded. "Safe journey."

In the parked car, Rose summarized her conversation with Franklin while Sabine sat at the wheel in pursed-lip silence. Christoph listened closely, tapping a finger against his jeans. When Rose finished, a beat passed before Sabine spoke.

"This place. Lakwali. It's a gold mine?"

Rose nodded.

"In the Congo?"

She nodded again.

"Her research could have been broader than just ivory and the LRA," Christoph said.

"Or she had an informant there. Someone who could help her." Sabine shook her head. "Congo. Fuck." She gripped the steering wheel as though to steady her. She looked exhausted, Rose thought.

Christoph reached across the console and touched Sabine's shoulder. Sabine flinched at the touch, though Christoph didn't seem to notice. "Let's find someplace to eat," he said. "We can reevaluate over dinner. It's been a long day."

The White Horse Hotel and Restaurant was newer and more chic than the Bomah, or any restaurant in Kitgum for that matter; in the dining room the handsome dark wood tables rested contentedly under blue tablecloths, and outside on the hotel grounds the pool was full and the foliage brushed up lushly against the spacious private huts. But Rose saw everywhere signs of menace: in the jagged orange reflection of sunset on the eerily still pool water, in the blazing-red dining room walls that seemed to her to be the color of fresh blood. She tried to focus on the plate of tilapia in front of her, but the crimson walls loomed too near, bringing back the sticky glistening wetness of Agnes's blood that morning. A wave of nausea caused her to set her fork aside.

She wasn't the only one without appetite. Sabine hadn't even picked up her silverware, and Christoph ate a few bites of chicken halfheartedly. They'd separated for half an hour or so to check into their rooms—it was too late to return to Kitgum tonight—and then had come together for dinner, where they went over Rose's conversation with Franklin again in greater detail, holding each piece to the light. Sabine said that while she was in her room she'd called a friend in Kampala who did some quick research online about Lakwali. There wasn't much information, but it appeared to be owned by an Australian mining company called Gladstone. According to a company press release, the Lakwali mine was poised to become one of the largest open-pit mines in Africa. Sabine's friend said she would look into it more and get back to them later that night or the following morning.

"But I have to wonder," Sabine said. "How do we know Franklin is even telling the truth?"

Christoph wiped his mouth with a napkin. "What reason would he have to lie?"

"Rose, you said he's involved in smuggling."

"Small-time," Rose said. "Fuel, cigarettes. Nothing like ivory or gold." She didn't leave anything out, except the fact that she'd known of Lakwali before this evening. She already sensed that Sabine didn't entirely trust her, and there was no reason to feed those doubts by admitting that she'd kept certain things to herself. Lakwali was out there now, known to all of them.

"What if Lily was about to expose him?" Sabine continued. "What would he do to prevent it?" She seemed distant, as if thinking aloud rather than speaking to them. "Lily wouldn't have suspected him, because she didn't suspect Ocen. She might have looked to Franklin as an informant. But he wouldn't want her to get too close. Maybe Lakwali is a distraction. Maybe she never left Arua."

"And what about Ocen?" Christoph shook his head. "You can't imagine Franklin would do anything to his own nephew?"

"Maybe he didn't have to."

Rose flushed with anger. "Ocen would never be a part of such a thing. He is a good man. An honest man."

"Honest enough to keep you in the dark about their plans?"

"He was protecting me. Lily had dangerous knowledge."

Sabine's voice was swift as a spear. "Dangerous to Ocen's uncle."

"The investigation was Lily's idea," Rose shot back. "Ocen was trying to help her. If something happened to him, the blame falls at her feet."

"Stop," Christoph said sharply. The word rang out between them. "Both of you, stop it. Sabine, I've met Ocen. He's a man of honor. And Rose, if they were traveling together, it was Ocen's decision, too. No one's to blame." He met each of their eyes in turn. "You're worried. People you love are missing. We need each other."

Rose felt buoyed by Christoph's defense of Ocen. "Sorry," she murmured, keeping her eyes low. Sabine's apology sounded to Rose to be equally reluctant, but Christoph seemed satisfied.

"Assuming Lakwali was their destination," he said, "what's our next point of action? The police should be notified. What about the UPDF?"

"No military," Rose said.

"No police," Sabine added.

Christoph gaped. "You can't be serious."

"Even if I thought we could trust them," Sabine said, "the Ugandan authorities don't have any jurisdiction in Congo."

"The UPDF is in Congo as we speak. Operation Lightning Thunder."

"That's a limited military action against the LRA in Garamba National Park," Sabine said. "Lakwali is hundreds of kilometers south. I very much doubt the Congolese military would look kindly on the UPDF broadening its mandate to include a gold mine."

Christoph looked doubtful. "For a missing American . . ."

"Who entered the country illegally?" Sabine shook her head. "No, there must be a way to get in touch with someone at the mine. Find out what Lily wanted there—find out if she ever arrived."

"Your friend—Rita—did she say if there was any contact information online?"

"Only Gladstone headquarters in Australia. She'll try calling, but with the holiday . . ."

"I'll go," Rose said.

The table fell silent. The patter of the waiter's footsteps echoed as he approached, and when he reached over the table to clear their plates, Sabine and Christoph leaned back slightly. Christoph waited for the man to leave and then said to Rose, "You absolutely will not." He had that expression Rose knew well: a kind of controlled furiousness, typically reserved for confrontation with uncompromising officials. Now he was using it on her—as if she were a child, as if she didn't understand what she was saying. But she understood better than anyone what such a journey meant.

"I will go to Lakwali," she repeated. "I will follow them there."

"It's not under discussion," Christoph said. "An excursion to Arua is one thing. The Democratic Republic of the Congo is something else entirely." He pressed his index finger against the blue tablecloth, pushing it into a wrinkle. Rose kept her eyes on the fabric while Christoph went on, his voice hushed and urgent. "This is a country that's basically been at war since independence. There's no stability.

No security. The UN is barely managing to keep its head above water. The roads will be patrolled by God knows what army—where roads exist at all." He turned to Sabine. "Help me out here."

Sabine nodded slowly. "All of that is true."

"It's brutal," Christoph went on. "The incidence of rape—" His voice caught.

Rose said, "And what do you think I have seen in my life? Only peace and sunshine?" Christoph blinked and her shoulder throbbed. She became acutely aware of her scar, the breath of space between her skin and the fabric that covered it.

His face was pale. "Rose, I can't stand to think of you going in there. A woman, traveling alone . . ."

"She won't be alone," Sabine said. She met Rose's eyes, and Rose saw a quiet fierceness there.

Christoph let out a cry of exasperation. "You're out of your minds."

"I feel it in my bones," Sabine said. "Lily is alive."

"You have to involve the authorities. How will you get around? How will you talk to people?" He threw up his hands. "You don't even speak French!"

"You do," Rose said.

For a moment no one said a word. The space around the table crackled with tension. Rose sensed something gathering strength, a swell of will and fear and hope. The crimson walls pressed ever closer.

Christoph heaved a great sigh. "We'll have to leave your car here, Sabine. We can inquire at the border about transportation to Lakwali and the security situation on the roads." He firmed up his voice. "If I deem the risks to be too great, I will not hesitate to alert the authorities."

Sabine looked first at Rose, who nodded.

"Agreed," Sabine said.

Christoph seemed resigned as he rose from the table. "We'll meet here tomorrow morning at seven. Let's all get some rest."

———

Rose had just stepped inside her room when her phone began to ring. She recognized her brother's number and gasped at the force of the desire to believe that it *was* him, that in the next second James's voice would come through laughingly on the other end of the line. She had to steady herself before she answered.

"Auntie, it is me." Grace's voice was small and timid, and Rose's heart clenched to hear it.

"Grace. My sweet. You're with Beatrice? And Isaac? Wilborn?"

"We are all here."

Warmth flooded her veins, and her grip on the phone became loose. "Thank God." She hesitated a moment and then asked tentatively, "And what news?"

But Grace did not respond, and in the pause Rose knew everything. She could not bear for the girl to have to say it aloud.

"It's all right," she said. "Don't answer." Rose found herself sitting on the bed, the sheets so crisply tucked around the sides. A mosquito net was tied in a neat knot overhead. The room felt clean and full of nothing. Where James was now—and Agnes, and their unborn baby— was it like this? Was it like this where her own son had gone, and so many others? Would it be so bad to be in such a place?

"Are you safe, auntie?"

Rose's throat tightened. "I am safe."

"When will you come back?"

She gazed out the window at the vestiges of sunset, the swift fall of night. "Soon," she soothed. She tried to imagine what tomorrow would bring: a crossing, or not. A journey, or not. Answers, or none. Her voice trembled when she said, "Take care of your cousins, Grace."

"I will."

"Kiss them for me."

"I will, auntie."

The stillness of the room after they hung up felt vast and weightless.

Rose lay back on the soft bed and willed herself to sleep.

CHAPTER 15

SABINE

December 29

Alone in her hut, Sabine sat on the bed, phone in hand. At Ocen's uncle's house and then at dinner, her mind had been churning with a hundred thoughts at once, grasping at the fragments that kept bumping against each other without cohering into a whole. Lily and Ocen; Ocen and Franklin; Franklin's illegal activities; Lily's investigation. Ivory. Gold. Truth. Lies.

Congo.

Despite her accusations at dinner, Sabine didn't really believe that Franklin was responsible for Lily's disappearance. She couldn't say why, exactly; it was a sense, an instinct. But was it like the instinct that told her Lily was still alive?—an instinct she gladly exploited to persuade Christoph to their side, but one she didn't entirely trust. Was she feeling only the desire toward instinct? A need to believe? The idea of Lakwali pulsed dangerously, magnetically from the unknown territory beyond the border. Sabine now knew why Lily had been studying the atlas at the peace center: it was no art project, no hobby. It was a guide. Online maps would be useless without a smart phone—forget about satellite coverage or GPS. Sabine wished she had that atlas, too, to prepare her for what was to come.

"Tell me, Rita," she said after her friend answered on the first ring. "Am I crazy? Is this whole idea insane?"

Rita sighed. "God knows I wish you wouldn't go."

"What did Peter say?" When she'd called Rita before dinner, she'd confessed her suspicions about Lily's research, the reason she might have had for taking such a risk; Rita had promised to ask the Australian journalist, Peter, for advice.

"He said if it were him, he'd keep the authorities out of the loop, too."

"But I could wait, couldn't I? I could try to get in touch with someone at the mine."

"And what if they say they don't know anything about her? Would you believe them? Would you call it a day?"

Sabine ran her hands along the taut bedsheet. "No."

They were quiet a moment.

"It's so odd," Sabine said. "I lived in northern Uganda for three years, and I'd never even heard of this place—Lakwali. I have no idea what to expect."

"How much do you know about the war in Congo?"

"Only what's reported on the BBC," Sabine admitted. It shamed her to know so little—yet the intensity of her job in Kitgum had demanded a near-exclusive focus on what was happening then and there. If she'd been transferred to Congo, she would have immersed herself as deeply in Congolese history, geography, and economics as she'd once done for Uganda, for Mozambique, for Ethiopia. But until a crisis was directly relevant to her work, she didn't have the capacity for any more tragedy. And even if she'd been offered a job in Congo, she probably wouldn't have taken it. There were some places that frightened even her.

"The conflict in Congo is probably the most complicated war in the world," Rita said. "Two wars, technically, in the last twenty years, but they overlap quite a bit. Nine African nations. Twenty armed groups. Five and a half million people dead, mostly from disease and starvation. Large-scale fighting has been occurring in various provinces since Rwanda invaded eastern Congo—it was Zaire, then—in

1996. Ever since, the country has been mired in one conflict after another."

There was no agreed-upon narrative for these conflicts, Rita explained, except that they were all thoroughly, relentlessly bloody. Northeastern Congo had some of the richest goldfields in the world— and without any governmental structure or authority, it was the usual story: executions, torture, rape, slaughter, stealing, smuggling. During the Ugandan occupation of northeastern Congo from 1998 to 2003, troops extracted some nine million dollars' worth of gold from Congolese mines. When the Ugandans pulled out, they left behind local rebel groups who scrambled to take over where Uganda had left off.

"There were international interests at play, too," Rita said.

"And that's what Peter was researching?"

"Exactly. The project he worked on looked primarily at a place nearby called Mongbwalu. They uncovered evidence that AngloGold Ashanti, a major player in global gold production, gave logistical and financial support to Congolese rebels in order to have 'safe passage' to conduct exploration activities around the mine. That rebel group killed thousands of civilians in the Mongbwalu area in a two-year period."

Sabine took a moment to absorb the information. "Could it be the same with Gladstone and Lakwali?"

"Hard to say. Peter didn't know anything about Lakwali specifically, and in the last few years he's been focusing on activities around Goma. The Gladstone Web site is awfully vague, and if they had any contact with rebel groups it's not like they'd be shouting it from the rooftops." She paused. "Do you have any kind of plan for transportation, communication?"

"Transportation will be tricky. We'll try to find someone on the other side of the border who's willing to drive us. Or we'll take a bus. Christoph speaks French. Hopefully that'll be enough."

"Do you trust him?"

"He's . . ." What could she say? That she wanted to pull him closer, inhale his smell? That he might have had an affair with her twenty-two-year-old niece? But she did trust him, and she told Rita as much.

"And Rose?" Rita asked.

Sabine thought of the poised Ugandan woman. Rose was inscrutable, a mystery. But the unease Sabine felt about her wasn't mistrust, she thought. She recalled the sense of closeness, the easy intimacy between Rose and Christoph—the way he'd let her work at Franklin's house, the unspoken signals between them. The discomfort in Sabine's gut wasn't doubt. It was envy.

"I think Rose wants to find Ocen as much as I want to find Lily," she said.

"I'm assuming you don't plan to contact the woman from the U.S. embassy in Kampala."

"Kathryn? Not a chance."

"What about Steve?"

"He'd be against it, no question."

"You don't think he has a right to know?"

"I think he'd be dialing CNN the second we hung up, and publicity is the last thing we need right now."

Through the window of her room, Sabine caught a glimpse of Christoph crossing the courtyard area, on the other side of the pool. The handsome profile of his nose and lips. He was moving slowly, his head down, hands in his pockets. Where was he headed? She craned her neck to follow as he passed out of view.

"It must be hard for him," Rita said. "Being so far away. He probably feels helpless."

Sabine pulled her attention back to the phone. "Steve's a good man. Hannah loved him. But he doesn't understand anything about Africa."

"Do we?"

Sabine half-laughed. It was better than crying. "No, I don't suppose we do."

The knock came just as she hung up. She opened the door to find Christoph with a grim look on his face. "*Guten Abend,*" he said.

"Come in."

There were no chairs, and Christoph glanced around awkwardly until she gestured to the bed. They sat apart, their legs dangling off the side. Christoph shifted a few inches toward her; Sabine, her neck prickling, stayed put.

"I talked to the hotel manager," he began.

Sabine felt a trickle of betrayal. "About our plans?"

"Just that we want to cross the border. I said we were tourists."

"He believed you?"

"It's not unheard of. He mentioned a Danish couple from earlier this year—they were driving from Cairo to Cape Town, via Congo and Zambia."

"They would have had an easier time through East Africa."

"Apparently they wanted the adventure," Christoph said. "In any case, the manager said he can arrange a ride for us to the border in the morning. We don't have time to sort out the paperwork on your car, and it's a rental anyway. We can leave it parked here for a week if need be. I asked about visas, too. He said we should be able to get them on the spot."

"Good."

"What if some of us get turned away?"

"We'll cross that bridge when we come to it."

He pressed his hands hard against his thighs. "You're serious about this, aren't you?"

"I am."

He stood up and began to pace. "They left Arua weeks ago. We need to be prepared for the possibility that this is as far as we can go."

"You can say that because you didn't love her." The force of her bitterness took her by surprise; the words had come out before she'd consciously formed the thought. Suddenly she was afraid of how he would respond.

Christoph stopped walking.

"You're right," he said. "But she reminded me of someone I loved."

"She did?"

"My sister," Christoph said.

Had she gotten his interest in Lily all wrong? A glimmer of relief and hope shimmered at the edge of her awareness.

"They were the same age," he said. "Céline would have been twenty-three in March." He sat back down on the bed, closer this time. Sabine felt a palpable sense of something being exchanged between them. "After I was born, the doctors told my mother she couldn't have any more children. She didn't—for fifteen years. Then, out of the blue . . ." He smiled. "Céline was a beautiful baby. I know everyone says that. But with her, it was true."

Sabine's stomach clenched with foreboding. "What happened?"

"I was hardly ever around. I left for university when she was five, and then I did my master's and Ph.D. . . . I came home for holidays, of course, but I was preoccupied. I didn't even notice how she was slipping away." He lifted his hand to the mosquito net knotted overhead and rubbed it between his fingers. "She overdosed when she was seventeen. Heroin. I can't help but think that if I'd been there for her earlier—if I'd seen the signs . . ."

Sabine knew the guilt he felt. She thought of all those curt replies she'd sent to Lily's e-mails from Kitgum, the cursoriness of her advice—how little attention she'd paid to Lily's struggles. A deep sadness tugged in her chest.

"I'm so sorry," she said.

He turned toward Sabine, his eyes moist. "Linda was right about Lily being disillusioned. She and I talked about it a lot. I wanted to help her."

Outside, the last patches of tangerine sky were darkened by the encroaching night.

"She told me a story," Christoph said. "A fairy tale her mother used to read to her when she was young. The Seven Ravens."

Talking ravens, glass mountains, siblings lost and found.

"I remember watching Hannah sit on Lily's bed at night with that book," Sabine said. "Our grandfather read it to us as children. We always loved the story of the seven ravens, too."

"It was a question Lily struggled with a lot—sacrifice," Christoph said. "How far to go to help others. She brought up the girl in that fairy tale quite a lot. She said she didn't know if she had that kind of courage." He met her eyes. "She believed you did. She admired you deeply, you know. She thought you had it all figured out."

"I didn't," Sabine said, suddenly helpless. "I didn't have anything figured out."

Christoph took her hand and squeezed. "Does anyone?"

She couldn't meet his eyes; she could only see the fine white-blond hairs on the back of his hand where he held hers, the subtle lines under his skin, his blood pulsing, his warmth.

"I know I'm not family," he went on, "but I felt responsible for her somehow. Protective. With Rose, too." He paused for a long time, finally releasing her hand. "She was abducted by the LRA when she was thirteen," he said at last. "She spent five years with the rebels. She's never talked to me about it. I found out from another expat who worked at the rehabilitation center where she arrived when she first came out of the bush. She's very private about those years."

Sabine didn't know what to say, and so she said nothing.

"I can't even begin to imagine what she's been through," Christoph went on. "And now, with Ocen missing . . ."

"I can see why you would feel protective," Sabine said.

"I want to help her, Sabine. I want to get her a better education, a better job."

The steadiness of his eye contact made her uncomfortable, and she looked away.

"You understand why we have to go," she said. "She and I both."

His voice was quiet. "I do."

"You don't have to feel responsible for me, too."

"You? Veteran of a hundred disasters?" He smiled. "The thought never crossed my mind."

———

The morning dawned chilly but clear. Sabine had said good night to Christoph with a prolonged hug—one that had left her dizzy, confused—then spent the rest of the evening packing and unpacking her bag, eliminating all but the essentials. It was strange to imagine Lily having done the same, weeks before: what had Lily chosen to bring? What had she left behind? What had brought her comfort on this dangerous journey? What was with her still?

She met Christoph and Rose at the breakfast buffet, which was laid out with fresh fruit and pancakes. Her body was tense and alert to Christoph's presence. After their conversation last night she had the feeling that something was shifting between them, and she was both exhilarated and nervous. She missed her sister with an abrupt longing. Hannah would recognize this terrain of in-between; she'd know the delicate balance of coyness and encouragement that would help the process along.

"Sleep well?" she asked him, bumping his shoulder ever so slightly.

He looked up at her with tired, red-rimmed eyes, and gave a small smile. "Didn't sleep much, I'm afraid." He turned blankly to the slice of pineapple on his plate. "I can't stop thinking about them. What might have happened."

And here she was, trying to flirt. How selfish to think of Hannah now; if Hannah were here, she'd have space in her thoughts for Lily and nothing else. Abashed, Sabine took a step away and said, "The best thing is to focus on the next step. For now we just need to cross the border and get to the mine."

Rose was as reserved as ever, her movements graceful and slow; Sabine's gaze fixated on the sewn-together sleeve that covered Rose's shoulder. The unconsciousness of her elegance left Sabine feeling gangly and stilted in her wake. How could someone who had been so profoundly crushed by tragedy hold herself with such poise?

What an odd trio we are, she thought: an unlikely band of rescuers. Yet this morning she found comfort in their strangeness. Yesterday she'd hoped their paths would split; today she was grateful she did not have to face the next steps alone. Christoph thought her tough, and she was. But today she was also afraid. Afraid that they would not be able to cross the border—and afraid that they would.

The road leading out of Arua toward the border was flat and wide and lined with greenery. Tall, spindly-trunked eucalyptus trees flanked the roadsides. *Bodas* and bicyclists passed in both directions, some holding their eyes a little too long on the car, and Sabine thought of Ocen's uncle and wondered if she was witnessing his network in action. The distance was less than ten kilometers, but the few minutes it took to drive felt as though they kept looping back on themselves, as if time was stuck and wouldn't move forward, as if she would stay suspended forever.

"Here we go," Christoph said as a meadow opened up to their right and the driver slowed. Half a dozen trucks were parked alongside the road ahead, and a series of huts and small buildings signaled the border offices. The driver pulled over and pointed to a small white building with a brown roof behind a ten-foot fence topped with barbed wire.

"Immigration," the man said as the three of them got out of the car.

"Thanks," Sabine said, handing him a twenty-thousand-shilling bill.

Christoph came up to the driver's side window and said to the man, "Can you wait a few minutes until we make it to the Congolese side?"

"No problem."

Christoph caught Sabine's eye. "Just in case."

They turned toward the building.

Two officers in khaki uniforms and black berets sat idly in the shade of a large tree. The officers glanced at their approach but showed little interest. They appeared to be manning a single barrier, one metal pole painted in alternating blocks of black and white; farther down the road were more small buildings, more parked trucks. Sabine went first through the gate in the fence, followed by Christoph and Rose. Her mind was alert, her body on edge. She'd crossed plenty of African borders as an aid worker, but relatively few as a tourist; without official credentials and a nongovernmental acronym to smooth her way, she felt small and powerless. She steeled herself for an interrogation, ran through the lines they'd discussed at breakfast: *Overland expedition through Africa, adventure in public transportation, headed south to Bunia, then west to the Okapi Wildlife Reserve.* They'd agreed that this invented itinerary seemed less suspicious, as it took them away from the military action in Garamba rather than toward it.

But the Ugandan officer hardly said a word; he took each of their passports and examined them morosely—he spent an especially long time scrutinizing Rose's photo—and then stamped them and waved them on.

"That's all?" Rose whispered as they left the building and exited the gate.

"They've only given us permission to leave Uganda," Christoph said. "Now we have to get permission to enter Congo."

One of the two police officers rose from his seat in the shade to check their passports before they could skirt the black-and-white vehicle barrier. Once past, they began to walk the short stretch of no-man's land between border posts. A cool breeze lifted the fabric of Sabine's shirt around her waist. With each step she took on the hard earth, her legs felt heavier. *Breathe,* she told herself. It's just another road. Just another blue sky. Just another signpost.

LA REPUBLIQUE DEMOCRATIQUE DU CONGO

VOUS SOUHAITE LA BIENVENUE

"The Democratic Republic of the Congo welcomes us," Christoph said.

"Yes," Rose said. "I am feeling very welcome." She turned to Sabine and smiled, and Sabine felt herself smiling back. Just another border crossing. Just another adventure.

The building and cars came closer. Leafy trees rustled gently alongside them. Four women chatted while resting in a shady patch of grass, buckets of green bananas and plump bags of sugar and avocadoes sprawled before them. It's really quite peaceful, Sabine thought: no one seemed stressed or hurried or angry. She hadn't seen a single gun or even a soldier in camouflage. She knew there would be refugees farther north, families fleeing the resurgence of LRA violence; she'd half expected to see throngs of displaced people trying to cross the border here. But the LRA attacks were so recent—they'd only started in the last week or two, since the start of Operation Lightning Thunder—and this border was hundreds of kilometers away from the fighting.

From the cluster of roadside traders, two children came out from behind their mothers and pointed at the *mzungus* and the one-armed girl as they passed; one boy was sucking on his finger, and when the other nudged him to go closer, he swatted him with the wet digit.

Christoph nodded at a low white building with a blue-trimmed roof. "Is that it, you think?"

"Must be," Sabine said. She halted and turned to him. "You can still turn back."

He squinted into the sun. "You know I can't do that."

She looked to Rose. "You, too."

Rose's expression didn't change. "And you."

They exchanged a nod.

The immigration building—identified by a hand-painted sign—was bordered by two others without markings. Outside one of them, three men stood in a small circle having an animated argument. Two were dressed in civilian clothes and a third was in a khaki officer's uniform. They were the only other people present; evidently the rest of the guards were busy with Franklin's fleet. The men weren't speaking French—that much Sabine could tell—but when she glanced at Rose, the Ugandan woman gave a brief shake of her head: *not Acholi.* One civilian kept pointing toward a parked truck, whose contents were hidden beneath a tarp. The officer responded angrily, flicking his hand against a piece of paper that seemed to be the flashpoint of the discussion. The front of the trucks faced east; they were coming into Congo rather than leaving. Just as Sabine was stepping into the immigration room, she noticed a figure exit the nearby building and insert himself into the arguing group. Her heart pounded in surprise: the man was white. Another *mzungu*? Was he a development worker? Missionary? Diplomat? He looked rather young, didn't he?—but she only caught a glance before she was inside the building, in the dimness, with a wall between them.

The room was sparsely furnished with two desks, six wooden chairs, and several sets of filing cabinets; a tall fan stood unplugged in one corner, dusty staplers and hole punchers crowded the top of the cabinet, and stacks of loose papers covered much of the desktop space. A smallish, round-faced man sat neatly behind the desk with pursed lips and glasses. From outside, the faint sounds of arguing drifted in.

"*Oui?*" the man said briskly.

"*Bonjour,*" Christoph began. Sabine couldn't follow the rapid-fire back-and-forth that came after; she mutely handed over her passport when Christoph told her so, and watched his face and the Congolese official's expression closely as they spoke. Christoph remained surprisingly cool—firm but polite, she thought—and the official gave nothing away. He barely made eye contact with Christoph, focusing instead on opening each passport in turn, flipping through the pages, then closing it again. When he went through all three, he began again. Sabine glanced to Rose, who stood quietly by, delicate beads of moisture gathering on her forehead. Sabine was sweating underneath her shirt. Why wasn't the fan plugged in?

"He says it's possible to get tourist visas," Christoph said in a low voice to Sabine and Rose. "Seventy-five dollars each."

"Will you accept euros?" she asked the man directly, in English. He cocked his head and looked at Christoph, who translated.

"*Oui,*" the man said.

Sabine nodded. "All right." She sensed Rose tense beside her, and touched the woman's elbow. "Don't worry, Rose. I can pay."

Upon the exchange of currency, the man opened a large ledger and copied their names and passport details painstakingly into the narrow columns, then wrote in each passport in tiny letters and stamped the page. As soon as the last stamp thudded down, Sabine felt both relief and terror. There was no going back. Meanwhile Christoph continued to ask a few more questions, to which the man replied curtly.

"The roads are secure south to Bunia," Christoph murmured to Sabine.

"What about west? Did he say anything?" She kept a smile on her face.

"I didn't ask. I thought it would raise suspicions."

"A casual inquiry wouldn't hurt."

Christoph seemed skeptical but spoke to the man again. The man put down his pen and clasped his hands on top of their passports, then lifted his gaze to meet Sabine's eyes.

"And what interest do you have in traveling westward?" he asked in crisp, precise English.

Sabine bit her lip. "We're considering a detour."

"Into a war zone?" he said archly.

Christoph straightened. "We know about the operation in Garamba. We weren't planning to go so far north. Has the fighting spread?"

"Kony's men have attacked villages all around the park. Dungu, Tora, Faradje . . ."

"We heard about Faradje," Sabine said. "The Christmas massacre."

His eyes were intense and bright. "These men are monsters. It is not our war, and yet we are suffering." He glanced at Rose then back at Sabine. "There is nothing for you in that place. It would be better if you went south." The last sentence felt to Sabine like a veiled threat.

Through the open door behind them, she heard a hearty laugh; she turned in time to see the group that had been arguing walk past cheerfully with the white man among them. In the half second they were visible, it looked like the white man was shaking the hand of the Congolese officer.

"Are the western roads quite unsafe then?" Christoph said.

The man removed his glasses. "How will you be traveling? You have no car. You have no driver. At least I assume she," nodding to Rose, "is not the driver." Rose seemed to shrink beneath his hard look.

"There must be a bus," Sabine said. "There are always buses."

He raised an eyebrow pointedly. "To Bunia, you mean?"

She felt a kind of desperation coming over her. Any moment now this official would change his mind. He'd cite security reasons or improper documentation. He'd keep their money, of course: a special tax on foolishness.

"We're going to Lakwali," she said.

"Lakwali?" His surprise was clear. "You're friends with them?"

"Them?"

He nodded toward the wall, in the direction of the border crossing. Sabine heard the sound of one engine starting, then another. *Them.* That group of men—they were from the gold mine? And the *mzungu*? As the engines revved, her thoughts raced.

"Why didn't they say anything, I wonder?" the officer mused. "They don't seem to be waiting for you."

A shadow darkened the doorway and Sabine saw the other officer lean in. He spoke rapidly with the round-faced man at the desk, who responded with a flare of anger, then stood abruptly.

"Stay here," he said to Sabine.

He followed his colleague out the door, where they turned away speaking in animated tones that quickly faded beneath the roar of engines. Sabine heard the distinctive mechanical hiss and groan of a truck shifting into gear. She craned her neck out the door and saw, through the driver's-side window of the nearest truck, an African man at the steering wheel and—there!—the *mzungu* in the passenger seat, facing ahead, now wearing dark sunglasses. The truck began to roll slowly forward—into Congo. *To the mine,* she thought frantically. *To Lily.* The truck in front with the tarp was already twenty meters down the road. She looked the other way and watched the two Congolese officers disappear into one of the side buildings.

"We've lost our chance," Christoph said. "There's no way he's letting us through now."

Sabine glanced around the yard. Aside from the women traders, the buildings were deserted. Her decision was swift. She grabbed the three passports from the desk. "He already did."

She pushed Christoph's passport against his chest and gave Rose hers. Rose took it and slid it neatly into her small purse.

"Do what you have to do," Sabine said as she stepped out of the room. "I'm getting on that truck."

Behind her she heard Christoph mutter, "*Merde*."

She gave the side building a final glance: no officers. Then she began to run. The second truck was a hundred meters down the road and gaining speed. Her senses focused; she could hear two sets of footsteps behind her—she turned her head briefly and saw Christoph and Rose following. If they didn't make it to the *mzungu*, they were done; even if they did, there were no guarantees. Her legs beat harder. When was the last time she'd run at a flat-out sprint? Five years ago? Ten? She felt she had never run so fast in her life, even with the heft of her backpack bobbing behind her. It was exhilarating.

She caught up with the truck just when it reached the speed of her gait.

"Stop!" she shouted. "Hold up!"

But the windows were up, and the driver couldn't hear. The truck let out a tremendous rush of noise and accelerated. The back bumper began to pull away from her grasp. She dug deeper. Christoph and Rose fell farther behind.

The bumper came into reach again, and in another second she was able to bang on the metal siding. "Stop!" she called out again. She wasn't sure she could go on any longer. Finally she saw the *mzungu's* reflection in the side mirror. His profile turned slightly, and the instant he saw her he shifted in his seat and said something urgently to the driver, who in turn put on the brake. Sabine slowed to a jog gratefully as the truck decelerated. She gulped air and tried to get her thoughts together. She came up to the passenger-side door just as the *mzungu* opened it a crack to get a better look at her. His feet came roughly to the level of her shoulders. She could see a small logo on the front pocket of his T-shirt. It read Gladstone.

"Hi there," the man said. "Can I help you?"

He spoke with such politeness, such earnestness—and with such a strong American accent—that for a second she forgot where she was. It didn't take long to remember.

"My name is Sabine Hardt," she said, breathing hard. "In a few minutes, those officers are going to come get me and my two friends and arrest us unless you help me. I'm looking for my niece. Lily Bennett. She crossed the border three weeks ago headed for Lakwali." She nodded at him. "Your gold mine."

Christoph and Rose came up beside her. Rose bent over at the waist to catch her breath.

The man took off his sunglasses, and Sabine realized how young he was: barely a boy. He couldn't be more than twenty-five. His eyes were startlingly blue and wide. But he didn't say a word.

"I don't know if she even made it there," she continued. "She's missing. She was supposed to fly home, but she never showed up for her flight." After a second's pause, she added, "She was traveling with someone. A Ugandan friend. His name was Ocen. Do you have any idea where they could be?"

The *mzungu* swallowed; his mouth seemed to be working, but no sounds came out.

Sabine closed her eyes. She could hear shouting distantly, from the direction of the immigration building. The officers would be here any minute.

The boy's eyes darted toward the border. Two running figures appeared in the road behind them. "They're coming," she said. She gripped the metal step of the cab. "Take us with you."

"You want to come to the mine?"

She couldn't tell if his look was of confusion or shock or unease; everything was happening too fast.

"It's the only clue we have," Sabine said. "Our last hope."

"You!" the smallish officer called out. "You! Stop!"

Sabine met the *mzungu*'s eyes. "Please."

At last the *mzungu* raised an arm and yelled out to the approaching officers, "It's all right, they're with us."

The officer slowed, uncertain. "They're with you?"

"Yup." He put down a hand to pull Sabine up into the cab, whispering, "Don't give them a chance to think about it too much." She grabbed hold and stepped up. "Atta girl." Sabine nodded to the driver and climbed between the seats to the long bench behind them. The boy pulled Rose up next, and she came to sit on Sabine's right, so that her left—whole—arm rubbed against Sabine's shoulder. The backseat held space for one more, and Christoph joined a moment later. It was snug, but everyone fit. Sabine's view through the side windows was cut off—she could only see straight ahead—but she watched the *mzungu* wave brightly as the truck took off. "Sayonara, suckers," he said through a smile. He turned back to the new passengers. "That was awesome! I hope my boss doesn't kill me."

"We don't want to get you in trouble," Christoph said.

"Nah, I'm just pulling your leg. No biggie." He stuck out his hand. "I'm Patrick, by the way. Patrick Flynn. Nice to meet y'all." He put back on his sunglasses and grinned. "Welcome to Congo."

CHAPTER 16

ROSE

December 30

Patrick Flynn. The words entered Rose's consciousness like the small hand of a child, reaching out to tug her skirt. She only half-heard Sabine make introductions. *Patrick Flynn Lakwali.* Not three names: only two. The man; the place.

"Sorry it took me a second to get it," Patrick was saying. "When you said Lily Bennett I wasn't sure who you were talking about—and then when you mentioned Ocen, I was like, oh, *Lily.* Except she told me her last name was Hardt." He paused. "No wonder I couldn't find her on Facebook." When he looked back, his face was grave. "But that's who you mean, right? Lily from Denver? I saw her just a few weeks ago. She and Ocen came out to the site."

Rose's temples tingled.

"They were there?" Sabine asked.

"Right at the beginning of December. They only stayed one night, though. I wish it was longer."

"I don't understand. What did they come for? Were they meeting someone?"

"Me."

"You?"

"I'm not enough?" he joked.

Sabine's tone was skeptical. "You were helping Lily with her research?"

Patrick frowned. "Research? Nah. We just hung out."

Rose saw Sabine and Christoph exchange a look. She could almost read their thoughts: *Unknowing informant? Romantic fling?*

"Was she asking questions about the mine?" Christoph said.

The truck rumbled heavily over a series of potholes—bigger than the ones outside Kitgum, Rose thought; she put her hand on the back of the driver's seat to keep her balance.

"Actually, we didn't talk much about the mine," Patrick said. "Didn't spark her interest. She was really curious about the community development project I'm working on, though. It was good to hear her thoughts, since she'd been volunteering over in Uganda." He paused. "I guess you already knew that."

"So why was she there?" Sabine's tone wavered between confusion and frustration, and Patrick in turn seemed baffled by her bafflement.

"I invited her."

"Maybe you should start from the beginning," Christoph said.

Patrick sighed. "I keep a blog, right? About my day-to-day life in Congo, the project I'm working on, weird food in the canteen, etcetera, etcetera. WiFi is pretty good on site. The blog is mostly for my family and friends back in Texas, but I guess Lily found it. She e-mailed me around Thanksgiving and asked a bunch of questions about the area, like if I'd done any traveling outside the mine, if the roads were secure, that kind of thing. She seemed nice, you know." A little sheepishly, he continued, "Look, I've been out here for nine months with no home leave and only a couple runs to Kampala. Do you know how many girls there are on site at Lakwali? Seven. None of whom, I might add, speak English, and my Lingala isn't so hot, either. So when a cute American girl e-mails me out of the blue about traveling through this general vicinity, I'm gonna pull whatever strings necessary to have her make a detour."

"You did all this for a date?" Sabine said.

"Hey now," Patrick said. "I was a perfect gentleman. And she had this guy with her anyway. Even if they slept in separate rooms, I wasn't gonna get in the middle or whatever."

Sabine fell silent. Rose sensed her trying to fit this new information into her understanding of Lily's intentions. At once, Rose felt a surge of frustration well up inside her—it peaked in anger, curled over, and crashed. Why did everything have to hang on Lily? Why was the *mono* girl at the center? *Lily's* investigation, *Lily's* contacts, *Lily's* disappearance. As if Ocen was a disposable element whose primary purpose was shuttling her here and there, taking her steadily toward some indefinable danger. As if he weren't also putting his life, his heart, at risk. This was Lily's doing, all of it. A rush of fury overwhelmed her. She wanted to shout at them, tell them that Ocen was a soft man who'd had a hard life; he was undereducated and overtrue. She wished he'd never met the *mono* girl. She wished he'd stayed in Kitgum with his *boda,* and if she could take back the word *coward* and all the other things she'd said, she would, she would.

On the other side of Sabine, Christoph finally asked the obvious: "If Lakwali was a detour, what was the original destination?"

"She didn't tell you?" Patrick said, puzzled. "Garamba."

The word hung there a second, shimmering, before Rose understood.

Her heart felt pierced by a thousand bullets. *Rat-a-tat-tat-tat-tat.* She had a flash of Ocen slashing his way through the brush, a gun slung across his back and a rusty *panga* in his hand. But it wasn't rust, it was blood, and it wasn't Ocen, it was Opiyo. She shook the vision off as if it were a spider that had dropped from the ceiling. Next to her Sabine had brought a hand to her slightly open mouth.

"Garamba," Sabine echoed.

"Sure," Patrick continued. "Best national park this side of the Nile. The ultimate African safari. Real wilderness. Zero tourism."

"Ivory," Christoph said heavily.

"Huh?"

"Lily was doing some research from Kitgum," Christoph explained. "Extremely sensitive information."

"What was her research about?"

"Connecting the LRA to the illegal ivory trade."

"Garamba?" Sabine repeated. There was a kind of desperation to her tone.

Christoph shook his head. "She must have thought she could do research on the ground—interviewing eyewitnesses, collecting information on poaching incidents. She would have known she couldn't tackle a full-on investigation in just a couple of weeks. But if she unearthed real evidence, she could pass it on to a professional journalist. Or maybe she planned to come back again."

"Why didn't you stop her?" Sabine said to Patrick. "The UPDF is dropping bombs all over Garamba as we speak. How could you let her walk right onto a battlefield?"

"It wasn't a battlefield then," he said defensively. "She traveled up December fourth. The UPDF didn't launch Operation Lightning Thunder until the fourteenth. And it wasn't like they were advertising their arrival. Surprise attack, remember? No one knew it was coming."

"The LRA has been in Garamba for years," Sabine said. "It's always been a war zone."

"Yeah, but the rebels were pretty quiet for most of that time. We don't bother you, you don't bother us. Last time I was in Bunia, I met a couple of Spanish aid workers who live in Goma—they spent a week in Garamba back in September. They had a blast. Granted, there was an attack in Dungu in November . . . but no one could confirm it was LRA, and in any case Dungu is still seventy-five miles or so from Garamba headquarters at Nagero. Seventy-five miles might not sound like much, but out here it's a lot. There aren't exactly any express lanes." He spread his arm at the road ahead. "The road we're on right now is only decent because Gladstone built it. And it's still shit."

Sabine was exasperated. "So you just sent her merrily on her way?"

"Nagero is well protected by Garamba's armed rangers. That's the park headquarters, where visitors stay. Like I said, the UPDF didn't come in until afterward, and Lily told me she and Ocen were only gonna be there a few nights anyway. She seemed like a pretty adventurous girl—very capable. Of course I thought about them when Operation Lightning Thunder happened. But I figured they were long gone." After a pause, he added, "If anything happened to her, I would have heard about it. Gladstone takes security very seriously. Anything in a two-hundred-mile radius involving a white person, they would have put me right on a plane. My boss wanted me out after the first UPDF strike, but I convinced him to let me stay. My project's so close to being finished. Look, if I could have gotten the time off work, I would have gone with her to Garamba, no question."

"That's supposed to make me feel better?" Sabine snapped.

But Rose felt she understood Patrick's cavalier attitude in some crucial way: when you spend enough time living at the periphery of anarchy, your perspective begins to shift. Normal becomes whatever surrounds you. You recognize that all life is risk, danger is relative, and death arrives equally by the swiftest machete or the tiniest mosquito. When the place itself is peril, there's no use building walls—the menace is in the air you breathe, in the sunlight and rain that fall across your face when you turn it to the sky. She was surprised Sabine didn't understand this, too; hadn't she lived in Kitgum during the war? And all those other countries in Africa—didn't she know what it was like to become accustomed to the knife-edge threat in every sudden shadow, every distant bark of a dog? Perhaps it was different imagining that her niece would feel the same, or perhaps Sabine had been too long away to remember.

"Let's look at the facts," Christoph said. "Lily and Ocen made it to the mine on their own. That has to count for something. We know they were headed to Garamba. There must be a way we can contact someone at the park."

"I'm sure we can find out at Lakwali," Patrick said. He held up his cell phone apologetically. "No service."

"So we must wait," Rose said.

The question—less a question than a statement—seemed to jolt the others. She'd said nothing since they'd gotten in the car. Her voice sounded strange even to her own ears.

Patrick turned his face toward her, though his dark sunglasses hid his eyes. "Ocen was your friend?" She nodded. Patrick's tone was earnest when he said, "I'm really sorry he's missing."

She choked back a sudden sob. "Thank you," she said, blinking as she looked away.

"Lily, too," Patrick said to Sabine.

Rose noted a glistening around Sabine's eyes. The woman swallowed and said, "How long until we're there?"

"Oh, five, six hours. Depends on the roads. And the fuel." Patrick patted the driver on the shoulder. "Full tanks, right, Pascal?" The driver nodded, and Patrick threw a glance at the backseat. "Pascal's a new recruit. Last time the trucks made a run from Uganda, the drivers siphoned off so much fuel to make a quick buck at the border that they ran out of gas halfway to Lakwali. We had to send a Land Cruiser to meet them. And *that* car got stuck in a pothole for two days before we could find another vehicle to tow them out. Which is why," he said, "I postponed my Christmas holiday home: so I could ride shotgun with the shipment and make sure everything arrived in one piece." His gaze fell on Rose again. "Hey, what happened to your arm?"

Rose felt Sabine stiffen beside her. No one spoke. It was the first time anyone—*mono* or Ugandan—had asked. Not even Ocen had probed the subject. In Kitgum you simply assumed: all scars were scars of war. Why make a person say the thing aloud?

"Sorry if I offended you," Patrick said. "I was just curious."

"I lost it in a battle," she said, "between the UPDF and the LRA."

Patrick's eyes went wide, and she turned her face away. In the sliver between the wall of the cab and the driver's seat, she could see out the window to the land beyond. The trees alongside the road into Congo were wild and green, the elephant grass tall and thick. Gnarled trunks of dead trees reached out like the burnt bodies of women in supplication. "It was five years after my abduction," she said. The army had ambushed them near their camp in southern Sudan. They were mostly women and children then. The commanders—their husbands—were away.

She watched the Congolese landscape blur past. The world was no different here than the territory of her youth around Kitgum, or that of her womanhood in captivity. Everywhere the same: trees bound by earth and sky; violence bound by birth and death.

"I had a child," she continued, so soft she was no longer sure she was speaking aloud, except for the magnetic attention she felt upon her from the others' eyes. "He was in his third year. I carried him when the attack came." She'd fled with the others, but they ran into trouble. "There were land mines." The woman just ahead of her—she was one of Rose's co-wives, she had two daughters alongside her—one second they were there, and in the next second, when Rose stepped down, the world came apart. She forced herself to keep her eyes on the green horizon of foliage out the window. Otherwise the memory would flood her and she would drown.

"Whoa," Patrick said.

"Rose," said Christoph, his voice seemingly disembodied coming from the other side of Sabine. "I didn't know you had a son."

"Maybe he survived," Sabine said. "You'd have no way of knowing."

"In the bush, if the mother falls in battle, the child who cannot run is left behind."

The quiet in the car became a cold and shrinking thing.

"Fuck the LRA," Patrick blurted. "Fuck them."

Nothing else was said.

The drive was long and the hours passed slowly. Conversation had halted; no one was able, or willing, to do anything but skirt Rose's grief silently. That was fine by her. They passed through several checkpoints manned by grim-faced soldiers wearing fatigues and dark sunglasses—some with outlandish patterns, leopard-skin and rhine-stones. "Just like the movies," Christoph murmured, and even Rose was surprised, as the LRA had never condoned such ostentatious displays. The soldiers studied each of their faces and then waved them on, gesturing casually with enormous guns. Between the checkpoints were long stretches of uncultivated land, dotted by vil-lages and isolated fields. Sometimes Rose caught sight of children playing in the clearing outside a hut, or groundnuts spread on a piece of fabric to dry in the sun.

A ways in they took a short break where the men from both trucks relieved themselves discreetly along the side of the road, and Rose and Sabine each strode a comfortable distance away. Afterward, back in the car, the disruption seemed to loosen the air, and Patrick and Christoph began to chat. Rose could sense Christoph's vague disap-proval of the reckless young American; her Swiss employer was a thoroughly transparent man, once you knew him. But Christoph's academic curiosity often outweighed his social instinct, and Rose listened with half an ear while he questioned Patrick on all matters concerning the mine. Lakwali, Patrick explained proudly, when it was in operation, would be the biggest open-pit gold mine on the continent.

"Was there mining in the area before Gladstone came?" Christoph asked.

"Oh, sure," Patrick said. "You can still walk around the ruins of the old Belgian equipment from before independence. It's super creepy. Locals say that during each war that comes through, more bodies get dumped down the well. When the Belgians jumped ship, artisanal miners took over—a bunch of guys out there on their own, digging in the dirt. Every so often the place would get taken over by Congo-lese military groups or foreign armies. The Ugandans extracted mil-lions of dollars' worth of gold when they occupied the town." He blew out a breath. "Honestly, I know the mine is pretty problematic from an environmental perspective and all that—and yeah, we're a

foreign corporation arriving in an underdeveloped country and ex-
ploiting the mineral resources. But before Gladstone came in, this
place was chaos. There was no stability, no education, no medical
facilities, no security. Now there's a free clinic and a school and real
jobs—most of my coworkers are locals. There used to be half a dozen
rebel groups operating out of the area. Now there are none. The village is growing; people are coming from outside to look for work.
You can't tell me that's not a good thing."

Good for whom, exactly? Rose wondered. They passed a development of new concrete houses—single-story boxes with empty frames
for windows and doors. Patrick gestured toward them.

"We're building all these, too. For everyone who has to get relo-
cated because of the mine. They get the same amount of land, the
same size house . . . We're even giving them money to plant new
trees like the ones they had."

In her heart was a rent, and through it seeped sorrow. The stories
of a hundred generations, summed up in a neat table: x many square
feet, two bedrooms, a mango tree. The lore of families, of lovers and
daughters and brothers and blood, swept away by the shuffling of
papers, the signatures of men in hushed offices a million miles away.

They turned a corner, and the mine came into view.

The landmark was unmistakable. Two green hills rose from a verdant valley, and marring the cupped earth between them was a vast
brown gash where the trees had been ripped up and the soil dug out;
one hill had been partially carved away, so that it looked like a half
wave, leaning forward. Heavy machinery was dwarfed by gray cylinders, which were in turn swallowed by the hollowed-out earth.
Roads snaked off from all sides, and Rose watched as trucks rumbled
slowly to and from the mine. From this distance they looked minuscule, like playthings.

"My God," Christoph said. "It's . . ."

"Epic, right?" Patrick said.

The view disappeared as trees came up on either side of the road.

A ways farther they passed a fenced-off airstrip much like the one in Kitgum. A Congolese flag flapped high on a pole, next to a second flag with the word GLADSTONE, stylized in the same way as the logo on Patrick's shirt.

"The airstrip is how I usually come and go," Patrick said. "It only takes a few hours to get to Entebbe, even with a stopover at customs in Bunia. Sometimes they make us go through Kinshasa, though, which is a huge pain in the ass. It's like six hours in the wrong direction."

"What are those things?" Christoph said, as they came alongside a long line of enormous gray cylinders like the ones Rose had seen distantly at the mine; now that they were right next to the trucks, she understood how massive they were: almost as tall as the Kitgum Mission. As they passed, Rose could look straight through the hollow circles to the other side. In some of them, she caught glimpses of men standing. Their heads didn't even reach halfway to the top.

"That's pipe for the hydroelectric dams we're building," Patrick said. "Eventually they'll supply the mine with all its power. And later on, when Gladstone pulls out, complete ownership of the entire project—the mine and the dams—turns over to the Congolese government."

"Who will no doubt let it go to waste and ruin," Sabine said.

Patrick sighed. "Yeah, well, we can't do much about that."

The truck came to a stop, and Rose strained to see around the driver's seat. The truck ahead of them had stopped, too; a tall fence with barbed wire barred the way ahead. Beyond it stood a series of buildings. Her body jerked as the truck ground slowly forward, behind the truck ahead, through an open metal gate. A moment later, the truck stopped again, and Patrick unbuckled his seat belt. "Here we are," he said. "Come on down."

Rose was the last to descend. She found herself stepping onto a dun gravel road, neatly marked by larger, evenly sized rocks painted alternately in black and white. The buildings were modest but solid, made of brick and concrete. A few looked like shipping containers, with corrugated sides, but she saw that even these were outfitted with air-conditioning units, boxes attached to the siding. Thick, trimmed hedges separated the buildings from the road. The premises felt quietly cared for, official. Tame. Four or five pickup trucks with the Gladstone logo painted on the side were parked at various wide points in the road. A few men in yellow hard hats strode unhurriedly past. Far in the distance, Rose saw the gash of the mine, the busyness of machines in the earth.

"This is the upper camp," Patrick said, hauling a backpack down from where it had sat at his feet in the cab. "These buildings on the right are mostly offices, and then the higher-ups generally stay in the prefabs. Hold on a sec while I find the camp manager. He'll get you set up with rooms."

"We're allowed to stay here? Just like that?" Christoph asked.

"Usually I have to get advance permission for visitors, but pretty much everyone's off site because of the holiday. Most of the rooms are just sitting empty."

As he bounded off, Christoph turned to Rose and Sabine. "This is completely surreal. Honestly, I imagined tents and mud."

"It is very strange," Rose agreed. "Very . . . controlled."

"I don't like it," Sabine said.

"Rubs you the wrong way?" Christoph teased.

"We're guests at a gold mine in Congo," Sabine said. "You can't ask me to feel good about that."

Patrick returned with three sets of keys jingling in his hand. "Sabine and Christoph, you're in Mangbutu . . . rooms three and seven." He turned to Rose. "You're in Watsa number ten. That's the room Ocen had."

Hearing him say Ocen's name sent a trill down her spine.

"Oh, and FYI, the camp manager just told me that Internet's out all over camp. I guess someone tried to download like seventeen gigs of porn and the tech guys shut him down, and then somehow the whole system went kaput. They're working on it, but I wouldn't get your hopes up. The real computer genius went on vacation to Thailand and won't be back for a week. Anyway." He gestured for the three of them to follow him. "I'll show y'all around."

Sabine said she'd rather call Garamba first, though, so Patrick took her to his office to get set up, leaving Christoph and Rose alone in the road. The late-afternoon haze made her drowsy, yet she felt the sharp awareness of being in an unknown place.

"Are you doing okay, Rose?" Christoph asked.

"I am . . . tired."

"You're a long way from home."

"Home?" She felt a rope of sadness twisting inside her chest as she thought of the ugly rented room she slept in, and her brother's hut—perhaps now burnt to the ground. "Kitgum is not my home."

"What is?"

"We are searching for him now."

He let a beat pass. "Ocen is the Acholi name given to a twin, isn't it?"

"Mm. The second to be born."

"Opiyo is the name given to the first?"

"Yes."

"And Ocen's twin—his brother, Opiyo. Where is he now?"

"He was abducted the same night as me. We were together in the bush." After a moment she said, "He died." The ease with which she spoke the words surprised her—as if she believed it, as if it were true. It probably was. It had been years, after all, since the last time she'd seen him. There were a thousand ways it could have happened.

"I'm sorry to hear that," Christoph said gently.

"Y'all ready?" Patrick called out as he approached.

"I think I'll stay with Sabine until she gets through to Garamba," Christoph said.

"Office is thataway." Patrick turned back to Rose. "Let's get you set up, shall we?"

———

The room into which Patrick led her was spacious and cold; the air conditioner hummed loudly, and her skin was prickled by goose bumps within the space of a minute. Rose took in the wide bed, chest of drawers, wardrobe, desk, chair, refrigerator, flat-screen television. Patrick fiddled with the remote control but couldn't get anything but snow. "They're still working on the DStv," he apologized.

"It's no problem," she said. She felt overwhelmed by luxury. "Thank you."

He opened the door to the private bathroom. "The water gets really hot, so watch out. Oh, and there's bottled water in the fridge. If you need more, just ask."

After he left, Rose stood a while in the center of the room, listening to the air conditioner rattle. Three and a half weeks ago, Ocen had stood in this place. His eyes had seen what she saw now. She walked to the chest of drawers and ran her hand along the edge, lingered on the handle on the top drawer, as if she might absorb his touch, his intentions, through the wood. She tried to imagine what thoughts had occupied his mind as he rolled this way and that at night, the blankets pulled tight around him; had he slept at all? What did he imagine would meet him there, in the north, where the rebels lay in wait? How much money had Lily offered to accompany her? Was it enough to buy his motorcycle—enough to pay for Rose's dowry? She pulled her hand back as if it burned.

There was a folded blanket on the chair next to the desk, and she wrapped it around her shoulders and sank into the seat. Tentatively, in the stillness, she probed inside herself for any secret knowing, any sense of what would come. She remembered the thing Sabine had said about knowing Lily was alive because she felt it in her bones. What did it mean, to feel something in your bones? If Ocen were alive, would Rose know it there?

A harsh knock at the door startled her from her reverie. "Rose!" It was Christoph's voice. "Come quickly!"

"Yes?" she said, alert, as she swung open the door.

"It's Sabine—she's on the phone with someone at Garamba right now." He caught his breath; he'd been running. "They have Lily's diary," he said, and in his tone she heard the dual-edged urgency of hope and despair. "Her journal," he said. "It's there."

CHAPTER 17

SABINE

December 30

"You're sure it says Lily—Lily Bennett?" Sabine gripped the phone with both hands and leaned heavily against Patrick's desk.

"*Sí,*" the woman said. "Lily Bennett. It is here, on the page." She spoke English with a thick Spanish accent; when she first answered the phone, she'd introduced herself as Daniela, park manager, and Sabine had hardly said Lily's name before Daniela gave a little gasp of recognition and said, "Ah! The diary. One minute, wait"—and put the phone down without another word, leaving her breathless. "Lily's journal," Sabine said to Christoph, and he'd rushed out to get Rose. In the meantime the seconds had ticked by, sluggish and uneven, while Sabine stood alone in the office trying to still her galloping heart, until Daniela returned a full eight minutes later to say she had the book in her hand, she was looking at it now.

"So Lily was there?" Sabine pressed. "She made it to Garamba? Did she leave the journal behind? Where is she?"

"Ah." Daniela half sighed. "No . . . Mm . . ." She seemed to be struggling with the words. "She don't come here. I never meet her. Our rangers find the book three days ago—out there, in the park."

"In the park?"

"At the camp. Where the rebels are."

A chill crept up Sabine's spine. "Say that again?"

Two shadows darkened the doorway, and Sabine glanced up as Christoph and Rose stepped inside.

"The rebels. LRA. Joseph Kony. You know?"

"Yes," Sabine said faintly.

"And the Ugandan army, they are in the park also . . ."

"Operation Lightning Thunder."

"*Sí*. The Ugandans are here for two weeks, they are chasing LRA. So LRA make camps in different places. But our rangers are also working, searching. Sometimes they also find camps. Sometimes LRA are there, sometimes no."

"And Lily's journal was in one of those camps?"

"*Sí*, exactly."

Desperation. "But Lily wasn't there?"

"No one is there. Only book, blankets . . . They leave hurry. The camp is old, a week, maybe. I'm sorry, my English . . . We speak here Spanish and French."

Sabine's throat and chest closed up, and she willed herself not to look at Christoph and Rose, though she could feel their eyes upon her. Christoph could translate, but she couldn't bear to give up the line; she needed the connection, this painful intimacy. She pressed the phone harder to her ear. "Tell me, please, what does the journal say inside? Does it give any hints about where she might be?"

"We don't read," Daniela said. "We only see the name. Wait . . ." Sabine heard the sound of pages turning. "The words are very small."

"Can you read them?"

Daniela exhaled. "Everything is English. It will take long." She paused to flip a few more pages. "You want to know about drawings? Many pictures are here. Some people, animals, buildings . . . There are huts, market, food. It's very nice."

That would be from Lily's time in Kitgum, Sabine thought. Her sketches of daily life. Those early drawings would have little to bear on her investigation, but perhaps . . .

"What about toward the back? Is there anything else?"

"Mm . . ." Again the rustling of pages. As the pause lengthened,

Sabine felt the coldness reach the back of her head, spreading around her neck and shoulders like hands preparing to choke.

"Ah—here," Daniela said. "There are maps. This one . . . It says Arua. And the border. Then roads . . . Lakwali?" she said, with some interest.

"Keep going," Sabine said urgently.

She turned a page with a soft *swippt*. "Oh! Garamba. Big map. Here is Nagero, our headquarters . . . There is the river . . . There are names of LRA camps, locations." *Swippt. Swippt. Swippt.* "That is everything. No more. Only empty." She paused. "I no understand. She is with rebels? She is journalist, or . . . ?"

"Lily's my niece. She's been missing for nearly a month. I'm at Lakwali now—we followed her trail here. We came from Kitgum. From Uganda. I came all the way from Germany."

After a beat, Daniela spoke. "Do you want I send the book to Lakwali? We have a truck, he is driving next week for supplies."

Sabine closed her eyes. Next week. So long? "No. I'll come to you. How do I get there?"

A moment later, armed with instructions based on known local bus routes, Sabine hung up. Christoph pounced the second the phone clicked on its cradle.

"What happened?" he said. "What kind of camp?" He stepped forward. "What did you mean, 'I'll come to you'?"

Sabine's arms hung uselessly at her sides; they felt almost as though they belonged to someone else. "Lily and Ocen made it to Garamba," she said numbly. "But they didn't go to park headquarters. Three days ago, the rangers found her journal left in an abandoned LRA camp out in the forest." She lifted her gaze to Rose. "There were no bodies."

Rose said nothing. In her peripheral vision Sabine saw Christoph rub the back of his neck. He, too, was silent. What was there to say? Each of them understood that this evidence, discovered in the circumstances described, could be explained by a chillingly limited number of scenarios. The possibility that the LRA had come across

Lily's journal without encountering her or her traveling companion was minuscule. And if an encounter had taken place—this, Sabine understood with terrible clarity—Lily and Ocen were either dead or captive.

Captive or dead.

And if Lily *were* alive among the rebels, what had they done to her? What were they doing to her right this minute?

Tears came involuntarily to her eyes. She did nothing to stop them. She'd remained steady over the phone, but now she could barely keep herself upright. By the time she realized the world was tilting, Christoph had already gripped her arm, murmuring, "Careful, careful. Take a deep breath. Good. Let's get you sitting down."

She found herself in Patrick's chair, blinking as if seeing the space for the first time. She felt dumb and blank. The objects presented themselves with painful ordinariness. On the plain wall behind Christoph was a round clock, a whiteboard with various lists of names and numbers, and a framed picture of Congolese President Joseph Kabila, dressed in a sharp blue suit and smiling smugly. A small table with an open Nescafé tin and an electric kettle stood askew from the wall. At once this crookedness pierced her senses: the feeling of something carelessly knocked aside, an accidental jostling. The casualness of it left her flailing and enraged. *No*, she thought simply. *The story is not over yet.*

"Hey y'all," Patrick said cheerfully as he entered the room. His smile dropped as he saw their grim faces. "Shit. What did they say at Garamba?"

Sabine looked away. She only half listened as Christoph summarized the situation. Out the office window she watched three African men on the other side of the road; they wore yellow hard hats and stood leisurely in conversation. One said something that made the other two chuckle. Their easy smiles seemed as distant to Sabine as the moon.

Patrick blew out a big breath. "I don't even—does that mean . . . ?"

"We don't know," Christoph said.

"What are you gonna do?"

Sabine cast a glance in Patrick's direction. "Daniela said there's a bus that travels from Bunia north to Dungu. It passes through the village next to Lakwali and would take me within a few kilometers of Garamba headquarters at Nagero. What time will it be here tomorrow?"

Patrick looked doubtful. "You want to go there yourself? With the war and everything?"

"What time?" she repeated.

He bit his lip. "Varies. Usually around eleven."

"How long will it take to walk to the pickup spot?"

"Hey, if you're serious about this," Patrick said, "you better talk to our security guys first."

"That would be very useful," Christoph said. "We'll need some up-to-date information."

His *we* wrapped itself around Sabine's heart and squeezed. She caught a glance from Rose, who gave a small nod, her eyes bright and sad.

"All right," Patrick said. "Let's go see who's around."

They spent an hour in the main security office with two members of the Gladstone "asset protection and crisis management" team: a grizzled South African who wore sunglasses indoors and a soft-spoken Congolese man whose fingers were long and delicate, entrancing Sabine as they traced back and forth across an enormous wall-hung map of Orientale Province. She appreciated the visual distraction—somewhere to focus her eyes, an object of scrutiny. The province extended north all the way to the Sudanese border, northwest along the border of the Central African Republic, and east to the Ugandan border. In the uppermost part of the province, the district of Haut-Uele included Lakwali as well as the entirety of Garamba National Park—which covered nearly five thousand square kilometers, Sabine learned, a number whose vastness, in comparison with the single very slender girl who had disappeared inside, she couldn't quite will herself to comprehend.

The map was overlaid with a series of color-coded splotches to indicate which areas were controlled by which military group. The list of groups in a side bar was disheartening: of the dozen or so groups listed, the only two she recognized were the *Forces Armées de la République Démocratique du Congo,* FARDC—the DRC's official army—and the LRA. There were several blue dots indicating the presence of UN troops. Sabine was relieved to see that the area immediately surrounding Lakwali belonged solely to FARDC and the UN; the more troubling mosaics appeared much farther south, in Ituri District. There was also a disturbingly wide swath of overlapping interests in Garamba and along the Sudanese border, where the locations of the recent LRA attacks on civilians were marked with small red flags.

"So many," Rose murmured, reaching out; her finger hovered just above the red flag marking the town of Faradje.

"It's not a drive in your grandmammy's buggy, that's for sure," the South African said. "But you'll be traveling in daylight, and I'm pretty sure the bus company that runs this route keeps a police officer on board. I'd be more concerned if you were in a private car or on a motorcycle. Then you'd be a sitting duck for thieves and thugs."

Sabine thought of Lily and Ocen, how small and vulnerable a *boda* was. Such easy prey. Had they been targeted before even reaching the outer boundaries of the park?

"And Garamba headquarters?" Christoph said.

"Nagero station," the Congolese man confirmed.

"Nagero, right," Christoph said. "Is the UPDF using it as a base?"

"Not as far as I know," the South African said. "But Nagero's got a good lot of rangers on hand. For keeping away poachers and rebels and what have you. You'll be all right there."

After dinner Patrick offered to let them use a satellite phone to contact the outside world since the Internet was still out. Rose said she had no one to call. Christoph tried his parents in Geneva, but no one answered, and he chose not to leave a message. Sabine considered calling Rita, but in the end declined; the situation still felt too fragile, too tenuous. She needed to hold the journal in her hands—to absorb the truth of the artifact's existence—before she could fully believe it, and until she fully believed it, she would not lay that burden on anyone else. Christoph suggested calling Steve, but here, too, Sabine demurred. Would it not be kinder, she said, to tell Steve: I am in the place Lily came to, and now I stand with evidence of her life in my hands, and I will—I *will*—take whatever next step I must?

After they left the office, Patrick guided them toward their rooms, through the outdoor maze of offices and sleeping quarters. The darkness was kept at bay by the severe light of bare bulbs outside the buildings, where buzzing insects circled and sparked. They dropped off Rose first, and then Patrick brought Sabine and Christoph to their building.

"I wish I was coming with you guys tomorrow," he said, hands in his pockets.

"I'm sure your parents would be glad to know you're not," Christoph said.

"Yeah, well." He kicked his boot in the dust. "Guess I'll see you in the morning. Canteen opens at seven."

Watching him go, Christoph said, "Ah, the invincibility of youth." He scratched the stubble that had begun to grow in around his jaw. "Didn't you say someone was looking into Lily's e-mails? Wouldn't they have found her correspondence with Patrick?"

"Steve told me that she opened a new account in October using the last name Hardt," Sabine said. "She must have used that one for her investigation."

He nodded. "She took every precaution."

"Except when she smuggled herself into Congo and headed straight into rebel territory."

"She thought she was doing something good."

"It was foolish," she said bitterly.

"Or brave."

"To risk her life for a story?"

Christoph appraised her. "Stories are what save us."

"No," Sabine said. "Stories only make us believe we're worth saving."

They'd come to Mangbutu building and stopped in front of Sabine's door.

"You don't have to come to Garamba," she said.

"Hey," he said, stepping closer. "You're not going to do this alone." He took another step. There was less than a meter of space between them.

Sabine felt the air change; an alert stillness settled in the hall. "Alone has always worked for me."

"Ah, yes. Two decades in Africa. The nomadic life of an aid worker." He leaned closer. "You're a fascinating creature, Sabine Hardt."

"Because I chose a career over settling down, having a family?"

"Because you won't admit what it is you're really looking for."

"And what's that?"

"Absolution."

"For what?"

"For being human."

She wanted him to come closer; she wanted him to leave. He did neither. He seemed to be evaluating her, reading her face for a question, or an answer—what was he looking for there? She had a sudden, overwhelming desire to be *seen,* to have all of herself exposed to this man—her failures, her flaws. It was embarrassing how base this instinct felt, how singular and forceful. If she let it loose, there was no telling whether she could control it. Her body tingled with a powerful sense of reciprocity—as if his body and hers were already in communication. But that couldn't be. It was the uncertainty of the last few days, the emotional roller coaster: that was all. And anyway, what would happen after tomorrow? After Garamba? When they returned to their separate cities, their separate lives? She swallowed hard and took a step back.

"Good night, Christoph."

He nodded; was that disappointment in his eyes? "Rest well."

Inside her room, with the door closed tightly behind her, Sabine turned off the air conditioning and opened the screened window to let in the thick, humid night and the sounds that came with it. Then the yowling of wild dogs and the chirruping of night insects became too much, and she snapped the window closed and started up the AC. But the stale smell of chemically cooled air made the space feel cramped and oppressive. She opened the window again.

It was the right decision to keep him out. When this was all over, when they'd found Lily—maybe something could happen. Not now. Silly to think on it further. She put it from her mind and started the water for a shower.

It was the right decision, too, to go to Garamba, she told herself as she scrubbed the day's sweat and dust from her skin. She hadn't come all this way to abstain from the final stage of the journey, whatever the danger.

For a brief, blessed moment, Sabine was grateful that Hannah wasn't alive to endure this grief. The gap between the worry Sabine felt now and the agony her sister would have felt was infinitely, unknowably vast. Sabine remembered with aching clarity the first time her sister had come back to Germany after Lily's birth: how resonant Hannah's voice had become, how changed her face, how centered and still. At the time Sabine looked on her sister's domestic contentedness with pity; motherhood didn't fit into her own humanitarian ambitions. When she asked Hannah how it felt to be a mother, Hannah replied, *It feels as though a piece of my heart exists outside my own body, in another person. And I can never get it back.*

This answer only confirmed to Sabine what she had already suspected about herself—that she would never have children—because why would you want a piece of your heart in such a precarious location as someone else's body? Why choose that uncertainty, that terror, that utter lack of control? As she grew older, this approach extended to lovers and friends, because how could she do her job if her heart was elsewhere? Love made you selfish; love made you choose some above others. And so, all these many years later, her heart was lonely, but whole. Unseen—but intact.

She changed into a fresh T-shirt, closed the window, and got into bed.

CHAPTER 18

ROSE

December 31

Rose passed a fitful night. Awake she was haunted by Ocen's ghostly presence in the room; asleep, by the image of him in the bush, his wrists bound, his skin slick and dappled by rain. She slept naked, having washed her only set of clothes in the hot shower the night before and hung them to dry on the air-conditioning vent, and the stiff bedsheets rubbed roughly against her skin. Sometime in the night she woke with a start at a great and terrible *crack,* the sound of an explosion. In the unfamiliar darkness it took her a moment to distinguish between the racing of her heart and the storm beating the ceiling, but then she understood the noise was thunder, not a bomb. Part of her wished she would fall back asleep and never wake.

By morning the storm had not yet cleared, and as Rose dressed in her clean, dry clothes, she watched through her window as sheets of water turned the ground into a raging, muddy mess. She couldn't help but imagine Ocen, exposed to the weather. Strangely, this thought brought her comfort: that the rain she would taste when she stepped outside was the same rain that had fallen over her lover in the night, whether the body that received it still breathed or not. She consciously steered her mind away from evaluating which of these options— breathing, or not breathing—was likelier, or kinder.

For a long time she'd believed she would rather die than face the

LRA again. Even now, with the road to Garamba ahead, her instinct rebelled. Her body felt heavy as a brick. Yet the thought of
Ocen tore her heart in half. She must continue. She must endure.

Out the window she saw Sabine and Christoph coming toward her
building to pick her up for breakfast, their figures hunched and hurrying under two large umbrellas printed with the Gladstone logo. Rose
felt a rush of thankfulness for her two traveling companions, despite
the many differences that lay between them. Christoph's protective-
ness was perhaps naïve, but sweetly so, and Sabine's ox-headed deter-
mination was galvanizing. Rose donned her travel purse and, for lack
of toothpaste, swished her mouth with water, then went outside to
meet them.

After a quick breakfast—Christoph kept encouraging them to eat
more, to build up strength for the journey ahead—they bundled into
a Gladstone vehicle so that Patrick could give them a ride to the clinic
in the village, where the bus would stop. The rain was relentless; Rose
was glad that she'd had the luck that morning in Kitgum to wear
sneakers and long pants instead of her usual attire of sandals and a
skirt.

After the solid, newly painted buildings inside the Gladstone
camp, the village surrounding the mine appeared positively shabby:
the little wooden lean-tos, the mud-walled huts, the boarded-up kiosks
that stood between gushing rivulets of runoff. Through the window
of the car, Rose caught the gaze of men and women watching from
the dark doorways of huts, their wary eyes following the vehicle as it
splashed by. She was glad to be leaving this place.

There were already a dozen people gathered under the overhang
along the side of the clinic to wait out of the rain's reach. They paid
the SUV little mind, aside from a brief flurry of tittering from three
young Congolese women wearing brilliantly colored skirts, sitting
on tautly bound sacks of what Rose guessed to be maize or yams
by the size of the lumps. Patrick parked the car and turned off the
engine.

"Might as well wait in here," Patrick said, settling into his seat.

"It's nice and dry. Oh—I almost forgot." He shifted to pull out a handful of bills from his pocket. "I'm assuming you didn't get a chance to exchange any currency at the border."

In the passenger seat, Christoph accepted the money. "Congolese francs. I didn't even think of that."

"It's only like thirty bucks," Patrick said. "But it should get you up to Garamba."

Rose thought of the slender stack of shillings folded inside her purse. So far the money had been left untouched; Christoph had paid for everything in Arua, and Sabine had paid for her visa at the border. She felt uncomfortable accepting their charity, but what else could she do?

"Hey, there it is," Patrick said, swinging his door open and popping open an umbrella. "Looks like we got here right on time."

Rose turned to the window and watched the bus approach, bumping slowly along the road. The vehicle was rusty under the splattered mud, and it juddered under the weight of the enormous pile of suitcases, food sacks, and jerry cans tied to the roof in an intricate zigzag of rope and twine, a heavy tarp concealing most of the items beneath. Rose followed the others as they exited the Gladstone car, Christoph and Sabine slinging on their backpacks, and joined the rest of the waiting passengers under the overhang. Rose's hair was dripping from the short dash, and cold lines of wetness traced their way down the back of her neck under her collar. Faces were crammed up against the fogged windows of the bus, heads turning as they caught sight of the three white faces and the woman with one arm.

"*La vie est un combat,*" Sabine read aloud from the side of the bus, the hand-painted letters blocky and bold.

"Life is a war," Christoph said.

"Weird name for a bus company, right?" Patrick said. The heaving vehicle shuddered to a stop and released its doors. An energetic bustle of off- and on-loading began, its chaos amplified by the battering storm.

"Hey," Patrick said, gripping Rose's good shoulder. "Be safe, okay? Say hi to Ocen for me when you see him." He pulled her into a hug before she realized his intention. His body was big and warm, his embrace tight, and she allowed herself to relax into him. When he pulled away, she saw his eyes were moist.

"Thank you for your help," she said.

"I wish I could do more." He shook Sabine's hand and then Christoph's. "Lily, too," he said. "Tell her she still owes me a round of rummy."

"You haven't seen the last of us," Christoph said. "We'll come through on our way out. We'll be counting on you for a ride back to the border."

"You bet," Patrick called behind him as he climbed into the truck. In another minute, the Gladstone vehicle was out of sight.

One by one, they boarded the bus.

Space inside was limited; the aisle was cramped with bags and small children and a pair of chickens, their knobby feet tied together with rope. The floor was slippery with rain and mud. An upbeat pop song throbbed powerfully through the speakers. Rose squeezed in at the front, seated on three thick sacks of grain next to the window; Sabine sat beside her with her feet out in the aisle and her backpack on the ground beside her. There was no seat back, only the legs and luggage of the people in the row behind them. Christoph edged onto the corner of the bench seat across the aisle, next to a man in a Congolese police uniform who had the butt of his AK-47 resting between his boots and the barrel coming up between his knees, the muzzle angled slightly toward Christoph, who kept shifting on the bench as if he might claim more than the six square inches available. As the bus jolted forward, Christoph lost balance and fell to the side, catching himself at the last second.

"Do you want to switch?" Sabine asked.

He grimaced. "I'm okay."

"I'm smaller than you are. I really don't mind."

"It's fine."

"Seriously, just let me . . ."

She started to rise and Christoph put a hand out to stop her. Quietly, he said, "I don't want this gun pointed at you."

"A true gentleman." Sabine laughed, but Rose sensed the softness beneath her words. She sensed, too, the sweet concern behind Christoph's gesture, and this intrigued her. She knew Christoph didn't have a wife or girlfriend at home in Switzerland, and in the many months that they'd worked together, Christoph hadn't been attached to anyone in Kitgum, as far as Rose knew; certainly she'd never seen his general friendliness venture into more flirtatious terrain. The thought of Christoph and Sabine together in this way made surprising sense.

But even as the warmth of this possible connection spread through her, Rose felt a deep, cold pang of loneliness. Christoph and Sabine were perhaps at the very tip of a vast beginning; Rose was nearly at the edge of the distant horizon, alone, unsure whether Ocen would be there when she arrived. There were so many things she'd never told him—so many things he was too good to ask. Had he died believing Opiyo would be waiting for him on the other side? Had he closed his eyes in his final moments, willing his twin to appear and guide him into the afterlife?

If Ocen was alive, if she found him, she would tell him everything, everything. He would know Opiyo's deeds, and the truth of the son she'd lost; he would know the agony of those eternal seconds before the blast, when her bundle had already begun to slip from her grasp. And then the blackness, and the whoosh of something slicing through the air, separating her from the arm that held him: and when she woke, she was in a gray room, miles from where the attack had come—miles from the place where her child's body would have lain, exposed to the birds, the hyenas, the rain. Ocen would know how she wailed, how she emptied herself into that dirty square space, emptied herself of sound, of sorrow, of soul. He would know how she had screamed for three days before falling silent and succumbing to her fate—to be a husk of herself, a thing that was supposed to have died but which was condemned to remain in the world of the living.

And then, when she had finished telling him everything, perhaps this curse, too, would be lifted, and she would be at peace at last.

For hours the bus drove north and the rain never stopped. Despite a lack of functioning windshield wipers and the presence of a perpetually lit cigarette in one hand, the driver maneuvered around potholes that had left other, less-skilled navigators stuck in the mud with their wheels spinning. While driving he turned up the music to a near-unbearable level, making conversation impractical. He only turned it down again when they paused at checkpoints, where—unlike when they were with the Gladstone convoy—a soldier or police officer would climb onto the bus and run his gaze unhurriedly up and down the aisles. Inevitably his eyes would linger on Christoph and Sabine, but thus far—after four such encounters—no one had asked about their destination or demanded a bribe or even spoken to them directly. On two occasions the officer had pulled a passenger off the bus, though it wasn't clear to Rose what the person had done to arouse suspicions. The policeman sitting next to Christoph never said a word nor moved to intervene. When the bus continued, those passengers were left behind. Rose did not like to think of what happened then.

After the fourth checkpoint, the rain stopped and the sky cleared. The greenery glistened, and people began to appear in the clearings outside huts or carrying hoes and baskets on narrow paths leading away from the road. The sun glimmered brilliantly off puddles and passing motorbikes, which multiplied on the road like insects emerging after a storm. As a motorcycle with one driver and one passenger caught up alongside them, Rose caught a glimpse of red and blue tassels on the seat, and she felt for a second that somehow the bus had traveled backward in time, and they had drawn parallel with a moment four weeks previous—Ocen and Lily riding north together, swerving around this pothole and that, passing the bus from Bunia. *Stop!* she wanted to cry out. *Please!* Then the motorbike pulled ahead and vanished over the crest of a hill, and Rose was in the present once again.

Shortly thereafter, the wide-scattered huts started appearing closer together, until they were dense enough to give the impression of a town. A handful of low brick buildings and a series of evenly spaced palm trees lining the road confirmed it. Pedestrian traffic increased, and signs of trade became apparent in small wooden kiosks and vegetable stands. The bus driver made a sharp left onto a wide road, and suddenly, as if the wind had changed and brought a new, distant sound, the hairs on the back of her neck rose. Her skin became clammy; her insides plummeted.

"This must be Faradje," Sabine said, her voice raised just enough to be heard.

Faradje. Rose remembered the name from the map. A tiny red flag had marked this place as a site of violence. Her body was so profoundly in tune with the passage of her past that she could feel the rebels' presence even after a week had gone by. She examined the expressions of passersby, their eyes, their hollow cheeks, and wondered: were you there? Did you see the faces of the men who descended upon you? Who is gone from you now? Did the earth split open to take in your dead? How many have you buried? How many remain?

She felt Sabine exhale as they left the densest living quarters behind them, and Rose noticed that she, too, had been holding her breath. In another few minutes, the huts became rarer, the twisting trees and brush filling in all the space between.

"Garamba's not far," Christoph said across the aisle. Rose could hear the buoyancy in his voice, the treble of anticipation.

The bus began to slow down.

"What is it?" Sabine said, craning her neck. But she could see as well as Rose: ahead was a bridge, wide enough for a single truck, and the bus driver was stopping to allow an oncoming minibus to finish crossing. She remembered seeing the river on the map at Lakwali; it meandered northward for a while, then turned west, eventually passing directly next to Nagero. They were close now—twenty kilometers, she guessed. With the engine idling and the wheels still, Rose felt distinctly like prey.

"Come on, come on," Sabine said under her breath.

They began to move, and Rose breathed more easily. The driver kept a slow pace as they crossed, and from her place at the window, Rose could see down to the swollen, brown river churning below. The sight reminded her of the Kitgum river where she'd last seen Grace and Isaac and Wilborn. She forced herself to look away.

There was another checkpoint just on the other side of the bridge. The driver stopped and dialed down the radio. By this time, the protocol was routine, and even as a steely eyed FARDC officer climbed into the bus, his black gumboots resounding in heavy thuds, Rose's thoughts drifted to Nagero, where Lily's journal lay on a table somewhere, or propped up on a shelf. What would this book reveal? What secrets of Lily and Ocen's mission? Secrets of their . . . togetherness?

She didn't realize she was being addressed until she felt Sabine's hand on her thigh.

"Rose? He's asking to see our papers."

Rose blinked. Sabine was already holding out her maroon German passport, and Christoph was unzipping his money belt while conversing with the officer in French.

"Is there a problem?" Rose whispered.

"It's okay," Christoph said after a moment. "He just wants to see the entry stamps."

Rose felt the gaze of other passengers as she slipped her Ugandan passport from her purse and handed it tentatively to the impressively outfitted young officer. He took all three passports with a grunt and began to flip through them. Rose remained silent, as did Sabine and Christoph, though Rose saw Sabine's impatience in the tapping of her heel against the floor.

Finally the officer tightened his lips and closed his hand around their passports. Rose watched with mounting fear as he slid them into the back pocket of his camouflage pants.

Under her breath, Sabine said, "What's he doing?"

Christoph tried to say something in French, but the officer cut him off briskly and turned around as if to exit the bus.

Rose knew what came next. They'd be taken away to be interrogated or tossed in the back of a truck or worse. The policeman next to Christoph looked away.

"I'll talk to him," Christoph said, standing up.

"What does he want?" Sabine asked. "Is it money? We have money."

Christoph stepped forward. "*Pardonez moi, monsieur . . .*"

The officer turned with both hands resting lightly on his rifle. The warning was clear, yet Christoph took another step. Rose's heart leapt into her throat.

"*Monsieur,*" Christoph said, "*s'il vous plait . . .*"

A shot rang out.

The window behind Rose exploded in a rain of glass; she heard a single piercing scream amid a rising commotion of voices. She bent at the waist and gripped Sabine's hand. Everything after that happened quickly. Out of the corner of her eye she saw the driver put the bus into gear, and Rose felt the acceleration with a hard jolt. The FARDC soldier toppled onto Christoph, knocking them both to the floor, and Rose slammed into the knees of the person in the seat behind her.

Christoph, Rose thought wildly, and in the same instant she heard Sabine cry out his name. There was no reply, but it was hard to hear anything except the straining of the engine and the rumbling of luggage on the metal floor. Rose felt the ridges of the road in her very bones; all around her, suitcases and sacks and legs rattled and bumped into one another while she kept a tight hold on Sabine's hand.

As the *rat-a-tat-tat* of shooting faded, Rose understood that it was coming from outside, not inside. They were under attack.

Then a swerve, and screaming, and weightlessness, and tumbling . . .

. . . and the world came to a vicious-loud-hard-crashing halt.

The softest skin. The smallest hands. His eyelashes are so tiny and dark; she brushes his puffy cheek with her fingertip and his mouth responds with a puckered yawn. The sky is blue and wide as a prayer, the world new and green.

She whispers his name—not the one given him by his father, but the one she calls him secretly when they're alone, the one she's never spoken aloud to anyone else. He giggles, opens his eyes. Her son.

All was still. Rose raised her head, disoriented. Everything rushed in—the wrong position of her body, the tilt of the bus onto its side; Sabine was beneath her somehow, as well as the policeman who had been sitting next to Christoph. The policeman wasn't moving. A trickle of blood traveled slowly along the curve of his forehead. Rose heard Sabine groan.

"Come," Rose said hoarsely. Their hands were still entwined.

Nearby, passengers began to stir.

"Sabine? Rose?" Christoph's voice came from behind them.

She turned to see Christoph's flushed face behind Sabine's panicked one; he appeared to be unharmed, and Rose felt a tiny rush of relief. More noises came from the jumble of people and things. Shouting; a man rose, staggering, cradling a bloodied elbow; the heaps began to shift and waken. Rose caught a glimpse of the FARDC soldier's uniform somewhere in the middle of the bus, where he must have been thrown back during the crash. She was overwhelmed by a powerful urge to flee. *Don't look back. Just go.*

"Out," Rose said. "Now!"

"What happened?" Sabine mumbled.

"Ambush," Christoph called out. "We need to get away."

A baby started to cry. Rose let go of Sabine's hand so that she could pull herself forward. With the bus on its side, the door faced upward, but Rose knew that if they lifted themselves through, they'd be exposed. The front windshield—cracked open during the crash— was the better option. She climbed over the driver's seat and saw the man's motionless body below, flecked by shards of glass. Beneath him the dark earth pressed against his window. The end of his cigarette glowed red. Stepping carefully around him, Rose used the gearshift to stay steady.

Sabine gripped her elbow. "Rose! Our passports."

"Leave them," Rose said. She found a piece of cloth and cleared enough broken glass to make space for an exit. The front hood had popped during the crash and was concealing what lay ahead; all Rose could see was earth and green. She squeezed past the dashboard and stepped out onto mud and grass. For a second the solidness of the earth made her dizzy. The air was fresh and still. Then her senses became focused and acute: she heard the faint sounds of men shouting in the distance. They would be here in moments.

In another second Sabine and Christoph were standing behind her, Sabine with a hand to her forehead, though there was no bleeding. Other passengers were beginning to clamber across the dashboard and out the windshield. The luggage on the roof had come loose from the ropes and now lay spilt among the brush.

"Are either of you hurt?" Christoph asked.

"My backpack," Sabine said. "The passports."

A quick succession of pops caused them all to duck reflexively.

"There's no time," Christoph said. "I have my pack. Follow me." He took a step toward the road.

Rose grabbed his elbow urgently. "That way is death."

"Where, then?"

This was what she knew: to flee. To hide. To disappear.

Her son's face appeared again before her: *tiny, perfect eyelashes; a sky as wide as prayer.* She faltered in the presence of this vision. He was so close! If she stayed here, if she allowed herself to be caught— if she became like the driver, like the officer, a light gone out—but another, elsewhere, in the land of the eternal dreaming, turned on—

"Rose?" Christoph's voice broke through.

She looked between him and Sabine, and the mirage vanished.

"Come," she said.

The brush parted before her, and she led them inside.

CHAPTER 19

SABINE

December 31

Sabine's heart pounded in her ears, her skin was hot, her mouth dry. No one spoke as they pressed on, stealthy and swift. Rose led with surprising skill, intense and purposeful as she took Sabine and Christoph around thick tangles of bosky undergrowth and between shoulder-high stalks of dun grass, whose sharp edges nicked at Sabine's bare arms, drawing blood. Her thoughts kept returning to the bus, the shots, the escape—then that baffling blankness, the lost moments before she woke with Rose atop her—and how, as they'd climbed out of the crumpled bus, she'd looked at the lifeless body of the driver and understood that the thinnest of lines separated him from her: a whim of fate; a lucky, or unlucky, draw. Sabine felt the softness of her own body with a startling terror: how fragile, how easily bruised. How easily extinguished. Now, she tried to brush those thoughts aside and concentrate on Rose's asymmetrical figure from behind, stepping where Rose stepped, ducking where Rose ducked. Christoph's rhythmic breathing behind her, and his occasional steadying touch when she lost her footing, brought some comfort. Still, there was no calming the fear that raged through her veins, humming with urgency.

At points early on she'd caught the faint sounds of gunfire from the direction of the crash site, but as they pushed deeper the noises faded and were finally replaced by birdsong and invisible insects and the swish and crackle of their passage. Her clothes absorbed the lingering wetness of the rain-drenched plants, and mud sucked at her shoes with every step. Above, the sky was eerily clear and bright, and every so often Rose would lift her face to check the position of the sun. The air tingled with alertness and danger. Several times they came across family homesteads, each a collection of three or four huts surrounded by circles of smooth earth. Most seemed deserted or abandoned, the mud walls crumbling in places, but twice Sabine caught glimpses of children, and once a group of adults, the women with their breasts bare, who watched Rose lead the group around the edge. One woman had a sculpted, narrow visage with exceptionally fine features; when she turned her head slightly, Sabine saw a long slash running the length of the opposite cheek. The skin around it was swollen and red—fresh, Sabine thought. Her eyes, and the eyes of the others, were hard and unfriendly as they followed the fugitive trio until Rose veered off into the brush; Sabine was relieved to put the homestead a ways behind.

They must have gone four or five kilometers before they came at last to a small clearing where Rose stopped. The space was sheltered by a barrier of trees with broad overhanging branches and slick dark roots twisting out of the soil. The ground was dry and scattered with a few boulders. Just beyond, Sabine saw a glint of sunlight flash on a glassy brown surface—a river. Rose kneeled to examine the earth, then stood, apparently satisfied.

"Here," Rose said.

"For the night?" Sabine said.

Rose nodded. "The animal prints are old. We shall not be disturbed."

Sabine looked down and saw that the patterns of indentation were indeed in the shape of large footprints. Quite large, in fact, she noticed with growing discomfort. One set was approximately the size of a dinner plate.

"We say *raa* in Acholi," Rose said.

"Hippopotamus," Christoph said as he set down his pack with a huff. "We can take turns keeping watch in any case." He squinted at the sun, which was dropping quickly behind the forest canopy. "Tomorrow we'll see if we can make it to Faradje—find the UN base."

"No," Rose said. "We go to Nagero."

"Back to the road?"

"Through the bush."

"But how?" Sabine asked.

"The river," Rose said. "It will take us there. I saw it on the map."

"Good thinking," Christoph said. He unzipped his backpack and handed Sabine a water bottle. "I stocked up at Lakwali," he said. "Drink as much as you need. I have plenty." As she drank gratefully, he handed another to Rose, then opened a third for himself.

"What about our passports?" Sabine said. "The soldier—he took them . . ."

"We'll have to manage," Christoph said. "Maybe the staff at Nagero can help us."

Sabine had never been without her passport, and she felt as naked as if she were without clothes.

"Did either of you see anything during the attack?" Christoph asked.

"LRA," Rose said. "They were there. I felt it."

Christoph lowered his voice. "Are we safe here?"

"Our tracks are easy to find, but they will not come looking," she said. "After a battle they would rather vanish into the bush. They will stay hidden. The only danger is if their path crosses too near."

"It will be dark soon," Sabine said. "Do we have anything we can use to light a fire?"

Rose shook her head. "The smoke would draw them to us."

Sabine felt a welling of frustrated tears, which she quashed. No fire meant no warmth, no light. Already the shadows were closing in around them. She thought of her cell phone, left behind in the crash; even if she couldn't call anyone, the green glow of its screen would be better than nothing.

"I have a headlamp," Christoph said, as if reading her thoughts. "And some peanuts," he added. "Maybe even a chocolate bar." He managed a smile. "Almost the right ingredients for s'mores."

"It will not be comfortable," Rose said matter-of-factly. "But it will pass."

Night fell.

Christoph distributed all the clothing in his backpack so that Rose and Sabine could change out of their wet clothes and get dry and warm. The humidity of the day became pierced with chill, and Sabine was grateful to drown in Christoph's soft, too-big sweater, which smelled both of fresh laundry and dust. There hadn't been time to build any kind of shelter, so they did the best they could with what they had. Rose had cleared twigs and rocks from a flat space next to two large boulders, and Christoph sat not far from Sabine, each of them with their backs against a tree trunk; Sabine was nestled into a hollow made by emergent roots, with her knees against her chest and her forehead resting lightly on the wood. She wouldn't sleep well, but at least she felt more secure in the tree's solid embrace than if she were sprawled out in the open air.

Sunset was muted over the river, the colors choked off by the darkening land. They decided to save the batteries in Christoph's headlamp, and it wasn't long before Sabine could hardly make out Christoph's figure not three meters from where she sat. She wrapped the sweater tighter around her and focused on the chorus of insects and birds singing the dusk away. The sounds were deeply familiar to her—the same as those she'd heard a thousand nights in Kitgum—and yet here they felt closer than ever before, and strange, and frightening.

"Rose," said Christoph, "would this qualify as a *wang'oo*?"

Sabine recognized the Acholi word referring to the nightly family gatherings around a communal fire, when elders would tell stories, riddles, and jokes, and people would discuss their lives. She recalled a former coworker in Kitgum who told her that one of the greatest casualties of the war was this essential piece of Acholi culture, which had become rare in the IDP camps.

Sabine sensed Rose stirring in the darkness. "We are not family," Rose said. "And we have no fire."

"But we have stories," Christoph said. When both women were quiet, he said, "All right, I'll start."

"You'll just tell a story, right off the top of your head?" Sabine asked.

"I wouldn't be much of a folklorist otherwise." He cleared his throat. "*Ododo-na-ni-yo?*"

"What does that mean?" Sabine asked.

"It means, 'May I tell my story?'" Christoph said.

From Rose's corner came a reply: "*Eyo.*" Yes.

Sabine paused. "*Eyo,*" she said at last.

He began.

Once there was a man who had seven sons but who wished desperately for a daughter. At last his wife gave birth to a girl, but the baby was small and sickly, and they decided to give her an emergency baptism in case she didn't survive. So the father sent his sons to the well to fetch some water.

"Hurry," he told them. "The time is precious."

Eager to please, the seven boys ran quickly, but when they reached the well, each of them wanted to be the one to fulfill the task, and in their struggle, the jug fell in.

The brothers didn't know what to do, but neither did they dare return home without the water. Meanwhile, at the house, their father became impatient, assuming that they had been distracted by play and forgotten their duty.

In anger he cried out, "I wish they would all turn into ravens!"

No sooner had he spoken the words than he heard a great whirring sound, and out the window, saw seven black ravens fly up and away.

By this point, Sabine had recognized the story: the one her *opa* had read to her and Hannah when they were children, which Hannah read in turn to Lily; the same story that Sabine and Christoph had discussed just the other night at the White Horse Hotel in Arua. Strangely, Arua seemed more distant now than her grandparents' house in Marburg, the smell of hearth and wood, the familiar heaviness of the quilt her *opa* tucked around her before bed. As Christoph continued, his voice transformed, becoming low and rich, and soon Sabine no longer heard the chitter of insects or the call of forest birds, but only the soft, alert breathing of her sister next to her in bed, and the flick of pages being turned, and her grandfather's bass tones, rising and falling in the wonderment of the fairy tale.

The father could not take back the curse, and together he and his wife mourned their sons. But their daughter soon grew healthy and strong, and they rejoiced in her beauty, which deepened daily. The man and his wife took care not to mention the raven-boys, and so the girl grew up believing she was an only child.

One day, while she was at the village market, she overheard some neighbors speaking about her as she passed. They said that she was indeed quite beautiful, but that she was to blame for the misfortune of her seven brothers. The girl was greatly troubled, and when she returned home, she asked her parents if what the neighbors had said was true. They finally confessed.

Though her parents reassured her that she wasn't at fault—her birth was the cause, but her role was innocent—the burden weighed on the girl's conscience day after day. She came to believe that it was up to her to redeem her brothers.

For months she agonized over what to do. One night she gathered her courage and set off secretly into the wide world, hoping to find her brothers and set them free, whatever it might cost. She brought nothing with her except a loaf of bread to satisfy her hunger, a jug of water to quench her thirst, a chair to rest on along the way, and a small ring to remind her of her parents and the home she'd left behind.

The girl walked on and on, ever farther, all the way to the end of the world. There she came to the sun, but it was hot and frightening, and ate children. She ran away toward the moon, but it was cold and wicked, and when it saw her, it growled, "I smell human flesh." So she hurried away again and came at last to the stars, each one sitting in its own little chair.

The stars were friendly and good to her, and when the morning star arose, it gave her a chicken bone. "Your brothers are inside the glass mountain," the morning star said. "And you can only open the glass mountain with this bone."

The girl thanked the star and took the bone, wrapped it in a cloth, and went on her way until she found the glass mountain. The door was locked, and she took out the cloth with the chicken bone so that she could unlock it.

To her horror, the cloth was empty. She had lost the good star's gift.

What could she do? She wanted desperately to rescue her brothers, but she had no key.

Then she had an idea. She took a sharp stone, cut off one of her fingers, and put it into the door.

The door opened.

When she went inside, a dwarf approached her and said, "What have you come here for, my child?"

"I am looking for the seven ravens," she answered, hiding her bleeding hand. "They are my brothers."

"The lord ravens are away, but if you wait here, they will return."

So she followed the dwarf into an enormous banquet hall, where he placed on the table seven plates and seven cups, and filled them with food and drink. Though her hand throbbed painfully, the girl took a bite from each plate and a sip from each cup, and into the last cup she dropped the ring that she'd brought.

Suddenly she heard a great rush of wings, and she became fright-

ened, and ran and hid behind a door. In flew seven ravens, who landed at the table, ready for their meal. One after another they said, "Who has been eating from my plate? Who has been drinking from my cup? It was a human mouth eating from my plate, and a human mouth drinking from my cup."

When the seventh one drank the last of his wine and turned over the cup, the ring rolled out. He recognized it as belonging to their mother and father. He cried out, "If only our sister were here, we would be set free!"

When the girl heard this wish, she came forth and revealed herself, and the ravens were restored to their human forms. They kissed one another and embraced, and went home happily.

With the final line, Sabine found herself thrown abruptly back to the present, the prickling chill, the Congolese night. The vision of her *opa* was extinguished.

"Is that a folktale from your land?" Rose asked.

"Do you like it?" Christoph said.

"I like the Acholi stories better."

Sabine heard a rustling from Rose's direction, and Christoph asked: "Everything all right, Rose?"

"I need to make a short call."

Sabine remembered the euphemism well; she'd taken to using it herself when in the field with Ugandan coworkers, who would have been mortified to hear their boss ask for directions to the nearest toilet.

"Take the headlamp," Christoph said as he switched it on. Sabine's eyes adjusted quickly to the dim glow of their little scene, with the flickering shadows of trees and the distinctly humanlike shape of Rose reaching out for the light.

"Don't go far," Christoph said. "Shout if you need us."

"I will."

The tiny light bobbed away behind a tree and was consumed by blackness.

"I haven't heard that story since Lily was a child," Sabine said quietly.

Christoph let her words hang for a moment before he said, *"Aboloi wi ngadi."*

"What?"

"It's part of the Acholi storytelling tradition. 'I throw it on so-and-so.'"

"Throw what?"

"The responsibility of telling the next story. I'm throwing it on you."

"I don't know any folktales."

"It doesn't have to be a folktale." After a moment's pause, he said, "Tell me why you became an aid worker. There must have been a reason."

Sabine pulled her knees tighter against her chest. "You don't want to hear about that."

She heard him moving; then he was sitting beside her. She could feel his pulsing warmth, close.

"I wouldn't have asked if I didn't," he said.

She was silent.

"Does it have something to do with your grandfather?"

"What makes you say that?"

"Just a hunch."

If there were ever a moment of reckoning, it was now, she thought. She was so tired. And this man, this earnest, cheerful man who sat near, who'd memorized the stories she'd grown up with—this man who, it seemed, *already knew* everything about her—why should he not hear this from her lips?

"I was fifteen when he died," she began. "I'd worshipped him, you know. Him and his Rhinelanders. What you said before, that he sounded like a gentle man. He was. But he was something else, too."

"It was a time of war," Christoph said. "Many people didn't have a choice."

"I don't mean his military service. He was an engineer. He helped plan roads and bridges. He never saw battle. Even if he had . . . I could understand that, forgive it."

"You're being cryptic."

"I found a hatbox," she said faintly, feeling distant from herself. "In his closet. The day of the funeral, when the rest of my family was out in the garden. They were arguing over the rabbits, trying to figure out whether they should sell them off or cook them for dinner. I couldn't stand to listen. I fled inside, wandering the empty house—touching the things he'd touched, sitting in the chair where he'd always smoked his pipe in the evenings after dinner. Eventually I came to the bedroom. It's . . . silly, maybe, but I wanted to put on his coat. The winter coat he wore when he tended the hutches in the snow."

"It's not silly," Christoph said, but she hardly heard him.

"That was when I found it. The hatbox. It was so curious, you know—he'd never worn hats. I pulled it down and opened it. There were papers inside, letters and official documents. The first letter I picked up was just a few months old, from March 1981. I still remember the words exactly; I read them over and over again. *'Sehr geehrte Herrn Hardt, thank you for your inquiry into the whereabouts of Herrn Ari Morgenstern of Marburg, Hessen, and his family. It is with regret that I inform you, our records do not show any persons of that name, nor possible relatives thereof.'* The next letter was from the previous year. *'Sehr geehrte Herrn Hardt, we would gladly assist you with your query; however, unfortunately our files contain no matches . . .'* At the very bottom of the pile, there was a letter from 1951. Nearly thirty years old. It said something similar. I read every letter in the box; all of them were the same."

"Morgenstern," Christoph said. "A Jewish name."

"My grandfather had included their last known address in his correspondence—it was the same street as my grandparents' house in Marburg. They were neighbors. The letters also referenced the time frame, the date the Morgensterns disappeared. November tenth, 1938."

"*Kristallnacht,*" Christoph said.

"I didn't know that then. It was the eighties; Holocaust education in Germany was still in its nascency. I'd heard things, of course. The facts were out there. I'd even seen parts of that American miniseries, *Holocaust,* on TV at a friend's house when her parents weren't home. But to speak of it directly—it wasn't done. To ask what role your father played, or your grandfather . . . it was tantamount to blasphemy." She paused. "But these documents . . . I thought they were evidence of something noble."

Christoph said nothing.

"My grandmother found me like that, hours later, with the letters all around me. I didn't even apologize—I just started asking questions. Who were the Morgensterns? How did they disappear? Why was it so important for my grandfather to find them? Had he helped them escape? She finally explained, just to shut me up, I think.

"The Morgensterns were neighbors, yes. And they had indeed come to my grandparents' door under the cover of darkness, the night of the tenth of November, 1938. The synagogue in Marburg was burning; Jewish homes and shops had been ransacked. The Morgensterns— Ari and his wife, Ewa, and their two small sons—were afraid.

"I asked her if *Opa* had hidden them behind the rabbit hutches, or if there was a secret cellar beneath the kitchen. She said, 'Your grand-father was a boy of twenty-two. Your father was a baby of three months. The risk was too great. There was nothing we could do.'"

"They sent them away?"

"Yes," she said. The word felt vast and hollow. "I never told any-one else. Not even Hannah. I kept up the search for a little while on my own, but nothing ever came of it."

"And then came aid work."

"I thought I could . . . balance it out somehow," she said. "I wanted to believe that if I had been alive—if it had been me at the door—I wouldn't have turned them away. I imagined that when my moment came, I would make the selfless choice. But I was wrong."

An insect chirruped from the direction of the river, and Sabine lengthened her legs out in front of her, took a deep breath. Probably no more than ten minutes had passed, but she'd gone elsewhere in the meantime, and her feet were numb; they prickled painfully with the return of feeling. She waited for Christoph to speak. If he felt disgust or anger or disappointment, he masked it well, Sabine thought, and surely he felt all of those things. He had the blood of righteous gentiles coursing through his veins.

At last he stirred. "How were you wrong?"

She felt a flare of frustration. Had he not been listening? "I told you about the woman with the baby in Kitgum, along the side of the road. That was it—that was the moment. I could have saved them and I didn't. I'm just like him." She felt a strain in her chest, something tugging for freedom—an unbinding.

She sensed his touch half a second before his hand actually came to rest upon her outstretched leg. The warmth of his palm seeped through her jeans against her skin. The blackness between them became charged and alive.

"You have to forgive yourself, Sabine."

"Forgiveness," she scoffed. "You think that makes it better? You think forgiveness fixes anything?"

He was silent.

"It doesn't bring anyone back," she said.

"No. It doesn't." There was just enough moonlight to see the outline of his face. "Neither does your guilt. You can't stay stuck looking back forever. You have to figure out a way to take what you've learned and go on."

"It doesn't matter," she said wearily. "Nothing matters. Nothing makes a difference."

"I don't believe you. This cynicism—I don't believe that's how you want to live."

"How do I want to live, then?"

"Like all of us. With love," he said simply.

As soon as he spoke the word, a spark of light appeared before her: the briefest of blinks, with a greenish tint. It was so quick she thought she'd imagined it.

Then another appeared, six feet away.

Then blackness.

Then two more tiny flashes, suspended in the air, a flickering dance. Fireflies.

First there were only a handful, circling around one another in miniature, slow-motion bursts of brilliance, then there were a dozen, two dozen. Some lights stayed on for several seconds, zigzagging dreamily through the blackness. Others sparked on and off, on and off, on and off in the scintillating dark.

Sabine was transfixed. As she watched, mesmerized, the flashes began to occur at more regular intervals, closer and closer together. Her vision became filled with dozens of fireflies blinking in perfect unison. Illumination, then dark. Illumination. Dark. On and off.

Something inside her split open. The borders of her self dissolved, and she felt the pattern's resonance as if it were the beating of her own heart.

The synchronicity lasted less than a minute before it fumbled, and the flashes became erratic. A breath later the fireflies went dark, apart from a few lingering blinks.

"Do you know what day it is?" Christoph said.

She still felt dizzy from the trance. "What do you mean?"

"The thirty-first of December. New Year's Eve."

"New Year's Eve," she echoed. The thought baffled her: had it only been six days since she'd landed in Entebbe? Two days since they left Kitgum? Uganda was a lifetime ago.

"It must be close to midnight," he said. "Should we count down?"

She felt in his voice an invitation—something like magnetism. There was more than exchange between them: there was collision, collapse. His hand was still on her jeans. His words came back to her: *You're a fascinating creature, Sabine Hardt.*

A branch cracked nearby, and Sabine snapped alert. "What was that?"

Christoph's hand stiffened with tension. "Rose? Is that you?"

Sabine only now realized how long it had been since Rose left

with the headlamp. But there was no reply, and no bobbing light—
only the last remaining fireflies, scattered.

"Maybe she . . ." But there were too many awful ways that sentence could end. Christoph didn't respond. Another crack came from
the darkness. *Wind?* Sabine hoped desperately. *Animal?* Perhaps it
was only the hippos, emerging from the water to graze.

Then she heard whispering. More than one voice. The sounds
were disturbingly near, but Sabine couldn't see anything in the pitch-
blackness beyond a few meters.

"Rose?" Christoph repeated, louder this time.

The whispering stopped.

This is how we die, she thought. Her throat locked; she couldn't
speak. Her legs were rigid. This was the calm before the attack, the
slowed-down seconds before it was over. The rebels had found them,
by intention or by chance. Sabine wanted to cry out for the futility of
it all, but her body wouldn't respond.

She felt Christoph's hand slide into hers. "I have a knife," he said,
so quietly it was barely more than a breath. He spoke urgently and
without hesitation. "On my signal, I want you to move as fast as you
can toward the river. Stick to the shoreline. Get to Nagero."

Run? She could hardly tremble. How could she explain that her
legs weren't working when her voice, too, had failed?

"Get ready," Christoph said, squeezing her hand.

No, she thought frantically. *Not yet. Not ever.*

But before he could say anything more, four figures advanced into
the clearing: two men and two women. Everything was in shadows;
Christoph sprang to his feet—how quickly he moved!—and stood in
front of her protectively. The approaching party halted, and for a
long moment all was still. Then, slowly, the two men lifted their
hands in a universal gesture of *we mean no harm.*

With relief, Sabine saw that none of them appeared to be carrying any weapons; each woman had a tightly wrapped bundle upon
her head. Sabine looked closer at the nearest woman's face, pale hints

of starlight defining the curve of her forehead—and there, a catch of unevenness. The line of a wound. In an instant Sabine recognized her: she was the one from the homestead they'd passed that afternoon during their escape. Without a word, the woman lowered the bundle to the ground and pulled back the folds.

Groundnuts. Chapati. Bananas. Tears came to Sabine's eyes.

The second woman revealed her gifts, too: a small pile of blankets, which she set on the ground before Christoph. Shakily Sabine rose to standing. Christoph put away his knife.

"*Merci,*" he said.

From the opposite direction, a thin beam of light cut through the dark, then grew steadily stronger. Rose appeared a moment later. When she caught sight of the newcomers, she hesitated half a second, then strode into their circle.

CHAPTER 20

ROSE

December 31

The four visitors did not stay long in the makeshift camp at the river. Before the villagers left, Christoph tried to give them the Congolese francs he'd gotten from Patrick, but they would not accept them. Their refusal touched Rose more profoundly than the food they'd brought. After a wordless farewell of clasped hands, they melted back into the blackness from which they'd come. The clearing seemed colder and darker without them there. Rose, Christoph, and Sabine ate the groundnuts and bananas in silence; afterward all that remained was a short stack of chapati, which they agreed they'd keep for the morning. By the light of Christoph's headlamp, they draped two blankets over an outstretched branch and pulled the bottom edges away, securing them with rocks, to make a sort of tent. Two people could lie down underneath comfortably—or as comfortably as possible, given the circumstances.

"I'll take first watch," Christoph said, setting himself up against a tree trunk. "You both try to get some sleep."

"Wake me in a few hours," Sabine said.

"Then me," Rose said to Sabine, who nodded.

Christoph kept the light aimed into the shelter until they'd crawled in and were each wrapped in a blanket, then he switched off the lamp and said, "Rest well."

Rose and Sabine were so close that Rose could feel the warmth emanating from the woman's body.

"You were gone for a long time," Sabine whispered. "Is everything all right?"

Rose felt a quick thrum of guilt. "I thought I was lost. But I found my way."

"I'm glad you're safe," Sabine said. Then Rose heard rustling as she turned onto her side, facing the other direction.

Rose thought back to those long moments in the darkness, before her return to the camp. She had not strayed far, knowing how easily one got turned around, and how many dangers lurked in the night, and she'd turned off the headlamp right away, afraid to draw attention to herself. She had been crouched within a thicket of grass perhaps twenty meters from camp when she heard murmuring nearby. Rose hadn't even dared to breathe. The voices seemed to be coming from another twenty or so meters in the direction of the road; Rose was roughly halfway between them and camp. She caught the subtle sounds of motion in the bush—humans who were accustomed to silence. Her mind raced: if she went back now, quickly and with great stealth, she might get there in time to warn Christoph and Sabine. But her present location was well hidden; if she stayed, she could remain undetected. *Go or stay?* She'd thought of Christoph, his formal white shirt and paper cranes, and Sabine, all that rugged toughness swaddling a tender core. She could still run. Then the murmuring came again, closer, muted by the dead air, and Rose squeezed her eyes shut and wrapped her arm around her knees and folded herself within the hollow of a bush. She stayed.

After the group had passed by, Rose crept out behind and followed them from a safe distance. From the voices and the noise Rose guessed the group to be on the small side; still, she took extreme caution, staying far enough behind that when the group finally did enter the camp, Rose from her hiding place couldn't quite be sure what was happening. It was too dark to see, and she heard no dialogue. But neither were there screams. She stole closer until she could make

out in the moonlight Christoph's glinting knife, poised but motionless, and a woman with a basket atop her head. Rose watched as she
set it onto the ground before Christoph. His stance instantly relaxed.
A second woman laid down her basket as well, then Sabine stood
behind Christoph, and Rose turned on the headlamp. She'd been
struck dumb by a second blaze of fear when she came into the clearing and saw the two other men with their heavy black gumboots; it
took her a second of fighting to breathe before she realized their hands
were empty.

Now, in the intimate space of their improvised tent, Rose listened
to Sabine's even breathing. It was a peaceful sound, almost a lullaby,
and Rose felt the weight of her own exhaustion settling upon her.
Outside, Christoph was shifting to get comfortable. Rose heard him
crack a stick in two and then begin to tap it against his jeans. *Tak
tak, tak tak tak.* Warm memories of childhood trickled through her,
the hollow half shell and its earthy smell, the cozy darkness, the
rhythm of her mother's patter. Ocen and Opiyo, small and naughty
and full of play.

She opened her eyes to the pale brightness of dawn. Her mind felt
swimmy and slack, and she struggled to focus: why hadn't she been
woken for watch? Was something wrong? She rolled over and found
Sabine still sleeping beside her. Careful not to rouse her, Rose
extracted herself from the blanket and crawled out into the fresh,
dewy air.

Two birds trilled from the trees above, but the scene was otherwise deathly quiet. There was no sign of Christoph. Rose noted the
undisturbed stack of chapati resting on a rock. A line of ants had
found its way to the food. Her heartbeat began to stutter. She made
a quick round of the clearing: no articles of clothing, no sign of a
struggle. Then she looked toward the river. Christoph sat on a boul-
der at the shore, facing the blue-gray water flecked with yellow light;
the sun was just beginning to appear over the canopy on the far side

of the river. As she watched, he took a tiny pebble, and with a flick of his wrist, sent it skittering across the surface.

She picked her way between the rocks and bushes and came to sit beside him. Christoph turned just once with a quick smile when he heard her approach.

"You didn't wake us," she said.

"I wasn't tired. You needed your sleep."

"Nagero is not so far," she said. "We will reach there by midday."

He nodded.

"It is better that we leave soon," she said.

Christoph didn't move.

"Come, let us wake Sabine."

He sent another pebble skimming across the water. "I was so scared, Rose," he said. "Last night. When those people came. I've never been so frightened in my life. And you—you *lived* like that. For years."

She reached out and rested her hand lightly on his shoulder. What could she say?

He gripped her hand with surprising force. "We'll be all right," he said. "We'll get out of this."

"Yes," she said, though the word felt hollow.

"You'll finish your education. I'll help you."

She felt a welling of tears. "Yes."

"And your brother," he said. "And his family. I can help them, too. *We* can help them."

A wave of pain washed through her. She hadn't told him. *But Grace,* she thought. *Isaac. Wilborn.*

"Yes."

He nodded, turning his face back toward the river. "We're almost there. It's so close."

"*Alunya loyo lakwong,*" she murmured.

"What's that?"

"The second surpasses the first."

"Meaning?"

"What follows will be more severe than what has come."

As the last tip of sun rose above the trees, Christoph said, "I hope your Acholi wisdom is wrong about that."

Ten minutes later, after folding and stacking the blankets and leaving them on a rock in the clearing—along with the Congolese francs the group had refused the night before—they were on their way. Sabine and Rose had changed back into their own clothes, dirty as they were; Christoph's were too big for comfortable trekking. Around her shoulder Rose still carried the little purse with its contents of shillings. Sabine, though annoyed that Christoph had let her sleep, looked visibly refreshed, and Christoph showed no signs of exhaustion. Rose felt fit enough, but in her chest a kind of dread had lodged overnight, and it grew with every step they took toward Nagero. Logically speaking, Nagero was safety: satellite phones, the protection of armed rangers and possibly UPDF soldiers. But it held, too, the truth about Lily and Ocen—their purpose, their pact. She was in no hurry to meet it.

Passage along the river was more difficult than through the bush. The riverbank was for the most part steep and snarled with shrubs and boulders, and where the shoreline flattened and became sandy, hippos or crocodiles often lay in the shallow, murky water beyond. Sometimes the river forked into smaller branches, and the group would have to make a long detour to find a suitable place to cross before following the branch back up toward the main channel. The sun grew in height and intensity, and the mosquitoes were vicious.

Once, the group had to take cover as a military helicopter flew almost directly overhead. It was the first sign of war they'd seen since the attack, and it shook them badly enough that they didn't dare move for a long time after the choppy thrum of the rotor had faded.

At least the sky was blue: no more rain. And there were, Rose admitted, moments of tremendous beauty: a flock of white egrets lifting in unison; two vervet monkeys in a tree overhanging the water, their faces intelligently attentive toward the humans' progress; and on a cliff on the far side, a vast colony of brilliantly colored birds with crimson bodies and turquoise heads. The staccato *rik rik rik rik* of their calls carried across the river in a rich chorus of cheer.

The group reached Nagero sometime after midday. Christoph was the first to spot the smooth slope of a building's roof, pronounced against the erratic curves of the tree canopy, a little ways in from the river. "Thank God," Sabine said as they quickened their pace. Rose's senses were on high alert for soldiers; surely there were men on watch, patrolling the periphery. But they met no one as they emerged into a wide, flat space crisscrossed by dirt roads and scattered with trees. It looked like a parade ground, Rose thought, where soldiers might do drills. A tall silver pole, slightly bowed, bore the Congolese flag at the top; the fabric drooped listlessly toward the earth. A handful of small buildings and huts stood around the periphery, a large mud-splattered truck was parked next to a brick shed, and the structure they'd seen from the river was just beyond, an imposing sight with tiered concrete steps and yellow archways all the way around. Rose nearly stopped at the vision; it was the grandest building she thought she'd ever seen—more magnificent, even, than the Kitgum Mission. Here lay her fate. Her footfalls became heavier with each step.

Two men appeared from behind the building, dressed in camouflage fatigues, black gumboots, and floppy wide-brimmed hats. Each carried an automatic weapon. They were walking in the other direction, following the dirt tracks toward a second largish structure—longer and lower than the first—a few hundred meters away. They didn't seem to have noticed the newcomers. They reacted quickly enough, though, as soon as Christoph shouted out and began to jog toward them. Rose halted and held Sabine back when the soldiers pivoted and dropped to one knee, rifles raised. Christoph stopped, his palms up. There was less than a hundred meters' space between them.

"Is this Nagero?" Christoph called. The soldiers stayed put. Christoph threw a glance back at Sabine. "What was the name of the woman you spoke with?"

"Daniela," Sabine said. Christoph repeated the name loudly for the soldiers, and they exchanged a look; one lowered his rifle and pulled out a black communication device from his belt. Meanwhile six other men had come running from the building and were forming a semicircle around the group, barking out orders between themselves.

"Please," Sabine said. "We're friends."

"*Amis, amis,*" Christoph said.

Rose closed her eyes and waited for the shooting to start.

It never came.

"Sabine Hardt?" a male voice called.

When Rose opened her eyes, a short Congolese man with big eyes was standing a dozen meters away, addressing them. He wore the same uniform as the others aside from a black beret in lieu of a hat. His stature was diminutive, but his person emanated power.

"I'm Sabine." Sabine stepped forward.

With the slightest gesture, the commander—for that's what he surely was—had his men at ease. He walked briskly toward Sabine and shook her hand.

"I'm Jean-Pierre Mutondolwa, chief warden."

Introductions were made with Christoph and Rose.

"We expected you yesterday," he said. "But we heard about the attack on the bus outside Faradje. We feared you were involved."

"We were," Christoph said. "We managed to get away. Rose led us to the river, where we camped overnight. We followed it here this morning."

The ranger trained his eyes on Rose. She felt uncomfortable under his scrutiny, as if standing under a very bright light in an otherwise dark room.

"It was LRA, wasn't it?" she said.

He nodded. "We think they had a dozen fighters. They've broken up into smaller groups now—ten to fifteen for raiding parties, fifty or so when the group includes families and captives."

"Where's the UPDF?" Sabine asked. "We saw a helicopter this morning. Was it theirs?"

"Probably. They're based in Dungu, a hundred kilometers west, but they've been crisscrossing the land northeast of here for a few days.

My guess is that they're responsible for flushing out the group that attacked the bus yesterday."

"What about the UN?" Christoph said. "Can't they do anything?"

"Limited mandate," he said.

A few beats passed before Sabine cleared her throat. "It's been . . . a difficult journey."

"Of course," he said, gesturing toward the building. "Come inside. There's food and water."

"Thank you, yes. But what I mean to ask is—do you have my niece's journal? We've come a long way to see it."

"Daniela will be here soon. She can tell you more."

Sabine and Christoph walked ahead, while Rose came alongside the chief.

"Were you at the camp where the journal was found?" she asked.

"I was."

"What else did you find there?"

"The things you might expect," he said. "Sandals, tarps, jerry cans, rubbish."

"Anything else?"

"Are you hoping for something in particular?"

"Lily was not traveling alone," Rose said. "She had a man with her. A Ugandan man. My . . . husband." The word was a lie, but it felt exactly right. "He wore a bracelet made of braided metal. If Lily's journal was there—if she left it on purpose—I thought maybe . . ."

He stopped walking and met her eyes. "I am sorry. We found nothing else."

They entered through a yellow arch and two wooden doors. Inside was a large room furnished with tables and chairs. No one sat.

A few minutes later, a white woman strode in looking rushed but composed, very pretty despite the tangled mess of her brown hair. She wore tall hiking boots and knee-length khaki shorts that showed off her lean, muscled legs. It was strange to see a woman here—surely this was a man's place, remote and rugged and rent open by violence.

"Daniela," the woman said, sticking her hand out. "Park manager. Welcome. You are . . . well?"

"*Nous allons bien*," Christoph said.

Daniela's face showed relief upon hearing the French, and she quickly responded in kind.

Christoph translated. "She says she's sorry that her English isn't very good. She's glad we're safe, she was worried about us after the attack on the bus."

"Lily's diary?" Sabine asked. "Does she have it?"

Another rapid-fire exchange in French, with Christoph translating concurrently. "She has it. She'll take us there now. After we didn't arrive yesterday, she put the journal in a secure location, a locked storage shed over near the office, where they keep the . . ." He stopped, then asked Daniela another question.

"*Oui,*" she said.

"Keep what?" Rose asked. "What do they keep?"

Christoph's face was pale when he turned back. "The ivory."

CHAPTER 21

SABINE

January 1, 2009

Ten minutes later, the group stood outside a brick shed, Daniela fiddling with a padlock while Sabine, Christoph, and Rose waited a few feet away. A handful of rangers had accompanied them and looked on. Sabine felt strangely calm. Or perhaps not so strangely: after all, behind this door lay a book that would, in all likelihood, reveal nothing she didn't already know. Certain details might become clear: how far Lily had gotten in her investigation, the people she'd spoken with, what exactly she planned to do when she got to Garamba. But whatever questions the journal addressed, the most essential one—*where is she now*—would remain unanswered. Sabine would find no closure here.

"Ah!" Daniela exclaimed as the key finally clicked and the lock opened. She tugged open the stiff wooden door and stepped inside. Sabine was the first to follow. The shed was approximately the size of the kitchen in her apartment in Marburg, separated into a front and a back space joined by a doorless frame; there were neither windows nor lightbulbs, and it took a few seconds for Sabine's eyes to adjust. Daniela strode ahead into the back space while Sabine halted abruptly. Behind her she heard Christoph enter and take a sharp inhalation.

"*Merde*," he said.

On the floor to their left was a stack of elephant tusks that nearly reached her chest in height. The tusks lay lengthwise on the ground, curves of different sizes—some as small as a child's arm, others taller than a man—linked into one another in a massive, grotesque sculpture. Their colors ranged from eggshell-white to splotchy brown to burnt black. Many of the tips were broken and jagged, as if hacked off in a hurry or with crude instruments.

"There must be hundreds," she said.

"More," Christoph said.

Sabine had known what the shed contained, of course; back in the main building, Daniela explained that this was where they stored everything the rangers confiscated from poachers when they were caught. But somehow the word *ivory* was too distant, too imprecise an object—it conjured delicate trinkets and polished white figurines— and Sabine had imagined that it would, in any case, be kept out of view. She was completely unprepared for the grisly sprawl before her. It must have been years' worth of seized tusks. She remembered from her cursory online research in Kitgum that this would only represent a tiny portion of what the poachers got away with.

She ran her hand along an enormous tusk that was lodged in the pile somewhere around waist height and ran nearly the length of the room. Its surface was covered in a vast network of dark hairline cracks. In black marker, someone had written directly on the tusk itself: *2.81 m, 53 cm, 46 kg.* Length. Diameter. Weight. It weighed almost as much as she did. She tried to imagine the majesty of the creature it once belonged to—the creature that had died for its beauty. She couldn't.

In the back room, Daniela was bent over a file cabinet, sorting through a dozen tiny keys. Stepping through to join her, Sabine was startled at the sight of fifty or so rifles, dark and long and hanging on racks; more were piled below, spilling over. Several had yellow labels taped around the middle. None looked new: the wooden stocks were chipped and worn. More seized booty, she guessed. How often had these rifles exchanged hands? She had never seen so many guns in one place, except perhaps when carried by a regiment of soldiers. Inert, the guns should have seemed harmless, she thought: just metal and wood. But so near the grim display in the room behind, the rifles pulsed with violence. They had no purpose but to kill. As Sabine stood there, it occurred to her that whatever truths Lily's journal held, it was this shed that told the real story of her fate: ivory at one end and guns at the other.

Vaguely, Sabine heard the tinny sound of metal drawers opening and closing. Then Daniela was standing next to her, presenting something. "*Alors*," she said.

In Daniela's hand was a large sketchbook, about the size of a normal sheet of paper and nearly an inch thick; the pages were bound together by two stiff blue covers and a spiral coil. The cover was scuffed, marked by streaks of dirt and splatters of discoloration, probably from rain. Sabine felt no sense of recognition. Should she? She took a short step forward, hesitant. How far this object had come, Sabine thought: through mud and rain and brush and fear. Her hand trembled when she took it.

She opened the cover; it was the only thing she could think of to do. The first page was entirely blank except for two words: *Lily Bennett*.

A rush of memories flooded in. That handwriting, loosely cursive. This was *her* Lily. Hannah's Lily. Lily of the bubbles blown at the neighbor's cat; Lily of the gardener's hat and Play-Doh; Lily of the hand-drawn maps and the cartographer's flourish; Lily of the talking ravens; Lily of the white-and-yellow flowers that bloomed in early spring in the grassy foothills of the Rocky Mountains.

Her chest constricted, and she felt the walls closing in around her. She needed air.

"Sabine?" Christoph said.

She pushed past him, the journal clutched to her chest. Past the weapons and the tusks, the whitewashed walls and unswept floor. Outside, she stumbled and caught herself. There was Rose—anxious, concerned—and the rangers. The scattered trees, the wide blue sky.

"What does it say?" Rose's voice was near, but Sabine heard it as if across a great distance. "What does she write about Ocen?"

"I . . ." Her speech faltered.

Christoph was suddenly at her elbow. "Are you okay?"

Daniela emerged from the shed behind them and swung the door closed, then threaded the padlock through the latch. Sabine brought Lily's journal away from her chest and examined it again. This was a sacred thing, she understood: the laying down of words. Lily's secret-most thoughts would be captured here; the things she never would have said aloud. What right did Sabine have to expose those senti-ments? She felt suddenly protective. And yet—she glanced at Rose, whose expression was attentive and pleading, right there on the verge of anguish. Rose had nothing of Ocen's. No physical anchor to give weight to this agony.

"Do you need a minute alone?" Christoph asked.

Alone. She recalled her words to him just a few days before: *Alone has always worked for me.* But had it, really? Her heartbeat slowed to the pace of a firefly, just one, twinkling. She met Christoph's eyes: two fireflies, blinking in unison. She looked at Rose. Three.

They began at the end.

Together, they laid the journal down on one of the wood tables in the main building, and Sabine, Rose, and Christoph squeezed in shoul-der to shoulder. Daniela had left them; she still had a park to run, after all. Christoph held the covers open. Sabine trusted the steadiness of his hands more than she did her own.

The back third of the book was blank. Christoph flipped toward the front, page by page, in silence. *So much emptiness,* Sabine thought. *So much left unsaid.*

Finally they reached the last entry. It was just as Daniela had de-scribed over the phone: a large map of Garamba, spread over two pages. There was Nagero, situated toward the bottom next to the river they'd followed that morning; Faradje, farther to the east, and Dungu to the west; and four tiny stars, the estimated locations of the LRA camps throughout the park's boundaries and to the west. Each had a name: Eskimo. Boo. Pilipili. Kiswahili.

"How did she possibly find out where they were?" Christoph said.

This had puzzled Sabine, too, ever since Daniela mentioned it. She looked closer at the squiggles connecting the LRA camps to nearby landmarks. The faint lines were accompanied by brief notes: *walk 3 days, pass 6 creeks, 1 river, radio tower here, follow park road 2 days.*

"Miriam," Sabine said.

"Who?" Christoph asked.

"The girl at the Children In Need center in Kitgum—the one who first told Lily that the LRA were smuggling ivory. She escaped from the rebels in September and arrived in Kitgum a month after that. She would have known exactly where the camps were." She thought back to that conversation: *I told Lily about life with the rebels,* Miriam had said. *The names of our people, the rivers, how we traveled, where we stayed . . .*

But why? Sabine wondered. Was Lily trying to determine smuggling routes? Or did she just want to make sure she would avoid areas close to the rebel camps?

Christoph turned the page. This, too, was as Daniela had said: a map that included both Arua and Lakwali as well as the roads between. Lily would have gotten this information mainly from the atlas and Patrick. Lily's detour through Lakwali made a lot more sense now, when the route was laid out on a map like this: even though she and Ocen might have taken a more direct road to Nagero if they went north from Arua instead of west, detouring to Lakwali split the journey into two shorter days instead of one long one, with the added bonus of secure shelter and hot showers.

Another page. This one had no maps or images of any kind; it was filled with handwriting, a more condensed version of the slack cursive Sabine had seen on the front page. Her heart quickened—maybe there were names here, informants or contacts. The notes were scrambled and messy, but Sabine detangled them bit by bit: a packing list, two phone numbers for Franklin in Arua, approximate distances between towns, times for sunrise and sunset, a handful of phrases with Lingala translations (*Can you help us? Can we buy food? How far to* _____*?*). The URL for Patrick's blog was there, too. Finally, boxed off near the bottom, she saw what looked like a rough itinerary that listed December second as Arua, December third as Lakwali, and, beneath:

Dec 4—Garamba???!!!

Sabine's stomach churned.

"Ready?" Christoph asked gently. She nodded.

On the next page the writing was more fluid, the phrases cohering into full sentences and even paragraphs.

In times of famine they eat wild plants, adyebo and anunu . . . The camps have 150–200 captives and 75–100 fighters . . . They stay in one place for months, sometimes years—women have jobs cutting grass for hut roofs, digging in the fields . . . They grow cassava, simsim, sweet potatoes, sorghum, maize, sunflower, groundnuts, rice . . .

"These must be her interview notes," Sabine said. "When she spoke with Miriam."

The room was quiet as they read further. *Soldiers form small hunting parties . . . The younger abducted girls are kept as* tingtings, *babysitters, before they're old enough to be married off, usually by 12 or 13 . . .* Then a separate list with the underlined title, 0 sightings, and the names of LRA camps followed by months:

Boo—Sept
Eskimo—Aug/Sept
Boo—July
Kiswahili—April/May
→ June?? Oct/Nov???

A code, perhaps? Sabine wondered. She looked at the title again. Zero sightings of what?

"That's odd," Christoph murmured.

"The sightings?"

"No," he said. "Haven't you noticed? She doesn't mention ivory once."

Christoph was right, she realized: nowhere was there a single instance of the word *ivory*, or *elephant*, or *smuggling*, or any direct reference to Lily's investigative object.

"Here," she said, pointing to the list. "This must be when Miriam saw evidence of poaching or smuggling."

Christoph pursed his lips skeptically. "I'm not sure. Why the letter *O*?"

"The zero? Maybe it's a placeholder—Lily was being cautious. Keep going," Sabine urged. "There must be something else."

Dutifully, Christoph turned another page. More notes from the rehabilitation center, though these were even less relevant—it looked like a rough draft for a funding proposal; Sabine had seen enough grants in her time to recognize the signs. Then a series of sketches of the children at play, the boys kicking around a soccer ball and the girls in traditional dance costumes or hunched over a piece of paper with a pencil. Christoph flipped past a few more pages. Still nothing.

"We're not getting anywhere," she said.

Christoph looked at her in surprise. "You want to stop?"

"What are we going to find? These notes are all too old to be of any use. Not even the locations of the rebel camps can help us now—Operation Lightning Thunder has seen to that." She flipped another page and saw a sketch of three cows in a field, or perhaps the same cow three times. Underneath was a to-do list that included things like *buy snacks* and *finish human interest story for CIN newsletter* and *Francis re: more art supplies.* "What good will this do us? What good will it do them?"

She began turning pages more rapidly now, frustrated and confused. More drawings, more flurries of notes—nothing about ivory, not a word. At the same time she chided herself: what did she expect? Flowcharts and diagrams, evidence of systematic research?

"Wait," Christoph said, stilling her hand with a touch. The feeling of his skin on hers was electric, and for a second she didn't even notice the page where he'd made her stop. Then her focus shifted, and she saw the portraits—nearly a dozen, all of the same person: a Ugandan man, youngish. Handsome. They were simple pencil drawings, not quite as detailed as the portrait of Miriam at the rehabilitation center, but the face was vivid and lifelike nonetheless.

Sabine heard Rose gasp. It was the first indication she'd made that she was still here, still attentive; she'd said nothing about the maps nor the interview notes nor anything else in Lily's journal thus far. Sabine glanced at her, watching as Rose brought her hand to her open mouth, unable to take her eyes from the page.

"It's Ocen," Christoph said softly. "Isn't it?"

But Rose couldn't even nod; she'd gone still as stone. Sabine looked again at the face in the sketches, the same somber expression in each. So this was Ocen. He'd clearly posed for Lily: his eyes stared unwavering out from the paper, his profile presented at precise angles. She felt an acute pang of anguish for Rose, to have to witness this proof of the intimacy that had so clearly existed between subject and artist. She touched Rose's shoulder. "I'm sorry."

Rose reached out quick as a flash and gripped Sabine's arm. "No," she said. "No—look." She let go to point to a sketch in the lower right, one Sabine hadn't picked out before, but now that she looked closer, it did seem different somehow. She couldn't quite put her finger on it.

"Are those supposed to be military fatigues?" Christoph said. "Huh." He squinted, trying to read the words underneath. "'Is this what he looks like now?'" He frowned. "I wonder what that means."

Rose's voice was hardly more than a breath: "Opiyo."

The word jogged something in Sabine's memory. "Say that again?"

"Opiyo," Rose repeated.

"Ocen's brother?" Christoph asked.

Sabine shook her head. "What are you talking about?"

"Ocen had a twin—Opiyo—he was abducted the same day as Rose."

"The sightings," Rose whispered. "*O* for *Opiyo*."

Christoph's hand flew to his forehead, his expression stricken. "Aboke. Lily thought she could—the night before they left, she was talking about—" He choked up, unable to finish.

Sabine desperately tried to put the pieces together. Ocen's brother? Aboke? The Italian nun and the schoolteacher who tracked the rebels into the bush . . .

With a quiet click, everything slid into place.

The simplicity was staggering.

The secrecy, Miriam's memories, *I told Lily about life with the rebels, the names of our people* . . .

O for *Opiyo*.

Lily's e-mail came back to her again: *For a while I just felt helpless, like no matter what I did here, there was no way to make a difference. But now I think I've found a way. It's about finding something that's bigger than yourself, and being brave enough to commit to it.*

The audacity. The foolishness.

It had never been about ivory. There was no secret investigation. Lily and Ocen weren't trying to avoid the rebels.

They were trying to find them.

"It was a rescue operation," Sabine said.

Christoph nodded, stricken. Turning to Rose, he said, "But you thought he died."

"I believed it was true."

Sabine felt dizzy. She had to sit down. "Rose," she said, her voice sounding faint even to her own ears. "You know how the rebels operate. Is there any chance . . ." She trailed off, then began again. "Is there any chance the LRA would let them go?"

Rose's silence echoed all around. It seeped into the walls and through the floor.

Dinner that night was beans and stew and rice, served hot on spotless white plates in the main building. Daniela had returned after organizing their sleeping arrangements: three huts, she said, spare but comfortable, among the rangers' quarters. There were other huts closer to the river—the ones they normally used for guests—but given the security situation, Daniela would rather that everyone stay within a tighter radius.

"She can help organize transportation back to Lakwali, or Arua—wherever we want to go," Christoph said. "She just needs a few days to set it up. And in the meantime, they don't have Internet, but we can use the phones to call out. We should be contacting everyone. UPDF, police, the American embassy, media outlets." He met Sabine's eyes. "Steve."

"Tomorrow," Sabine said.

"The sooner they know—"

"Tomorrow."

He didn't press.

Sabine surprised herself with her appetite. She and Rose said little, leaving Christoph to carry the conversation with Daniela, the chief warden, and a few other staff members, who all kept their voices low out of respect; Sabine didn't even ask Christoph to translate.

Afterward, Daniela brought a change of clothing for both Sabine and Rose—Christoph still had his backpack—and showed them the wooden stalls the staff used for showers. Each had a bucket filled with river water that had been boiled then cooled enough to use. The water felt sublime against her dirty, sweaty skin; the shower at Lakwali seemed a hundred years ago instead of two days. Sunset streaked fiercely overhead, brutal in its splendor.

Exiting the shower, Sabine caught a glimpse of Rose slipping her blouse on in the next stall. Her single arm was lean and skillful, doing the work of two. What would Rose return to, Sabine wondered, in Kitgum? What awaited her there? Christoph had said that he wanted to help her, but for a woman who'd lost her adolescence, then her child, and now her partner—what balm could soothe those wounds?

When they were dressed, the chief warden met them with a

flashlight and walked them across the parade ground, past the low administrative offices and the Congolese flag, past the mud-spattered trucks and the brick shed and the trees and a single-room building that read SALLE DE POLICE. The warden's stride was slow and powerful, the fabric of his fatigues swishing softly, boots creaking, rifle and radio clicking against one another every few steps. Sabine carried Lily's journal against her chest. The warden pointed out the three huts Daniela had prepared for them and gave them each a key, then aimed the light toward the drop toilets a few dozen meters from the periphery.

"If you need to leave your hut for any reason during the night, take a flashlight and stay alert. Hippos come through here regularly, and we've had leopards as well."

"I'm the only one with a headlamp," Christoph said. "We lost most of our gear in the attack on the bus."

"I've got an extra flashlight at my hut, if one of you wants to accompany me there. I can send someone to take another over."

"Let me come," Rose said.

Christoph nodded. "I'll stay with Sabine."

They stood outside Sabine's hut and watched the warden and Rose disappear into the night.

"Will she be all right?" Sabine asked.

"I trust the warden completely," Christoph said.

"I mean in Kitgum. When she goes back."

Insects and birds chittered from invisible places in the grass. After a long time he said, "I don't know. She has family there—a brother and his wife—but I don't think they're close. Her reintegration has been difficult, even with her own clan."

Brisk footsteps and a bobbing light approached from the darkness: the ranger sent by the warden. When he got close enough for Sabine to see his face, she realized how young he was: barely more than a boy. As she accepted the flashlight and mumbled a word of thanks, she felt a sudden, crippling tenderness toward him, this young man who faced down poachers and rebels, day in and day out. She pictured the fortune of ivory in the brick shed—hundreds of thousands of dollars' worth, at least—and the single padlock on the wooden door. Yet he, and all the other rangers at Garamba, chose this: to trudge onward in obscurity, unrecognized by the outside world, unacknowledged even by the creatures they risked their lives to protect. As he walked away, she felt an abrupt urge to send a prayer out behind him: that he would weather whatever violence raged across his path, that he would grow old and die in his own bed, surrounded by people who loved him.

Christoph followed her into the hut while she made a quick scan with the light. The space was cramped but clean. The bed was covered by a taut blue sheet, and a mosquito net hung from the thatched roof; a water basin stood next to the door along with a pair of rubber sandals. A gecko ran across the wall, but there were no snakes under the bed nor spiders on the ceiling.

"What about you?" Christoph asked. "Will you be all right?"

She held up the flashlight. "I promise to look both ways."

"You know that's not what I meant."

"I . . . can't," she said. "Not right now."

Neither of them spoke for several minutes, and finally Christoph turned to leave. Before she realized what she was doing she'd reached out and taken hold of his hand.

"Stay with me," she said. "Just a little longer."

They sat together on the concrete step outside the door. Sabine had left Lily's diary on the nightstand inside. Christoph was silent, making space for her to begin. But she didn't want to talk yet. She was thinking of her first memory of Africa: when she landed at the airport in Addis Ababa those many years ago, seeing the flat green land all around and hazy mountains in the distance—how raw the land had seemed, how promising and untamed. She'd known even then that it wasn't just about making up for the sins of her forefathers; she'd made this choice for her. *She* was the selfish one. Other people's tragedy would be a platform for her redemption. She was special.

She was kind. She would map goodness on a suffering land. She'd acted the part of the noble savior with a terrible, secret satisfaction. The people she professed to be helping—when had she stopped to ask for their permission? What insidious, invisible harm had she done? Was it still possible, after everything, to claim that imperfect action was better than none?

In novels she'd read—novels that had been passed around among aid workers starved for evening entertainment—there were consequences for a person's actions: every scene served a purpose; every decision, no matter how minute, affected the greater arc. But if you lived this way you would be paralyzed, unable to decide whether to have coffee or tea. In life things happened and you didn't always feel the effects. The consequences came later or not at all. Or they happened to someone far away.

Was there such a thing as a final equation? A moral balance of variables?

Beside her, Christoph waited.

"What's the first thing you'll do when you get home?" she asked at last.

He thought about it a while. "Ice skating."

"Ice skating?"

"There's a rink, a *patinoire*, in the Parc des Bastions, right in the heart of Geneva. I used to take Céline there when I came home from university for the holidays, when she was six, seven, eight years old. She loved the cold. She refused to wear mittens, even when the temperature dropped below zero. It was amazing, though—when I held her hands, her skin was always warm to the touch."

Sabine had never been to Geneva, but she could picture it exactly: Christmas lights strung from trees, a kiosk selling hot chocolate, children in puffy winter coats, dashing blond Christoph arm-in-arm with a laughing, barehanded little girl. The image suffused her with sadness.

"Back in Lakwali," she said, "you told me stories save us."

"They do."

"How can you say that?"

"Maybe the choice to believe is as powerful as the belief itself."

"But then it's just fantasy. It's like your folklore, your fairy tales. It's not real life."

"Fairy tales don't tell us about what happened or didn't happen," he said. "They tell us about ourselves. The things we long for, the decisions we make. The ways we fail. The possibility that next time will be different."

"And when there's no 'next time'?"

She sensed him hesitate. Then he leaned forward and cupped her chin gently in his hand. She understood his intention with a kind of panic. But when his mouth touched hers, something released in her chest: a tiny knot, unraveling. She wanted to struggle against it—there was too much at stake, too much grief locked up behind—but she couldn't, the release had already started, and she kissed him back, hard. A moment later they had to pause for breath.

"Inside," she whispered.

"Are you sure?"

She took his hand, rose, pulled him with her. With the door shut behind them there were no more restraints. They undressed jerkily, elbows bumping in the tiny space. They laughed at their own awkwardness, then found themselves standing face-to-face, both naked, suddenly shy.

He ran the back of his hand from the hollow beneath her jaw to her collarbone, light as a feather's touch; he kept going, running a line down the center of her chest and then grazing outward to her right hip.

As their bodies leaned into one another, a noise came from outside the hut—what sounded like heavy breathing. The muted crunch of grass.

Sabine froze. "Someone's there."

Christoph held a finger to her lips and looked up, listening. As the sound repeated—louder now, like snorting—a smile crossed his face.

"Hippos," he said.

Then kissed her again.

CHAPTER 22

ROSE

January 1

"Here," the chief warden said. "Take this. I changed the batteries yesterday."

"Thank you, Mr. Mutondolwa." Rose accepted the flashlight and flicked it on. The beam was focused and powerful, a tunnel of brightness cutting through the night.

"Please, call me Jean-Pierre."

They stood in the packed dirt outside the warden's hut, which looked just like all the others, despite his rank. Through the open door she got a glimpse of the spartan room inside; it was almost as poor as Ocen's hut near the airstrip in Kitgum. Thinking of that hollow space pinged her with fresh grief, and she was relieved when Jean-Pierre closed the door and said, "Let me walk you to your quarters."

His pace was unhurried, and his composure seemed to permeate the space around him. Her mind had been in turmoil all evening, reeling with the revelations of Lily's journal, and she clung to the steadiness of the warden's quiet assurance with gratitude. They passed a young ranger, and Jean-Pierre spoke a few words with him, gesturing briefly at his own flashlight and nodding in the direction of the hut where Christoph and Sabine waited. The ranger strode off purposefully.

"How long have you worked at Garamba?" she asked.

"Three years. My wife, Sincere, and our children have been living in Faradje so the young ones can attend school. I prefer to stay with them, but my work often keeps me here."

"Faradje? The Christmas attacks . . ."

"They're fine. I've arranged for them to come to Nagero for a while. There are family quarters south of the station, toward the main road. They arrive tomorrow morning. It is better for them to remain here until the present unrest has passed."

"The LRA will not stop attacking civilians," Rose said. "Now that they have been driven from their camps, they will need food and supplies. They will raid villages and then vanish into the bush. It's what they know."

Jean-Pierre nodded. "All the UPDF has succeeded in doing is stirring the hornets' nest. They have made our work very difficult."

He stopped in front of a hut tucked behind a copse of trees, unlocked the door, and stepped in confidently, running the beam of the flashlight under the bed, checking for snakes, Rose guessed. She almost wished there would be one, so that he would stay a bit. She wasn't ready to be alone, not with her thoughts creeping up in her consciousness like a hungry river rising.

Opiyo—alive, alive, alive.

The words lapped against her ears. This was the truth that had come between her and Ocen before he left, not money troubles or another woman. Rose recalled Ocen's all-night absence at the end of October, when she'd waited for him in his hut until dawn—that was the day he'd found out. And afterward, his moodiness through November—it wasn't a phase. It was disgust, thinly disguised.

Ocen had not died believing his brother would meet him on the other side of the eternal border. He died knowing he'd been lied to by the woman he loved.

"Rose?" Jean-Pierre's voice brought her back.

"Yes," she said. "Thank you for your assistance."

He aimed the flashlight out the open door to the toilet stalls in the distance, dimly illuminated with the diffuse beam. He politely refrained from voicing an explanation. "Our on-duty rangers will be patrolling the perimeter all night. Others will sleep in the huts here and here," he said, pointing out nearby huts with the light, "if you need anything before morning."

"Are you from here? From this place?" she asked. She would have asked anything to get him to stay, just a moment longer.

"I am from here," he said, "but I spent fifteen years as a park warden in Kenya."

"Fifteen years? So long?"

His low chuckle reverberated. "I am nearly an old man. But I was once as young as you. In fact, I studied in Kampala."

That surprised her. "In my country?"

He laughed again, his white teeth glinting in the moonlight. "Yes, in your country. Kampala is an exciting city. Very stimulating."

"I was never there."

"I am sure you will see it someday."

After he left, she lay awake for a long time thinking of his words. Kampala felt like something out of a story; people might speak of it, but it wasn't real. In fact, the entire world beyond her bed might be an illusion, she thought. If she only closed her eyes, it would stop existing at all.

By the time Rose made it out of her hut in the morning—she'd slept hard and late—the sun was already above the surrounding canopy and everyone else seemed to have been up for hours. Rangers were doing drills in the parade ground as she crossed to the main building, feeling discomposed. Inside, Christoph and Sabine were nowhere to be seen. A Congolese woman with a severe expression brought a plate of pineapple and cold toast without asking, then retreated into the kitchen area and, with a few sharp words Rose could only assume were at her own expense, elicited a peal of laughter from a second woman whose large bum Rose glimpsed through the open door. Alone at her table, Rose ate the toast in embarrassed silence, which subsided only upon the arrival of Jean-Pierre, whose smile she returned with tremendous relief.

"Christoph and Sabine are in the office," he said. "There is no Internet, but they already started making calls."

"Thank you, I will go to them." She stood. "And your wife and children? They have arrived well?"

His smile broadened. "Very well."

The joy in his voice was palpable, and it both pleased and pained Rose to hear it. No one would ever speak of her like that again, except perhaps Grace.

"Let me return the flashlight," she said. "It is in my hut still."

"Keep it for now. You may need it another night."

She thanked him and left, skirting the rangers on the parade ground and approaching the low, green-roofed building that housed the administrative offices. Of the six doors she counted, only one was open. Peering inside, she saw Christoph standing with a phone to his ear, speaking in French; Sabine sat behind a messy desk concentrating on the clipboard in her hand, tapping a pencil against the paper. In front of her was Lily's journal, laid open. Both Sabine and Christoph possessed an energy about them that felt incongruous with the depressed lethargy from the day before.

Sabine looked up as Rose entered. "Rose! Good morning. Did you sleep well?"

"I slept . . . too long."

"You must have needed it. Here . . ." Sabine handed the clipboard over. "This is the list I've come up with so far. Can you think of anything else?"

Rose took the clipboard hesitantly. The first item—*Contact UPDF re: possible sightings, request for temporary ceasefire*—already had a checkmark next to it. She read further: *Contact embassies re: lost passports (Kinshasa??) . . . Notify Steve/Rita/U.S. & international media . . . UN involvement? U.S. military? Hostage protocol? Negotiation team? Photos of Lily/Ocen? Reward?*

As she read, Rose became confused. "What is this?"

Sabine gave her a puzzled smile. "We're organizing the search team."

Christoph swiped the clipboard from Rose's hand and wrote down a series of numbers. Then he said a few last words into the phone and hung up. "That was the Swiss embassy in Kinshasa," he said. "They gave me the number for the German and Ugandan embassies as well. The process should be about the same for all of us. We'll need to file police reports—we can do that here, I think, or in Faradje—and have people back home fax them copies of our birth certificate or driver's license, some kind of identification. It will mean going to Kinshasa in person—I'm not sure about transportation, it's a long way . . ."

"You know," Sabine said, "if FARDC didn't recover our passports from the bus, they must still be in the wreckage somewhere. The rebels will be long gone. Let's ask Daniela if one of the rangers can drive us this afternoon."

"It would certainly avoid a lot of hassle," Christoph agreed. "And then we don't have to be so quick to leave. We can keep our focus on what's happening here." He put a hand on Sabine's shoulder, and she reached up to squeeze it. Rose watched this newfound intimacy with a curious sense of detachment.

"Rose," Christoph said, turning to her, "there's a lot to catch you up on."

"We got through to the UPDF this morning," Sabine said.

Rose shifted warily. "The UPDF?"

"Now that we know it was never about ivory, it doesn't make any sense to withhold information from them," Sabine said. "Our first priority is to prevent any additional military actions against the LRA until we find out exactly where Lily and Ocen are. The UPDF commander I spoke with couldn't agree to this on the phone, but he's taking it back to his superiors. He did at least confirm that there's been no report of Lily's body in any of the rebel camps targeted so far during Operation Lightning Thunder. He seemed quite certain." She paused, apologetic. "They couldn't be sure about Ocen . . ."

"But," Christoph cut in, "if they took Lily captive, there's no reason to believe they would treat Ocen any differently. Remember Aboke? Both the Italian nun and the Ugandan schoolteacher were unharmed."

"That's what you believe?" Rose said. "They're still alive?"

Christoph and Sabine exchanged a glance.

"We're cautiously optimistic," Sabine said.

"And you will remain here to look for them?" Rose asked.

"Until we get our passports, we don't have a choice—we can't leave the country."

"But Rose," Christoph said, "if you want to get back to Kitgum, the UPDF can arrange transport. They're already bringing a group of women and children they've rescued from the rebels. Even without your identification documents, we could vouch for you—make sure you're taken care of."

Rose's thoughts went back to those weeks in the UPDF barracks four years before—the interrogations that began the day she was released from the hospital. The soldiers had kept her for weeks, asking a thousand questions about the rebels' movements, their strategies, their communication systems. She'd told them what she could—but not everything. If they'd known it all, if she were discovered, they would have kept her a hundred days more. She would not go through that again.

And Kitgum held nothing for her. Well, the children, of course—but would she be allowed to see them? Would she have to stalk Grace outside the schoolyard, observing her from a distance? Even if Rose were cleared of any wrongdoing in Agnes's death, she would have no job after Christoph left. The warden's words from last night came back to her: *Kampala is an exciting city. Very stimulating . . . I am sure you will see it someday.*

Why not? She still had her purse with the little bundle of shillings, and her much greater savings at Stanbic Bank; she could slip into Kitgum just long enough to return Christoph's equipment to his room at the Bomah and send a secret farewell message to Grace. She didn't have to wait for the UPDF to take her there—it would be easy enough to leave Nagero without notice and travel by bus as far as the border. If Franklin's thugs could cross without issue, surely she, a single woman who carried no cargo, could evade detection. In Kampala, she might begin again. No one would know her. No one would know the horrors that lay dormant in her blood.

"You don't have to decide now," Christoph said. "It's a lot to take in." He turned back to the clipboard. "So. The German embassy can wait . . . We need to ask Daniela about a ride to the crash site."

"Let me find her," Rose said.

"That would be very helpful. She told us she would be in the air for an hour or so . . ." He checked his watch. "She should be back now. If she's not in her office down the hall, try the headquarters or ask one of the rangers. They'll know where she is."

Rose was still puzzling over the phrase "in the air"—was that a metaphor for something?—when Christoph turned back to Sabine.

"Do you have the State Department woman's number at the U.S. embassy? She'd know how we can get in touch with American military."

"Everything's at the bus," Sabine said.

Christoph considered a moment. "I have Linda's contact info stored in my phone. She can get a number for the U.S. embassy in Kampala. They must have contact information for Steve, too."

"It's the middle of the night in Colorado . . ."

Sabine's voice faded as Rose exited the room, leaving them to their logistics and their eagerness. Meanwhile she was forming her own plan: to leave the next morning before dawn, without even saying good-bye.

She tracked down Daniela in a back room of the main building, where she was leaning over a map of the park and speaking into a walkie-talkie, her tousled brown hair escaping in wisps from her ponytail. With her were three Garamba rangers in green fatigues—including

Jean-Pierre—and a police officer in blue. Daniela asked a question into the communicator, and a moment later a male voice crackled through. Everyone's faces fell. Jean-Pierre noticed Rose and came to her at the doorway.

"Is everything all right, Rose?"

"Sabine and Christoph have a question for Daniela," she said quietly. "But maybe you can help? They would like to return to the site of the attack on the bus, this afternoon if possible. Our passports, documents . . . Everything was left behind."

"I'm afraid we can't spare any vehicles today."

"I will inform them. I'm sure they will understand."

"Maybe I can arrange something for tomorrow."

Daniela spoke briefly into the walkie-talkie and pressed her finger simultaneously against the map.

"What's happening?" Rose whispered.

"Daniela does an aerial survey of different areas of the park every morning in our small plane," Jean-Pierre said. "This morning she spotted a large group of vultures about twenty kilometers northeast of here." He paused to listen to the ongoing conversation between Daniela and whoever was on the other end of the walkie-talkie. "We sent a team to investigate," he continued in a hushed voice. "They arrived just a few minutes ago and confirmed that it was a herd of elephants. Twenty-two, all dead. The tusks are missing."

"Was it the rebels?"

"No. There are no footprints leading to and from the site—only around the bodies. It appears . . . it appears that the adults huddled around the calves, trying to protect them." He stopped, and Rose saw the emotion in his eyes. "But they could not shield them from above."

"From above?"

"Our team says many of the elephants were killed by bullets to the top of the head."

It took her a few seconds to understand the implication. "The UPDF helicopter we saw yesterday. It was flying north."

He nodded gravely. "Greed knows no borders. This is war of another kind." He looked back at the team assembled around the map. "If we are not willing to die for these creatures, they will be gone."

When she returned to the office to inform Sabine and Christoph that the vehicles were unavailable, they hardly even seemed disappointed; tomorrow, they said, would be fine.

"Rose, good news," Christoph said. "We found out there are U.S. military advisors working with the UPDF on Operation Lightning Thunder. It's all very hush-hush."

"That's good news?"

"Now that we have hard evidence about Lily, the media is going to pick up the story for sure," Sabine explained. "The U.S. military will be under a lot of pressure to get involved. They're already on the ground—they'll want to act as quickly as possible."

"I see," Rose said.

Christoph came around the desk to stand at her side. "Ocen is a part of this, too. We haven't forgotten him. It's just easier to spur people to action when it's an American life at stake."

The injustice of this truth should have outraged her. Tens of thousands of abducted Acholi children, tens of thousands more slaughtered at the rebels' hands; how many dead and dying in IDP camps? How many dead and dying in Faradje, in yesterday's bus attack? Ah, but should a *mono* girl be among them! Then we may intervene; then we may act.

She felt nothing. She'd heard this story before.

"I wish you luck," she said. "Please, I told the warden I would assist him in some matters."

They let her leave without argument. Instead of crossing the parade ground for the fourth time that morning, though, she turned south, toward the main road. It didn't take long to reach the family quarters Jean-Pierre had mentioned. Rose saw children playing, women hanging brightly colored laundry on lines, chickens pecking, a small dirt soccer field. A rooster crowed. She approached a woman sweeping the hard-packed ground outside a hut and said, "Sincere?" The woman pointed toward a hut some twenty meters away, where two children were scratching in the dirt with sticks. As Rose approached, a woman came out from the hut with a basket hitched on her hip. Her face showed signs of age, but her body moved with grace and purpose.

"Sincere?" Rose asked again.

The woman paused. "*Oui?*"

Rose fumbled through the only French she knew. "*Je* . . . Rose. *Amie* . . . Jean-Pierre."

"You may speak English, child," Sincere said gently.

With relief, Rose said, "My travel companions are occupied, and I have nothing to do. Your husband has been so generous—I thought I might be of assistance to you and your children, helping you settle in . . ."

Sincere good-humoredly appraised her. Under her mothering gaze, Rose felt herself becoming a girl again, shy and in need of comfort. How sharp this longing was! She caught her breath.

"Come, sit with me," Sincere said. "I have great plans to shell this entire basket of groundnuts before noon."

And so Rose passed the day as a kind of daughter, listening to Sincere speak of life as a ranger's wife, here and in Kenya. Their two oldest children were already grown, she said, now with babies of their own; the two young ones here—a twelve-year-old girl, Nicia, and her younger brother, Serge—reminded Rose of Grace and Isaac. With Sincere, Rose was at ease; the comfort was like that which she had experienced sometimes with Ocen, when he made her feel taken care of, as if she belonged. Over a background of the chickens' *buckkaws* and the children's laughter, Sincere acknowledged the fear of watching her husband leave for work, knowing the dangers he faced—the perpetual doubt that he would return. And yet she loved him for his dedication, his passion; she could never ask him to give it up.

"Why does he care for these creatures so much?" Rose asked.

Sincere smiled. "Once, in Kenya, he came upon a baby rhinoceros that had gotten stuck in a mud pit and was struggling. It was close to exhaustion, and its mother could do nothing. There was an elephant nearby—a cow. Jean-Pierre watched her wade into the mud and push the baby out, even while the mother rhinoceros was attacking her. She would risk her own life to save another." She stroked the grinding stone in her hand absentmindedly. "He has loved them ever since."

"The elephants are his family, too," Rose observed.

Sincere sighed and crushed a shelled groundnut. "Except you can teach your wife to wield a gun. The elephants have only their tusks, and that is no defense at all."

Late in the afternoon, Rose returned to the headquarters to hear what progress Sabine and Christoph had made. The office where they'd been working was empty, though the clipboard remained on the desk, and Lily's diary lay open to the map of Garamba. Rose approached it carefully, as if the object held some kind of dark power. She let her hand hover above the paper a moment without touching it; then she flipped the page, and again, and again, and again, until she reached the place where Ocen's profile appeared. Outside she could hear the sound of a truck engine growing loud and then fading.

Looking at the face of the man she loved, she was filled with remorse. If she'd told him everything from the beginning—if she'd said, *Opiyo is alive, but he is no longer the boy you remember*—Ocen would have understood. She was sure of it. He would have known that rescue was madness. They would still be together in Kitgum; Lily's revelations would have meant nothing. The girl would have set aside her naïve notions of heroism and returned home to America.

She shut the journal and closed the office door behind her when she left.

Sabine and Christoph were not in the main building, either. One of the rangers who spoke a little English told Rose that he had seen them heading toward the sleeping quarters. Rose started in that direction, but halfway across the parade ground she saw Sincere carrying a basket of onions and tomatoes toward the kitchen. Rose decided to join. She would meet Sabine and Christoph that evening at dinner.

She and Sincere walked around the side of the building to a small outdoor cooking area next to a door leading to the kitchen inside. The two Congolese women who'd served breakfast welcomed Sincere jovially but eyed Rose with rather less bonhomie until Sincere said something that seemed to break the ice.

"You must forgive them," Sincere whispered to Rose. "They never served an African woman before. Only African men and whites."

Rose glanced around the pots and pans and various boxes of supplies sitting on wooden crates nearby, and pointed at a package of Pembe baking flour, then to herself. "Samosas," she said to the two cooks. The women hooted and laughed and waved Rose cheerfully toward the jerry cans filled with water and oil.

Twenty minutes later, she was so focused on the dough that she didn't notice Sabine's approach until the woman was sitting right beside her on the mat.

"Rose," Sabine said. "There you are. Christoph was worried when we didn't see you at lunch."

Rose exchanged a glance with Sincere, who pointedly rose from her place peeling potatoes and took her bowl into the interior kitchen. "I was around."

"Well, we haven't been able to speak directly with anyone at the U.S. embassy in Kampala yet," Sabine said, "but my friend Rita is working on it. We left a message for Steve, too—he's Lily's stepfather—so he'll whip the media into a frenzy." Sabine smiled, though Rose saw it was pained. "I'm sorry that the search has to focus on Lily at this point. I'm confident, though, that when we find Lily, Ocen will be with her."

"Why do you say *when*?"

"Sometimes . . . the choice to believe is more powerful than the belief itself." Sabine paused. "And I choose to believe that if Lily and

Ocen found the rebels, Opiyo wouldn't hurt them. Ocen is still his brother."

Rose continued to knead the dough. For a moment she thought it would be better to say nothing; if Sabine wanted to hold on to this hope, however empty, then let her do so. But Rose had made this mistake with Ocen, hadn't she? Wasn't that lesson enough? And what did it matter now, if Sabine heard everything that Ocen should have known from the start?

"Opiyo . . ." Rose said. "He was that, once."

"He was what?"

"Kind."

A long pause. "You were taken together?"

"We were . . . promised to each other. The rebels found us kissing." She almost smiled to remember. "When we marched to Sudan, Opiyo took care of me. He brought me extra food and water. He made sure I was not cold. He gave me strips of cloth from his own shirt to protect my feet from sores, so that I would not fall behind." Her voice grew faint. "When we were forced to beat someone who was too slow, or who tried to escape, he met my eyes. He helped me not to cry. They kill you if you cry."

"I know what happens to abductees," Sabine said. "What they make you do."

"You know nothing," Rose said.

This time, Sabine remained silent.

"We were lucky," Rose said. "For two years we were kept together, in the same group. I was a *tingting*, caring for the children of one of the commanders. We were both given guns and trained to fight, but I stayed behind. Opiyo would leave for months at a time. It was dangerous for us to communicate, but he would find ways to give me small messages."

She began to roll pieces of the dough out on a flat stone.

"When I was fifteen, I was old enough to become a wife, and one of the commanders chose me. I was . . . innocent. I had never been with a man before. Perhaps it will surprise you. The rebels are very strict in this way. The men must stay pure, and the women—we belong to our husbands. If a man is caught with a commander's wife, the punishment for both is death.

"The night before the ceremony, Opiyo found me where I slept. He was careful to wake no one else. Together we went into the darkness. He was risking his life, he knew this." She felt tears dampen her cheeks, but she ignored them. "He was gentle with me. It was . . . a gift. So that on my wedding night I would not be afraid."

Before her, the rolled-out dough sat in a neat round pile. She had nowhere to put her hand.

"I met my husband the next day. I let him do what he needed. He did not suspect."

And nine months later, everything changed. Yes, Rose thought, she must tell this part, too: how her son was born and given a name she did not choose; how she gave him another name, a secret name. How Opiyo, in the face of this evidence that she belonged to another man, turned hard and mean, but because he could not defy the commander, it came out in other ways. How the mischievous streak that had been so charming when he was a boy now became ruthless. How he became a man without mercy. How she'd grieved to watch him drift further into the blackness, while she held her baby tightly against her breast and wished they could go back to how it was before.

But hope meant nothing. They could never go back.

"Rose?" Sabine's voice came floating in.

Rose gathered her words. As she opened her mouth, something caught her eye in the distance behind the building, across the clearing where the low grass crept right to a thick border of trees— a flicker of shadow, a movement so subtle she might have imagined it. A bird? A trick of the light?

In the same instant her skin was prickled by goose bumps and something in her chest dropped like a stone. The moment hung suspended. Her senses narrowed and the world became unnaturally bright, surreally sharp.

"Run," she whispered to Sabine.

"What?" Sabine tilted her head.

The first shots came from the opposite direction, near the administrative building; another burst followed from the trees toward the river. A flurry of shouts rose up from various points—the offices, the *Salle de Police,* the headquarters—and then more gunfire, originating in the clearing where Rose had seen the shadow. Within seconds Rose saw Garamba rangers hurrying to take position, running in low crouches with their rifles at the ready. Rose seized Sabine's hand. "Inside!"

Just on the other side of the door frame, she came face-to-face with Sincere, whose expression was panicked; the two Congolese cooks clutched each other behind her.

"What's happening?" Sincere asked. "Is it an attack?"

"The rebels are here," Rose said.

Sincere's hand flew to her heart. "The children," she breathed.

"Nicia is clever. She'll take Serge and hide."

"Christoph's at the office," Sabine said urgently. "If we can get to him—"

"It's too dangerous," Rose said. She glanced around the kitchen. "But here is not secure. Come."

The five women hurried into the dining room, where two rangers were running toward the main doors, their boots thumping heavily against the floor. As the first ranger exited, a quick succession of *pops* came from outside, and his body jolted then thumped onto the concrete steps. One of the Congolese cooks let out a wail, and the second ranger hit the ground in a crawl position. A round of bullets whizzed through the main door and splintered the table next to Rose. The two cooks retreated to the kitchen, but Sincere grabbed Rose's hand. "Here!" She led them toward a side room; coming in last, Sabine closed the door behind them and turned the lock. The three of them stood in the dimly lit space breathing heavily, listening. The room appeared to be a storage area, with batteries and blankets and mosquito nets and stools. High on the wall was a window open to the outside, through which gunfire and shouting echoed.

"Why would the LRA come here?" Sabine asked. "They know Nagero's protected."

"They attack when they need supplies," Rose said. "Food, fuel, equipment."

Sabine's face went pale. "The ivory. That shed—it was full of guns. If the rebels get to it . . ."

"I told him," Sincere said faintly. "I told him they had to move the stockpile, it wasn't safe. But there was never time. And where would they take it? There is nowhere."

They waited several minutes in silence. Rose tried to empty her mind, but she couldn't stop the assault of memories. Every bombardment, every ambush, every time she'd swept up her son and scrambled for cover; the first attack, the night of her abduction; and the last, in those final seconds before everything came apart. It was all happening again, right now—right in this room.

Sabine sniffed the air. "Do you smell that?"

In another second, Rose smelled it, too. Smoke.

"It's coming from the main room," Sabine said.

"This way." Sincere took them through a back door that led into an attached garage area, bereft of vehicles and open to the outside except for a tin roof. Sabine and Sincere pressed themselves against the wall while Rose glanced around for anywhere they could run. From here, the administrative offices lay several hundred meters diagonally to the left; in front of her and to the right lay an equally far-reaching meadow of patchy grass, with slim options for shelter until the start of the forest at the far borders. To the right, where Rose had seen the figure in the shadows at the start of the attack, a termite mound loomed—a possibility for a single person, but not for three. Straight ahead, a tractor was parked about thirty meters away underneath a tree. There was a large supply truck some twenty meters beyond that. Rose couldn't see any soldiers from her position; the shooting seemed to be coming from everywhere. The smoke was getting stronger by the second.

"Sabine! Rose!" A male voice carried from the direction of the supply truck.

"Christoph," Sabine whispered.

"First the tractor," Rose said. "Go! Now!"

There was a brief lull in the shooting, and the three made a dash for it. A spray of bullets clanged the metal frame of the tractor just as Sabine slipped in behind Rose and Sincere. After a moment's pause, they braved the second leg to the truck, where they found Christoph leaning in a half-sit against the truck's oversized tire. When he saw them he startled at first, then came forward, his face slack with relief. He took Sabine's face in his hands and kissed her forehead fiercely. "Thank God you're all right."

"Where's the warden?" Rose asked.

"He was with me in the office when the shooting started. He went right out with his men and ordered me to stay behind. But I—I couldn't. I tried to get to the main building where I knew you'd gone. This was as far as I got."

"You should have stayed," Sabine said, her eyes wet. "You should have stayed."

Next to the truck was a pile of cut lumber, a stack of tires, and a row of red and black metal barrels marked with the Shell logo and the word FLAMMABLE.

"It is not safe here," Rose said.

Christoph flinched as a bullet pinged a board in the lumber stack. "Where else can we go?"

Rose looked around. If they could make it into the forest, she thought, they'd be able to hide until the rebels retreated. The closest trees still stood some hundred meters away across a dusty clearing that was interrupted only by a small wooden shack at the far edge and the body of a Garamba ranger, sprawled in a lifeless heap. Where had he been running to? Which direction had the fatal shot come from? There didn't seem to be any crossfire now; all the shooting sounded like it was coming from the main building behind and the parade ground to the left.

"Straight ahead," Rose said. "Into the bush. We must run."

"We'll be exposed," Sabine said.

The passenger-side window of the truck shattered, and they all ducked.

"We're exposed here," Christoph said. "We can take cover at that lean-to."

Rose nodded. "Two people at a time."

"We'll go first." Christoph took tight hold of Sabine's hand.

Rose took a swift look left and right: she saw no one. She could only hope that no one saw them. "It's clear," she said.

Christoph kissed Sabine's forehead a second time.

They set off.

Rose watched them sprint, hand in hand. She counted the seconds.

One, two, three . . .

No gunfire yet.

Six, seven . . .

Halfway there.

Nine . . . ten . . .

Just a few more meters . . .

Twelve . . . thirteen . . .

An odd sort of moaning began to rise from Sincere just as Sabine and Christoph made it to the shack and disappeared from view. Unsettled, Rose turned to Sincere to check for wounds—had a stray bullet caught her side? The woman appeared to be unharmed, yet the groaning continued. Rose followed Sincere's gaze to the right, past the termite mound toward the trees beyond. Her heart quickened at the sight of a dozen figures at the edge of the forest: a line of rebels and, strung between them—

Children.

Five of them. Including one familiar shape, a slender girl . . .

Sincere's scream was a piercing, ragged thing. Before Rose could hold her back, Sincere was sprinting toward the slain ranger's body in the clearing. With surprising agility, she knelt at his side, unwound the rifle from his grip, and carried it as she raced headlong toward the line of rebels. Exactly what Sincere planned to do, Rose didn't know: if she started shooting from this distance, she was in danger of hitting her own daughter; if stealth was her aim, she was failing miserably. Yet Rose in that moment understood *why*. She understood that Sincere was not driven by strategy but by need.

She knew how this would end.

And still she watched as the woman, afire with motherly instinct, lessened the distance between herself and her daughter's captors. The seconds dragged on. The rebels and their prisoners continued weaving into the brush, as if nothing were amiss. Rose found herself suddenly lifted by hope: *she's going to make it. They haven't seen her. She's going to reach them and—*

A burst of gunfire rattled across the clearing, and Sincere crumpled into the low grass. She did not rise.

Rose looked again at the rebels and saw that one had deviated from the line and was now stalking toward Sincere's body, taking large steps in his black gumboots. Rose slammed herself back behind the lumber, pulse pounding. Had he seen her, too? No—he was too far. Surely too far. She squeezed her eyes shut. Don't think. Don't look.

She counted to thirty then peered around the edge of the lumber pile. The rebel was gone, and so were the others with the children. Now two bodies lay in the long meadow before the trees. Rose swallowed the scream that threatened to expel itself from her chest. She looked again both ways: clear. With a gulp of air she pushed off and began to run, counting backward.

Thirteen, twelve, eleven . . .

Don't think. Don't look.

Eight . . . seven . . .

The lean-to was just ahead—but where were Christoph and Sabine?

Four . . . three . . .

Fear bolted through her: had that rebel spotted them? Had he made it all the way here?

Two . . . one . . .

She swung around the shack and straight into Christoph's shoulder.

"Rose! We heard the shots . . ." He looked behind her; when no one followed, realization crossed his face. "*Merde.*"

"We can't go into the forest," Rose said. "The rebels are there. They are everywhere."

"Quick—inside," Christoph said. He jiggled the door of the little shack and shoved it open.

Yet Rose couldn't look away from the wall of foliage. The edge of the clearing stood so close now—almost, Rose thought, as if it were reaching out to her, inviting her to step across its boundary line. It seemed shimmery, like a veil to another world.

"Here," Sabine said, grabbing Rose's hand. "No one saw us come this way, right?"

Rose turned away from the trees. "No one saw."

Into the musky darkness they crawled.

Time seemed endless. The shack was cramped and dark and smelled of rotting wood, and the three of them were pressed against each other in tense silence. The sounds of battle raged around them, sometimes so close Rose could make out the words the rebels shouted—it was her language, after all, that they spoke. Other times, the sounds were muted and distant; it seemed that one side was getting pushed out.

With her eyes closed in the blackness, Rose thought of other things. The rhythmic scratching of a thatched broom across a dusty *dye-kal*; the smell of simmering stew; the peal of laughter in a schoolyard at break. Memories from before, when life was uncomplicated. Did that life exist for anyone, anywhere?

After a while, there was only quiet.

This, too, went on for an eternity. All was still.

Then the first bird of evening. Rose recognized its song from Kitgum: like water pouring from a bottle.

"How long do we wait?" Sabine whispered.

"I haven't heard movement in a while," Christoph said, though he, too, kept his voice barely above a breath. "It must be—"

At the sound of approaching voices, he halted.

They were speaking Acholi.

Despite the dimness, Rose could see the shapes of two figures as they came up to the shack and tried to peer in. They whispered back and forth.

"Is there more here? Can you see anything?"

"Eh, it's too dark."

Rose didn't dare to breathe. Sabine and Christoph were rigid beside her.

"I found the door."

The sound of scratching came through as they worked the latch.

"It's stuck."

"Let me."

There was no time. There was no escape.

The door opened.

Rose called out, *"An Rose Akulu, dako pa Lapwony."* Her voice was shaky but clear, and the rebels swiftly raised their rifles and shouted back—but did not shoot.

Rose repeated herself, slowly, to make sure they understood. The nearest soldier gestured to Sabine and Christoph, who remained crouched and quiet, and the second soldier swiveled his rifle in their direction.

"Pe!" Rose's voice cut shrilly through the space. "They must not be harmed. All of us come, or none of us."

The first rebel hesitated, then nodded slowly. The second trudged forward and prodded Sabine and Christoph to standing. They both kept their hands behind their heads as they stumbled forward through the open door, the soldier's bayonet nudging them onward. Rose followed, and the second soldier came behind her after making a quick sweep of the room.

Outside, the main headquarters building was ablaze and the sky flashed crimson and orange in the last streaks of sunset. The battle wasn't over—Rose could still hear scattered gunfire from the direction of the main road—but the parade ground and surrounding infrastructure appeared to have been secured by LRA. The bodies of rangers and rebels lay where they'd fallen. Rose blinked away tears at the sight of Sincere, unmoving, her blood darkening the earth beneath.

All around, rebels looted supplies: Rose saw jerry cans, sacks of food, and barrels of fuel spirited away into the trees where Nicia had been taken earlier. Far across the parade ground the door to the brick storage shed was open, and Rose could make out tusks being passed out along a line of soldiers.

Nearby, two rebels stood behind a hut, and Rose and the other prisoners were shuffled over and made to sit.

"What's going on?" Christoph said urgently. "Rose, what did you say back there?"

"I told them who I am."

"I don't understand," Sabine whispered. "You recognize these men from before?"

Rose glanced around at the faces of the rebels who stood guard. No one looked familiar, but in the growing darkness it was difficult to tell. Still she felt their stares boring into her, their wary eyes.

"No," she said. "But they know me."

"Why would they know you?" Sabine pressed.

Rose looked back across the parade ground at the bodies of those who would never rise again. *He* had done this. *He* had wrought this hell.

"Because," she said, "I was Joseph Kony's wife."

***

Again I looked and saw all the oppression that was
    taking place under the sun:
I saw the tears of the oppressed—and they have no
    comforter;
power was on the side of the oppressors—and they have
    no comforter.
And I declared that the dead, who had already died,
    are happier than the living, who are still alive.
    But better than both is the one who has never been
    born,
who has not seen the evil that is done under the sun.

Ecclesiastes 4: 1–3

PART III
THE DEAD

CHAPTER 23

SABINE

January 2

After they were taken at Nagero, they marched through the night without food or rest. The rebels carried flashlights, which they swung around at sporadic intervals in a dancing sea of lights; at other times Sabine had to stay almost on top of the boy in front of her in order not to lose the trail in the darkness. Their hands were left unbound so that they could carry supplies. Even Rose had been given a jerry can full of cooking oil, which she balanced atop her head and steadied with her hand. Christoph and Sabine carried two enormous elephant tusks between them, Sabine in front and Christoph a few paces behind; they bore the ivory on their shoulders like the poles of a royal litter or gripped the tusks in their hands to give their shoulders a break. No matter how she shifted the weight, her skin chafed raw around her neck and on her palms, and her muscles ached beyond the point of trembling. Her feet stumbled forward mechanically through brush and mud; she hardly saw where she stepped, focused only on staying upright and awake. She had no sense of direction, and when, during a few minutes' pause at dawn, Christoph murmured that he'd been paying attention to the position of the moon and stars and thought they were headed north, it took all her strength just to nod. Then a guard shouted for the convoy to continue, and she silently took the narrow ends of the tusks and waited for Christoph to take the bases so they could lift the load into the air together.

Even in daylight it was difficult to get a sense of how many they were: they walked in a long line, one after the other, so Sabine mostly saw the captives around her—they were perhaps a dozen altogether, including a girl whom Rose seemed particularly protective toward—and various soldiers who passed periodically to keep an eye on them. The rebels spoke little and never smiled. Dressed in loose-fitting combinations of green- and camouflage-patterned fatigues and black and brown gumboots, they carried an array of weapons. Sabine recognized AK-47s and rocket-propelled grenade launchers, but others were mysterious to her, and therefore even more frightening. Some of the soldiers wore shoulder belts of glinting bullets. All handled their firearms expertly, even when the weapon was almost as big as the boy who wielded it.

The way was hard going, and collectively they were slower than when it had just been the three of them following the river to Nagero. There were other differences, of course, too: then, she'd had the sense of moving toward something—refuge, shelter, answers. Now all that was behind them, and the way ahead was immeasurable and bleak. Even when the sky arced crisply above, a pure blue pebbled by shadows of trees or a flock of startled birds, Sabine saw the peril of brightness, and she swayed in the drowsiness of heat. She felt between worlds: presumed dead, probably, by Daniela and Linda and Rita and Steve, but alive enough to suffer. Every now and then she'd hear Christoph's voice drift up softly, asking if she was all right; the question made no sense, she thought—how could anything be all right?—but still she murmured an affirmative, because his continued presence was the only comfort she had.

She was too exhausted to be truly frightened, yet fear was the only thing that kept her lurching forward, step by fumbling step. In her half-awake, half-dreaming state, she sometimes thought she might wake up and be in her bed in Marburg, ready to take Bruno down to the frozen River Lahn, where she'd watch a man in black

waders rescue a swan stuck in the ice. In this vague fantasy, the man—
who became Christoph—waited afterward on the opposite shore, and
they struck up a conversation, met the next day for coffee; they became lovers, and he showed her his grandfather's handmade wooden
chest and gave her a bird in a cage for her birthday. This gift, though,
she couldn't abide, so she fled to Uganda in the blurry way of day-
dreams, and from Uganda she was sucked into a current that pulled
her west across the border, and with a rush she blinked and was here
again, or here still: trudging onward through the tall grass and the
undergrowth. Even her reveries always led back.

The second night, they finally slept. Christoph flattened some grass
and cleared small stones from the ground for the two of them, and
Sabine collapsed into a dreamless sleep. In the morning the captives
shared a pot of overcooked rice, and between the food and rest, Sabine felt almost superhumanly refreshed. She began to think with
greater clarity. She knew they'd been half an instant away from death
in the shack at Nagero, saved only by Rose's quick words and the
rebels' grudging acquiescence. It was quite possible that whenever they
got where they were going—wherever that was—the rebels would
revert to their original intention. In the meantime, rescue was a profound improbability, and if the group came under fire by UPDF or
FARDC, Sabine and Christoph and Rose were just as likely to be
killed by indiscriminate bombing or shooting as they were to emerge
unscathed. No: they would have to escape. That was the only way out.

Yet this, too, was preposterous. Even if they managed to slip away
unnoticed, untracked, where would they run? The wilderness around
them was vast. They had nothing with which to communicate with
the outside world, nor supplies of any kind, nor anything with which
they might protect themselves against weather or injury or predators.

The only choice was no choice: to keep on, to keep up. To lift, to
carry, to bear. To relish in the briefest respite and hope for another
minute's rest before the march began again.

On the fourth dawn, Sabine was wary when, after the now-standard pot of rice, the rebels herded the captives into a small area under a copse of trees that was shaded from the sun and any military reconnaissance missions that might pass overhead. A single soldier was posted at their periphery. As concerned as she was for this change in routine, she was also grateful for the break, particularly because Christoph had fallen ill the evening before—fever and nausea—and Sabine suspected malaria. His breathing was shallow as he lay back and rested his head in Sabine's lap. She stroked his forehead and noted the hair that stuck to his skin. Rose sat nearby with her legs folded to the side; her hand lay between her thighs, and her expression was vacant. The young girl, Nicia, sat a few feet away with her knees up against her chest and her face buried between them.

It was the first time Sabine had been allowed so close to Rose since that first night. *Joseph Kony's wife*. One of how many—fifty? Sixty? Sabine couldn't remember the figure.

"Rose, do you know why we stopped?" Sabine whispered.

"I do not know."

Christoph managed to get up onto his elbows. "Will we camp here?"

"I do not know."

The arrival of a new figure at the edge near the guard pulled Sabine's attention away. The man was dressed like a rebel but looked significantly older than the boy soldiers she'd seen—he might be middle-aged, she thought—and instead of a gun, he carried a duffel bag in his right hand and wore a backpack. Sabine looked back at Rose and thought she saw a flicker of emotion cross the woman's face.

"Do you recognize him?"

"He is a doctor."

The man caught sight of Rose and nodded subtly.

"Is he a good man?" Sabine said under her breath.

"He is a good man." As he began in their direction, she added, "But he is one of them."

He squatted before Rose and took her hand, and they spoke quietly in Acholi, him looking down and she away. Sabine watched him closely, curious at the familiarity with which they spoke. No other rebels had addressed Rose directly since that first encounter. The soldiers had no problem prodding other captives with their rifles, but Rose they only watched vigilantly with chary eyes, maintaining a few meters' distance at all times.

Now the doctor brought his fingertips toward Rose's scarred shoulder and they hovered just above the skin, as if absorbing its story through the air. After a few seconds he enclosed her hand in both of his, said a final word, and turned to Sabine.

"I am Lieutenant Benson Ochola. I'm a medic with the Movement. I'm sorry I couldn't check on you earlier. I've been busy with our injured soldiers." His speech bore traces of a British accent, a surreal collapse of worlds. Sabine noted his use of the term *Movement* instead of *LRA*; she remembered that this was how the rebels sometimes referred to themselves, that they'd once been the Lord's Resistance Movement rather than the Lord's Resistance Army. He continued, "Are there any wounded among you?"

"Not as far as I know," Sabine said. "But"—she gestured to Christoph—"he's got a bad fever and he shook all night with chills. I think it's malaria."

Leaning forward, Benson reached for Christoph's forehead, but Christoph jerked away, weak as he was. "Don't touch me."

Benson took no offense. "As you like. I'm afraid I don't have any antimalarial medication with me anyway."

"None at all?" Sabine asked. "Not even from Nagero?"

"We didn't make it as far as the clinic. Shame, because I'm nearly out of everything—bandages, antibiotics, ARVs . . . I do what I can, but with so few supplies, that usually means very little. Hopefully the other unit will have had better luck in Faradje."

"Other unit?" Christoph asked.

"We'll meet up with them tomorrow, I think."

"And then?"

"I expect we'll stay put for a little while. We'll be across the border by then."

"In Sudan, you mean," Sabine said.

"Central African Republic."

His openness surprised her, and she decided to take advantage of it. "Do you know anything about an American girl being taken captive?" she asked. "Lily Bennett is her name. Her journal was found in an abandoned LRA camp in Garamba last week. She's my niece."

Benson shook his head. "I'm sorry, I haven't heard. We've been scattered since the UPDF strike began. We've spoken with other units but only to learn where they are, how many casualties, where the enemy last attacked. We were spread out before the strike, too. The unit we're meeting tomorrow—I haven't seen them in six weeks."

"What will happen to us when we get there?" Christoph asked.

He shook his head. "That, I do not have the answer to." Gently, he added, "And perhaps it is better not to ask."

He moved on to the other captives, examining each in turn. The minutes stretched into a quarter hour, then a half, then Sabine couldn't tell anymore. Christoph's head was heavy in her lap, his skin hot to the touch. He began to doze. Tiny white and yellow butterflies rose and disappeared in the grass at the edge of the glade. Rose and Nicia napped side by side. After so much marching, it felt luxurious just to sit for a while in daylight. She watched Benson wrap a girl's feet in banana leaves so that she would no longer have to walk barefoot.

"Benson," she said, "why has the group stopped?"

He checked to make sure the leaves would hold, then came to sit beside Sabine, wiping his hands on a cloth. "The soldiers are hunting."

His words seemed ominous. "Hunting for what?"

"Food."

"Nothing else?"

Benson gave a pointed glance at the elephant tusks that lay in a haphazard pile at the base of one of the trees. "They may seek other objects of value as well."

"Is that why you attacked Nagero? For the ivory?"

"Yes."

"There were weapons in that shed, too."

He nodded. "The Movement has financial backers, but the UPDF strike has created something of an urgent need."

"Aren't you afraid of reprisals by the rangers?"

"We destroyed their radio room, their towers, their communication equipment."

After a pause, she asked, "Why are you telling me all this?"

"Why not?"

"You're not afraid of giving away military secrets?"

He appraised her. "And who do you plan to tell?"

They sat quietly. In the distance she heard the faint sound of gunfire, then a second burst, and a third. Then quiet again. The soldier standing watch scratched his chin with the butt of his rifle. Benson picked a blade of grass and rubbed it between his thumb and middle finger.

Sabine looked down at Christoph's face, his brow wrinkled and the muscles of his jaw tensed even in sleep. Beads of perspiration glistened at his temples. His fever was getting worse.

"How much farther will we have to walk until we reach the other unit?" she asked.

"Not far."

"I don't know how much more he can take."

"I will try to find some fresh fruit for him to eat. That will help. And then, let us pray that the other unit has had success with medicine." He called to the guard, who wiped his nose and spoke a few words in response. "He says there may be pineapple and passion fruit. I will find out. Unfortunately it is not the season for fruit."

The guard spoke again, and Benson smiled, this time with a trace of humor.

"What did he say?" Sabine asked.

"He said you're a good wife, looking after your husband."

Sabine opened her mouth to object, but found herself hesitating;

a warmth crept up her chest and she thought, *What harm to let them believe?*

"Have you been with the rebels a long time?" she asked.

"Thirteen years."

"You were abducted?"

"From my ancestral home outside Gulu. I was only home for a short visit. I was in my third year studying medicine in London, on a scholarship. The commander who took me was quite pleased. There's a shortage of doctors, you see."

She lowered her voice, flicked a glance at the guard. "You must have wanted to escape."

"At the beginning, of course. But I saw how much they needed me. There was . . . so much suffering."

"Surely you don't support the cause—the things they've done to children, to innocent civilians."

The question seemed to trouble him, and he waited a long time before responding. "It is a privilege to heal," he said at last. "Are the soldiers here less deserving than you? Than me? Most of them did not choose this life." Softly he added, "We are all far from home."

The hunting party returned shortly thereafter, with fresh tusks thrown onto the pile, smeared with blood and clotted dirt. Some were so small she wondered if a larger piece had broken in two, but the shapes were whole, from hollow base to rounded point. Young elephants. Calves. Farther into the bush she caught a glimpse of two rebels carrying some kind of gazelle or antelope on poles between them. Her stomach rumbled at the thought of fresh meat.

"I must return to sick bay," Benson said, standing and reaching for his bags. "They'll need me when they start to move the gurneys." He paused just before he left. "I'll check on him when we reach the camp tomorrow."

"Thank you."

Christoph and Rose roused, and the convoy was soon under way. Though he was clearly struggling, Christoph bore his share of the ivory without complaint. At sunset they stopped again, this time for the night, and Christoph passed directly into a fitful sleep. They had no blankets; Sabine wrapped her body around his to try to keep him warm. She thought of the night they'd spent together at Nagero, that incredible collision of passions, the sweat-slick skin, all that was unspoken. It had felt as though through this holy act they were staking a claim, planting a flag in the ground for aliveness, for hope. As she pressed herself against him now, feeling his body racked with chills through the fabric of their clothing, she thought: maybe that's all we get. A single instance of fusion, a single collapse of two into one— and when they extracted themselves from one another afterward, something new was created between them that had not been there before. A thing in which each of them had left a part of themselves.

This was what they meant, she realized. All of them. When they spoke of love.

Amid the insect symphony that surrounded them, Sabine heard another, eerier call, lower and longer and rumbling across the savannah and into the trees: trumpeting.

Some of the herd had survived.

She fell asleep to the sounds of their grief.

A rustling woke her in the night. She lay still for several minutes, listening to the forest sounds, letting her eyes adjust. The dark was nearly total; starlight and the crescent moon provided only enough light to make out the shapes of a dozen slumbering bodies around the clearing and the start of brush at the edge. Christoph slept deeply beside her. Nothing moved. Nearby she could make out the outline of a rebel's long rifle. The boy it belonged to breathed slowly and rhythmically. Even the seasoned soldiers had been pushed hard.

She had a sudden need to relieve her bladder. Moving cautiously, she rose and treaded a little ways into the undergrowth, then undid her jeans and squatted to pee, a handful of soft leaves in her hand.

Her senses became sharp and alert; who knew what lurked in wait? She'd heard stories of LRA captives getting picked off by lions on their marches through the bush. Just within her field of vision, the pile of stolen tusks gleamed against the dark foliage.

The rustling came again—closer this time, and matched with a gentle kind of creaking. Charged with electric fear, Sabine fumbled with her jeans zipper as an enormous shape loomed out of the far shadows. She froze.

The elephant didn't seem to notice her as it approached the tusks. It must have smelled her, she thought, but perhaps to the elephant Sabine was simply part of the larger human element. She was mesmerized by how carefully the creature moved through the brush: astonishingly silent for its massive size, its heavy sway. Only the crack of sticks beneath its feet and the brush of leaves against its hide sounded its position.

Sabine remained in a half crouch just a few meters away. She'd never been this close to an elephant before—not even when she watched the stampede from the Jeep all those years ago—and the thrill and danger rippled through her body. She was near enough to hear its heavy breathing punctuated by soft, chuffy snorts. The silhouette of its long, supple trunk lifted up and forward in a graceful S, probing the stack—feeling, searching. The elephant paused over the miniature tusk of a calf, and Sabine felt a world of sadness open up inside her.

After another moment, the great creature turned and melted back into the blackness, and Sabine returned shakily to her place beside Christoph, hoping that when she closed her eyes, a different dream would come.

In the morning, Sabine noticed large, circular indentations in the earth around the ivory, but there were no looming shapes in the brush nor trumpets in the distance. She turned her focus to Christoph, who had descended into a kind of hallucinatory state: his fever had risen again, and he mumbled incoherently with his eyes fluttering behind closed lids. Sabine wondered what visions he saw there, whether he glided on ice skates, squeezing a smaller hand than hers. When Benson came by with a quarter pineapple—which Christoph wasn't conscious enough to eat—Sabine gripped the doctor's elbow.

"He can't walk like this," she said.

"He won't have to. We received word this morning to stay where we are. The other unit is meeting us here."

"Thank God. How soon?"

"Soon."

A thought came to her, and she checked to make sure Rose wasn't within hearing distance. "Benson, do you know a soldier named Opiyo? He would be in his early twenties, I think."

His gaze was steady and gave nothing away. "Rose's friend?"

"They were abducted together. Many years ago."

"I know him."

Sabine lowered her voice. "Will he be there today?"

"The last I heard he was somewhere far, perhaps Sudan."

She wasn't sure if it was disappointment or relief that she felt, and Benson's expression stayed carefully neutral.

"He is Kony's aide-de-camp, you know. His personal envoy."

She realized the implication in Benson's statement: that if Lily and Ocen had managed to find Opiyo, they would have met the rebel leader himself. Her skin went clammy, and she swallowed a surge of nausea.

"Come," Benson said. "I'll show you where to get water. You'll need to keep your husband hydrated."

Stay present, she told herself firmly. *Christoph needs you now.* She asked Rose to look after Christoph for a moment then followed the doctor through the brush. It was the first time she'd really seen the layout of the unit. Strange, how small it was—she estimated no more than twenty soldiers, some building shelters with tarps, others organizing supplies. She saw two boys swinging *pangas* at tree trunks. The notches, she realized, formed a kind of ladder. Lookout stations. She recognized the two rebels who'd found them in the shack—her skin crawled at the hard stare the taller one gave her as she passed.

Benson led her to a creek that had been dammed up with a plastic sheet set with rocks. He dipped a jerry can into the slow-swirling pool and let it fill.

"He'll die, won't he?" she said quietly. "If the other unit doesn't have medication."

Benson lifted his head and handed her the jerry can. It was heavier than she'd expected.

"I'm afraid that is the most likely outcome, yes."

She nodded, mute, trying to blink back the tears that blurred her vision.

He considered a moment, then gently took the water jug back from her. A few drops splattered her wrist. "Here, let me."

She heard some commotion behind them and turned to see more rebels stepping out from the tall grass, their faces as sober and un-yielding as those that greeted them.

"The other group is arriving," Benson said. "I should find their medic."

Sabine had a jolt of fear for Christoph's safety; what if the new commander saw no use in a gravely ill prisoner? Rose alone might not be able to protect him. Sabine wouldn't be any greater defense, but she knew she had to be there, to put herself between Christoph and any threat, physically if necessary.

"I have to be with him," she said over her shoulder, leaving Benson and the water jug at the little pool. The new rebels were already inte-grating into the camp. As she hurried between tarps and cooking fires, Sabine was surprised to see women and children walking freely—some of the women even carried guns. Soldiers' wives, she realized: families. She saw one woman with a rifle slung across her chest and a baby tied to her back.

A moment later Sabine emerged from the thicket into the small clearing where the captives were gathered. Her heart pounded to see three new soldiers here, too, but they appeared to be ushering more prisoners into the circle, not attending to those who were already there. The number of new captives was astonishing. There had to be dozens, and more appeared every second from the surrounding foliage: skinny children with torn clothes and grave faces. Sabine saw Rose kneeling by Christoph's side, and she hastened over.

"He is bad," Rose murmured.

"The doctor will ask about medicine," Sabine said under her breath. "But we can't let them see how sick he is." She cast furtive glances about the clearing, studying the newly appeared rebels for signs of menace. "If they think he's too much of a burden, they might . . ."

She stopped. Her voice: gone. The arrivals had parted—briefly and casually, in the normal course of being shuffled about—and she'd seen . . . What had she seen?

A vision. Her younger self: dark haired and uncertain, in dirty jeans and a dark T-shirt. Precisely how she must have looked that morning in Lalibela when the men confronted her outside her tent, a memory that came back to her with astounding lucidity. The ghostly girl's pale expression had been an exact reflection of her own twenty-two-year-old fear dimly seen behind a curtain of false bravery. How vivid and strange it was! She gave her head a little shake; was she feverish? She touched the back of her fingers to the underside of her jaw. Craning her neck, she looked again. The crowd opened.

It was no vision.

"Lily," she whispered, the ground tilting, her hands grasping—fumbling; she heard her own voice, as if from far away, echoing, "Lily!"

Her younger self looked up; their eyes met. Everything else fell away.

The force with which their bodies came together—Sabine could not wrap her arms hard enough, or tightly enough; she pressed Lily's head against her chest, pressed her mouth against Lily's hair, smelled the sweat and oil and a faint trace of soap; her fingers clutched at Lily's body, her shoulder and arm and the narrow waist—real, real, all real, flesh and muscle and bone. Both of them were crying. Sabine felt the shudders of Lily's sobs, and the wetness that seeped through to Sabine's collarbone. She couldn't stop saying her name, "Lily, Lily . . ."

"I have to sit down," Lily said, half gasping. "I'm—oh, God." She crumpled out of Sabine's embrace and sat in a broken heap on the ground, choked for breath, ruddy cheeks and puffy eyes, grimacing in pain.

"What is it? Talk to me. What did they do to you?" She was seized with horror—*a pretty* mzungu *girl, a prize*—but then she saw Lily clutching her foot. Her ankle was bound in a crude splint made of two semiflat pieces of wood cinched with torn cloth around the lower calf and under the heel. She wore no shoe, and her ankle was swollen to the size of a grapefruit. Slowly the rest of the world came trickling back to Sabine: where they were. How they came to be here. How far away from safe. Sabine knelt. "Is it broken?"

"I don't think so," Lily said. Her hair fell in greasy tangles across her face. "It must just be a bad sprain. But I've been walking on it for days, there's no ice or anything."

"There's a doctor here. Benson. He'll figure something out." Hushed, she added, "Is there anywhere else they hurt you?"

Lily shook her head, and the relief Sabine felt made her lose her breath in gratitude.

Lily noticed Christoph's prone figure. "Christoph! Why is he here? Oh my God, is he—?"

"Malaria." She squeezed her niece's thin shoulder. "But he's alive. We're all alive. And now we're together."

Tears made clean passage down Lily's earth-streaked cheeks. "I'm sorry," she said, hiccuping into a sob. "I was so selfish. I can't believe I thought—I'm so sorry. I'm so sorry . . ."

"Shh." She held Lily's face to her chest again, this time softly, as if cradling a baby. Sabine's eyes—stinging and wet—lifted, and she blinked into the sky, so piercing sweet above them. When she looked levelly again, across the clearing, she saw him.

That face.

Like he'd walked right off the page and into this day.

CHAPTER 24

ROSE

January 7

At first Rose didn't understand what she was seeing. There was Lily, just as she remembered the American girl—though more ragged now, her body held at sharper angles—and the tearful reunion between aunt and niece. Rose watched their embrace as if through a veil. Their emotion was profound and palpable, and yet Rose felt nothing, no stirring inside her chest.

She had made up her mind the first night: she was already dead. Nothing could move her.

But then Sabine's face had lifted, a shadow crossed it, and Rose followed her eyes to the figure that had just emerged from the grass. Broad shoulders and a familiar red T-shirt and dark jacket and— there, a glint of copper around the wrist. His lip was cut and his cheek bruised, and when he saw her, his eyes became wide and full. She stood up, swayed; tried to take a step forward but couldn't—her knees buckled and she was crouched, her hand on the ground, her breath gone. She found his face again. *Ocen.*

He rushed toward her, but in an instant two soldiers leapt in front of him, rifles aimed, one shouting in Acholi, "Stop where you are! Stay back!"

Palms raised, he halted, surrendering, though Rose could see his confusion and desperation. He sank to his knees. They looked at each other across the space. The air felt as impenetrable as stone. She witnessed Lily and Sabine next to her, holding onto one another. The distance between Rose and Ocen was a thousand miles.

"It is you," he said softly.

Just to see him alive—a kind of lightness had entered her heart. She thought: *now I can die, because I have seen his face again.*

"Did you find him?" she asked. "Is he here?" There was no need to say his name; they both knew whom she meant.

He shook his head once, shortly. "They have told me nothing." Without drifting from her gaze, he spoke to one of the rebels who stood between them. "Let me go to her. Please."

But the guard's tongue was sharp. "She belongs to Kony. She is one of his."

Ocen's eyes never left hers, though she wished they had, so that she would not have to see the shock there. He said nothing, asked no questions—but the question didn't need to be said aloud. Neither did her answer.

She didn't know how long they sat like that, unspeaking, the few meters between them stretched into an entire country, a landscape for which there was no map. Her neck ached from the weight of the jerry can, but there were other, greater aches that consumed her. Vaguely she sensed things happening around them. The rest of the captives settled in, cautious not to breach the invisible territory that at once connected the silent pair and kept them apart. An atlas of lies, of loss, of love, of all the things they could not say, all the futures that were not theirs to hope for. Benson appeared with a jerry can of water and a packet of tablets that he administered to Christoph, who remained unconscious. Sabine and Lily spoke to one another in urgent, hushed voices, talking over one another, filling in the gaps of their journeys. Nicia, Sincere's daughter, was there as well, watching on silently. Rose saw and heard everything, and she saw and heard nothing at all, nothing but his face, his breath. Eventually the rebels decided they could let down their rifles, that Ocen understood the rules.

At last she broke the quiet. "I lied to you."

"Not only about Opiyo." His voice was strained, and he looked away. "But I understand."

She kept her hand as still as a stone, though it wanted to be a bird, aching to fly toward him. "I kept secrets."

His eyes glistened. A muscle in his neck strained. "I chose not to ask. There were things I didn't want to know."

"I had a son," she said.

"You forget: I have seen the scars."

The gentleness in his tone felt like an offering, and she clung to it gratefully. Though they stayed rooted to their places at opposite ends of this dangerous, uncharted topography, the words that traveled between them began to find safe passage. She explained how Sabine and Christoph and she had come together to find them, the clues that had led them to Arua and Lakwali, the bus crash at Faradje, the attack at Nagero.

"We were with the unit at Faradje," Ocen said. "They kept us hidden in a storeroom. They'd killed the farmer and his family who lived there."

His face was so haunted. The things he would have seen.

"But why?" she asked. "What made you think you would reach him?"

Ocen glanced over to where Lily and Sabine had moved, a dozen meters across the clearing; together they ministered to Christoph. It didn't matter anyway if they were within hearing distance; they couldn't understand Acholi. "Lily's conviction was . . . contagious. She made me believe." He paused. "I wanted to believe."

Slowly, carefully, as if uncoiling a length of rope, Ocen described the events of the previous months, casting all the way back to July, when he first became Lily's regular *boda*. She was eager and earnest, he said, and kind. After a while it became easy for him to talk about his experiences of the war, the death of his parents, and the abduction of his twin. She had lost her mother, too, and in a way shared some part of his grief. Rose listened to him speaking, his low and rhythmic voice, and burned with jealousy for the closeness he'd shared with the American girl. But she did not interrupt.

He said that Lily first learned Opiyo was still alive at the end of October, when Miriam and the other former abductees came to the rehabilitation center. Lily recognized Opiyo's name and told Ocen at once.

"That was the night you never came," Rose said.

"I was angry. And confused."

Shame made her look down.

He went on, explaining how Lily came up with the plan to rescue Opiyo; he would never have thought it possible, but she was convinced that her whiteness would be a shield. She went over and over the story of the Italian nun and Ugandan schoolteacher who rescued a hundred girls kidnapped at Aboke. Miriam gave precise descriptions of the secret LRA camps in and around Garamba, sharing details with Lily that she hadn't told the UPDF during her interrogations. Lily cross-referenced everything with Google maps and the old atlas at the National Memory and Peace Documentation Centre. And at the end of the day, Lily told Ocen, if they got themselves within a close enough radius, the rebels would be just as likely to find them first.

But there was something else.

"Juba," Ocen said.

"The peace talks," Rose murmured.

"Yes. Lily was following the negotiations very closely. There was still some hope that a deal would be reached. The government had come up with an agreement that would offer amnesty to all rebels not included in the International Criminal Court indictments. If Kony signed, Opiyo would return home. He would be free."

"But Kony did not show," Rose said, remembering. "When the team went to the assembly point at Ri-Kwangba. They waited for him for two days, but he never came."

"We heard the news on the last day of November. The government had repeatedly said that it was the LRA's last chance for peace. There were rumors circulating that Museveni had already put together a plan B, and he would act quickly."

"Operation Lightning Thunder."

"We didn't know how quickly. Lily was leaving Uganda in three weeks. There was no time."

They were meticulous in their preparations, he said. No one could know. Not Lily's family, not the expats in Kitgum. Not Rose.

"When I knew you had left together, I thought there was something else between you," Rose said.

Ocen looked down. "A part of me wanted you to think that."

His bracelet caught the light. It was late afternoon now; evening would fall soon.

"Paddy told me that you had ideas about money," Rose said. "I took this to mean that Lily was paying you for your assistance, the way I earned from Christoph."

"Lily gave me enough to purchase the *boda*, so that we could travel without worry. I planned to sell it again when I returned to Kitgum, so that I could help my cousin."

She forced herself to ask: "You had no plans for a dowry?"

For a long time Ocen was quiet, and Rose wondered if this was meant as a kindness. Maybe it was better not to hear it aloud. His posture flagged. When he finally spoke, his voice was pained. "If I did not return, it wouldn't matter. And if I did, it would only be with Opiyo." He hesitated. "I thought you would choose him. You had always chosen him."

She saw them both before her: the smiling twin and the shy twin; blessed by *jogi*, two halves of one whole. Her love for one felt impossibly interlinked with her love for the other. Opiyo's cunning; Ocen's gentleness. Both had saved her. The boy who kissed her by the river and stole rations so that she would not starve; the man who took her back, who tethered her to earth when she watched the airplanes rise and disappear into the boundless blue. Ocen could not have given her what Opiyo had: as a boy he'd been too sensitive, so easily swayed. But Opiyo couldn't accept her once she'd belonged to another. If it had been him waiting in Kitgum, he would have cast her aside. Ocen forgave.

"I choose you," she said.

Even as she said it, she knew it was too late, and in Ocen's eyes, she saw that he knew, too. There was no afterward, there was no more choice. Their future lay among the rebels; their fate would be chosen for them.

"Your son," Ocen said. "What was his name?"

She thought of the name Kony had given the boy, a name that meant nothing, just a collection of letters, strange syllables. Her child had worn the name like a costume that didn't fit. His secret name— the one she'd heard as clearly as if a bell had been rung the first instant he'd come into the world, when she held him to her breast while bombs began to fall—that was the name that meant everything.

"Adenya," she said.

A smile crossed Ocen's face, authentic and unfiltered and too brief. "Adenya," he echoed.

Rose felt the looming presence of a guard overhead.

"Get up," the guard said. "Follow me."

Ocen's eyes became wide and worried. "Where are you taking her? Why can't she stay? I gave my word not to approach!"

"She must be kept separate."

Rose stood stiffly as Sabine and Lily came over, the girl hobbling on her injured foot.

"What's happening, Rose?" Sabine asked. "What's he saying?"

"Separate," the guard said in English.

"But why?" Sabine said. "She's been with us for days."

The guard shrugged. "He made the order."

"Who?" Lily pressed.

"The chairman." The guard's expression didn't change. "He arrives tomorrow."

Familiar words skipped among the assembled: *Lapwony is coming,* the soldiers said, *Baba will be here.* The names the man had chosen for himself were generous: teacher, father.

"The chairman . . . ?" Lily glanced at Ocen.

"Kony," he said.

Rose saw the horrified faces of Lily and Sabine; she sensed Ocen watching her as the young rebel led her away into the trees. But she did not speak. She felt peaceful and calm. She kept thinking of Ocen's smile, the way he said her son's name—the shape of the word, from his mouth: it sounded like prayer.

She heard the whispers pass by and around her all evening and into the night.

Baba Kony is coming here. Where shall he sleep? The old Mbororo hut, the one we used last time, are the walls still intact? Maybe the Sudanese are with him, to collect the ivory . . . Will they take supplies from Khartoum? I used six magazines at Nagero, now I have only four left! Eh, six magazines! The battle was not so long . . . I used only three. How many wives are with him? What about this one here?

There were stories that Kony had sixty wives or more, but Rose knew the number was much smaller than that—a dozen at most. He had chosen each one with care. When he selected Rose from the other girls, he'd touched her cheek with his thumb and said, "Don't be afraid. God has many plans for you."

Eh, this one, a guard said. *He will decide when he arrives.*

Is he with the large group? one asked. *With one hundred more fighters, we will be strong.*

Eh, the large group comes later, another replied. *Now Lapwony comes with his personal escort only.*

The High Protection Unit, the other said with awe.

Then they spoke of Kony's bodyguards, their bravery, the way they would spread out like a spiderweb around their leader, alert to any danger: the slightest threat at one side would cause the whole web to shift. Kony was always in the middle, unreachable. The UPDF would never reach him by ground, the soldiers bragged among themselves, and an aerial assault would never take them by surprise.

Rose ignored all that was said. She sat where she'd been brought, beneath a makeshift shelter of broken branches and fallen palm fronds and two green plastic tarps; she ate from the pot placed before her, though she could not taste the food. Something had caught fire inside her: a minuscule spark, grown to a smolder. The longer she sat—the darker the night became, the colder the wind—the closer she cupped her thoughts around this tiny flame, fanning it with the breath of possibility. She knew what she had to do. It was the only way to be free. She saw this now: clear as rain.

She just had to wait for the right moment, and she could be with her son again. In the last pure place.

Sometime in the night she heard rustling outside the shelter. The beam of a flashlight bobbed at her feet and then shone directly in her face. Blinded, she squinted and shielded her eyes. The beam lowered again to the ground, and she blinked away the blackness.

For a few seconds all she could make out was a looming figure crouched before her. Slowly her eyes adjusted, and she took in the military fatigues, the black gumboots, the rifle. The man rose to standing and turned his back before she could see his face—but she'd already recognized the breadth of his shoulders, the bones of his wrists, the sound of his breathing.

"*Apwoyo,* Opiyo."

He halted a few feet away, his back to her, saying nothing.

"Will you speak?" she said.

He'd kept the flashlight on and aimed low, so that the ambient brightness showed the stiff folds of the tarp that shielded them on three sides. From beyond the shelter she heard the muted sounds of a guerilla camp at night: hushed voices, the crack of twigs, sporadic insect song.

"Please," she said.

Still he did not turn. His voice was cold. "He will see you tomorrow."

"Is that all you came to tell me?"

"I had to check to make sure it was you. I did not believe Lieutenant Ochola."

"Now do you believe?"

He snapped around. "What is Ocen doing here? Why did you bring him?"

In the dimness his features were indistinguishable from his brother's, and she was taken aback; in her mind he hadn't aged, he was the same as the last time she'd seen him, four years before. This was the boy who'd kissed her among the maize fields. The boy who bound her feet with banana leaves. The man who led her into womanhood, though they were both children still.

"Ocen did not come with me," she said. "He came with the American girl. They were searching for you. They wanted to take you home."

He raised his lip, rested a hand on his weapon. "I am a captain in the Movement, *Lapwony*'s personal envoy. I do not need rescuing. I will return to Acholiland when the government has returned what was stolen from us. Our land, our wealth, our culture."

"That is rhetoric. The strength of the Movement diminishes every day. Operation Lightning Thunder has scattered you. Museveni will not rest."

"Neither will we."

"Their strikes have made you weak. How many fighters are left? Three hundred? Four? You are too few."

Opiyo cut his hand through the air. "The spirits protect us."

"Spirits," she scoffed. "When Kony tracks the position of the enemy by satellite and claims to have learned it from a voice in his head—that is not God speaking. That is his madness."

His voice became low and deadly. "Careful, Rose."

Suddenly she felt very tired. It didn't matter: she would soon be at peace. She leaned back against the tree trunk, brought her knees to her chest. "What will happen to me tomorrow?"

Opiyo shined the light at her missing arm. "It depends on whether the chairman believes you can still be of use to the cause."

"My companions?"

"The foreigners mean nothing to him."

She expected no different, and yet the sadness she felt took her breath away.

"And Ocen?" she said at last. "What will be his fate?"

Opiyo looked away, but not before she saw a shadow of emotion cross his face. He was not stone after all. "He is too soft for this life. He would not survive."

"Release him," she said. "It is within your power."

"Then I would be too soft."

"Go together. Escape. Leave this life behind." He eyed her skeptically. "There have been other defectors, Opiyo. They are given amnesty by the government. The clans are performing *mato oput.*"

Opiyo squatted before her so that their eyes were level. "We cannot be cleansed, even by the bitter root."

"Forgiveness is there," she said. But he knew her too well, he could see through the plea. She thought of the words whispered behind her back—*killer, rebel, whore*—and the hostile looks flung her way when Christoph couldn't see. Still she insisted, "You can return."

He smiled a humorless smile and traced his finger along the ground where the beam of the flashlight shone. She made out the number eight, followed by a seven. "That is the number of people I have killed."

All those bodies—stillness. "You had no choice."

Opiyo brought his hands together. "Last week we met three women crossing a road. They begged us to let them go, but the spirits had already spoken." His tone was even, matter-of-fact. "'The lips that would denounce us must be cut off. The ears that would hear our secrets must be slashed. The eyes that would spy on us must be gouged . . .'"

"Stop," she said quietly. "Please."

"Such orders are nothing new," he went on, "as you must recall. But the spirits weren't finished. 'Those who beg in a foreign tongue must eat the flesh of their betrayal.'"

Her stomach churned, and she suppressed a shudder. "You are a good man underneath."

"I was a good man," he said sharply. "Until you gave yourself to *him*. Until you bore his son."

"Your son," she whispered.

Opiyo's lips opened as if to speak, but nothing came out; not even breath. For an instant she saw the hardness vanish, and his face was open and new. She could see him thinking back, trying to remember— *was it possible?* In the bush, the months blurred together, one upon the next; she could see him calculating, wondering how she could be sure . . .

He stood abruptly. "You lie."

She squeezed her eyes shut so that the tears would not be released.

His heavy footsteps started for the exit. "I'll hear no more."

"Do you remember how we used to meet at the river in Kitgum at midnight?" she said softly. "We stole candles from the teacher so that we could find our way in the dark."

She heard his footfalls pause.

"You'd take your slingshot and shoot bats by moonlight," she went on. "You did it so that I would be impressed, so that I would let you kiss me."

She opened her eyes and saw his head move subtly to the right, as if the slow-moving river was there, reflecting a rippled canopy of stars. She saw the boy he'd been, the impish look in his eye when he stretched a pebble back in the band and let it loose—the *twang* of rubber, the *thwipt* of a direct hit.

His grip tightened around his rifle.

Without looking back he said, "I remember nothing of that life."

Then he was gone.

CHAPTER 25

SABINE

January 7

After the guard took Rose from the clearing, Sabine stood, mute and dumb at the suddenness of what just occurred and how little power they had to stop it. The place where Rose had been sitting now felt jarringly empty. Sabine looked across at Ocen, who was slumped, his face in his hands, and then at Nicia, who was watching the place in the trees where Rose had disappeared, her young eyes bright with panic. Sabine felt Lily's hand slip into her own and squeeze.

"I'm afraid," Lily whispered.

Sabine squeezed back. "It's going to be all right."

In the half hour since they were reunited, Sabine had stepped firmly into the role of guardian, however thin the solace was that she could offer. She'd listened in silence to Lily's tearful accounting of the previous months—the revelation that Opiyo was still alive, the possibility of amnesty if Kony signed the peace agreement, the awful news when he failed to show at the assembly point at the end of November. The desperate last resort, the secrecy, the breathless journey across the border, the slightly disingenuous e-mails with Patrick. Everything Lily said confirmed what Sabine and Christoph and Rose had pieced together via her journal.

"And the ivory?" Sabine asked.

Lily's confusion was answer enough. "What ivory?"

There was more that the journal hadn't revealed: the trek through Garamba, following Miriam's directions and Lily's maps; the first moment when Camp Boo came into view, the two lines of rebel soldiers that appeared from the foliage and surrounded them, rifles raised. At first, Lily said, everything went miraculously smoothly—after their initial skepticism, the rebels were courteous, treating them more as guests than captives; the soldiers seemed awed by Ocen's mirror image of a man they all knew and feared, and Lily was given a loose freedom among the women and children. A meeting with Opiyo, Lily believed, was imminent.

A week later, the first bombs fell. The rebels' attitude toward Lily and Ocen turned mistrustful; they bound their hands and guarded them closely, even during the chaos of the UPDF's aerial attacks. "They accused us of being spies," Lily said, her eyes filling. "They thought we'd given away the location of the camp." Just before the soldiers confiscated Lily's backpack, she left the journal behind, hoping it would get found. "I didn't know what else to do. I didn't even know what day it was. I thought it might still be before Christmas, and you wouldn't even be worried yet . . ."

As Lily spoke, Sabine's heart twisted at the astounding scale of her niece's audacity, the arrogance that had allowed her to claim Ocen's cause as her own. Lily had seemed to view the war as a game—as something romantic and dangerous, a problem she could solve. It shamed Sabine to think that Lily was forming these ideas without Sabine noticing—yet what would she have said, if she'd known?

When Lily's story caught up with the present, Sabine detailed the chronology of their search in turn, the previous two weeks of panic and frustration and unexpected breakthroughs.

"We can't give up," she told Lily. "The U.S. military, UPDF . . . they know we're here. Christoph and I were able to make some calls at Nagero before the attack. They're out there looking for us right now."

And in some strange way Sabine had begun to believe it: they were together, the seekers and the sought. Surely there was something powerful in this convergence. Benson's appearance with antimalarial tablets seemed to confirm the changing of the tide toward a more hopeful outcome. After all, Sabine thought, Lily herself had been brought back from the dead; Christoph would recover; Opiyo was with Kony, somewhere far away . . .

The illusion shattered the moment Rose vanished at the point of the rebel's bayonet. Their group had come together only to be rent brutally apart.

And the guard's parting words. Kony was coming. They awaited his judgment.

"What will they do to Rose?" Lily said. She hadn't let go of Sabine's hand.

"It's going to be all right," Sabine repeated, though the conviction in her tone rang hollow.

Lily's eyes widened. "Opiyo—he'll be there, too."

Sabine pulled her niece close and stroked her tangled hair. "All we can do is wait."

In a few hours, Christoph's breathing began to steady, and the worst of his fever seemed to pass. Ocen sat at Christoph's side with Sabine and Lily, but he said nothing, his thoughts clearly elsewhere—with Rose, no doubt, and his brother, whom he would meet tomorrow for the first time in a decade. Sabine had been examining him surreptitiously throughout the afternoon, startled at how perfectly Lily had captured his likeness in such few strokes on the page. It was odd to be suddenly so near to him, this person for whom Lily had taken such an unfathomable risk. Sabine thought of all the ways she'd pictured him—as kidnapper, as lover, as assistant, as anonymous *boda* driver—and nothing, nothing came close to the unassuming young man before her. Why Ocen? He seemed almost random, an act of whimsical charity.

Or—Sabine wondered—had Lily needed him more than he needed her?

She looked at her niece's troubled face, so young: so young and so lonely. At once she saw Hannah's features stand out in bold relief: the constellation of freckles across the nose, the soft sculpted eyebrows, the shy prettiness Sabine had always pretended not to envy. A memory came back to her of Hannah at hospice, during those last draining days. Sabine had flown in from Tanzania when it became clear the end would come soon. She and Lily kept vigil at Hannah's bedside, talking of silly things, or nothing at all. Sometime during that blur of hours—morning and night seemed one and the same— Lily left the room to pick up some food from the deli down the street, and Hannah reached out and gripped Sabine's hand with surprising force. *Sie weißt,* Hannah breathed. She knows.

Was weißt sie? Sabine said gently. Knows what?

Hannah coughed. *The morning star,* she said in English.

Sabine thought of the fairy tale, the girl who flees the sun and the moon in search of her raven brothers. Hannah's thoughts had become increasingly tangled, her mind muddled, and in Sabine's exhausted state she only stroked her sister's bony wrist and said, *Yes, she knows. They all live happily ever after.*

Now, in a blaze of understanding, Sabine saw it in a different light.

Morning star: in German, *Morgenstern.*

She knows.

Hannah had known about their grandfather's dishonor, too. That was why she eloped, why she escaped to the States, why she stayed in Colorado, even after her marriage fell apart. She would have used their family history as a lesson for Lily—*we must rise above the place we come from.* With a jolt, Sabine saw herself from Lily's perspective: evidence of the noble choice, sacrificing safety and comfort in the service of a grander ideal. When Sabine returned to Germany, Lily would not have seen it as defeat, but as quiet triumph. Kitgum was not the site of Sabine's surrender, but the place where atonement could be made.

How devastatingly wrong they all had been.

Lily's voice drifted in. "Aunt Sabine? Are you okay?"

"I . . ." She took in the low dun grass stamped down in the clearing, the green brush at the edges, the tiny hovering gnats backlit by the sinking sun, the dozens and dozens of silent children under a dome of sky. She didn't know what came next.

Christoph coughed, and Sabine heard Ocen's low voice: "He is waking."

She looked down and saw Christoph blinking. His eyes fell on Sabine's face, then moved to Lily and Ocen. He turned questioningly back to Sabine, clearly discomposed. Sabine put her hand to his forehead. It was warm but not hot.

"They're real," she said. "We're all together now."

"Safe?"

She stroked his hair away from his temple. "No."

He pushed himself up onto his elbows and glanced about the clearing. There were five rebels guarding them now instead of one, and they eyed the group of foreigners with obvious suspicion. As Christoph absorbed the changed scene, the solemn, scared faces of the abducted Congolese children looked at him, then away.

"You had malaria," Sabine said. "You've been out since morning."

"Where's Rose?"

"They took her away. Kony is coming. He'll be here tomorrow."

His arms trembled, the muscles too weak, and he lay back down and closed his eyes. For a long moment no one spoke.

"It's a lot to take in," she said. "You should rest."

"Paper."

"What?"

"I need paper."

Sabine looked around uselessly. "I don't . . ."

"Here," Lily said, pulling a piece of paper, folded into quarters, out of the back pocket of her jeans.

Sabine looked at her in surprise. "Where did you get that?"

"It's a blank page from my sketchbook. I was going to try to send a message, but they took my pen."

Christoph struggled to prop himself up again, and Sabine helped him scoot a few feet to the right where he could lean against the trunk of a tree. She watched, baffled, as he unfolded Lily's page and smoothed out the creases against his jeans. She glanced up as a guard narrowed his eyes and began to stalk toward them.

"What are you doing?" she whispered to Christoph. He didn't reply but folded the page diagonally until the sides aligned, then carefully ripped off the leftover rectangle. Then he folded the triangle in half again so that the two acute angles touched. She noticed the raw blisters on his palm—from carrying the heavy tusks—and felt her own hands throb in sympathy.

The guard was coming closer; he was almost upon them. Sabine's heart raced. Christoph stayed completely focused on his task: folding and pressing and unfolding, making new triangles and squares and diamonds. "Christoph . . ."

The rebel loomed over them, his heavy rubber boots quashing a few last blades of grass as he stood, the barrel of his rifle aimed at Christoph's busy hands with an unmistakable message. But Christoph was already finished: he spread his palms to reveal his creation.

It was a bird. Sabine was unsettled by the sharpness of the angles, the precision of the lines—and yet the creature it was meant to represent was manifestly visible, the beak and tail and two folded wings.

Christoph lifted his palm toward the rebel. "Crane." He gave a small smile. "*Owalo*."

The guard hesitated for a few seconds, then took the paper bird delicately, pinching the very tip of one of the wings between his thumb and index finger. "*Owalo*," he echoed.

As the rebel examined the fragile object, Sabine noticed the slenderness of his waist, the bagginess of his uniform. He had a long scar running from his neck up in front of his ear across his cheek, which from a distance made him look fierce—but up close she saw how young he was. He couldn't be older than fifteen. Around his right wrist he wore a fraying cloth band. Perspiration stippled his forehead.

"*Owalo*," he said again, this time nodding toward the patch on the shoulder of his uniform. When Sabine studied the image closer, she saw an intricately embroidered insignia with two green palm leaves under a crested crane. The boy tucked the paper bird into his pocket and walked away.

"I remember that story," Lily said quietly. "The girl from Hiroshima. We read it in school. A thousand paper cranes is supposed to grant you a wish."

Christoph's eyes followed the young rebel as he settled back into position on the periphery. "Let's hope one crane is enough."

Christoph continued to recover throughout the evening. Sometime after dark had consumed the last remnants of daylight, Benson came by to check on him as well as all the new arrivals and brought clean materials to replace Lily's splint. He had Sabine hold the flashlight while he laid two sections of a dried palm frond stem on the ground; they were stiff as wood and cut to just the right length for a brace. He put a strip of cloth along the concave insides, then set each vertically against either side of Lily's ankle and bound them together with medical tape. Lily winced at his touch but did not cry.

"Keep it elevated," Benson said. "Tomorrow the pain will be less."

"How's Rose?" Sabine asked.

"You should put her from your minds." He walked off before she could say more, leaving them once again in utter darkness, aside from the stars spread lavishly across the night sky. Sabine couldn't pull her eyes from this astounding cosmological display: so much vaster and deeper and more dazzlingly real than anything she thought she'd ever seen. Or perhaps it was that as long as she was looking up, she would not have to cry.

"She'll be there tomorrow," Christoph said. "She must."

"Maybe we can convince Kony to let her go," Lily said.

"Never." Ocen's voice came as a surprise to Sabine, who hadn't realized he was still awake. The sadness in his tone was excruciating; it resonated with surrender. "He would rather see her die."

No one answered.

Eventually, one by one, occupied by their troubled imaginations, they drifted off to sleep.

The rebels came to fetch them in the morning. The Congolese children watched silently as four soldiers—including the boy with the wrist band and scar; the three others looked almost as young—surrounded Sabine, Christoph, Lily, and Ocen and prodded them forward. Christoph, still a little dizzy, leaned on Sabine's shoulder, and Ocen walked a half step behind Lily.

It was a blue-sky day, the temperature mild. Birdsong drifted from the forest depths. They were led out of the clearing but away from the main camp where Benson had brought Sabine the day before to fetch water. Sabine had a sudden image of getting led off into the bush just to be shot. Maybe Kony was never coming at all, there was no third unit, they'd have no chance to plead their case. The end would be unremarkable: a branch shorn from a tree, a plant crushed underfoot, a flock of birds taking flight. No one would ever find their bodies. It had happened a thousand times before; it would happen a thousand times again.

Just as desperation overcame her, they came into a clearing. She looked around for any sign of rebels, but it was empty aside from banana leaves that had been spread on the ground; in the center was a basin filled with water, and next to it a small bar of soap.

One of the guards barked out an order, and Ocen translated: "We must wash first." He paused. "Before we meet him."

The four of them shuffled awkwardly around the plastic basin. Ocen was the first to kneel. He splashed some water on his face and rubbed the soap into a lather between his hands. His movements were graceful and slow, and Sabine felt distinctly like she was witnessing an act of devotion. When he was done, he rose and let his hands dry in the warm air. Lily knelt and followed the same procedure, though Sabine saw her hands were shaking. Then Christoph. Then it was her turn. She bent on one knee and cupped her hands in the water that was now not entirely clean. In the glassy surface she saw the silhouette of her face and shoulders against the brightness of the sky. The reflection was too dark to make out her own features. She closed her eyes and brought the water toward her, felt its cool touch. There was something strangely sacred about the action; her hands possessed a profound serenity that originated outside her body. When she was finished, she rose, not with a sense that she had been cleansed, but clarified.

They were led away again along a narrow path through the brush, Sabine in the front behind two guards, followed by Lily, Christoph, and Ocen; the last two guards brought up the rear. After a few dozen yards, the rebels halted. Sabine craned her neck to see around them, but there was nothing ahead, only more trees. The foliage was dense and tangled. Why had they stopped? Her panic returned.

The soldier in front of her turned; it was the boy with the scar. He glanced around as if nervous. The rebel next to him whispered something in Acholi, and the boy made a quick movement to readjust his rifle and pull something out of his front shirt pocket.

It was a tiny strip of paper—smaller than the length and breadth of his finger—and Sabine recognized the stiffness and slightly off-white color as that of Lily's journal. She thought of the crane Christoph had given him last night. As she took the slip, she saw that something was written there: a name, *Okwera Emmanuel,* in clumsy lettering. She looked up in confusion and saw his eyes wet with tears.

"If you return to Uganda," he said in English, "please find my mother and father. Tell them I am alive."

The soldier behind him stepped forward and handed her a second strip of paper. Another name.

"Please," the second soldier said quietly. "My parents. Tell them I miss them."

Sabine's eyes pinched with tears. From the left, out of the thicket, more soldiers appeared, furtive and cautious, each with a roughly edged rectangle bearing his name. Some slips had two names or more. A boy would emerge, hand over his paper, whisper a *please* or *thank you* or *apwoyo,* and vanish back into the bush. Much of the handwriting looked the same, as if a small number of rebels had taken dictation for the others.

When the last soldier had come and left, Sabine was left with a palm full of paper, thin and crumpled as packing confetti. Did any of the names she held match the ones on the banner back in Kitgum? She closed her hand around the pieces and tucked them into the tight front pocket of her jeans. The boy with the scar—*Emmanuel,* she thought firmly, *that's his name: Emmanuel*—inhaled sharply and gave a quick nod.

"It is time," he said.

They walked forward.

After a few minutes, they came to a new clearing. As Sabine followed the two guards out from the brush, she felt her stomach plummet at the sight of a group of heavily armed soldiers, unsmiling, standing in a row behind an empty brown plastic chair; they wore military fatigues and an assortment of berets and wide-brimmed caps, all in shades of camouflage and green. They held their weapons loosely in front of their chests. Surreally, Sabine saw Ocen among them, then quickly corrected herself: Opiyo. His eyes were fixed on the approaching group but showed no sign of emotion. Sabine's foot caught on an exposed tree root and she stumbled; Christoph's hand steadied her.

Behind the soldiers was a mud-and-thatch hut in poor condition and several bamboo lean-tos that appeared to have been hastily erected. A handful of young children stood shyly around the lean-tos, and two women, each carrying a baby on her back, went about domestic chores: one fanning the flames of a small cooking fire and the other swishing laundry in a plastic basin filled with soapy water. Neither looked up at the captives' arrival, but the woman at the fire did cast a glance at another figure, who was seated some distance from both the lean-tos and the soldiers, her knees folded to the side, her left arm resting lightly in her lap, a single rebel standing guard behind her. Sabine's throat closed.

"Rose," Christoph said, his voice choked. Rose kept her face in profile; she would not meet their eyes.

The guards led the four of them to two makeshift bamboo benches that were arranged side by side facing the brown chair. Sabine and Lily sat together on one bench; Christoph and Ocen, on the second. Opiyo's face was still hard, his stance unwavering. The soldier next to him casually waved away a fly.

From the doorway of the hut, a figure appeared. He paused a moment in the sunlight; unlike the other rebels, he was dressed in all white—white T-shirt, white pants: brilliant, blinding white—and wearing, bizarrely, flip-flops. He had no hat; his fuzzy black hair was shorn close to the scalp. His eyebrows were faint, his mustache trimmed, and his chin showed the shadow of new stubble. The rest of his jaw and neck were smooth-shaven. Sabine recognized him instantly.

This was Joseph Kony.

His expression as he looked upon his visitors seemed to Sabine to be the same as in the photograph she'd seen hanging in the National Memory and Peace Documentation Centre in Kitgum: somewhere between puzzled and concerned, a seemingly guileless display of wonder and worry. There was no savagery or madness in his face or bearing, no ruthlessness, not even a hint of rage. In fact, what Sabine first felt upon laying eyes on this man—*messiah, monster, myth*—was an overwhelming sense of ordinariness. Here was a middle-aged man of average build, with pleasant features that one might even call handsome. He walked slowly, without strutting, and took a seat in the brown plastic chair, crossed one leg over the other, and leaned forward, holding his knee with both hands. He was surprisingly close; Sabine could see a small cut on the hollow of his left ankle, just starting to heal. Finally he spoke.

"Would you like tea?"

His voice was soft, slightly hoarse, and impeccably polite. He didn't wait for a response before calling over to the two women in Acholi, gesturing with slender fingers; a silver wristwatch glinted in the light. Without a word the woman doing laundry pushed herself to standing and went around the back of the lean-to, disappearing from sight.

They waited in silence. Sabine's heart pounded. Her hand found Lily's. A moment later the woman returned with a blue thermos and four tin mugs; she set them on the ground before the benches and knelt to serve the tea. Reluctantly releasing Lily's hand, Sabine took the mug offered to her and held it awkwardly above her lap. The heat stung her blistered palms.

"Please," Kony said earnestly. "Drink."

She dutifully brought the mug to her lips. The tea was the sweetest she'd ever tasted. Beside her, Lily did the same.

Kony leaned back and broke into a smile. Sabine noticed a small gap in his upper teeth, from misalignment or a broken tooth. It gave him a weirdly jolly demeanor.

"It is good that you have come," he said. "You are very welcome here with us, the Lord's Resistance Movement." He gestured toward the structures behind him. "It is a shame, you see us in such a bad situation. The UPDF is making our lives very difficult. Even me, Joseph Kony, I am escaping only with my life."

No one responded. This was not a dialogue, Sabine knew; it was a speech. His tone became more serious.

"Maybe you believe you know something about us. About the war we are fighting." He pursed his lips. "I read the newspapers, I listen to the radio. I know what they are saying about me. They call me a terrorist. They say I am evil. Fundamentalist, madman, demon . . . They say I am killing only innocents, that we took twenty thousand children from their homes. Eh!" He spread his hands. "Where would we keep twenty thousand children in the bush? These children here," he waved vaguely toward the lean-tos, "they are my own sons and daughters."

Several more young children appeared while others vanished into the trees, apparently bored. Sabine caught the eyes of a girl who looked to be about four; she had her fingers in her mouth, staring unabashedly at the *mzungus*. A slightly taller boy slapped at her hand until she turned and followed him into the brush.

"They say that I cut off ears and noses and lips," Kony went on. "But how can I cut off the ear of my brother? How can I harm my own people, the Acholi?"

His fist cut swiftly through the air. "It is propaganda—this is all propaganda Museveni made. The UPDF is the one who is killing. The UPDF kills civilians and says it was LRA. But that one is not true. We were never there. We never did those things they say."

He was gesturing passionately now, punctuating his statements with a lifted hand, a pointed finger, as a preacher might during a sermon.

"I am a freedom fighter. We are fighting for the freedom of our people. It is Museveni who put millions of Acholi into camps, where they suffered and died. It is Museveni who keeps the people penned up like cattle so he can steal their land."

Sabine recalled the truly horrendous conditions she witnessed in the camps around Kitgum—the tens of thousands of people crammed into a few square miles, the cholera outbreaks, the alcoholism and rape. People stripped of dignity and hope. And the land-grabbing was real—huge tracts of good farming and pasture land snatched up by outside interests while the owners remained trapped in the camps, unable to dispute those claims. She'd spoken with too many witnesses to LRA brutality to believe that part of Kony's story, but as she listened, creeping into her mind was a new understanding. The camps—which, at the peak of the conflict, housed nearly two million people—were supposed to be temporary, but as the years went on, and the NGOs multiplied, it had become less and less urgent to find a solution. After the World Trade Center attack on September 11, Museveni's government was rumored to be receiving fifty million dollars a year from the United States to fight the LRA "terrorists"; a large portion of that money likely never left Kampala, either by straight-out siphoning or through lucrative military equipment contracts. War was good business as long as the violence stayed in the hinterlands of the country, where Acholis were killing Acholis; they'd never voted for Museveni's party anyway.

Was Operation Lightning Thunder intended to end anything at all? The viciousness of Kony's forces may have been the focus of media attention—but Sabine had heard plenty of stories of atrocities committed by the UPDF. And Museveni's political maneuvers were killing the north slowly, genocide by economic suffocation, while the government benefited financially and Museveni's moral shortcomings were given a blind eye by Western powers.

And suddenly it was this distant, pale specter of the West that loomed sharper and more horrifying than anything else. Those unbloodied hands gesturing vaguely around long, polished tables, claiming the role of the savior one minute and ushering in new waves of calculated, convenient complicities the next.

Abruptly Kony's manner changed again: now he was chillingly calm.

"Colonel Otim says that you are spies. He says you gave away our position to the enemy."

"No," Lily blurted. "That's not it at all. You don't understand."

Sabine's heart nearly stopped. "Lily, quiet," she said under her breath.

But Kony furrowed his eyebrows and said, "Please, continue."

Lily's voice was trembling. "We were looking for Opiyo. Ocen's brother." Opiyo's expression stayed unreadable. "We just wanted to find him, to bring him back home to Kitgum."

Kony listened intently. "How did you find our camp?"

"I met a girl who lived here with you. With the LRA, I mean. In Garamba. She helped me with the locations. I never shared it with anyone, I swear."

"What was her name, this girl who claimed to know us?"

Lily seemed to realize she was treading into dangerous territory. "I can't remember."

Kony turned to Sabine with a piercing gaze. "You came at a different time. After this one was already here."

"She was missing, we had no idea what happened . . ." Sabine trailed off; where could she even begin? What was he accusing her of? Firmly, she said, "We didn't come out here and track you down. We were at Nagero—your soldiers kidnapped us."

Kony nodded slowly. "This girl, why is she so important to you?"

Sabine found herself choked up. It took a moment for her to get the words out. "She's my sister's daughter. She's family."

"Yes," Kony exclaimed, growing animated. Sabine was relieved to have given a correct answer. "Family," he repeated. "That is what I mean. The Acholi people, they are my family. And I see them suffering. I am fighting for them not to suffer. Museveni says I don't want to talk peace, but that one is not true. We are separated from our Acholi family for too long here in the bush. It is not good for families to be separated."

He turned at last to Ocen. "That is also why I understand your reasons for coming to find your brother. You can see he is here. You have found him." His tone became smooth, as if giving instructions to a small child. "But I will tell you this: he has no wish to return to Uganda. None of us will come back—only when our cause succeeds, when we remove Museveni from power. Then we will return together, victorious, in the glory of God."

He clasped his hands and looked between the captives. "Now, you all have your answer. It seems our business is concluded."

Sabine's temples tingled. Concluded? What did that mean?

"You will see for yourself," he went on, "that I am not an evil man. The Somalis, they would keep you hostage and demand fifteen million dollars. In Sierra Leone they would cut out your intestines and make you eat them. We are not like that. These criminals, they are not people like us."

He leaned back slightly in his chair and raised a finger. Opiyo bent his head, and Kony whispered something into his ear. Opiyo nodded and strode away from the chair, tapping one of Kony's bodyguards to follow. They crossed the clearing and Opiyo murmured to the boy soldier with the scar—*Emmanuel*, Sabine thought faintly.

Emmanuel kept his eyes down as he joined the two in approaching the benches.

"Up," Emmanuel said softly. The bodyguard was not so gentle, prodding Christoph with the barrel of his rifle.

Sabine looked back and forth between the soldiers and Kony. "What's happening?"

Kony flicked his hand. "I release you."

"Release us . . . ?" Now the bodyguard pressed his rifle hard against her ribs, and she was rising from her seat, fumbling to set the tea mug onto the bench; her knee jostled the bamboo and the mug tipped with a clatter, spilling liquid onto the grass. Lily bumped into her, and Sabine felt her niece's hands gripping tightly at her waist. She heard Lily inhale sharply—her ankle, of course. Sabine nudged her shoulder under Lily's armpit to help her walk. Christoph appeared on Lily's other side. "Easy now," he said. Emmanuel and the bodyguard were herding them from behind, pressing forward out of the clearing in the direction from where they entered.

In the confusion it took her a moment to realize they were only three.

She looked back; Ocen was still seated on the bench, his back to them. Opiyo stood with his hand clamped down on his twin's shoulder. To the far right, Rose hadn't moved from her place on the ground. *It is not good for families to be separated . . .*

"Ocen," she said breathlessly. "Rose."

A rifle pushed hard into her lower back. "They stay."

She caught Kony's eyes. His unblinking, unshakable calm.

"This is not your war," he said.

It was happening too quickly: the steely jabs against her back, her own feet stumbling traitorously forward; Lily limping; even Christoph was pressed onward, onward, away from Ocen's seated figure and Rose's lowered head, her unmet eyes. The foliage came up on either side and the path narrowed; Sabine's mind spun. The long green leaves brushed against their bodies and closed behind them. No chance to refuse; no final embrace. No good-bye.

Five pairs of feet moved methodically through the verdant under-growth: *swish, crack, crush, creak.* Words did not exist in this universe. Everything around her seemed appallingly alive, heady, humming: the lush green plants, the whistling birds, the yellow grasshoppers that landed on her shirt, clinging with their tiny hooks until they sprang off again.

She knew she should be relieved. They were going home. Lily was safe; their ordeal was nearly over. But every step brought them far-ther from Rose, farther from Ocen. Any number of times she was seized by the conviction to go back—and in the next instant, she knew how futile it would be. Their return would save no one and would clinch their own doom. Even Christoph must have understood, because even he made no move to turn around, though tears rolled silently down his cheeks.

They hadn't gotten far when Lily tripped and crumpled to the ground, gasping.

Kony's bodyguard stood over her, gesturing with his rifle and speaking harshly in Acholi. His meaning was clear enough.

Lily clutched her ankle. "I can't."

"She's injured, can't you see that?" Christoph said. He, too, had lost strength in this short time, Sabine saw; his face was pale and his eyes sunken.

The bodyguard responded with a sneer, but before he made any further moves, Emmanuel spoke a few quiet words and the body-guard appeared to acquiesce, though unwillingly.

Emmanuel turned to Sabine. "Rest."

Christoph sat heavily next to Lily; Sabine walked a few paces away with Emmanuel. "Where are you taking us?"

"Village."

"What will happen to the people back there? Rose and Ocen?"

He paused for a long time, and when he spoke, his voice was so faint she wasn't sure he said anything at all. "I don't . . ." He didn't go on.

They'd stopped on the top of a rise, with the forest at their backs and a long landscape of savanna sloping down before them. In the valley Sabine saw a herd of water buffalo grazing in the tall grass, with dozens of white cattle egrets perched on their thick hides. From the forest came an echo of an elephant's trumpet. Sabine thought of the gruesome pile of tusks back at the rebels' camp and wondered where they would travel next, who would purchase them, what trinkets they might be shaped into for display on a shelf an ocean distant. The lines linking this place to that, the invisible networks that traversed the surface of the earth: she saw them stretching before her, reaching outward, illuminated in a vast and complex web of connection, pumping like veins, pumping money and oil and gold, greed and hate and guilt and fear. She thought of the European explorers, the colonialists, the armies, the missionaries, the bureaucrats—and now the journalists, the aid workers, the diplomats, the saviors.

We never should have come, she thought.

She looked at Emmanuel. From this side of his profile, his scar was hidden, and Sabine thought she could glimpse the boy he'd been before: studious and shy, assisting in domestic chores without complaint. *How his mother must miss him.* The names in her pocket filled her with sadness—and purpose. She could still do this small good.

From the direction of the camp came the muted *crack* of a shot; the flock of egrets took wing in the valley below. Sabine caught Christoph's horrified eyes.

Lily let out a choked sob. "Oh, God."

An awful silence throbbed in her ears. Then Kony's bodyguard shouted an order, and Emmanuel said, almost apologetically, "We go."

No one moved.

"Go!" the bodyguard repeated.

More gunfire sounded from the forest: a heavier exchange. Sabine looked to Emmanuel, whose face showed new signs of worry.

The bodyguard swiveled his head and listened as the *rat-a-tat-tat-tat* continued, his body tense and swift. Sabine watched his alarm with growing concern. Whatever he imagined was taking place at the camp was clearly not what he'd expected. When he turned back, his expression was distorted with anger. His eyes were on Lily.

"Spy," he hissed.

He raised his gun.

What happened next felt slow. The seconds were stuck together, gluey and long. Sabine had time to take everything in: the white crescents on the man's pale fingernails wrapped around the wooden grip; a bead of sweat trickling down the back of his neck; two dragonflies hovering dreamily at her kneecap. Silence had dropped like a swaddling blanket over the earth. Her mind formed no conscious thought—but her body knew.

She hurled herself at him. *Thunk* came contact, followed rapidly by jolting stabs of metal and wood and elbow and bone. The gun went off a fraction late and she felt the kickback as they were falling through the air, a nanosecond before they hit the ground hard. The rifle thumped lightly away and the bodyguard made a small *uhmf* sound as the wind was knocked out of him.

She heard the sound of trumpeting. *Odd,* she thought; the herd had been so far away. Dazed and shaken, she tried to push herself up, but her wrists gave out. The rebel scrambled for his gun, picked it up. Took aim. At her.

Now the seconds sped up; there was no time. Still she tried, tearing at the grass, digging her feet into the soil . . .

He fired.

She felt no pain. A lightness spread throughout her body, an expansion of tingling luminescence. She broke into a trillion tiny parts.

Her vision cleared, and she saw Kony's bodyguard, standing, breathing heavily, hunched over his gun. Emmanuel held position behind him, rifle stiffly raised, though his hand was nowhere near the trigger.

Lily, clambering. Her features were twisted in anguish, her mouth a gaping hole: no sound that Sabine could hear. She was reaching for something, for someone . . .

Oh. It was *her* she was reaching for. Sabine tried to take a breath; failed. How strange, how laughable to see her own chest open to the sky, blossoming.

With a gush her senses returned: the remote noise of gunfire at the camp, Lily's ragged screaming, the smell of something burnt in the air. Her body felt as if it were on fire. She longed for an extinguishing. They were right up against the trees, almost under their shade, but not quite.

Christoph's hand was in hers.

"Hey," he whispered. "It's me. I'm here."

His hand was weirdly cold, and hers, warm. She thought of scarves, and skates, and circles on the ice, spirals getting gradually bigger, gaining momentum . . .

"You can't die," Lily sobbed. "It's my fault. It should have been me. It should—"

. . . the spirals dizzied her. Could she have done more, or done differently? Of course she could have. There was always more to be done. It felt so horribly unfair that death came like this, before you were ready, before you were redeemed—but then, maybe, that was it after all. Redemption was not a state you could achieve, a place you could enter once and live inside forever. One had to make peace with the grappling. Just because it ended for her did not mean it ended.

She needed to tell this to Lily, to make her see that she could carry this failure forward with grace, that the questions had no answers but must be held nonetheless in one's heart with care. But her voice didn't want to work. When was the last time she took a breath?

"Please," Christoph was saying—not to her, but to the soldier who was taking aim again. Sabine saw them both through a gauzy haze. "Please, please . . ."

From out of the forest came a revelation of thunder. The earth rumbled and a great wind rushed past. Christoph threw himself across her body and she felt Lily do the same, her niece's arms crossing Christoph's, their pulsing, living skin. She turned her head sideways, squinting through the clamor and the dark spots that had begun to appear. She could no longer see the soldiers.

The elephants were in the way.

Gray, massive, grand—and ferocious, their ears flapping wide, legs stamping, tails swinging. Their bodies were almost baffling in their enormity and their force. They must have been spooked by the gunfire, she thought, and then the thought became untethered, loosely drifting. All thoughts became so. Memories hovered like fireflies, flickering, radiant, pulsing in sync with one another. Her world dimmed.

Nothing needed forgiveness, here. Everything went on.

Their long white tusks flashed as they charged past, the herd parting around the fallen like water around a rock, meeting on the other side.

CHAPTER 26

ROSE

January 8

What Rose felt when Sabine, Lily, and Christoph were led into the trees was, overwhelmingly, relief—relief so brutal she could not bring herself to watch. Watching their figures disappear would mean saying good-bye, and if she did that, she would cry, and if she cried, whatever small chance she had left to save Ocen's life would be gone. She prayed that Lily's ankle would hold up, that Christoph's malaria would not relapse, that Sabine would stay stubborn as ever, that they would find their way home.

Meanwhile, there was silence. Kony brought his hand to his mouth and nibbled on a fingernail. The soldiers in his High Protection Unit appeared both serious and at ease. Opiyo stood behind Ocen, his hand pressed upon his brother's shoulder as if without it, Ocen might become weightless and float up heavenward. When they'd first brought Ocen into the clearing, Rose thought her heart might burst right out of her chest; yet she'd seen no fear in Ocen's face, no reluctance in his stride. Even now he sat tall and composed, a man surrendered to whatever fate fell upon him. She felt her skin pulling away from her muscles and bones, toward him, her limbs tight and pulsing.

At last Kony broke the quiet.

"Rose, Rose," he tutted. "I am surprised to see you here."

It was odd: as long as he'd been speaking with the others in English, she could almost pretend he was a different man—a smaller, less powerful man. But in Acholi, he spoke as fluidly as the preacher from Agnes's church in Kitgum, the language a puppet in his skillful hands. This was the man she'd known: the man who'd taken everything from her. Despite her role, she'd seen him rarely during her years in the bush; he traveled often with his High Protection Unit and was rumored to have a house in Khartoum. Most of the time she remained with her co-wives and the wives of other commanders, harvesting crops, tending to the children. He'd used her perhaps two dozen nights in as many months. But those nights she remembered with painful clarity: the roughness of his touch, his wordless grunts. Most of all she recalled his smell. He was fastidiously clean, but no matter how much soap he used, how often he anointed himself with shea butter oil, there lingered a distinct scent of burnt milk.

"They told me you died in Sudan," he said. He flicked his eyes to her scarred shoulder. "I see you only survived in part."

"It is by God's grace that I survived at all." The words were hollow to her, but she had to tread carefully. She'd spent the night preparing, and still she could not be certain.

He assessed the rest of her frankly, without smiling. "Did you miss your husband?"

She forced herself not to look at Ocen. "Of course."

Softly: "Then why did you not come to me?"

"The UPDF watched us too closely. I could not leave."

"And yet you are here." His voice had taken a dangerous turn, but she stayed calm.

"The army was distracted by their operation. I took the chance that I would find you."

He leaned back as if considering this answer, and she looked casually toward her former co-wives who continued their chores at the lean-tos, now without returning her glance. She'd recognized them at once: one had been among the rebels when Rose was first abducted; the other came when Rose was pregnant. For the first, Margaret, Rose had no love. She was mean and jealous and had often accused Rose of petty infractions. If she felt Kony was favoring Rose, she would beat her on the head or toss her out of the hut to sleep in the rain. But the other girl—Fatumah—had been so young when she was abducted, only ten, and was a *tingting* for all the years that Rose was in the bush. Rose wondered if it was her own escape that precipitated Fatumah's elevation from babysitter to bed-sharer.

"And what is your relation to this one?" Kony asked, indicating Ocen.

Rose kept her face neutral. "None."

"You agree, then, that he is a traitor to the Movement."

She feigned indifference, but her pulse quickened. "Eh, he is harmless, this one."

"Harmless? He tried to lure away my personal envoy. His presence disrupted my troops' movements and their ability to follow orders. He would have sabotaged my entire strategy if given the chance. Are those acts not deserving of punishment?"

"In this way," she said, "you speak the truth. But can a man not repent for his crimes? Imagine the blessings you shall receive with both twins together, fighting at your side. Imagine how the spirits will rejoice."

"Don't presume to speak for the spirits."

Chastened, she quieted her voice. "Then let him return to Kitgum. Let him tell the Acholi that he met *Lapwony Kony*, that he met the teacher, and that you are fighting on behalf of his people. Let him tell them that you are prepared for peace."

"The Acholi know what I am fighting for."

"You have been away from northern Uganda for two years. Some have forgotten. It is easy to believe Museveni's lies, when that is all people see."

Kony's eyes met hers. For a long time—too long—he said nothing.

"I am not a fool," he said at last. "You did not come to Congo looking for me." With a raised hand to silence her unspoken objection, he turned to address Ocen for the first time. "The penalty for sleeping with a commander's wife is death."

Rose looked back and forth between their faces, her heart sinking as she saw that Ocen's expression equaled Kony's in coldness.

"Punish me instead," she begged.

Kony toyed with his wristwatch. "I still have need of you, Rose. Even though you are less than whole, you will be very useful to me." He gestured toward his other wives. Margaret went behind the lean-to and came back a moment later with Nicia beside her. The girl was terrified, her skinny legs stumbling. Three small children scattered at the commotion while two others drew nearer. Kony watched Nicia with calculating eyes. "I need someone to help my next wife adapt to her new position."

Rose's mind began to spin. It was too much, Ocen and Nicia, one directly after the other—she inhaled so sharply that her breath caught. "No," she gasped. "No—you can't. I beg you, *Baba*, please. *Lapwony*. Husband. Let her go. I'll do anything."

Kony narrowed his eyes, and Rose knew she had erred, perhaps fatally. She'd stepped out of her role, had acknowledged the unacknowledgable: *being your wife is no honor.*

But Kony ran a finger around his lips. "All right," he said. "I agree. I will release this girl."

She blinked, afraid to believe. "You will?"

"Yes." His voice was almost cheerful. "But in return, you must prove your loyalty, Rose. You understand why I cannot be certain otherwise."

"Of course I am loyal," she said. Her rocking world had begun to steady, and though she didn't want to trust it, she had no other option. "What would you have me do?"

Kony gestured at Opiyo. "Give her the *panga*."

Wary, she watched Opiyo release Ocen and lower his hand to the *panga* that hung at his side. When he turned her direction, she caught the grim expression on his face, and she realized what Kony would order, what he had planned for all along. It dropped upon her like a collapsed roof, swift and total. All she saw was darkness, all she breathed was dust.

"The traitor has received his sentence," Kony said. "You will carry it out."

She didn't move, but it didn't matter. Opiyo was coming closer, carrying the weapon with a loose grip while his other hand rested on his rifle. He came to a stop in front of her kneeling figure.

"Stand."

"Please," she whispered. "Find another way."

He prodded her stiffly with his boot. "Get up."

Slowly, awkwardly, she rose. Ocen's profile did not turn. As Opiyo handed her the *panga,* he leaned in a second longer than necessary; his words were barely a breath in her ear. "Quickly and he will feel no pain."

Rose startled at the plea in his voice. When their eyes met for an instant, everything that was hard between them melted. She felt his despair as intimately as if it were her own.

Kony's voice, darkly teasing, pulled her away. "You remember how to use it?"

The girl's body—stillness.

Opiyo stepped back and she closed her slender fingers around the worn wooden handle. Suddenly her body was infused with a sense of peace, the same peace she'd felt during the night, before Opiyo's visit, when she had decided to die.

She'd imagined a different end than this: by her own hand, perhaps—a cooking knife or a stolen gun or a swollen river—or, if the chance arose, a purposeful charge into enemy fire. The only reason she hadn't tried last night was the possibility, however slim, that her acquiescence to Kony's will would spare Ocen's life.

She hadn't foreseen an opportunity like this.

In the years since she'd lost her right arm, she'd grown competent enough with her left; she could write, type, dress, cook. Wielding a weapon was something else—for this she needed a strength she wasn't sure she possessed. Most likely that was why Kony gave her a *panga* instead of a gun: he wanted to watch her struggle. He wanted her to need more than one swing.

She brought her eyes to the place where Ocen sat. His back was tall, and his hands were on his knees, and still he did not look at her. A subtle shifting of light caught the metal bracelet on his wrist—three shining strands: copper, iron, brass. She looked at Opiyo. Two golds and a silver, forever intertwined.

Slowly she made her way across the clearing, lessening the distance between her and her object until she stood at the midpoint between Ocen and Kony. Two strides separated her from each man.

There was no choice to be made.

Outsiders might have thought it strange that no one in the LRA had attempted it before. Without Kony, the theory went, this war would crumble. Many had gotten close enough to him to swing a fatal blow. All those nights in Kony's hut in Sudan, when Rose could have reached out quietly for a hidden knife—and didn't. How to explain the perpetual fear, the terror living inside you like a parasite, colonizing your courage, making you small? How to justify the shameful belief churning deep within, the secret voice that said, *The spirits protect him, he cannot be killed.*

And—though this, too, seemed beyond belief—there had been times when Kony had saved her, had taken water from his soldiers to give to her so that she would not die of thirst. He'd saved her from Margaret's beatings when he learned of them. He was a monster and also a man. And this understanding—that he was human, that he breathed, he bled—was what she clung to now. Perhaps the spirits would enact their vengeance upon her, but what had she to fear? She would be dead, murdered by Kony's bodyguards. Ocen would no doubt suffer the same, though maybe without the kindness of speed. This would be her final cruelty. But then it would be over, for both of them, and if Agnes's God was right, if Rose had sinned too greatly to meet her son on the other side, then Ocen, at least, knew his name and would find him there.

As she stood before him, Ocen finally lifted his eyes to hers. In them she saw sorrow and fear and forgiveness.

"I'm sorry," she said.

She turned away.

Time slowed. She saw Kony's semipuzzled expression of anticipation, his too-white costume; the perspiring faces of the men behind him, relaxed but alert. She would have to be swift and accurate. Near the lean-tos, Margaret had Nicia's thin arm in a tight grip, while the girl looked at Rose with half-fearful, half-hopeful eyes. *I am sparing you, too,* Rose wanted to say, but she couldn't be sure it wasn't a lie.

It was a day like any other: warm and blue and green and alive. The two children who'd stayed to watch stood by blankly, their naked brown legs streaked with dirt.

"Rose," Kony said, "I am waiting."

She gripped the handle tighter. She would need all her focus, all her might. *The softest skin. The smallest hands.*

A third child stepped out from behind the lean-to and joined the other two. Leafy shadows rippled about him as he stood shyly back. As Rose took in the particular curve of the boy's elbows, the fullness of his eyelashes, she felt something inside her chest come open. It wasn't him—it couldn't be—yet the image of her son was so real, so perfect, that she had to blink her eyes to believe. But then there were tears blurring her sight, and the boy's face became indistinct, his features obscured. She felt panic rising up. *Don't leave!* She scrambled to find his face again, rubbing her good shoulder against her eyes to banish the tears—but when her vision cleared, the boy was gone. Two children remained. *Come back,* she begged silently, frantically, sinking to her knees. The *panga* fell from her hand. *Don't leave me here! You must lead me to the other side—please, please, come back.*

Kony waved his hand dismissively. "She has no will. Kill him."

Rose lifted her head as Opiyo raised his rifle—the moisture on his cheek and jaw could have been sweat, could have been tears—and pulled the trigger. A single, deafening shot rang through the clearing. Ocen's chest jerked backward and he slumped off the bench, clattering the tea mugs and spilling liquid to the earth. Rose felt struck as if by a physical blow. Her breath left her body. The *panga* lay still in the dirt, inches away from her hand. Meaningless. Everything was meaningless now.

"What of her?" Opiyo's voice came distantly.

Rose closed her eyes and begged for the vision to return, for her son to lead her across the divide between life and death. She let the hoarse ringing in her ears drown out any response Kony might make. The ringing morphed into a high-pitched drone. Was this the sound of a soul leaving earth? She sensed a sudden tension around her: a suspended moment of absolute stillness.

A cool, brief shadow.

A plane.

Kony jolted from his seat, knocking over the brown plastic chair. Two bodyguards rushed to Kony's side while the others fanned out. The entire unit fled into the undergrowth with Kony in the middle. She caught a last flash of white as Kony disappeared into the trees.

Margaret released Nicia's arm and the girl dropped instantly to the ground in a fetal position, hands covering her ears. Fatumah and Margaret scooped up a child each and shouted at the others to follow as they raced behind the men. From the direction of the main camp came the sound of automatic fire, shouts, screams. Rose stayed perfectly still, as still as Ocen's body, as still as the empty chair that lay on its side, as still as a lone rubber flip-flop left behind in the dust.

Opiyo had not fled. He hesitated over his brother's body. The fighting was escalating, coming nearer.

"Stay with me," Rose said. "Drop your weapon. They will not harm you."

"No," he said softly. "You made your choice. So have I." He looked up a last time. "Bury us well."

A spray of bullets thudded the tree trunks and kicked up tufts of earth and grass. Rose pressed her cheek to the earth and watched as

Opiyo returned fire blindly into the forest and then—without looking back—ran after Kony and his men. A second burst of fire zinged over her head. Near the laundry basin a tin bowl, kicked by an errant boot, rattled and went still.

There was a lull in the fighting while the attacking force awaited return fire. The clearing was eerily calm, apart from Nicia's low sobbing. Rose dragged herself along the ground, clawing into the dirt and grass, to reach Ocen's body where he'd fallen from the bench. When she reached him—the glistening crimson blood on his soiled shirt marking the shot to the chest—she was surprised to realize he was still breathing, if barely, through parted lips. Frantically, she felt for a pulse. It was faint, but beating. His eyes were closed, and his wrist was warm and soft. It was the first time she'd touched him since the night they'd fought in Kitgum, a universe ago.

"Ocen, can you hear me? Help is coming. They're almost here." She had no idea if it was true, but she hoped, she hoped. She pressed her hand against his chest to control the bleeding.

His eyelids fluttered. His hand fumbled for hers.

"Rose," he whispered. Then: "Adenya."

With a flurry of shouting, three soldiers entered the clearing. They were African, speaking a language Rose didn't know, and though their rifles were aimed they held back fire. Still gripping Ocen's hand, she tried to make out the insignia on the soldiers' shoulders: a white circular patch with a green symbol inside. Where had she seen this symbol before? Not UPDF. Not FARDC. Not UN . . .

A fourth soldier emerged from the trees, and Rose recognized Garamba's head ranger. Her body flooded with relief. "Jean-Pierre!"

He turned briskly, then saw beyond Rose to Nicia, who lifted her head at the sound of her father's name. The instant the two locked eyes, Nicia leapt from the ground and Jean-Pierre raced toward her. The space between them clapped into nothing. The girl disappeared inside her father's embrace. For a long second nobody breathed.

"Please," Rose called out. "He's been shot."

Jean-Pierre guided Nicia toward one of the rangers, then hurried to kneel at Ocen's side. Ocen's breathing was labored, and he'd slipped into unconsciousness. Jean-Pierre pulled a rag from a pouch around his waist and put it between Rose's hand and Ocen's wound.

"It is bad," Jean-Pierre murmured. He spoke into a crackling communication device, listened to a clipped reply, then turned again to Rose. "We have vehicles not far from here that can take him to a clinic. We have also sustained casualties, though not many. We were able to take the camp by surprise."

"You tracked us all this way?"

"The elephant carcasses were visible from the sky."

"Kony was here," Rose said. "He fled as soon as he heard the plane. He has a dozen men with him, and women and children." She choked up on the word *children*. The vision she'd seen had seemed so real, but she knew in her heart it was a lie. The truth was here in front of her, dying.

Jean-Pierre gave brisk orders to the other soldiers, who nodded and went back the way they came.

"They'll retrieve a vehicle," Jean-Pierre said, taking Nicia back under his arm.

"You won't pursue Kony?"

"He was not our objective." He closed his eyes and pressed his forehead against his daughter's. "And now we have other, more precious concerns."

"Sabine," Rose realized. "And Christoph and Lily—they were released, they are twenty minutes gone . . ."

"Daniela has a visual," Jean-Pierre said.

Rose looked down to Ocen's face, already fading. But there was still light in the day, and he was strong. She'd seen how strong he was. And the way he'd said her son's name, Adenya—in that moment it became more than a name, it became the separate Acholi words, clear and whole: *he opens the path before you*. She kept her hand pressed against the cloth, against Ocen's skin, his ribs, his heart; the grass, the earth, and whatever lay below. And somewhere deeply, vastly through, was another earth, another body, another deserving hand pressing to hold in the life, and beyond—the sky and stars, the smiling moon, waiting for its turn to rise.

AUTHOR'S NOTE

While this is a work of fiction, *The Atlas of Forgotten Places* is set against the backdrop of real locations and events.

Operation Lightning Thunder was a military offensive by Ugandan, DR Congolese, and South Sudanese troops against LRA forces in Garamba National Park. It began on December 14, 2008, and was supported by the United States Africa Command; an excellent article by Jeffrey Gettleman and Eric Schmitt in *The New York Times*, "U.S. Aided a Failed Plan to Rout Ugandan Rebels" (February 6, 2009), outlines the action and U.S. involvement.

In response to Operation Lightning Thunder, the LRA attacked civilian populations in northern Democratic Republic of the Congo, including Faradje, on Christmas Day and in the month that followed, slaughtering more than 865 civilians and abducting at least 160 children. These attacks, which became known as the Christmas massacres, are described in a Human Rights Watch report, "The Christmas Massacres: LRA Attacks on Civilians in Northern Congo," from 2009.

The LRA attack on Garamba National Park headquarters on January 2, 2009, resulted in the deaths of fifteen African Parks staff members, including at least two rangers and two rangers' wives; the kidnapping of two children by LRA forces; and an estimated $2 million worth of damages.

Lakwali and Gladstone are inventions; however, the reference to

AngloGold Ashanti and its ties to a local armed militia in Mongbwalu is documented in a 2005 report by Human Rights Watch called "The Curse of Gold."

In the time since I began writing this novel, the link between the LRA and ivory smuggling has been firmly established by extensive field research conducted by advocacy groups and investigative journalists. Two of the most in-depth resources are the Enough Project's "Tusk Wars: Inside the LRA and the Bloody Business of Ivory" and the series of reports by Bryan Christy and photographer Brent Stirton in *National Geographic*.

For more information about the long and complex history of the Acholi people in northern Uganda, including the formation and evolution of the LRA, below are some of the books I consulted during my research. I am also indebted to an *Acholi Times* article listing numerous Acholi proverbs and English translations. Any inaccuracies that remain in the novel are, of course, my own.

Allen, Tim, and Koen Vlassenroot, eds. *The Lord's Resistance Army: Myth and Reality*. London: Zed Books, 2010.

Amony, Evelyn. *I Am Evelyn Amony: Reclaiming My Life from the Lord's Resistance Army*. Edited with an introduction by Erin Baines. Madison: University of Wisconsin, 2015.

Behrend, Heike. *Alice Lakwena and the Holy Spirits: War in Northern Uganda 1986–1997*. Translated by Mitch Cohen. Oxford: James Currey, 1999.

De Temmerman, Els. *Aboke Girls: Children Abducted in Northern Uganda*. Kampala: Fountain Publishers, 2001.

Finnström, Sverker. *Living with Bad Surroundings: War, History, and Everyday Moments in Northern Uganda*. Durham and London: Duke University Press, 2008.

Girling, Frank Knowles. *The Acholi of Uganda*. London: Her Majesty's Stationery Office, 1960.

P'Bitek, Okot. *Song of Lawino* and *Song of Ocol*. London and Ibadan: Heinemann, 1984.

GLOSSARY OF ACHOLI TERMS

apwoyo—thank you; also used for greetings

boo—a northern Ugandan dish made of boiled leafy greens, sometimes mixed with groundnut paste

boda—motorcycle taxi; can be used to refer to both the motorcycle and the driver

cen—vengeful spirits or ghosts that haunt or inhabit people who have committed murder or other significant social transgressions

chapati—round, flat bread of Indian origin, commonly served across East Africa

dye-kal—common compound/living area for Acholi families

jogi—spirits

lapidi—an older child who cares for a younger sibling

larakaraka—Acholi courtship dance typically performed during weddings

malakwang—a northern Ugandan dish made of boiled leaves of the malakwang plant (similar to spinach) and groundnut paste, often served with cassava, millet bread, or sweet potatoes

mato oput—traditional Acholi ceremony of forgiveness; literally "drinking the bitter root"

mono—Acholi term for white person or foreigner

mzungu—Kiswahili term for white person or foreigner; in widespread use across East Africa *panga*—machete-like tool

owalo—crane; the national bird of Uganda

samosa—small triangles of dough filled with varied meat, vegetables, and
spices, of Indian origin, commonly served across East Africa

waragi—Ugandan liquor, similar to gin

A NOTE ON THE PRONUNCIATION OF NAMES

The "c" in Acholi is pronounced like the "ch" in the English word "church";
thus, the name Ocen is pronounced "O-chen." The word "Acholi" is also
often written as "Acoli," with the same pronunciation; I have used the
more common "Acholi" throughout.

The name Kony is pronounced "Koh-nee" by Westerners; in Acholi the
name is a single syllable pronounced like the word "cognac" minus the "ac"
(thanks to Oryem Nyeko for the description).

The name Sabine is often pronounced "Suh-been" by English speakers; in
German it is "Zah-been-uh."

BOOK CLUB READERS' GUIDE

Warning: spoiler alert! To preserve enjoyment of the novel, please review this section after you've finished the book.

1. How much did you know about northern Uganda before you read the novel? Do you feel like your perspective has changed?
2. Who did you connect with more, Rose or Sabine?
3. What is justice in this novel? Can wrongs be righted?
4. Did Rose's revelation about her ties to Joseph Kony take you by surprise? Would it have changed the way you felt about her if you knew the truth from the start?
5. Sabine's career choice was shaped in large part by her guilt over her grandfather's secret. Do you have family secrets or parts of your family history that have influenced your choices in life?
6. Was Lily's decision to search for Opiyo noble, or was it selfish? What if she had been investigating ivory smuggling—would that change how you see her?
7. What does forgiveness mean to you? Can a person be forgiven for many years of wrong acts by a single good act? What about the reverse? Should a person be condemned for a single wrong act after many years of doing good?

8. The Aboke abductions in 1996 were given little attention by the U.S. media. On the other hand, the 2014 kidnapping of 276 Nigerian schoolgirls by Boko Haram sparked worldwide outrage and demand for international action—the hashtag #BringBackOurGirls was even shared by First Lady of the United States Michelle Obama. Do you think this disparity can be attributed solely to the rise of social media? Or have attitudes shifted in the eighteen years between these incidents?

9. Do you think a single person can make a difference? Why would it be dangerous to think so? Why would it be dangerous not to think so?

10. What do you think lies ahead for the characters in this novel?

11. The author has said that she feels the novel ends hopefully, if not happily. Do you agree? Why or why not?

ACKNOWLEDGMENTS

The Atlas of Forgotten Places began years before the first word was written, when I was a volunteer with the Lutheran World Federation Uganda/Sudan in 2006; many thanks to the entire staff of the LWF for welcoming me so graciously into their fold. I was lucky enough to have the guidance of experienced aid workers Sarah Moldenhauer and Wiebke Hoeing, both of whom also provided invaluable feedback on drafts of the novel and who remain dear, if faraway, friends. During that period and on subsequent visits to Uganda and the Democratic Republic of the Congo, I relied heavily on the generosity and openness of countless colleagues and acquaintances. Thank you especially to Henni Alava, Akoch Emmanuel, Craig Kippels, Barbara Meier, Preston Nix, Karin van Bemmel, and the staff and rangers of Garamba National Park for insight, logistical support, and pointing me toward further resources.

Teachers & Writers Collaborative, the Rockefeller Foundation, and the Elizabeth George Foundation have, at various moments, provided financial support and encouragement exactly when I most needed both. The faculty of the Brooklyn College MFA program taught me unparalleled lessons in craft; my fellow MFA cohort, lessons in life (Jonas, Heidi, Michelle, Anna P., Anna H., Ria, Julia, Alberto, Nikita, Joanna, Susan, and Catherine: thank you!). Special appreciation to Richard Bausch for encouragement and for bringing together a wonderful group of writers in our Chapman workshop. And huge thanks go to my agent, Marly Rusoff, who has been a source of wisdom and an advocate for this novel from the beginning, when it was still a handful of chapters and a lot of big ideas.

Atlas benefited enormously from readings by Christian Acemah, Stephanie Bosch, Erika Mailman, Sarah Menkedick, Helen Mugambi, and others whose names I've already mentioned. In all other matters, Katie Bellas, Jenny Diamond, Jenine Durland, Sylvana Habdank-Kolaczkowska, Christina Olivares, Sarah Richmond, and Jeevan Sivasubramaniam have been voices of reason and love for decades and more. Thank you to Sarah Moldenhauer and Marisa Handler, whose words I have shamelessly borrowed in two of the most important lines in this book; you said it better than I could ever have. The women of Write Club are wonders of strength and solidarity. The '17 Scribes community has been terrific. And my Binders! You know who you are. It's been a pleasure and a privilege.

I could not have been luckier for *Atlas* to find a home with Quressa Robinson, whose brilliant edits saved the book in more ways than one. I'm also deeply grateful to Laurie Chittenden and Lisa Bonvissuto, for stepping in to usher *Atlas* through its final stages. It's an unfortunate truth of publishing that one must submit the final manuscript before becoming acquainted with all of the excellent people who will shepherd the novel through publication, often invisibly. My heartfelt thanks, therefore, to the entire Thomas Dunne/St. Martin's Press team—designers, copy editors, production managers, publicists, and many, many others—whose commitment to bringing this book to the world with integrity and grace is so dearly appreciated.

Gratitude to my parents, Scott and Sheelagh Williams, for giving me my most treasured inheritences: a yen for adventure, unflagging curiosity, and always a loving home to return to. Geoff: thank you for a million hours of road trip reading, for joining me at the tide pools on countless summer days, and for humbling me with your incisive wit.

And, Sebastian: in addition to conversation and companionship and all those nice things that make marriage worthwhile, thank you for making homemade ravioli and other gourmet dinners on nights when I would have eaten popcorn if left to my own devices. *And all I know of comfort / is that I shot an arrow into the sky / and built a home where it landed. / All I know of love is that it is a rope / best tethered to moving objects.*

ABOUT THE AUTHOR

JENNY D. WILLIAMS has lived in the United States, Uganda, and Germany. She holds an MFA from Brooklyn College and a BA from UC Berkeley. Her award-winning fiction, nonfiction, poetry, and illustrations have been published in *The Sun*, *Vela*, and *Ethical Traveler*, as well as several anthologies. A former Teachers & Writers Collaborative fellow and recipient of an Elizabeth George Foundation grant for emerging writers, she currently lives in Seattle with her husband and dog.

35674056355291